13/1/22

THE BOAT GIRLS

THE
BOAT GIRLS

Margaret Mayhew

BANTAM PRESS

LONDON · TORONTO · SYDNEY · AUCKLAND · JOHANNESBURG

TRANSWORLD PUBLISHERS
61–63 Uxbridge Road, London W5 5SA
A Random House Group Company
www.booksattransworld.co.uk

First published in Great Britain
in 2007 by Bantam Press
an imprint of Transworld Publishers

A CIP catalogue record for this book
is available from the British Library.

ISBN 9780593057162

Addresses for Random House Group Ltd companies outside the UK
can be found at: www.randomhouse.co.uk
The Random House Group Ltd Reg. No. 954009

The Random House Group Ltd makes every effort to ensure that
the papers used in its books are made from trees that have been
legally sourced from well-managed and credibly certified forests.
Our paper procurement policy can be found at:
www.randomhouse.co.uk/paper.htm

Typeset in Sabon by
Kestrel Data, Exeter, Devon.

Prined and bound in Great Britain by
Clays Ltd, St Ives plc.

2 4 6 8 10 9 7 5 3 1

To the valiant captain and crew of
the narrowboat *Grebe*:

James, Tilly, Ella, George,
Charlie and Sarah.

Acknowledgements

My thanks to Olga Kevelos for giving so generously of her time to tell me about her experiences working on the narrowboats in wartime. I am also very grateful to David Blagrove, boatman and author of a number of excellent books and videos about the canals, for all his help, as well as for his kind permission to quote from his song 'The Chestnut Bloom'.

The books written by former boat girls Eily Gayford, Susan Woolfit, Emma Smith and Margaret Cornish have all given fascinating accounts of what it was like to be an 'Idle Woman', as well as much useful information.

And I thank my editor, Linda Evans, my husband, Philip Kaplan and, finally, James, Tilly, Ella, George, Charlie and Sarah – the captain and crew of the narrowboat *Grebe* who took me along for a trip.

O thou who didst make for the Children of Israel a highway through the Promised Land, we pray thee to bless the highways of this country, especially its canals and waterways. We would remember before thee all who trade thereon. Be thou to them a Father, a Saviour and a Guide. Bless all who work amongst them for their spiritual good. Guide them by the light of the Holy Spirit that many souls may be won for Christ. We ask this for thy own name's sake.

Prayer for canal boaters:
Revd W. Ashbury Smith, 1940

Foreword

At the outbreak of the Second World War, the inland waterways of this country were taken over by the Government and all canal companies came under the control of the Ministry of War Transport. Canal work was classed as a reserved occupation but there was, nonetheless, a shortage of skilled boatmen, and the wartime importance of that system of transport was soon realized. Canals could save valuable space on the railways and evade the constant attacks suffered by east coastal shipping from German U-boats and E-boats.

In 1942 The Grand Union Canal Carrying Company agreed with the Ministry to implement a scheme for training women to handle pairs of narrowboats and help maintain a steady movement of vital supplies between London, Birmingham and the coalfields round Coventry. Advertisements were placed in newspapers and magazines and the women who responded, and survived the gruelling training, still had to learn to work alongside the real boat people whose families had lived on the canals for generations and who inhabited a very different world.

One

Carlyons had lived at Averton in Dorset for more than three hundred years. The first of them, a swashbuckling seafarer called John de Carlyon, had made a fortune as a buccaneer during the seventeenth century, preying on galleons on the Spanish Main and relieving them of their rich cargoes of gold and silver. He might well have ended up on the gallows, but, instead, had given up buccaneering and settled down to a respectable life on Dorset acres acquired through a shrewd marriage to a landed widow. He had built a large and very beautiful house of golden Ham Hill stone in a protective fold of undulating country-side, only five miles from the sea, and had added a church beside it. His first-born son and heir, given the name Vere at his baptism in the church, had later called his own son John. Thereafter, down the centuries, de Carlyon heirs were named, alternately, John or Vere.

The family fortunes had flourished. In the eighteenth century a Vere de Carlyon who had inherited some of the bravado and charm of his seafaring ancestor had found favour at court and been rewarded with a baronetcy. His heir, Sir John de Carlyon, had brought back an Italian wife from his Grand Tour who had further enhanced the beauty of Averton by creating formal gardens in the style of her native country, while her husband contributed stable blocks and a dovecote.

At the beginning of the nineteenth century, Sir Vere de Carlyon had given the house a classical front, a fine new staircase in the hall and a charming stone orangery in the gardens, but after his death a succession of profligate heirs had squandered the major part of their fortunes so that by the finish of the century, Averton had been reduced to a shadow of its former glory. The house and outbuildings had been neglected, the gardens allowed to grow semi-wild. At the end of the First World War, the family – now plain Carlyon – were struggling to keep their heads above water. Sir John Carlyon, who had fought courageously in the trenches of Flanders, had come back a broken man and, after the early death of his wife, had withdrawn from life to spend his days pottering about the old orangery, raising orchids. His only son and heir, Vere, had

14

joined the RAF three years before the Second World War. He had been posted to Bomber Command and reached the rank of Wing Commander by the age of twenty-five. His sister, named Frances like other Carlyon ladies before her, was seven years younger and incarcerated at boarding school until the summer of 1943 when she returned to a near-empty home. Except for Mrs Crocker, the elderly cook, and an even more elderly gardener, Didcot, assisted by a young lad, the Averton staff – such as they had been – had gone off to war. A Mrs Briggs, also well past her prime, came from the village on her bicycle to fight a losing battle with dust and cobwebs.

In September, on her eighteenth birthday, Frances presented herself at the local recruiting offices for the women's army, navy and air force, only to be told by each one, in turn, that recruiting was temporarily suspended. She waited impatiently throughout October and November and the recruiting officers grew used to, and tired of, the sight of her appearing before their desks. A volunteer job dispensing tea and buns in a canteen in Bridport occupied her for a while, but the other helpers were all old women and there was a battleaxe in charge.

'I thought I told you not more than *one* sugar is allowed per person, Miss Carlyon, and only *one* bun. There happens to be a war on, in case you're unaware of it.'

She carried on slipping extra rations to service men and women when the battleaxe's back was turned, but then there was a row over her breaking some cups and another over the way she slopped the tea into the saucers and another about chatting too much to the customers. 'Careless talk costs lives, Miss Carlyon. We never know who may be listening.' After a few weeks she left and went back to pestering the recruiting offices.

Aunt Gertrude, her father's sister, phoned from her flat in London to invite herself for Christmas. A First World War widow, her chief pleasures were cards, cigarettes, Gordon's gin – which she drank with warm tap water – and betting on racehorses. She was a lethal bridge player, unbeatable at most card and board games, and won considerably more than she ever lost with her bookmaker.

'Any hope of Vere being home, darling?'

'I shouldn't think so. We haven't heard from him for ages.'

'Too busy killing Germans, I dare say. How's your father these days?'

'More or less the same. He spends most of the time with the orchids.'

'Personally, I can't understand what he sees in them, but it keeps him happy – that's the main thing, isn't it? How about you, Frances? What are you doing with yourself?'

'Waiting to join up – but nobody seems to want me.'

'Who have you tried?'

'WRNS, WAAF, ATS. They've all stopped recruiting for the moment.'

'Well, I dare say they'll start again soon. Get Vere to pull an RAF string for you.'

'He wouldn't do it. He'd say I had to go through the proper channels. You know how stuffy he is.'

'He can seem it, I grant you, but it's a fault on the right side.'

Frances carried her father's lunch tray down the draughty stone passage leading from the kitchens to an even colder hall, and out of a side door to the pathway that led to the orangery. Every day it was exactly the same lunch: a shrimp-paste sandwich and a thermos of unsweetened tea. He had countered all Mrs Crocker's efforts to vary the sandwich filling simply by leaving anything different untouched – like some picky old dog.

The graceful eighteenth-century orangery stood apart from the main house at the top of the three-tiered Italian pool garden. It was easily the best-kept building at Averton and by far the warmest. Most of the coke ration went on feeding the voracious furnace which kept it at around

17

seventy degrees, while the temperature in the house rarely rose to fifty except in high summer. The orchids came before everything else, and her father would have mortgaged the estate for a rare blue one.

Visitors were not encouraged inside. They brought in bacteria, fungi, algae and pests, and breathed germs over the plants, and whenever Papa was occupied with the delicate business of sowing seeds with sterile test tubes and pipettes and eye droppers, a large KEEP OUT notice was pinned up on the side door and the lunch tray had to be left outside. He was liable to post it at other times, as well, but there was no notice to be seen this time so Frances balanced the tray on one arm, opened the glass door, went in and shut it very quickly behind her. Draughts, as well as microbes, were death to orchids, who lived like pampered creatures in their hothouse world. Beautiful they might be, but they never touched her heart. They were too perfect; too still – as though they weren't living things at all. They had none of the charm of, say, roses rambling over a garden wall, or daffodils nodding in the wind, or even common daisies studding the grass.

The orangery orange trees had gone with the Great War. Instead, long wooden benches held rows and rows of orchid plants. She could see her father bent over one at the far end, absorbed

18

in some delicate task. The summer-flowering kinds were dormant but there were others that produced their blooms in winter – exotic apparitions among their sleeping fellows and, to her eyes, all wrong in the grey English light of December.

She watched her father for a moment, un-noticed. As a small child, she had heard him crying out in his sleep at night – inhuman shrieks of terror that had made her cower under the blankets. Just nightmares, her mother had ex-plained. Nothing to worry about. But the nightmares had gone on through the years and they still happened, though less frequently. Once upon a time, he must have been a normal person, only she had no memory of it. He was perfectly kind and very sweet, but talking to him was like trying to communicate with a ghost – someone who had already departed. According to Aunt Gertrude, he had been badly affected by fighting in the war – shell-shocked it was called – which was a polite way of saying that he had gone to pieces. He had been engaged to her mother before he had left for the trenches and soon after his return they had got married in spite of the shell shock. Mama had helped him get better and the orchids had been her idea. She had bought him a few plants as a hobby, and books to read and learn about them.

Frances had been twelve and in her first year at boarding school when Mama had died. The headmistress had sent for her and had told her to sit down before giving her the bad news. Apparently, it had been very sudden and quite unexpected – the kind of thing that almost never happened to anyone. She had sat there in stunned silence while Miss Moorehead had explained that Mama had been bitten on the leg by some unknown insect and the bite had become infected and spread uncontrollably. The hospital had tried to save her but nothing could be done. The inquest had recorded that her death was from septicaemia. Frances had gone home for the funeral and then been sent straight back to school afterwards. The other girls had kept staring at her and then looking away, as though she had caught some disease and might somehow contaminate them.

She carried the tray to where her father was working and set it down on the bench.

'I've brought your lunch, Papa.' He didn't seem to hear so she tapped him on the shoulder. 'Your lunch, Papa.'

He glanced round vaguely, a small knife in hand. The only way to get any positive response was to say something about the orchids.

'That looks awfully tricky . . . whatever you're doing.'

He nodded. 'Must be careful . . . so easy to get

it wrong.' He bent over the pot again, like a surgeon using a scalpel.

She wandered about the orangery, looking at the exotic flowers with their spots and stripes and strange markings. In Edwardian times they had been particularly prized, she knew, and gentlemen had worn expensively raised orchids in their buttonholes to impress the ladies. The paler colours looked better than the gaudy ones, and white was best of all. There was one that always bloomed around Christmas in a long spray of small white flowers and she found it at the far end of a bench. It would look beautiful in the house, where it would die very quickly from cold.

Papa seemed to have finished whatever delicate operation he'd been carrying out, so she went back to him.

'Aunt Gertrude phoned. She's coming for Christmas, as usual.'

'Ah . . . that's good.'

'She asked me whether Vere would be here too.'

'Oh . . . I shouldn't think so, would you?'

'No. I expect it'll be just the three of us.'

'Mmmm . . .'

He bent over another pot and she knew he had either already forgotten that she was there, or was hoping that she would go away very soon. Sometimes she longed to grab hold of him and shake him, shout at him and *make* him pay some attention, but, of course, it was hopeless.

'Well, don't forget to eat your lunch.'

At the door she glanced back to see him intent again with the knife. He probably would forget.

She wandered into the morning room where a fire smouldered sulkily in the grate and, for something to do, picked up *The Times* from the sofa table and sat down to flick through the pages. The news was mostly about the war, of course: photographs of Allied troops squelching through thick mud in Italy, another of a very handsome American fighter pilot climbing out of his plane, another of a captured German U-boat crew looking bitter and resentful. Papa never read any of it – never even looked at the paper or mentioned the war. She turned another page and an article caught her eye.

Appeal for Volunteers

There are vacancies for more women volunteers to be trained to work canal boats. Training usually lasts about two months, during which women will be given full instruction in the management and handling of canal craft and the method of working the locks. They will live, eat and sleep on the boats which travel along the canals, carrying essential cargoes. Payment during training is

22

at the rate of £2 a week and a week's leave, without pay, may be taken at the end of each trip, which normally takes about three weeks.

She read on with interest.

On completion of training, if found suitable, women are given control of a pair of boats, consisting of a motor boat with a 'butty'. The earnings accruing from the tonnage moved are shared by the three members of the crew and are subject to a minimum wage of £3 a week. Above this minimum the earnings of the crew depend largely on their own experience and exertions. Canal boat workers are entitled to extra rations of tea and sugar. Fuel and light are free. Leave is granted at regular intervals, including one week annually with pay. Only women of robust constitution are advised to apply. The main qualifications are grit and spirit of service.

She tore the article out.

Aunt Gertrude came three days before Christmas, arriving in the local station taxi in time for tea. A blazing log fire made the drawing room bearable as long as one sat within a radius of eight feet. Aunt Gertrude, who had been born and brought up in the house, had come well prepared in her ankle-length musquash coat with several

23

layers of clothing beneath it. Her clothes and jewellery all dated from the twenties – ropes of beads, drop-waisted gowns, long cardigans, pointed shoes with splayed heels – and even her hair was cut in a twenties bob. She had discovered, when living through it, that the period suited her, and had never seen any reason to move on.

Papa put in a brief appearance before disappearing to his study with some mumbled excuse. Aunt Gertrude stuck one of her cigarettes into her ivory holder and lit it.

'I've been having a think, Frances. Would you have any objection to my coming to live down here for a bit? It looks like this wretched war's going to drag on and I'm getting sick of spending it in London. There are troops swarming all over town, prostitutes on every corner and the Americans pinch all the taxis . . . I'd like to shut the flat up and get away for a while. Do you think your father would mind?'

'I shouldn't think he'd even notice. And I'd love to have you.'

'Not much fun here on your own, is it? Not that I'd be much help in that department. You want other young people for company, not old aunts. Any luck yet with the service applications?'

She shook her head. 'Nothing doing. I've just tried them all again.'

The woman in the WAAF recruiting place had been quite frosty. '*We'll let you know. Please don't bother us again.*'

She said, 'I saw this thing in *The Times* the other day which sounded rather interesting. What do you think?'

Her aunt read the article. 'It sounds right up your street, Frances. Something quite different.'

'Only I don't know anything about canal boats. I've never even seen one. Or a canal either, come to that.'

'That wouldn't matter. They'd train you. And you've done plenty of sailing. It's all water. I think it sounds rather fun. Probably much better for you than one of the services. You'd be out in the fresh air, cruising along the waterways – very pleasant, I'd have thought, and all part of the war effort. Essential cargoes, it says. Grit and spirit of service . . . that's what they're after. You've got both those, haven't you?'

Frances smiled. 'Would you say I had a robust constitution? That's what they want too.'

'I'd say you were fit and healthy. Not liable to keel over or faint at a bit of hard physical labour.'

She said, 'I found an old book about the history of the canals in Papa's library. It was all rather fascinating. Did you know that the Romans built several of them when they were over here?'

'No, I can't say that I did.'

'Nor did I. Then nothing happened for years until Queen Elizabeth's reign when another canal was dug at Exeter. Things didn't get going properly until the Industrial Revolution when people found out canals were ideal for hauling coal and raw materials about the country cheaply, in barges pulled by horses. They built them all over the country and lots of people made pots of money. And everything went swimmingly until the nineteenth century when the railways started to be built. Bad luck for the canals – they couldn't really compete. I say, you don't think they *still* use horses, do you?'

'No idea. Rather nice, if they did.'

Late on Christmas Eve, Vere arrived unexpectedly. Frances hadn't seen her brother for months, and there were lines and shadows on his face that she couldn't remember from before. On Christmas morning they walked over to the church, minus Papa who had escaped to the orangery. There had been a heavy frost during the night and the countryside glistened white. Inside the church, the congregation, cocooned to the eyes, breathed vapour clouds into the air. Vere read the lesson.

And Joseph also went up from Galilee, out of the city of Nazareth, into Judaea, unto the city of David, which is called Bethlehem . . .

Frances watched him from the family pew. He had a nice speaking voice, as good as any actor, and he looked better after a night's sleep, standing there tall and straight in his RAF greatcoat with the wing commander's insignia on his shoulders and all the gilt buttons. The local girls in the congregation were paying lots of attention, and the WAAF girls at his station probably paid lots of attention too. He was the heir, the latest in a long line of de Carlyons – the first one, the Spanish Main pirate, lying in his respectable tomb only a few feet from where she sat. Sir Johns and Sir Veres and their wives were under other flag-stones marked by brass plates. Mama, though, was buried outside in the churchyard beneath a hawthorn tree. She refused to think about the frightening idea that Vere might be killed in the war and buried here, too. Stuffy he might be, but he was her brother. Her *only* brother.

There was a goose from the home farm for lunch, with roast potatoes and sprouts, and Papa had brought up wine from the cellar. Afterwards, Frances and Vere left Aunt Gertrude beside the log fire and Papa back in the orangery and took the dogs for a long walk across the estate. Vere had changed out of his uniform and looked more like a brother, but he was still bossy and interfering. For a start, he didn't like the idea of her joining any of the services.

'It was all right in the beginning, but you get all sorts of girls now.'

'Sorts? What sorts?'

'Not the kind you should be mixing with.'

'*You* mix with them, don't you?'

He said coolly, 'I don't, as it happens. And I'm not joking, Frances. I'd far sooner you thought of something else to do.'

'Such as?'

'There must be plenty of suitable jobs locally – helping out in a canteen, for instance.'

'I've already tried that. It was deadly boring.'

'Well, VAD work in a hospital.'

'Emptying bedpans? No, *thanks*.'

'We all have to do unpleasant things we don't necessarily care for in wartime.'

She wondered if Vere lectured his squadron about having to put up with unpleasant things, and decided that he almost certainly did.

They reached the brow of a hill. Beyond, the frosty landscape switchbacked towards the Channel five miles away, and the day was clear enough to catch the steely glint of the sea in a gap. Her brother stood beside her, hands thrust into his coat pockets, collar turned up, hair ruffled by the wind. The irony was that there was a strong resemblance to the pirate's portrait hanging in the hall – same long straight nose, same slightly hooded eyes, same colour hair – but *he* couldn't possibly have been remotely stuffy, like Vere, and he sported a large emerald in one ear to prove it.

She said, 'Papa's not getting any better, you know.'

'I'm afraid he never will. Still, he seems perfectly happy with the orchids. Which is really the main thing.'

'That's what Aunt Gertrude always says. Did she tell you she's planning to come and stay for a while?'

'Yes, she did mention it. I think it's an excellent idea. It'll be good for Pa and it'll be some company for you.'

'I may not be here – if I get called up.'

'I told you, Frances, it's much better if you find something to occupy you round here. There's absolutely no need for you to leave Dorset.'

'I don't want to be occupied, Vere. I want to *do* something useful.'

'You can. Go and be a VAD. That's extremely useful.'

'And I told *you*, I don't want to be one. It's not up to you to tell me what to do.'

He said, 'Frances – you're only just eighteen. I have a responsibility to look after you – since Mama is dead and Pa isn't up to it – and I'd much prefer that you stay here at Averton.'

'And I'd much prefer that I didn't. It's all very

well for you, Vere, you've been off having a lovely time – heaps of excitement and adventure.'

'Which shows how little you understand what fighting a war is about. The reality is anything but lovely.'

'You mean people getting killed? I understand that perfectly well.'

'I doubt if you do.' He glanced at his watch. 'I ought to be getting back. I have to be on duty first thing in the morning.'

He whistled to the two springer spaniels and they walked down the hill in the direction of the house, the dogs following. It looked very beautiful and serene, snug in its safe hollow with the winter sunlight touching the golden stone and masking all its imperfections – sagging roof, crumbling stonework, wonky guttering, peeling paint. She did love it and sometimes, like at this moment, she envied Vere that it would be his one day; at other times she was glad that she wouldn't be saddled with the burden of caring for it.

As they neared the house, she said, 'As a matter of fact, there *is* something else I could do. There was an appeal in *The Times*.'

'An appeal?' He frowned. 'What about?'

She told him. 'Aunt Gertrude's all for it.'

'Well, I'm *not*. You don't know what kind of other women would apply, or what the conditions would be, or anything about it. In fact, I think it's

30

an appalling idea. Working like some bargee! I absolutely forbid it, Frances.'

He had stopped walking and so had she. They faced each other. 'Is that clear?'

He was looking his very stuffiest, his most bossy.

'No, it's not. You said yourself that we all have to do unpleasant things in wartime. They need women to help move essential cargoes. It's really important – not just filling teacups and emptying bedpans. I think I'd enjoy it.' The truth was that she'd been rather uncertain on that point, but now she was determined. 'Mama would have approved. I know she would.'

'I very much doubt it.'

'Well, you can't actually stop me, can you? So, bad luck.'

She walked away from him, on down towards the house. He shouted after her, but she pretended not to hear.

Two

Every weekday morning for the past two years, Prudence Dobbs had left the house in Lime Avenue, Croydon and walked with her father down the front path and out of the gate to go to work at the bank. They left at precisely eight fifteen in order to arrive well before opening time and, as they approached the building, Prudence would hang back a little in order to allow her father to precede her, in deference to his position as chief clerk. Once he had entered the premises, she would then follow to take up her duties.

She had been named Prudence because it was a virtue much admired by her father, especially in a woman. After leaving school at sixteen she had begun work at the bank as a junior, filing cheques neatly in boxes, in date order, and making the tea for all the staff. After eighteen months she had risen to become a ledger clerk, writing the daily balances of customers' accounts into a heavy, bound book. It was her job to sort the cheques alphabetically and then post the figures neatly into her ledger – the debit entries and the new balance for each account at close of business for the day. There were five hundred accounts in her particular ledger and she had had to learn to recognize the signatures of all the customers she handled, and to write the figures very clearly and beyond doubt. Mr Holland, the manager, always preached what he called the Psychology of Accuracy. Any discrepancies in the day's final figures were dealt with as a very serious matter. All staff were required to stay at work until the mistake was found and rectified and her father, as chief clerk, oversaw the investigation.

In the course of her work she had also learned to match the faces of customers to their signatures, and to spot Mrs Harper, Miss Peabody, old Mr Cuthbertson, young Mr Lewis and so on, whenever they came into the bank. Mrs Harper would have been hard to miss, in any case, as she always made such a to-do at the counter, insisting on being given brand new notes. She quite often demanded to see Mr Holland who came hurrying out of his office at once – probably because she was their richest customer.

When Prudence had first started work at the bank, the war had been going on for nearly two years and Spitfires and Hurricanes were a familiar sight in the skies overhead. During the summer of 1940 they had watched them dogfighting with the German planes and the town had had its share of German bombs. The first and worst time had been in August, when the Luftwaffe had attacked Croydon airport and made a terrible mess of the aerodrome and houses and factories around it. Her father had been at work and she'd been at home having lunch with her mother. Halfway through the cold ham and lettuce she'd heard a sort of thump in the distance, and looked out of the window to see a puff of black smoke rising from the direction of the airport. The siren hadn't sounded and when she'd pointed out the smoke, Mother had told her to get on with her food and stop imagining things. Suddenly, there'd been more thumps and more smoke, the approaching roar of the German bombers, and the whistle of their bombs as they fell. RAF Hurricanes had come shrieking overhead and the ack-ack guns had started up. She and Mother had dropped their knives and forks and dived straight under the table. In the rush, the salad-cream bottle had got knocked off and spilled all over the carpet, which had upset Mother more than the bombs. The Bourjois soap factory had been badly hit, as well as two hundred houses, and more than sixty people had been killed. The salad cream had left a permanent stain.

Since then, they'd all got used to the war. Used to hearing the sirens wailing all during the Blitz and used to going out to sit in the cold, damp Anderson shelter beside the rhubarb patch at the end of the garden, listening to the bombs whistling and exploding and the ack-ack guns booming, and waiting patiently for the long note of the all-clear. They'd got used to the blackout and the rationing and the queuing and the shortages of food, paper, petrol, string, rubber, batteries, coal, material, glass . . . almost everything you could think of, except potatoes. At the bank, Mr Holland had insisted on regular stirrup-pump practices and practices for putting out incendiary bombs with sand, or using a long-handled shovel and rake to manoeuvre them into a metal box. Father had been put in charge of the practices and of the staff Fire Watch rota, and when he went off on duty at night he wore a tin helmet instead of his bowler hat. Mr Holland, as manager, was considered too important to take part.

On Christmas Eve 1943 Prudence walked with her father to the bank, as usual. Mr Holland had kindly permitted coloured paper chains to be strung above the cashiers' counter and holly to be placed on the window sills, and, at the end of the day, when work was finally finished – with no mistakes – he invited all his staff into his office for sherry. Miss Tripp, his secretary, dispensed the British sherry from a bottle – exactly half a glassful each – as if she was pouring out a dose of medicine, which was what it tasted like. They stood awkwardly around the room while Mr Holland delivered his annual speech, reminding them of their good fortune in working for the bank and of the vital importance of the Psychology of Accuracy, before he wished them a merry Christmas. Mr Simpkins, the senior cashier, was standing close behind Prudence and when he leaned forward to speak, she could feel his breath puffing into her right ear.

'I wonder if you would care to go to the picture house on Boxing Day, Miss Dobbs? They're showing an American film, but I understand it's quite good.'

It wasn't the first time that he had asked her out and she always refused him. 'It's very kind of you, Mr Simpkins, but my aunt and uncle are coming to visit.'

'Another time then.'

She suspected that he mistook her reluctance for shyness and awe of his position at the bank, talking directly with the customers. It would never do to tell him the truth – that she found him repulsive – in case he found ways of making trouble for her. He was years older than her, with thin, scurfy hair and eyes that glinted at her through wire-framed spectacles. Whenever his hands touched her – which they did if he got the chance – her skin crawled in disgust. Once, he had hinted at his good prospects at the bank. A senior cashier could expect to rise, in time, he told her, to become chief clerk and, one day, manager. Father, she knew, had his own sights set on taking Mr Holland's place in the private office behind the big leather-topped desk, dictating letters to Miss Tripp, issuing orders and delivering the Christmas Speech.

As usual, she left the bank a little before her father and waited for him outside in the dark. Miss Tripp passed her with a sharp 'Goodnight' and walked away, her lace-up shoes with metal bits on the heels ringing loudly on the pavement. Nobody knew where she lived or anything about her life outside the bank, and nobody much cared. She had never been known to smile – maybe because she had nothing to smile about after working there for thirty years. Prudence shivered. *Thirty years!* It was like a prison sentence. All those days and weeks and months spent shut up in a place where the windows were made of frosted glass, so you could never see what was happening outside or even what the weather was like. If she wasn't careful she might end up just like Miss Tripp, with only retirement to look forward to and a presentation clock to go on the mantelpiece.

There was a way of escape, though, now that she was eighteen. She could leave the bank to join one of the services, the ATS or the WRNS or the WAAF, or go and work in a munitions factory. Making bullets or guns, or aeroplane parts to fight the enemy seemed a lot more useful than posting endless figures about other people's money in a book. But when she'd suggested it to Father on the way to work one day, he'd told her he'd never allow it. Over his dead body, he'd said, striking the pavement with the steel tip of his rolled-up umbrella . . . a daughter of his mixing with common servicemen or with girls of loose morals. And, in any case, working in a bank was of vital importance to the war effort. Banks were needed to make everything run properly, he'd said. Where would the country be without them, he'd like to know? In chaos, that's where it'd be. When the conscription age had come down from nineteen to eighteen years old, she'd hoped that she'd be called up, whether he liked it or not, but so far it hadn't happened.

Father came out with Mr Holland and the bank door was locked as carefully as if it was the Bank of England chock-full of gold bars. Mr Holland went off towards Chestnut Drive where he lived in a detached house with a big garden and a gravel driveway, and Prudence walked home with her father to the semi-detached in Lime

Avenue with a sun-ray gate and a crazy-paving front path.

Christmas Day was the same as it had been for as long as she could remember. In the morning they went to church before they sat down for lunch in the dining room – Mother, Father and herself – with the best dinner service and the silver-plate cutlery and cruets brought out specially and polished for the occasion. Mother had queued for a small joint of beef at the butcher's, and roasted it with potatoes and boiled cabbage and Yorkshire pudding, and she'd made a sort of Christmas pudding out of breadcrumbs and dried fruit and carrots. Afterwards they sat down in the lounge to listen to the King's Speech and when the drums rolled for 'God Save the King' at the end of it, they stood up – Father ramrod straight as a soldier on parade. Then it was time to open their presents. Mother and Father had given her a book on the Royal Family and she had given Mother a pair of woollen gloves and Father a pair of socks. Mother had given Father a grey scarf that she had knitted and he had given her a marcasite brooch. After that, Mother got out her knitting bag and carried on with a balaclava helmet for the Forces Comforts, while Father read *The Illustrated London News* and Prudence opened her Royal Family book and looked at the photographs of the King and Queen and the two Princesses doing their bit for the war, including stirrup-pump practice. In the evening they listened to the Home Service on the wireless and to the nine o'clock news before they went to bed.

On Boxing Day, Father's brother, Uncle Ted, and Auntie Dot came for lunch. Auntie Dot had short, wavy hair, eyes as bright as a bird's and a chuckling voice. After lunch, they played racing demon and snap. Father didn't like card games and he left the room while Mother went into the kitchen to make the tea. Uncle Ted was shuffling the pack with loud zipping noises when Auntie Dot took a piece of paper out of her pocket and gave it to her.

'I saw this in a magazine, Prudence, and thought of you.'

The cutting featured a picture of a young woman in trousers, standing on the deck of some kind of boat, holding a long wooden pole and smiling happily, as though she was having a wonderful time. Underneath it said, CANAL JOBS FOR WOMEN. TRANSPORT MINISTRY'S CALL. *Women volunteers are needed for training to operate canal boats . . .*

'It sounds fun, doesn't it, dear? You earn £2 a week while you're training and then £3 after that. Wouldn't you like to do something like that, instead of working in the bank?'

She said, 'I don't know anything about boats. I've never even been on one.'

'You don't need to. They train you. I think it'd be just the thing for you.'

Prudence stared at the picture of the smiling, carefree girl again – it *did* look as though it was a lovely thing to do. Out in the fresh air and sunlight, sailing up and down on the water – not stuck indoors all day, sitting at her desk, sorting cheques and posting figures. And no creepy Mr Simpkins. No sour Miss Tripp, either. No Mr Holland and his Psychology of Accuracy. The escape she had been hoping for. *Praying* for.

She handed the cutting back with a sigh. 'Father would never allow it. Over his dead body, he'd say.'

Auntie Dot smiled. 'Leave him to me, dear.'

Mother wheeled in the tea trolley and Father came back and sat down in his chair. Auntie Dot waited until the tea was poured and the paste sandwiches passed round before she spoke.

'I expect Prudence will be called up any day now, won't she, Arnold?'

Her father frowned and stirred his tea vigorously. 'No reason why she should be, Dot. She's got an important job in the bank.'

'But it's not *reserved*, is it? She wouldn't be exempt. And now they've lowered the age, the Government could call her up at any moment.

Our neighbours' daughter has just been sent into a factory. She works a twelve-hour day, testing nuts and bolts, and the man in charge of the women takes all kinds of liberties with them, she says, and they can't do a thing about it. And, over the road from us, the Taylors' daughter has had to join the ATS. They're not very happy about *that*, I can tell you. Well, you've heard the rumours, I dare say, Arnold. Specially now the *Americans* have come over . . .' She let the words hang ominously on the air for a moment. 'You're a man of the world – you know what goes on. I heard a shocking story, just the other day—'

Her father interrupted hastily. 'Prudence will be staying at the bank.'

Auntie Dot wagged a forefinger at him. 'But what if they tell her she can't? We're at war. The Government can do anything they like. Order people about, send them wherever they're needed. They've got *powers*. Now, if I were you, and Prudence was *my* daughter, I'd make sure she wasn't sent into a factory or some military camp where she'd be at the mercy of unscrupulous men. I'd find something else for her to do before that happened – something respectable. Something nice and *safe*.'

Her father frowned again. 'Such as?'

The magazine cutting was produced and played deftly like a good card. 'I just happened to see this in a women's magazine the other day. An appeal for women to do essential war work on the canals. It's from the Ministry of War Transport. All above board and *very* respectable.'

Her father took the cutting and looked at it doubtfully. 'Canals? Canal boats? I've never heard of women doing such a thing. It's a man's job.'

'Not necessarily – not these days. Women are turning their hand to all kinds of things, and this sounded a very nice idea to me. Out in the fresh air. Very healthy. Working with other women – no men to bother them or take advantage. Something you could be proud of her doing – *essential supplies*, it says. And she could always go back to the bank as soon as the war's over.'

He examined the article more closely. 'The woman in this picture's wearing trousers. I don't call that very respectable. A woman in trousers!'

'Well, you wouldn't want them to be climbing around the boat in skirts, Arnold, would you? Going up and down ladders, and things. It wouldn't do at all. Would it, Kathleen?'

Prudence held her breath. If Mother thought it was a good idea, then there was a faint chance that Father might come round to it.

'No, I suppose it wouldn't, Dot. And I certainly wouldn't want Prudence to go into any of the services.' Her mother lowered her voice, leaning towards her father. 'Look what happened to Mrs

Watson's girl, Arnold. The air force sent her home in disgrace and everybody's been gossiping about it.'

'You don't want any trouble like that with Prudence, do you?' Auntie Dot said. 'Think of all the talk there'd be at the bank.'

Her father laid the cutting carefully on the table beside him and took a sip of his tea. 'I'll give it my consideration, that's all. I'll think about it.'

Auntie Dot winked at her.

Three

Rosalind Flynn had begun her professional acting career at six years old when she had played the part of an extra fairy in an open-air production of *A Midsummer Night's Dream*. Her father had taken the role of Theseus, Duke of Athens, and her mother that of his betrothed, Hippolyta, Queen of the Amazons. The company toured the country during that summer of 1931, performing in gardens and among old ruins and on village greens, rain or shine. When autumn arrived it disbanded. Her parents joined a repertory company in the west of England and appeared in supporting roles in a long string of popular plays, while Rosalind was given other walk-on, non-speaking parts and was sent to the local school. Later, they moved on to join other companies, taking work wherever they could get it, 'resting' when they could not and always waiting and hoping for the day when they would finally take the leads and see their names up in lights.

There had never been any doubt that Rosalind would follow in their footsteps and, as their own hopes gradually faded, those dreams were transferred to her. She had the looks and the voice and she had already learned that the smell of greasepaint was the headiest scent in the world, and that the most thrilling sounds were the swish of the curtain and the applause of an audience. By the time she was thirteen she was playing small speaking parts, and every so often the drama critic of a local newspaper would single her out as promising. At fourteen years old she was growing rather tall, which was a disadvantage, but, as her mother often said, there were always plenty of tall male actors, and height lent presence on stage.

And then the Second World War broke out and everything changed. Actors were called up, theatres and cinemas were closed down, finding work became even more difficult and her parents 'rested' for longer and longer periods. Her father's health – never good – deteriorated. The bronchitis that had plagued him for years became much worse and, even if there had been good parts offered, he would have been unable to play them. When a doctor advised sea air, her parents took out their savings and cashed in an insurance policy to buy a run-down terrace house in a side street of a south coast town where they let rooms to commercial travellers. As the war progressed and the need for entertainment was recognized, theatres began to open up again and Rosalind was occasionally given small parts at the Winter Gardens – maids, country girls, younger sisters, attendants, Dick Whittington's cat in the Christmas pantomime. The Germans had occupied Europe and the sound of their guns could be heard firing on the other side of the Channel. Before long their fighters came swooping over, rattling away with their machine guns, and their bombers droned overhead en route to attack airfields and London. The expected invasion, though, was thwarted by the RAF and the war took another turn, to be fought out in Greece, and Crete and Italy and north Africa, and in the Far East against Japan.

When she was sixteen, Rosalind left school and worked as a waitress while she auditioned for acting parts. Unfortunately, her height and her looks worked against her. The patriotic demand was for delicate English roses rather than for long-legged redheads of Irish descent.

Now that the Germans seemed unlikely to land on the beach at any moment, the run-down terrace house was sold and a better one bought on the sea front, not far from the Winter Gardens. Actors and actresses, coming and going in productions there, replaced the travelling salesmen and theatrical gossip was part of life again. There was talk of a completely new company being started up in a provincial theatre by a legendary Shakespearian actor. It was, Rosalind's mother told her, her big chance. She must take the train there and walk straight in. Beg the great man for a part – *any* part, however small. Once she was in and he saw how good she was, the rest would follow.

She had some trouble finding the theatre, wandering around dingy streets past bomb-damaged houses and heaps of rubble inhabited by cats and rats. The theatre had been damaged, too. A tarpaulin had been stretched over a part of the roof and the house doors had been blown out so that she was able, literally, to walk straight in. She opened an inner swing door leading to the back of the stalls, which was in darkness. The stage, though, was lit and two actors were rehearsing. She stood, motionless and unobserved, listening to Orlando and Jaques speaking familiar lines from *As You Like It.*

Rosalind is your love's name?
Yes, just.
I do not like her name.
*There was no thought of pleasing you when she
    was christened.*

What stature is she of?
Just as high as my heart.

Jaques made his exit and Rosalind her entrance
– a slight, blonde-haired girl, just the right heart-
high size for her rather short Orlando. An English
rose.

I pray you, what is 't o'clock?
You should ask me, what time o' day; there's no
*   clock in the forest.*
Then there is no true lover in the forest; else
*   sighing every minute and groaning every*
*   hour would detect the lazy foot of Time—*

'Nadine, darling, *do* try to pitch your voice
lower and strut about like I showed you – you're
pretending to be a boy, remember? A *saucy*
lackey. Orlando would rumble you in a second.'

The rich, theatrical voice had come from the
centre of the darkened stalls.

The actress said sulkily, 'I *am* trying. It's the
best I can do. Anyway, Paul wouldn't notice if I
came on stark naked.'

'Don't be bitchy, sweetie. It doesn't suit you.
Take it again from *I pray you* . . .'

They got as far as *Where dwell you, pretty*
youth? when the voice interrupted again –
wearily.

'All right, let's stop there for the moment, shall

we? I think we *all* need a rest. Is anyone capable of making a decent cup of tea?'

She moved then, walking boldly down the central gangway towards the stage.

'I am.'

Heads turned to stare from the front row and the two people on stage shaded their eyes, peering in her direction. The actress, Nadine, said, 'Who the hell's that?'

'I'm Rosalind Flynn,' she said. 'I'm looking for work. Any work.'

'You've got a nerve, barging in here. Hasn't she, Lionel?'

The voice spoke languidly from her left. 'She certainly has, darling. But I'm quite prepared to forgive her if she really can make a good cup of tea. Are you sure that you can, Miss Flynn?'

'Yes, quite sure.'

'Show her where it's kept, somebody.'

A plump, middle-aged woman who had been sitting at the front took her backstage where there was a cupboard-sized kitchen with a sink, a cold-water tap, a gas ring, a kettle, some dirty mugs, a teapot, a half-full bottle of milk, a soggy bag of granulated sugar, a metal spoon and a packet of Mazawattee tea.

'There's a tray around somewhere,' the woman told her. 'And there should be some matches.' She smiled at her. 'I'm Beryl. I do the character parts.

Sir Lionel likes his tea nice and strong, just a dash of milk and one sugar. Good luck, dear.'

The matches were in a drawer and she was well used to lighting temperamental gas rings in theatrical lodgings. While the kettle was boiling she emptied the teapot of a wad of old, cold leaves and rinsed out the mugs. She found a tin tray under the sink, and used a rag draped over the waste pipe to wipe off the old ring marks before putting out the clean mugs. When the kettle began to sing, she warmed the pot, made the tea – strong – and poured it out, adding milk. Since there was no sugar basin, there was no alternative but to put the soggy bag on the tray, together with the spoon. One of the mugs was larger and better than the rest and she put one spoonful of sugar in it and stirred it carefully.

The great man, Sir Lionel, was still sitting in the middle of the row, smoking a cigarette. He was wearing, she saw, a black cloak draped around his shoulders, and his thick silvery mane was long enough to reach its velvet collar. She handed him the best mug and he drank from it, paused dramatically, mug aloft, and drank again.

'Excellent. You're hired, Miss Flynn. Tea-maker and general dogsbody. Seven shillings a week.'

Beryl, the kindly character actress whose husband was away in the army, offered her the spare room in her rented cottage outside town for four shillings a week and included a hot meal once a day; otherwise she lived on pork pies and Smiths crisps from the local pub. The seven shillings was often late appearing, but somehow she managed. At the theatre, she did everything: making the tea, sweeping the stage and the auditorium, cleaning the Ladies and the Gents, painting scenery, moving props, mending costumes, running errands and prompting from the wings. Nadine, who had resented her arrival from the first, resented even more any prompts she had to be given by Rosalind.

'Does that girl have to shout, Lionel? She's supposed to whisper. I'm not deaf.'

'Don't keep blowing your lines, darling, then she won't have to say a word.'

The plays – by no means always Shakespeare – changed regularly, attracting respectably large audiences and sometimes leading drama critics: *The Tempest*, *Major Barbara*, *Much Ado About Nothing*, *The Constant Nymph*, *Hay Fever*, *Uncle Vanya*, *She Stoops to Conquer* . . . Sir Lionel always directed and very occasionally took interesting supporting parts himself, effortlessly eclipsing the rest of the cast whenever he did so. His company, Rosalind soon realized, was made up of actors and actresses who were either too young or too old to be called up, or were unfit for military service. Paul, the actor who had played Orlando, for instance, had flat feet, while the one who had been Jaques was so short-sighted he kept bumping into scenery, and Nadine was quite a bit older than she had looked from the back of the stalls.

Whenever the air raid warning sounded during performances it was ignored. The audience stayed firmly put, the play continuing without pause to the accompaniment of ack-ack guns booming. A near miss did some more damage to the roof and to the auditorium ceiling, which showered down plaster particles like a fall of snow. One day, as she was sweeping the gangway during a rehearsal, the great man beckoned her from his seat in the stalls. When she stood before him, broom in hand, he looked up at her and smiled.

'*More than common tall* . . . like your name-sake. You'd make a lovely Rosalind, darling, if we could only find you a matching Orlando. Perhaps one day . . . Meanwhile, I'll see if I can find a little part for you soon . . .'

She played one of the spirits attending on Prospero in *The Tempest*, and then Dorcas, a shepherdess in *The Winter's Tale*. The seven shillings went up to nine, though their payment was just as erratic. After that she was given small speaking parts and then longer ones, praise from Sir Lionel and catty comments from Nadine. Over one of the hot meals in her cottage, Beryl warned her.

'You want to be careful, dear.'

'What of? Nadine doesn't worry me.'

'I'm not talking about her. It's him.'

He took her to dinner at a restaurant one evening. Heads swivelled as they made an entrance and were ushered to the table and there was a flutter of applause, gracefully acknowledged by Sir Lionel. He was a charming dinner companion and an attractive man, in spite of being old enough to be her father – actually, almost her grandfather. He was seriously considering her, he told her, laying a hand softly on hers, for the part of Gwendolen in *The Importance of Being Earnest*, but, first, he'd like to hear her read a passage or two.

The reading took place in his nearby flat where the walls were hung with framed photographs of famous actors and actresses, and a great many of Sir Lionel himself in his younger days as Romeo, Hamlet, Laertes, Henry V, Oberon, Petruchio . . . She dutifully admired the broodingly handsome looks, the chiselled lips, the perfect left profile, the thick, dark hair, well aware of what was coming. As her mother had explained long ago, sleeping with people who had influence in the theatre was the necessary price of getting good parts. She'd already had several unpleasant experiences – one, especially, that she preferred to forget – but luckily Sir Lionel was as charming in bed as he was out of it. He gave her a pair of very nice silver earrings and the part of Gwendolen, opposite the flat-footed Paul as Jack. The local newspaper critic praised her performance. *A fresh and exciting new talent . . . I hope we see more of Rosalind Flynn – next time in the West End?* Nadine, who had played Cecily beneath several layers of make-up, wasn't mentioned at all.

Other good parts followed: the Princess Katharine in *Henry V*, Titania in *A Midsummer Night's Dream*. The nine shillings rose to eighteen. Nadine left in a huff and presently another and younger actress joined the company – another English rose with porcelain skin and Cupid's bow lips, called Felicia. Like Rosalind, she began by tea-making and sweeping and dogsbodying but, before long, she was walking on, then speaking, then taking minor roles.

At the restaurant one evening, Sir Lionel let slip casually that he was thinking of putting on a new production of *As You Like It* later in the year. 'I've always thought that you'd make an interesting Rosalind. Do you think you could do it, darling?'

She was sure that she could, and do it well. It was the part she had always wanted to play. The part that she had been named after and which perfectly suited her looks, her voice, her style . . . swaggering about in boots and breeches, teasing, mocking, daring. But when the time came to cast the play several months later, it was Felicia who was given the role. Felicia who was being taken out to dinner and to the flat, Felicia who was being given the good parts while she was back to playing minor roles.

'I did try to warn you, dear,' Beryl said. 'It's always like that with him. I've seen dozens come and go. They never last long.'

Rosalind packed up her few belongings, including some clothes filched from the theatre wardrobe in lieu of the three pounds still owed her in wages, and she kept the earrings. She went home to spend Christmas at the lodging house on the south coast. Her bedroom, she discovered, was occupied by an actress playing Dandini in *Cinderella* at the Winter Gardens, and the other rooms were taken by Buttons, the Fairy Godmother, and one Ugly Sister. She slept on the sitting-room sofa and spent the days walking along the promenade, keeping away from her parents who had not concealed their disappointment that she had thrown away her big chance. The beach, mined and barbed-wired against the enemy, was deserted, the wind cold, the sea grey and rough. She sat on a bench, watching the waves curl over and crash in endless succession onto the shingle, and wondered what to do next. In less than a week she would be eighteen, which meant that she was old enough for war work. They might send her off to toil at a bench in a munitions factory. She'd heard what that could be like from a girl she'd talked to on a bus: twelve-hour shifts drilling hundreds and hundreds of holes, all exactly the same. Or, almost worse, she might be made to join one of the women's services – put on some horrible uniform and march about saluting. As she contemplated this prospect, a group of khaki-clad ATS girls came striding along the promenade, chests stuck out, arms thrusting away like pistons, feet crunching in unison. At their head stomped a female officer even uglier than all the rest put together. *Left, right, left, right, left, right* . . . She watched them march away out of sight.

On the way home, she stopped at a seafront café, bought a cup of tea and a stale rock cake and sat by the window. The oilcloth on the table was smeared with slopped tea and gritty with crumbs, the ashtray full of cigarette butts. Someone had left a dog-eared magazine lying on a chair – a women's magazine of the kind she never normally read, full of handy home hints and recipes and knitting patterns and romantic love stories with impossibly happy endings. She picked it up and glanced idly through articles which told her the best way to unpick knitting wool, how to patch a shirt and turn cuffs, how to reconstitute dried eggs and how to make Savoury Tripe Casserole. At the end there were letters from anxious readers:

I have been going steady with an RAF sergeant until he was posted away. At first we wrote to each other every week, but now I haven't heard from him for more than three months. Do you think he's stopped loving me?

And an intriguing response to an anonymous reader.

To Worried Brown Eyes, If you will supply a stamped addressed envelope, I will send you a confidential reply that may help you with your unfortunate problem.

She flicked through the magazine again and found a feature on rotating crops in the vegetable garden and how to prepare the soil properly for early plantings, illustrated by a drawing of a jolly-looking woman with her foot plonked on a spade. On the opposite page, there was a photograph of an equally happy-looking girl gripping a very long pole and standing on what seemed to be the deck of some sort of boat. *Appeal for Volunteers*, it said underneath. *There are vacancies for more women volunteers to be trained to work canal boats.*

Rosalind took another bite into the rock cake. Were there indeed?

Four

Dear Madam,
In response to your letter, I enclose an application form and an explanatory letter about the Women's Training Scheme for work on canal boats. I should advise you that before continuing with an application it will be necessary for you to consult your local Labour Exchange.

I should be pleased to interview you if you could come to these offices next Thursday at 2.00 p.m. The necessary medical examination could take place on the same day to save you two journeys. Kindly telephone to confirm your attendance.

Yours faithfully,

The letter had been sent from the offices of the Ministry of War Transport in Stratton Street, London. Frances took the train to London and at two o'clock presented herself at Stratton Street. She was shown into an office where the writer, a grey-haired woman who looked like a school-teacher, was sitting behind a desk.

'Do you have any experience of boats, Miss Carlyon?'

'Well, I've done quite a bit of dinghy sailing.'

'I'm afraid that won't help you in this case. Work on narrowboats is completely different.'

'Narrowboats?'

'That's what they're called – not barges. Barges are much wider – at least a fourteen-foot beam, or more. The narrowboats are seventy-two feet long but under seven foot wide and specially designed to travel through narrow canals and locks.'

'Do they use horses?'

'Some of them do, as a matter of fact – old traditions die hard on the canals – but the Grand Union Canal Company narrowboats that you'd be working on are all fitted with diesel engines. The Company have been good enough to cooperate in the training scheme for women. There's a shortage of men, you understand. Canal work is a reserved occupation, but, nevertheless, a number of boatmen have joined the services and mean-while the narrowboats have become an important means of transporting vital war materials, especially coal. Using the canals saves space on the railways, and keeps supplies out of the reach of the U-boat attacks at sea. Tell me, Miss Carlyon, why didn't you apply to join one of the women's services?'

'I've been trying to for ages but they kept turning me away. I got fed up with waiting.'

'I see.' There was a pause. The woman was looking at her closely. 'The idea of going on the canals probably seems rather romantic and attractive to you, Miss Carlyon, but, in fairness, I should warn you that the work is very hard, very dirty and more or less continuous. Do you think you'd be up to it?'

She shrugged. 'I suppose I won't really know until I've tried.'

'Very true. Well, so far as the training is concerned, the hard work begins immediately. You will train under a woman trainer with two other recruits. You will be required to do a trip from the London docks at Brentford or Limehouse, carrying supplies up to Birmingham for delivery. You will then go on to Coventry to load up the empty boats with coal to bring back for delivery at various destinations. When you have completed two trips satisfactorily, you will be expected to be capable of working your own pair of boats.'

'A *pair* of them?'

'Narrowboats work in pairs, usually with a crew of three. The motor boat, which has an engine, pulls the butty which is without one. Did I mention pay? You'll be paid two pounds a week while training and are then entitled to a week's leave without pay. After that you'll receive three pounds a week and one week's paid holiday a year, with a short leave after every three trips. Light and heat are provided free and you receive extra rations of tea and sugar. There's no uniform provided and no extra clothing allowance, I'm afraid. By the way, can you swim?'

'Yes, of course.'

'Believe me, there are many who can't. Have you any questions you'd like to ask?'

Given time, she could probably have thought of plenty, but at the moment her mind was blank. 'When would I start?'

'As soon as possible. Assuming you pass your medical.'

The doctor was brisk and raced through the examination, listening to her chest, peering down her throat and into her eyes, firing off questions. 'Have you had any serious illnesses? When did you have your tonsils out? Appendix still present? Any other operations?'

She passed and there was another encounter with the schoolmarm in the office.

'Can you start at the beginning of next week, Miss Carlyon?'

'I don't see why not.'

'Your trainer will be Miss Rowan. She's very

good and I'm sure you'll like her. If you report to the Grand Union Canal Company depot at Bulls Bridge, Southall, they will tell you where to find her. Take as little luggage as you can – there won't be much room for storage on board. You'll need some bedding, towels and sensible clothes . . . thick jerseys, a waterproof jacket, warm socks, stout shoes, and a good strong leather belt, if you have one. I don't suppose you happen to have trousers of any kind?'

Frances caught the train home. Aunt Gertrude had already moved down to Averton and helped her assemble the sensible clothes. There was the dark-blue guernsey that she'd worn sailing and Vere's school trunk up in the attics produced old skiing trousers, a cricketing sweater and some thick grey woollen socks, while she still had most of her old school clothes – a belted gaberdine raincoat, Viyella blouses, striped pyjamas, Chilprufe vests and a pair of brown lace-up walking shoes. It was all serviceable and undeniably sensible. Some more ferreting round the attics unearthed a canvas kitbag from her father's army days and a padded sleeping bag of Vere's from his scouting ones. There were plenty of towels in the airing cupboard and she raided spare-room beds for a blanket and a pillow, and snaffled a leather belt from Vere's chest of drawers, punching an extra hole in it with a kitchen skewer to make it fit.

Aunt Gertrude gave her the keys to her London flat so that she could stay the night there before travelling out to Southall. 'I gave Vere a set as well so he could use it if he wanted whenever he's in London.'

'Well, I hope he doesn't turn up while I'm there. He'll throw a fit when he hears what I'm doing.'

'I shouldn't worry too much. Your father seems to approve.'

Approval didn't exactly describe Papa's reaction to the news. He had barely listened when she'd told him, his attention being entirely fixed on a new orchid that he had acquired.

'*Stanhopea tigrina* – gold and blood-red six-inch flowers with a very strong scent. Very special, don't you agree?'

'Yes, it's lovely.' She had marvelled politely at the dormant, flowerless thing in its pot. 'You think it's a good idea, then, Papa?'

'What idea?'

'For me to go and do war work on canal boats . . . like I just said.'

He was examining his new possession intently from all angles. 'Yes, I should think so. You like boats, don't you?'

'Aunt Gertrude will be staying here – to keep you company.'

'So she will. That's good.'

To her relief, Vere didn't arrive at the London flat – the ground floor of a house only a stone's throw from Harrods – and she had the place to herself. Rather disappointingly, there was no air raid that night – nothing at all to disturb the peace except some drunken American servicemen stumbling about in the blackout and swearing loudly.

In the morning, as instructed, she caught a suburban-line train out to Southall, complete with her kitbag and a bundle of bedding tied up with rope. It was a cold three-mile walk to the depot at Bulls Bridge and she carried the kitbag over her shoulder and the bundle clutched in one hand. The kitbag kept slipping off and the bedding kept tripping her up. At the depot she found corrugated iron sheds and brick buildings, offices and workshops, boiler-suited men hurrying about. There was no sign whatever of any canal. One of the workmen directed her to a door marked Enquiries, and she sat on a bench in a room for a long time until a man appeared to tell her that she'd find Miss Rowan down at something called the lay-by.

'You'll see a row of boats tied up at the wharf. Hers are *Cetus* and *Aquila*. She'll be there.'

She followed the directions given and lugged her luggage past more sheds and buildings and out across a big yard and on and on, arms aching, until she saw the canal for the first time. It lay before her. Not exactly the willow-lined, sparkling waterway of the sunny recruitment picture and of her imagination – more a trough of scummy water bordered by scrubland, cinders and mud. She also had her first view of the narrow-boats.

They were moored by their sterns to a long concrete wharf, tied with ropes to iron rings and packed together so neatly and closely that it looked easy to walk all the way across the row, from one to the next. The magazine picture had only shown a part of a boat but now she could see the whole. They were not only very narrow, they were also very long and painted in bright fairground colours with highly polished brass trimmings. Smoke curled up from chimney pipes, washing was pegged out to dry on lines rigged across empty holds and, ashore on the wharf, women in long black skirts, with shawls and scarves over their heads, were scrubbing away in zinc tubs. A man stood smoking a pipe on the stern of one boat and ragged children were playing a noisy game on the wharf, screaming and running about, mongrel dogs barking at their heels. They all looked like gypsies.

Years ago, when Frances had been nine, gypsies had trespassed at Averton. They had set up camp in a clearing in the woods, close to a stream, and she had ridden by on her pony and spied on them from behind a tree. Spied on the dark-skinned, black-haired people in strange clothes with their painted caravans, skewbald horses, chickens and goats and lurcher dogs, the big black kettle suspended on a hook over a wood fire. She'd watched for some time, her heart thudding with a fearful fascination. If they saw her, they might catch her and carry her off against her will to live with them for ever.

She's gone with the raggle-taggle gypsies, O!

Her pony had whinnied at the horses and one of the men who was standing by the fire, smoking a pipe, had turned, caught sight of her and smiled. She'd been hypnotized by his handsome looks and by his smile and by the golden hoop in his ear and the red scarf knotted round his neck. He'd beckoned to her and she'd got off her pony and walked towards him as if drawn by invisible silken threads. Close to, he had been even more handsome. Glossy black hair, dark eyes, teeth gleaming as he smiled and beckoned. The other gypsies had fallen silent, staring as she had followed him up the wooden steps into one of the pretty crimson and green caravans.

My mother said
I never should
Play with the gypsies in the wood . . .

A woman had been sitting inside, stirring something in a pot on an iron stove. She'd worn long black skirts, a yellow shawl and a purple silk scarf tied round her head; there had been golden earrings in both her ears and golden bracelets on her wrist. Her eyes were black as sloes and she'd talked in a strange language as she'd showed Frances the flowers painted over the woodwork, the bunk bed with its patchwork cover, the gingham curtains at the little window above. She'd opened cupboards and then a big locker under the bed, motioning to her to bend down to look inside, just like the witch in *Hansel and Gretel*. Given her a push.

She'd fled in terror from the caravan, bursting out of the doorway, down the steps, past the man, scrambled onto her pony and galloped away.

The memory still haunted her; still made her heart thud faster; still fascinated and frightened her, both together. And she still dreamed of her dark and smiling gypsy.

After a moment, she collected herself and started down the slope towards the wharf.

When she reached the boats, she could see that there were pictures painted on them – pictures of fairy-tale castles, of trees and rivers and mountains – and patterns of hearts and roses and diamond shapes. The company initials GUCCC were written along the sides and the number and name on the sterns: *Andromeda, Auriga, Delphinus, Libra, Pegasus, Polaris* . . . all constellations, unless she was mistaken. As she walked along the wharf, searching for *Cetus* and *Aquila*, the women looked up from their washtubs and their gossiping and fell silent. They had lined and dark-skinned faces like gypsies, but they were unsmiling. Neither hostile, nor friendly; they merely stared. The sensible thing would have been to ask them where to find Miss Rowan and her boats, but their silence and their stares were unnerving. One of the dogs ran up and bared its yellow teeth at her. She reached the man she'd noticed standing on the stern. He wore a flat cap and a dark jacket with cord trousers and heavy boots, and his face was sharp as a weasel's. He watched her with the same unreadable stare as the women, and in the same silence. As she passed him, he took the pipe out of his mouth and spat over the side of his boat.

She came across the *Aquila* first, and a woman poked her head out of the cabin doors. She was youngish and wirily built, with short brown hair and wearing what looked like sailor's serge trousers, a navy pea jacket and peaked cap.

'You'll be one of my new trainees. Come aboard!'

Frances scrambled clumsily over the side, hauling kitbag and bedding bundle after her.

There was no real deck to speak of – just a small well at the stern which also accommodated a large wooden tiller and led to some kind of cabin.

'Come down backwards. It's easier. Hand me your kit first, though. Thank God, you haven't brought too much. Some of them bring trunks and there simply isn't the room.'

She lowered herself gingerly backwards into the cabin, cracking her head in the process.

Miss Rowan was heaving her luggage onto a side bunk. 'This is the butty cabin. It's a bit bigger than the one on the motor because there's no engine – that's why I use it. I sleep on the cross-bed. You can have this one here, if you like. The other two trainees will have to go on the motor. First come, first served.'

Frances rubbed her head, looking round. The gypsy caravan had been very similar but this was even smaller – no more than a few feet square, not much more than five feet high, and every inch put to use. The walls were lined from roof to floor with cupboards and stained with brown varnish. The cross-bed, breezily referred to, was invisible. Every shelf was crammed full, something hung on every hook and over every rail, and a miniature cooking stove was scorching her left trouser leg. But it was the brass that she noticed more than anything; it winked at her from every side. Brass knobs and handles and rails and hooks, and brass without any purpose other than to adorn – old horse brasses, old brass door handles and old brass bed knobs.

'It's traditional,' Miss Rowan said. 'The boat people love their brass. So do I. You can put some of your stuff in that long cupboard above the bunk and there's a locker underneath, as well as the little cupboard there at the end. Keep the space under it free, though, so you have somewhere to put your head at bedtime. While you're getting yourself sorted out, I'll make us a pot of tea.'

Frances emptied the kitbag contents into the long cupboard and into the locker which was already partly occupied by a frying pan, tins of evaporated milk, sticks of firewood, a bottle of disinfectant, bars of soap, and what looked like a car battery. The small cupboard was useful for the oddments – her alarm clock, sponge bag, hairbrush and comb. Miss Rowan, meanwhile, had put the kettle on the stove, taken mugs off their hooks and lowered a hinged panel, revealing shelves stuffed with canisters and tins and an assortment of crockery.

'Our larder. I'm afraid the milk's tinned. Do you have sugar? Take a pew on the coal box there.'

She sat down on the lid of the coal box, which

71

did double duty as a step. Miss Rowan had fixed the hinged panel so that it was propped on the edge of the side bunk.

'Our table.' A spare plank of wood fitted neatly across the cabin's width. 'My seat.' She poured out the tea into the thick china mugs. 'I think we'll manage quite well, don't you? By the way, which trainee are you? What's your name?'

'Carlyon.'

'I meant your Christian name. We always use those on the cut.'

'Frances.'

'I'm Philippa, but everyone calls me Pip. Cigarette?'

She accepted the Players and puffed away, though she had hardly ever smoked before. It was snug in the cabin and, after a while, she found that it no longer seemed quite so claustro-phobically small – as though the space had somehow magically expanded around her. Pip talked about the trip they were to do, taking a cargo from the docks all the way up to Tyseley near Birmingham, then onwards to load the empty boats with coal from one of the coalfields around Coventry for dropping off at canal-side factories on the way back.

'It'll take us at least three weeks from start to finish, I'm afraid, as this is a training trip. An experienced crew could manage it in about ten days and the real boaters in a week, but then they've been doing it all their lives.'

'The real boaters? You mean the people I saw just now on the wharf? They didn't seem at all friendly.'

'Some of them are and some of them aren't. We're a bit of a mystery to them, you must understand that. They know nothing about us or our world. Their whole lives are lived on the cut – it's always called the cut, by the way, never the canal – and that's all they really know. The cut, working the boats, their own very particular ways and customs. It's important for us to respect them. After all, they've been here for a long time – two hundred years or more. We're the newcomers who have to learn to fit in. They can teach us a lot, if they're minded to, and help us when we get into trouble, which we often do. Sometimes, but not very often, we can even do *them* a good turn and they never ever forget that.'

'I got the impression that they resented us.'

'Who wouldn't? A lot of strangely dressed young women, playing at boats, shouting at each other in la-di-da voices, doing everything all wrong, and getting in their way and holding them up. I don't blame them, if they do. And, by the way, never call the boats barges or the boaters bargees, and never go on board without their permission, or look inside their cabins, or even lean against one of their boats, and never be overfamiliar, especially with the men, and never *ever* compare them with gypsies. It's a great insult.'

'I thought that's what they were, at first. They look awfully like them.'

'So would we if we'd spent all our lives in the open air, living on a boat and always on the move.'

'You mean, they actually *live* in a tiny space like this? All the time? Don't they have homes?'

'The boats are their homes. They're born in them, they live in them and they die in them. And they bring up their families in them. Some of them have as many as twelve children, though they don't usually all survive. Don't ask me how they manage to cope, but they do. Most of them keep their boats neat and clean as a whistle – others don't, it has to be said. They live with their work and it's a very tough life, especially for the women.' Pip drained her mug. 'Drink up and I'll give you a tour of the boats.'

A metal bowl with a wooden handle, known as a dipper, was unhooked from the wall and the mugs rinsed out in a few inches of water poured from a can. Water, Pip explained, was precious. The boats carried big four-gallon cans on the cabin roofs. There was no convenient tap to turn on and the cans had to be refilled at water taps along the canal that were, Pip said, few and far between. The dipper apparently did service for washing many things – vegetables, dishes, clothes and themselves. Water used for cooking was kept for boiling eggs, egg water for making tea and cocoa.

The motor, *Cetus*, lay alongside the butty, *Aquila*. At first sight, there had seemed little difference between the two, but Frances soon learned otherwise. For a start, the tillers were quite different – the butty's a long, thick piece of wood, curved and tapered like a steer's horn, while the motor's was metal banded in red, white and blue paint and bent like a swan's neck. On the motor, the steerer stood on a flat counter at the stern, not down in a well as on the butty, and the propeller blades and helm were protected by fat rope fenders hanging at the stern. The cabin on the motor was even smaller to allow space for the engine housed beyond the bulkhead, but otherwise it looked much the same as on the butty. She inched her way after Pip along the narrow gunwale that led round the edge of the cabin to the engine-room doors, where she was shown the shiningly kept green National diesel engine and, not so shining or impressive, the enamel bucket that served as the lavatory.

'You empty it over the side into the cut,' Pip said cheerily. 'Bucket-and-chucket. A bit primitive, but you'll soon get used to it.'

The gunwale came to a stop at the end of the engine housing and, to go further, they had to climb up onto the roof which also accommodated an old and rusty bike. Beyond and below lay the yawning chasm of the empty cargo hold. Pip's lecture continued.

'Both of the holds together can carry up to fifty tons. When we're loaded up, you'll see how low the boats go down in the water. Right now, they're riding high.' Pip glanced sideways at her. 'Think you can walk the plank?'

The hold was divided into three by wooden cross beams placed across the width of the boat. Supported by these, a long and sagging pathway of single planks ran from the cabin roof to the fore-end of the boat. There was, Frances saw, no other way of getting there. She gritted her teeth. 'I'll try.'

It was a terrifying journey. The planks were no more than a few inches wide and the only handholds along the way were the uprights fixing them to the cross beams. If she lost her balance on the stretches in between, she'd fall straight into the bottom of the empty hold, a good eight feet below. And, just to add to the fun, the planks bounced up and down as she walked. The idyllic recruiting picture hadn't shown any of this, nor had it been mentioned in the interview. She made it to the far end and turned to watch

Pip run across after her as easily as a tightrope walker.

The top planks had finished at a tarpaulin-covered framework called the cratch – another test in the obstacle course. She followed Pip round a narrow gunwale, clinging to the tarpaulin strings, until they finally reached the fore-end deck where an iron hatch covered a snake pit of coiled ropes and straps. There was also a head-light mounted on an iron stand.

'Not allowed to use it except in tunnels,' Pip said. 'Blackout regs and all that. Same on the cut as everywhere else. Well, now that you've done all that, let's go and have some dinner in the canteen. They call it dinner – remember that – not lunch.'

The depot canteen was crowded with workmen and wreathed in cigarette smoke. A wireless was going at full blast with a comedian telling jokes to roars of audience laughter. There was a long table down the centre and smaller tables at the sides, where the men were sitting and eating from plates piled high with hot food.

'Mechanics, painters, carpenters, glaziers, blacksmiths . . .' Pip told her. 'Nice chaps.'

She seemed to know most of them, exchanging smiles and greetings on their way to the counter. 'Hallo there, Bill. Is your wife better? Good to see you, Pete. Hallo, Tom.'

Tom stopped her with an arm outstretched like a barricade. 'Who's the young lady, then, Pip?'

'This is Frances. She's just started training with me.'

'Not another Idle Woman! Don't know as we can put up with many more of you.'

'You'll just have to make the best of it, Tom. You're stuck with us till the war's over.'

He gave her a nod and a grin, raising his mug of tea to Frances. 'Good luck to you, miss. You're goin' to need it.'

They queued up at the counter at the far end of the canteen. The food was served by women who were as friendly as the men.

'What'll you have, love? The toad's very nice today.'

They collected eating irons from a box and found room at one of the tables. As well as the Yorkshire pudding and sausages, Frances's plate contained a small mountain of mashed potato and boiled cabbage.

She said, 'They don't really think we're idle, do they? Like Tom said.'

Pip laughed. 'They know we're anything but.' She tapped the front of her pea jacket. 'See this badge I'm wearing. What does it say?'

'National Service.'

'What's under that?'

78

'It looks like the initials I W. With some waves underneath.'

'IW stands for Inland Waterways. But *they* say it stands for Idle Women and that's what they call us. It's only a joke. They don't really mean it.'

'Do I get one of those badges, too?'

'When you've completed your training – if you do. How do you feel about working on the boats – now you've seen something of them? Do you think you're up to it?'

She said cautiously, 'I should think so.'

'Well, you walked the plank all right and that's a pretty good test. Some of the girls never even get that far. They take one look at the boats and scarper. Actually, it's best if they do it then rather than going through all the training and then pushing off. That's a big waste of everyone's time. Other girls find they just can't cope, for one reason or another. They're not strong enough, they get ill or injured, or they just plain hate it. Somehow, I think you'll probably be all right, but only time will tell.'

Frances was far from certain that she shared Pip's optimism. The obstacle course had been alarming and, cosy as the cabin was and decent as Pip seemed, the prospect of sharing such cramped quarters, in such primitive living conditions, was daunting. No bath, no proper lavatory, only a hand bowl for washing in a few inches of water.

And, so far, Pip hadn't said a word about how they actually handled the boats. Over cigarettes and cups of very strong tea at the end of their dinner, she brought up the subject of locks.

Pip sighed. 'Everybody worries about them, but they're really very simple. Just think of them as steps in a staircase. The land across England's not flat, so sometimes you have to go up the stairs and sometimes you have to go down. The steeper the rise, the closer together the locks. Only, of course, boats can't climb stairs so you have to help them go up and down, using the water as a kind of lift. A lock has two sets of watertight gates with a chamber in between, big enough to take the boat – usually *two* boats, in fact, side by side. If the water in the chamber's at the *same* level as the boat when you arrive, then you can go straight into the chamber, shut the gates behind you and let the water in, or out – depending if you want to go up or down the staircase – by working the gate paddles that control the sluices. When the boat's at a level equal to the way you're heading, you open the other gates in front and off you go. But if the water in the chamber was at a higher or lower level than your boat when you came along, then the lock's *against* you and the boat has to wait outside while you bring the water up, or down, to its level. It's all done by gravity and water pressure and manpower. See?'

'Sort of.'

'You will, once you've seen one working for yourself. We've got time to take *Cetus* out for a little spin up to Cowley lock this afternoon. Before that, we must do a spot of shopping so we're ready to get going when the other two arrive tomorrow.'

They bought tinned baked beans and sardines, margarine, bread, Camp coffee, tea, jam, sugar, tins of evaporated milk. Frances offered up her emergency ration book with the extra coupons for tea and sugar.

The little spin up to Cowley wasn't quite so simple as it had sounded. First of all, the engine on *Cetus* had to be started. This involved another shuffle round the motor's gunwale and some bewildering instructions about handles and levers and rods and flywheels.

'I'll take the starting handle to turn her over and when I think she's ready I'll begin counting. When I get to *three* you push the compression lever down. Ready?'

Pip swung the handle vigorously – for all her small size, she was very strong. Round and round and round. 'One, two . . . *three*!'

Frances was too late the first time and jumped the gun on the second. Pip, patient as ever, began all over again. This time she got it right and the engine burst into a pulsating throb. Back round to the stern again where Pip fitted the swan-neck tiller into its hold.

'Important lesson. Tillers reach all the way across the counter. They have a nasty habit of swinging about if left unattended and can knock you clean off the boat. That can be very dangerous on the motor if you fall near the propeller blades. If that ever happens to somebody, put the engine into neutral immediately. Got that?'

'Yes.' Another terrifying hazard.

'You steer holding the tiller *behind* you. Engine controls are right here, just inside the cabin where you can reach them. Only three gears: forward, neutral and reverse. No brakes – you use reverse to slow down. The steerer needs all the space available for manoeuvre so anybody else on the counter has to perch forward on the gunwale – which means you in this instance, as I'm steering. Don't worry, it's quite safe. You can lean against the cabin sides and hang onto the ledge.'

They untied – narrowboats, according to Pip, didn't cast off, nor did they have port and starboard, but simply left and right, or inside and outside, the inside being the side nearer the towpath. You held in, or you held out. *Cetus* nosed its seventy-two-foot length from its place in the row and out into the cut. One arm of the Grand Union Canal turned towards the docks and the other, which they took, headed for the

Midlands. So far, the scenery was a big disappointment. There were fields and hedges on one side, but the other bank was lined with ugly wharves and warehouses. The only pleasant smell came from the Nestlé's cocoa factory – tantalizing whiffs of chocolate wafting around on the air. Pip shouted to her at her precarious perch on the gunwale.

'Another lesson: keep to the *right* of other boats on the Grand Canal, but stay away from the banks if you can. The cut's about twelve feet deep in the middle but the mud piles up at the sides and you're liable to get stuck in it if you're not very careful. Catch the rudder in the mud and you've lost control so your bows go careering into the bank. It happens a lot at bad corners, but luckily there aren't any on the way to Cowley.'

'What do you do, if you get stuck?'

'You use a shaft to try and shove the boat off. If you're lucky, it works. If you're not, you hope for a snatch from another boat passing – they tow you off, in other words. Like I said, the boaters will usually help if they aren't in too much of a hurry.'

It was hard to imagine the silent washerwomen, or the weasel-faced man, helping anybody but their own kind.

Cetus trundled on slowly and steadily. The pace was tortoise-slow – no more than about four miles an hour – and she began to see why it took so long to get anywhere.

'Bridge coming up,' Pip shouted. 'Keep your head down.'

They chugged under the archway of an old brick bridge. With the motor unloaded and riding high, the arch wasn't much above their heads. Soon afterwards the scenery improved, with fields on both sides and a magnificent group of beech trees just below the lock. They tied up and walked along the towpath running beside the cut. It was blowing an icy wind, and Frances found a silk scarf in her raincoat pocket and tied it over her head.

'It's an uphill lock,' Pip said. 'You're going *up* the staircase. The bottom gates are open, as you can see, and the water's down at our level, so if we were on the boat we could have gone straight in. We'll go up onto the lock-side so we can see properly.'

Frances peered gingerly over the edge at the water ten feet or so below. The brick walls of the lock sprouted ferns and weeds and were dank and slimy with moisture. At the far end, the heavy wooden gates were closed against the water above the lock. Pip was pointing and giving more lessons.

'The gates are V-shaped to withstand the weight of water, and those big wooden balance beams sticking out each side are for pushing them open and shut. There's a walkway along the top of them over the gates so you can get across, holding onto those iron rails. You can't see the paddles because they're always underwater, but they're worked by ratchets on each side which you turn with a windlass.' Pip cocked her head, listening. 'We're in luck. Here comes a pair of boats. Now you'll be able to see how they work through a lock. If they're boaters they'll be very quick. Watch carefully but for heaven's sake stay out of their way.'

Frances watched them approaching, the motor boat pop-popping along far ahead of the butty, which followed on a long tow rope. Both boats were loaded, black sheeting strung tent-like over the cargo, their gunwales only a few inches out of the water. The motor slowed to come into the lock below, the boatman steering it with one hand behind him, the other hand forward on the engine lever. The butty was steered by a fresh-faced girl of about her own age, nothing like the old crones at the lay-by. She was wearing a shabby-looking coat and a woollen scarf wound like a turban round her head. As the butty came gliding silently into the chamber the man unhooked the tow rope from the motor stern and threw it onto its fore-end. He shinned up the ladder in the wall and pushed the bottom gate shut on his side. The girl was already on the opposite lock wall, tying the butty to a bollard before she shut her gate. The boatman passed close to Frances as he headed for the top gates and he gave her a nod. He was young, too, and dressed the same as weasel-face – flat cap, jacket, waistcoat, cord trousers, boots – but he had a nice face. She watched him winding up the ratchet with a bent piece of iron and the girl doing the same on the other side.

The water in the bottom of the lock began bubbling and swirling and rising and the pair of boats rose with it. When it had stopped, the man pushed his gate open, leaning his weight on the beam. The girl was back on the butty and he stepped onto the motor's counter, now at his level. The engine pop-popped throatily as the boat moved forward, nosing the other gate open. As he came abreast of the butty's fore-end, he scooped up the tow rope and fixed it to the motor's stern again. The butty, tugged along, followed docilely, its wooden rudder trailing a flowing plume of horsehair. The girl had one arm hooked over the tiller and was mixing something in a bowl. As she passed Frances, she gave a smile and a wave of her wooden spoon.

'Nice scarf yer've got there. Wish I 'ad one loik that.'

She would gladly have handed it over, but the butty was out of reach. The whole lock process had taken a matter of minutes, and yet neither the man nor the girl had seemed in any great rush. Every movement had been unhurried, the big boats controlled with ease. They had made it look quite simple.

'This,' said Pip, holding up a bent piece of iron like the boatman had used, 'is a windlass. *My* windlass. I'll give you one of your own later and you must *never* lose it. And don't ever lend it to anyone else either. Now, we'll shut the top gates and drop the paddles. I'll do this one and you do the one on the other side.'

The other side meant walking yet another plank – the narrow and slippery walkway over the bottom gates – not so bad now that the lock was full, but it was still a long way down to the water on the outside. She held onto an iron rail until she reached the lock-side and ran up to the top gate. The heavy balance beam refused to budge an inch.

Pip was leaning against her beam, walking backwards and pushing rather than pulling. She shouted across. 'Go round the other side and put your back into it, it's much easier and a lot safer.'

Frances copied her and after a few desperate shoves the beam started to move; once she'd got it going, it swung over smoothly.

Pip came across to show her how to drop the paddle. 'You put the windlass just on the end of the spindle, give a half-turn back, release the safety catch, then take the windlass off quickly and down she goes.' The ratchet rattled down with a crash. 'Now, we'll open the bottom paddles to let the water out of the lock. Cowley lock's always left ready for uphill boats. The lock-keeper usually sees to it, but we'll save him the trouble.'

Winding the paddle up was a lot harder than dropping it. She found that she barely had the strength to turn the windlass on the spindle, and Pip had to take over and finish the job for her.

'You need to build up some muscle power, that's all. And always make sure the safety catch is properly engaged; if the ratchet slips when you're winding, the windlass can fly off and hit you.'

With the paddles up, the lock chamber was emptying fast, the water churning and whirl-pooling outside the gates as the lock water escaped into the cut below. When the levels were even, they opened the bottom gates ready for the next boats.

'Time to go back,' Pip said. 'But first we'll have to wind the motor – that means turning round.'

Winding the seventy-foot-long narrowboat in the canal was akin to turning a huge lorry in a narrow country lane, but Pip managed it smoothly without getting stuck on any mud.

'Have a go on the tiller now, Frances. Let's see how you do. Remember, push it the opposite way to where you want to go – right to go left, and left to go right.'

They swopped places, Pip perched out on the gunwale, while Frances stood on the counter, gripping the metal tiller behind her. She could feel it vibrating, expectantly, awaiting her commands. *Right to go left and left to go right.* Mercifully, the cut went straight for a while until they came to a gentle right-hand bend.

'Don't cut your corner,' Pip said. 'Keep going right round the bend.'

She pushed the tiller a little to the left and the *Cetus* responded obediently, her fore-end swinging round to follow the curve of the bank.

Pip beamed. 'I think you're a natural. It's instinctive with some people, you know. Others never quite manage it.'

After the bend, though, she was dismayed to see a pair of boats bearing down on them and taking up what looked like most of the cut.

'Keep to the right,' Pip reminded her. 'But well away from the bank. Pass as close to them as you can.' She leaned over and tweaked the tiller a fraction. 'You can move over a bit more. You've got *loads* of room.'

They passed within a few feet of the other motor, so close that Frances could see that the steerer had blue eyes when he turned his head briefly in their direction and nodded.

'How d'you do?'

The remark had been addressed to Pip, who

called back above the combined put-putting of the two engines. 'How d'you do?'

The butty, following at the end of its sixty-foot tow rope, took a while to reach them and the boatwoman steering repeated exactly the same terse greeting to Pip, who gave the same answer. No waves or smiles, just nods and those few words.

They arrived back at the depot lay-by just before dark, and *Cetus* was returned to her berth beside *Aquila*. The wharf was empty now except for a dog or two, sniffing about. Boat doors were shut, hatches closed, portholes covered, no chinks of light showing for enemy bombers to see. Pip was going off to have supper with friends in Ealing and invited her along, too, but she felt too tired to eat and too tired to make the tedious journey all the way back to Aunt Gertrude's flat.

'You can sleep on the boat tonight, if you like,' Pip told her, apparently still fresh as a daisy. 'We'll stoke up the stove and you can make yourself some tea, or cocoa. There's tinned food in the larder, if you get hungry. I won't be late back.'

When Pip had gone, she sat down wearily on the side bunk. There was no room to walk around, barely room to stand upright – not that she felt like moving. Her legs and arms were aching, there was a huge and painful bruise on her shin and it felt as though she'd done something nasty to her stomach, either from winding up the paddle or heaving at the lock gates. On top of all that, her brain was spinning like a top with everything she had been taught during the day, most of which she would never be able to remember.

After a while, she roused herself to stoke the fire, put the kettle on the stove, take down a mug and the cocoa tin – all reachable without moving from the side bunk. Later, she cut a slice of bread and spread it with margarine and plum jam. Then she made up her bed with Vere's padded sleeping bag and Aunt Gertrude's pillow and blanket, and wound up her alarm clock. No point in setting it as she had no idea what time she was supposed to get up. She poured some water into the dipper, washed her face, cleaned her teeth and undressed – awkwardly in the cramped space – wriggling into her pyjamas before switching out the light. Pip had lowered her previously invisible bed out of a cupboard in the wall and her feet touched the end of it, while her head was stuck in the hole under the little overhead cupboard.

The unwelcome thought crossed her mind that Vere had probably been right. Life on a narrow-boat was going to be much less romantic and carefree than she had imagined. One short day had been enough to demonstrate that bald fact, let alone the three long weeks of training that lay ahead. She was aware that Pip had been watching her closely, noting everything she did, or failed to do. She could walk the plank without falling off, and maybe she would learn to steer all right, and maybe she'd be able to work the locks, eventually, but what of all the other tests and trials lying in wait that she didn't even know about yet?

She could hear men's voices on the wharf outside, only a few feet away from where she was lying. Rough voices, rough speech, the scrape and crunch of heavy boots, the smell of strong tobacco. Boatmen.

After a while, the voices stopped, the footsteps faded away and another sound reached her ears from further along the wharf: someone was playing an accordion and singing. Another boatman.

A cold winter's night, an' I run by the light
Of Waddington's headlamp, the moon.
The fore-end is boastin' a thin skim of ice
An' I reckon 'twill thicken up soon.
The goin' is slow and there's two miles to go
And the boozer there shuts in an hour,
But 'tis just the same way on a mornin' in May
When the chestnut bloom's in flower.

There were several more verses on the tribulations of narrowboat life, each finishing with the same refrain about the chestnut blooming. Her brain had stopped spinning, her senses were calmed. She lay quietly in the dark, listening.

Five

The girl said, 'I'm not at all sure it's going to suit me. I'll have to see.'

She had climbed into the same train carriage, carrying a heavy suitcase and a bulky roll of bedding which Prudence had helped her put up onto the overhead rack. Then she had plonked herself down on the seat opposite and started to munch a bun produced from a paper bag. She was a large girl with big hands and feet and a square jaw. Her name was Janet and she was a trainee as well, she announced, having spotted Prudence's bedding also up on the rack. There were more buns in the bag, but she didn't offer one. She went on talking through mouthfuls.

'I've been in two minds, haven't you? I mean, how can they expect us to do men's work? We won't have the strength.' From the way she'd carried the suitcase and the bedding, she seemed just as strong as a man. 'I didn't fancy any of the services, you see, and I thought this might be a good idea, but now I'm not so sure. We have to work from dawn to dusk, you know. They don't give us any time off until we've finished the first trip and, even then, we only get a few days' holiday before we have to start the next one. I told the woman at the interview that we ought to get more days off but she just said it was the way it worked. I don't know how they think we'll cope, do you? And I'm not going to be put upon. I won't stand for that.'

She talked most of the way to Southall, devouring two more currant buns. Prudence soon learned that she had been a shorthand typist with a lace-making company in Nottingham, that she had an elder brother called Rodney who was at sea in the Merchant Navy, and that she lived with her widowed mother. Her mother had seen the advertisement about canal jobs for women in the *Nottingham Guardian* newspaper and thought it sounded quite nice, and that it would keep her out of the services.

'She didn't want me getting called up, you see, and being preyed on by soldiers. A lot of service girls are immoral, she says, specially in the ATS.'

Her mother had thought much the same, but Prudence couldn't imagine soldiers preying on Janet who looked capable of taking care of herself.

They arrived at Southall station to discover that the van which was supposed to meet them wasn't there. Janet said she'd a good mind to go straight back home but, after twenty minutes or so, it turned up and took them to the depot of the Grand Union Canal Carrying Company at Bulls Bridge. A man in the office sent them to find a Miss Rowan and the training boats, *Aquila* and *Cetus*.

The boats, tied up in a long row along the wharf, were painted in lovely bright colours but the people on them were not so lovely. They stared in silence, and when Janet asked one old woman where Miss Rowan's boats were she went on staring as though she'd been spoken to in a foreign language.

Janet sniffed. In a loud voice she said, 'Dirty gypsies. I hope we don't have anything to do with them.'

They found the boats eventually, but not Miss Rowan. Instead, another trainee called Frances appeared and said that she'd arrived the day before and that Miss Rowan had gone over to the workshops for something. Meanwhile, she helped them get their luggage onto one of the boats and down into the cabin.

'Pip said you're to share this one. It's a bit smaller than the cabin on the butty because you've got the engine, but there's no difference otherwise.'

Janet had hit her head against the ceiling as she'd clambered down. She looked round, open-mouthed.

'We have to live in *here*? *Both* of us? I can't even stand up properly.'

'There's more room than you think. I'll show you where everything goes.'

The girl opened up cupboards, let down a flap that became a table and pointed out the cooking range and the box under the step where the coal for it was kept. There was scarcely space for them to turn around and look while she explained it all.

Janet said slowly and sarcastically, 'Would you mind telling us where we're supposed to sleep?'

'Well, this is one bed – the side bunk – and there's another bed that folds up into that cupboard at the back during the day which is much wider. I'll leave you to unpack, shall I? You'll have more room without me.'

When she'd gone Janet exploded.

'It's disgraceful! They got us here under false pretences. Nobody said anything about putting us in a place like this.' She sat down heavily on the side bunk. 'I'll have to have the other bed. This one's much too small for me. And there's not going to be nearly enough room for my things.'

There wasn't, which meant she took up most of Prudence's cupboard space as well.

Miss Rowan returned and called down into the

cabin. 'How are you two getting on? May I come in?'

She was about half Janet's size, but very firm when Janet immediately began to complain.

'The cabins are small because the important thing about narrowboats is the cargo they carry, so as much space as possible is given over to the hold. I'm sure you'll get used to it – most girls do. Why don't you both come over to the butty cabin and we'll all have a cup of tea together before I show you both round the boats. We won't have long, I'm afraid, because we should be getting our orders soon – which means we'll have to leave straight away. You'll be learning as we go along.'

They climbed across to the boat tied up next door where the girl, Frances, had boiled a kettle on the range and was making a pot of tea. There was just room for the four of them to squash round the let-down table and Miss Rowan, who asked them to call her Pip, offered some digestive biscuits; Janet, Prudence noticed, took two. After that, they were taken round both the boats.

She followed in Janet's stolid wake, clutching at every available handhold and trying to pay attention to what was being said. Miss Rowan – she must remember to call her Pip – was talking about snubbers and shafts and studs and straps and sheets. She struggled to take it all in, but it was impossible. They came to the room where the engine lived and were lectured about that as well – about handles and flywheels and compression levers. Also, about the bucket.

Janet, who seemed rather wary of Pip, and had been unusually silent, found her voice again. 'You mean we're supposed to . . . to use *that*?'

'You'll soon get used to it,' was the brisk answer. 'Now, let's see how you both manage the top planks.'

A very long and very narrow walkway of planks had been erected across the length of the empty hold, leading to the front end of the boat, far away. Pip went across first and Janet, who seemed to have no nerves at all, bounced after her to the other side. Now it was Prudence's turn and she was rooted to the spot with fear.

Pip shouted encouragement. 'Come on, Prudence. You can do it. Just walk across, looking straight ahead.'

She put one foot on the first plank and then the other; the plank bounced and she froze, petrified.

'Come *on*, Prudence.'

She forced herself to take another step, and then another, stopped, wobbling, with arms outstretched, trying to balance herself.

'Don't look down. Just keep going. You're doing jolly well.'

Part of the way across there was a piece sticking up that supported the planks and she clung onto it desperately, but Pip was soon nagging her again. She stuck just the same at the next handhold and managed the last part in a desperate rush.

Pip said kindly, 'Don't worry, you'll find it quite easy after a while. You'll soon be running across.'

Names were called out over a loudspeaker from the depot offices. 'Calling Ron Burbridge . . . please report to the office for orders. Calling Alfred Carter . . . please report for orders. Calling Bill Stokes . . .' Engines started up and boats began to leave. By mid-afternoon, though, Pip was still waiting for her orders. She was giving them a lesson in knot-tying when the call finally came.

'Calling Miss Rowan, calling Miss Rowan. Please come to the office for orders.'

Pip rushed off on her bike and Janet started grumbling again.

'I think it's shocking, don't you . . . the way they expect us to live in these disgusting conditions? Nobody warned us what it would be like, did they? And that woman seems to think we should just put up with it. She keeps saying we'll get used to it.'

Frances said, 'You can always leave, if you want. Nobody can make you stay.'

'Oh, I know that. But they should have warned us before – it's not right.'

Pip came racing back, clutching papers. 'We're to leave at once. Limehouse. Steel billets arrived from America. Frances, you help me with the engine. Janet and Prudence, you go ashore and be ready to undo the stern ropes.'

Cetus's engine thumped into life and smoke puffed out from the chimney. Pip called to them from the tiller.

'You can untie us now – then you two hop aboard the butty. We'll tow you on cross straps, close up, so there won't be any need for you to steer.'

They moved off, went under a bridge and turned sharp right into another arm of the canal with Pip honking a horn loudly as they went round the corner. Before long it started to rain and Janet went down to shelter in the cabin while Prudence chose to stay at the butty's stern, getting wet. For one thing, Pip and Frances were out in the rain so she felt she ought to be as well, and for another she was glad to be away from Janet and her never-ending moans. It was fascinating to be journeying along the canal, seeing the backs of buildings instead of the fronts and looking into windows. A girl at an office desk lifted her head to watch them go by; Prudence could see her wistful expression through the sooty glass. That was me at the bank, she thought. I was just like that.

They carried on slowly but steadily along the canal under more bridges, through Greenford and then Perivale until they reached Alperton at dusk where they stopped for the night. The boats had to be tied together, side by side – Pip called it breasting-up – which meant running about in the rain and grabbing hold of slippery ropes and trying to remember how to tie them properly. To Prudence's relief Frances and Janet were given the job of walking across the planks to the fore-end.

When, at last, it was all done, Pip cooked the supper on the butty cabin stove – baked beans, spam and potatoes, with tinned rice pudding heated up for afterwards. They ate round the let-down table and finished with cocoa made with evaporated milk and some digestive biscuits. It was very snug with the doors shut against the rain and the dark, the curtain pulled across the little porthole, the brasses gleaming in the electric light. Prudence thought that the supper had been rather nice; Janet, however, hadn't thought so at all. The minute they got back to their own cabin on the motor, she started off again.

'I'm still *starving*. I don't know how they can expect us to do all this work if they don't feed us better. I thought we'd get extra rations.'

'We get extra tea and sugar.'

'I meant meat and butter and things like that.'

The paper bag rustled. 'Lucky I've still got one bun left.'

She chewed away ravenously. Prudence wondered if the prospect of extra rations might have been more of a reason for Janet volunteering for canal work than the threat of preying soldiers. The last of the last bun went down in a noisy gulp.

'Anyway, I've made up my mind that I'm not putting up with it. We got soaked to the skin, doing all that tying up. Enough to give us pneumonia. I'm leaving first thing in the morning. Soon as it's light, I'm off. There's an Underground station right by here – I spotted it when we arrived. I'll get the first train and if you've got any sense, you'll come with me.'

'We haven't given it a proper try yet.' She sounded a lot more confident than she really felt. 'And I think we ought to.'

Janet was emptying drawers and cupboards and repacking her suitcase. 'Suit yourself. But I think you're barmy, if you stay.'

'Shouldn't you tell Pip that you're going?'

'Not likely! She'd give me a long lecture. Anyway, I've a perfect right to leave if I choose.'

They made up the two beds, Janet commandeering the larger one that came down from a cupboard across the back of the cabin. Prudence took the bowl off its hook and poured in some warm water from the kettle. She washed her hands and face and cleaned her teeth and then went to tip the water over the side into the canal. When she came back Janet was already in bed and asleep – a big snoring hump under her eiderdown. She sat down on her narrow side bunk, twisted and turned to get out of her clothes and into her nightie, and then wound her hair up in curlers before switching out the light. As soon as she lay down, she realized that she'd forgotten to kneel and say her prayers, so she said them where she was. *God bless Mother and Father and keep them safe from harm.* She paused, listening to the piggy snores. *And please give me courage. Help me to walk the top planks and do everything else all right, and don't let me give up, like Janet.*

Janet was up at dawn, bumping and banging around. She had gone to bed in her clothes so as soon as she'd rolled up her bedding and put on her coat, she was ready to leave. Prudence helped her haul her things out of the cabin and onto the bank. It had stopped raining and there was a clammy mist hanging low over the canal.

Janet gave her a pitying look. 'Poor you, staying here. You'll be sorry.'

As she stumped away without a wave or a backward glance, Pip's head popped out of the butty cabin.

'Gone, has she? Oh well, I can't say I'm too

103

sorry. You're not thinking of leaving, too, I hope?'

'No.'

'That's good. Come over and have some breakfast as soon as you're dressed. It's all ready.'

Frances was stirring a saucepan of porridge on the butty cabin stove. They ate it in bowls with syrup drizzled over the top and evaporated milk poured round the edge. And they had cups of tea and thick slices of bread and margarine and jam.

'We needed a decent breakfast,' Pip said, lighting a cigarette. 'It'll be a long day and it's going to be hard work with one short, but we'll manage it. It's rather a useful training stretch between here and Limehouse, actually. A bit of everything for you two to experience – bridges, locks, a tunnel, bends, mud and lots of traffic. We'll go breasted-up all the way, except for the tunnel where we have to single out. You can stay on the butty, Prudence, so you won't have to worry about steering just yet. Frances will be on the motor with me, so she can get some practice at it. After we've loaded up, you'll take a turn with me. But before we leave, I'll have to phone the office to see if they can arrange for a replacement trainee to meet us somewhere.'

She disappeared ashore to make the call while they washed up the breakfast things and put them away.

'Good riddance to Janet,' Frances said. 'Pip guessed she'd go, sooner or later. She thought you might go with her – that she might talk you into it. I bet she tried to.'

'Yes, she did.'

'Well, I'm glad you stayed.'

As soon as Pip came back they untied and went on their way, Prudence alone in the butty which was tied alongside the motor. The canal snaked its way through London, meandering past back streets and houses, under road bridges and railway arches, past parks and pubs and shops and more streets, offices and factories, a school, a hospital, a cemetery. People stopped to watch them from bridges and men whistled at them from windows and workshops. Loaded boats were coming up from the docks: Grand Union Canal narrowboats painted in their red, white and blue, other boats in different company colours and great barges towed by horses, the bargees lolling at their tillers like kings.

The locks were terrifying: the thud and clang of the heavy gates, the slimy walls, the whirling, churning water. There were several close together, and, each time, Pip handed over the tiller to Frances and jumped ashore. The lock-keepers helped with the gates and with the winding and unwinding. What exactly they and Pip were doing was a mystery, but the water rushed out and the boats sank down, and the lock walls grew deeper and darker and slimier.

Further on, there was the tunnel – even more frightening. The boats had to be singled out to leave room for others coming the other way, and the butty was now towed on a short rope behind the motor so that Pip and Frances were the boat's length ahead of Prudence. The headlights gave hardly any light and icy drops of water kept plopping onto her hair. The noise of the engine was so loud that nobody could have heard her shout if anything had gone wrong.

The further they went towards the docks, the smellier and uglier everything became. Slums and skinny children in dirty clothes with dirty faces playing on the towpath, broken glass, rubbish bobbing in the water – old tyres, tin cans, a drowned cat horribly bloated with legs stuck in the air. Rubbish dumps, scrapheaps, bombed buildings, and, to her horror, more locks, more clanging gates, more swirling filth and slime. Finally, they came down into Limehouse where they tied up alongside other boats and barges, end on to the high wall of the dock. On the other side of the basin, she could see the hulls of sea-going ships and, tethered in the skies above, silver barrage balloons.

Pip went off and came back to say that they wouldn't be loaded until early the next morning.

'We'll have a cup of tea,' she said. 'Then we'll get the boats ready. The stands and the top planks and beams have to come out and the holds left completely empty. We'll start with the motor boat and you can both help me and learn how to do it. Tomorrow, after we've been loaded, we'll have to sheet up. That means covering the cargo completely with waterproof canvas sheets. If it were coal we wouldn't need to bother, but as it's steel we must keep it and the boats dry.'

They clambered down into the holds and Pip showed them how to take out the stands and top planks and how to knock out the beams and unscrew the rigging chains. They collected up stray brooms and mops and tools and put them away. They also collected bruises and splinters. When at last they had finished, Pip announced that, as a reward, she would take them to a Chinese restaurant for supper. They climbed up the vertical iron rungs in the wharf wall and walked out through the dock gateway into a dark street, groping their way by torchlight past shuttered shops and bomb sites and black alleyways.

The restaurant had crimson walls decorated with writhing golden dragons, paper lanterns hanging from the ceiling and a doorway at the back covered by a curtain of coloured beads. The beads moved with a tinkling sound and a tiny Chinaman appeared. He wore embroidered silk robes, a black

107

hat on his head and slippers on his feet and, as he turned to show them to a table, Prudence saw a thin pigtail hanging down his back like a piece of tarred string. He kept nodding and smiling and speaking to them in a funny sing-song voice but she couldn't understand a word.

Pip said, 'Mr Lang suggests the noodle soup. And the pork foo yung. And maybe some special fried rice and mixed vegetables and bean curd in black bean sauce. Does that sound all right for both of you? He cooks it all himself and it's usually pretty good.'

The curtain beads tinkled again as Mr Lang left the room. Before long, more customers came in – dock workers and a group of foreign merchant seamen. The three of them were the only women in the place, but Pip knew one of the workers and chatted to him across the room. The sailors were gabbling away in some strange language and one of them kept staring at Prudence.

The food, when it came, was served in different dishes and nothing like Prudence had ever seen or tasted before. The foreign sailor kept on staring; she could feel his pale-blue eyes fixed on her all the time while she was eating the funny food and trying to listen to what Pip was saying about what they had to do the next day. They were to be up before dawn to have breakfast and be ready for loading as soon as it was light. Once loaded, they would have to put the beams and stands and things back and do the sheeting-up. It sounded like an awful lot of hard work.

Pip said to her, 'Before we leave, I think we ought to try and get something warmer for you to wear, Prudence, otherwise you're going to freeze to death on the cut. There are some seamen's shops in Commercial Road. We'll see if we can find a jersey and maybe some trousers instead of that skirt – they'll be off points and very cheap.'

When they left, the Chinaman bowed low to them with his arms tucked up the sleeves of his robes. As Prudence passed by the foreign sailor at his table, he gave her a look that made her blush.

She slept on the narrow side bed again, though she could have taken down the cross-bed if she'd wanted to. The bed felt damp after all the rain but Pip had lit the stove for her to warm up the cabin and it was nice to lie close to it, seeing its friendly glow in the dark and listening to the water slapping gently against the sides of the boat. She wondered if there would be an air raid. The Germans always went for the docks, didn't they? That was why there were all those barrage balloons floating about. And the docks must be very easy to find because of the river; she'd seen the burned-out buildings and the rubble lying all round the docks. But the siren didn't go and after a while she stopped worrying about German bombers and thought, instead, about the sailor. No man had ever looked at her in that way before. Mr Simpkins's creepy sidelong glances had made her skin crawl with disgust, but the foreign sailor's stare had made her insides flutter with a quite different feeling.

It was still dark when Frances banged on the cabin door in the morning. The stove had gone out and Prudence dressed as fast as she could, unwound her curlers and brushed her hair. It was easier to do it all sitting down on the bunk. The butty cabin was lovely and warm and, once again, there was hot porridge, thick slices of bread, and tea.

Pip said cheerfully, 'Looks like you've been bitten in the night, Prudence.'

'Bitten?'

'Bedbugs. Just a couple of bites on your cheek. I'm afraid most boats seem to get them. The company fumigates them regularly, but they always come back.'

She put a hand up to her cheek. 'Oh.'

'It's really nothing to worry about. You'll get used to it.'

They started the loading soon afterwards. Slings of long steel bars were lifted from the quayside by a giant crane, swung out over the boats and manoeuvred by the dockers down into the holds, almost without a bump. The boats sank lower and lower until the gunwales were only just above the water. Frances was sent to make more tea for the men and Prudence passed round the mugs. The dockers thought it was all a great joke.

'You'll be after our jobs next, I dare say,' one of them said to her, grinning. He'd been down in the hold, manhandling the steel bars. 'We'll 'ave to look out for you lot.'

When the loading was done, their work began – the sheeting-up that Pip had tried to explain. Back went the beams and the rigging chains, screwed up tight enough to pull the sides of the boat together. Then the stands had to be wedged into place, the top planks put back, even higher up than before, and fixed with screws and ropes and uprights so they were safe to walk along. Then the sheeting-up began – scrambling about the hold, unrolling the black tarred canvas from the boat sides, uncoiling tarry strings and throwing them over the top planks to be laced through an eyelet on the other side. Tightening those up meant a terrifying crawl on hands and knees along the top planks with Pip shouting instructions from below. The three top sheets, which weighed a ton, had to be hauled out and hoisted up over their heads to cover the hold from the front end down to the cabin, and every top string had to be threaded through a metal ring and tied off all along the edges. Prudence added a lot more bruises to the ones collected before, as well as cuts and blisters all over her hands. Her arms

111

and knees were aching, and the bed-bug bites on her face were itching.

'Well done both of you,' Pip said in her nicest and most encouraging voice, but Prudence didn't feel she'd done at all well; she only felt exhausted.

Pip left Frances to guard the boats and took Prudence off to get the jersey and trousers. The shop in Commercial Road sold all kinds of sea-men's clothes – boots and overalls and trousers and jerseys and vests and long johns crowded the front window and hung from the ceiling inside. The cockney woman at the counter called her 'duck' and went off to find a jersey that didn't swamp her and the smallest pair of bell bottoms. The jersey came down to her knees and the serge trousers had to be rolled up, but no clothing coupons were needed and they only cost seven shillings. Pip said she'd need a leather belt so she bought one for two and sixpence and the woman punched some extra holes in it for her. On the way back to the dock gate, Pip stopped at a phone kiosk to ask about the replacement trainee and came out looking rather pleased.

'They're sending one to join us at Bulls Bridge. Let's hope she's keener than Janet.'

Off they went again, out of the dock basin and back to the canal, and through the locks – uphill this time – and under the bridges. Frances came on the butty with her to steer and, instead of being tied up close to the motor, they were towed on a rope about ten feet long. The laden boats, sunk so low in the water, seemed to behave quite differently. Frances, struggling with the tiller, kept making mistakes and the *Aquila* kept charging off in the wrong direction. Once it charged straight into the bank and got stuck firmly in the mud. That was when Pip shouted to Prudence to go up to the front with a long shaft to try and push them off. She had to walk the top planks to get there, carrying a heavy wooden pole that was at least twice her height, like a circus balancing act. It wasn't quite so frightening with the hold full. If she fell off she'd slide down the sheets into the water, but it didn't seem nearly as bad as falling headlong into an empty hold. She reached the fore-end safely, stuck the pole into the bank and pushed with all her might. Nothing happened however hard she tried and, in the end, a passing barge stopped and the bargee, a huge man, clambered aboard the butty, took hold of the pole in his great fists and with one shove they were free.

They got back to Bulls Bridge before dark and tied up at the lay-by for the night. Pip cooked the supper – tinned stew and tinned peas and mashed potatoes – and Prudence fell fast asleep over her plate. They were allowed a lie-in until seven the next morning, but as soon as breakfast

113

was finished and cleared away they had to clean the cabins, black-lead the stoves, polish the brass, fill the coal boxes, chop the firewood, scrub the decks and cabin tops, refill the water cans – Janet would have grumbled like anything. When all that was done to Pip's satisfaction, she gave them another lesson on tying knots and a demonstration on how to splice ropes – mending broken ones by winding the strands together.

The replacement trainee turned up at midday. Pip had gone off to the depot office and Prudence and Frances were practising rope-splicing in the motor cabin when they heard someone call outside. They stuck their heads out to see who it was.

She was standing at the edge of the wharf above – a tall, slender and very beautiful girl with russet-red hair that reached to her shoulders in a mass of curls. Her face was pale, her lips painted scarlet, and the silver earrings in her ears dangled like miniature chandeliers. She was wearing the strangest clothes: a green velvet cloak over a leather jerkin and corduroy breeches tucked into high red boots, and, on her head, a Robin Hood hat with a long quill feather sticking out of it. A carpet bag lay at her feet and a roll of bedding was tucked under one arm. She gave them a dazzling smile.

'Hallo there,' she said. 'I'm Rosalind Flynn. I've come to train.'

Six

She realized that they had no idea what to make of her. Maybe it was the theatre-wardrobe clothes, or maybe they'd expected someone quite different, or maybe she was just in the wrong place.

She said, 'This *is* Miss Rowan's boat, isn't it? *Cetus*. That's what they told me.'

One of the girls – the fair-haired one – nodded. 'Yes. She'll be back soon.' The rest of her emerged from the cabin doors. 'I'm Frances Carlyon. And this is Prudence Dobbs. We're both trainees.' She held out her hand. 'How do you do.'

Rosalind shook it politely and did the same with the other girl – the shy one with the sausage curls and what looked like bedbug bites all over her face. She indicated the old carpet bag at her feet and the rolled-up blankets and pillow that had done many years' faithful service on all manner of couches in all manner of lodgings. 'What do I do with these?'

They helped her on board and guided her down, backwards, into the cabin which made her feel like Alice in Wonderland after she'd drunk from the wrong bottle and grown too big. Sausage-curls said that she could have the bigger bed that came out of a cupboard at the back, if she liked. The fair-haired girl told her that she slept on the butty next door.

'The butty?'

'The boat without the engine. This is the motor – it has one to pull the butty. That's why this cabin is a bit smaller.'

They showed her where to store her things, and where everything else was kept, and how the dolls-house stove worked. And then they all inched their way along a very narrow ledge outside the cabin to where the engine was, and the bucket.

'You get used to it,' the one called Frances said. 'After a bit.'

Neither of them, she guessed, had ever come across anything like it before. Lavatories, in their lives, would have been made of white china and come with chains to pull and torrents of flushing water. But she had known buckets before, and outside privies, and chamber pots under the bed.

They clambered back along the ledge to the cabin, their feet almost in the water. The boats were all loaded up and ready to go, the fair-haired girl said. They'd been down to Limehouse docks for the steel billets and now they were going to take the Grand Union Canal north up to Tyseley near Birmingham to deliver them. After that, they'd go to a coalfield somewhere near Coventry and fill up the empty holds with coal for factories on the way back.

Rosalind said, 'I'm afraid I don't know a thing about barges. I've never been on one in my life before.'

The fair girl grinned. 'Don't worry, we hadn't either, had we, Prudence?'

The other one shook her sausage curls and scratched at the bites.

'And they're called narrowboats, never barges – just to warn you.'

Miss Rowan appeared and introduced herself as Pip. She was bossy but not bitchy. Some of the theatre-wardrobe clothes, she explained kindly, were going to be a problem. The cloak would get dangerously in the way and the hat would fall off. The breeches were quite practical, especially the leather belt that held them up, and so was the jerkin, but the smart red boots would get ruined in a trice. Did she have any other footwear? Alas, no. In the end it was decided to make do for the time being with the breeches, the jerkin and the boots, and Pip lent her an old jacket to wear on top. It would be a good idea, she added, still very kindly, if Rosalind tied her long hair back or it would blow about and stop her seeing properly and might get caught in machinery. A piece of string should do the trick – there was plenty of it on the boats.

They had thick spam sandwiches and cups of strong tea in one of the cabins and, afterwards, three bent pieces of iron were handed out ceremoniously like precious gifts. They were for winding up things called paddles in locks and for letting them down. They must NEVER be lent, lost or dropped overboard, but kept safe and worn tucked securely in their leather belts. Assisted by the girl, Frances, who obviously had more of a clue than she'd let on, Pip gave a demonstration of how to start up the engine which seemed to require a combination of brute force and split-second timing.

Rosalind was given the job of untying ropes from iron rings – she managed that all right – and hopped onto the back of the motor boat which Pip was driving, balancing on the ledge at the side, to keep out of her way. Frances and Prudence were in the one they'd called the butty, towed along behind them on the end of a piece of rope with Frances doing the steering. They pottered off along the canal, the engine making loud pop-popping noises. A row of urchins, leaning over a bridge, shouted rude things and hurled clods of mud. Pip took no notice.

'Pointless shouting back or getting angry – it only encourages the little perishers.'

After a while, they came to a lock – the first one she'd ever seen. The gates were standing wide open and in they went, the butty sliding in beside them. Pip, who had undone the tow rope, chucked it neatly onto its front end as it passed.

She followed Pip up some slippery steps to help heave the gate shut on their side. Frances was struggling with the gate on the opposite side of the lock, while Prudence was holding the butty on a rope, like a dog on a lead.

'We have to lower the paddles,' Pip said. 'Watch carefully.' The bent piece of iron was fitted onto the end of some sort of winding gear and given a quick turn and, hey presto, there was an ear-splitting rattling as the thing unwound. The other gate was still half open, Frances still struggling. 'Come on, Frances, put your back into it!'

They ran up to the gates at the top end and Pip said, 'Got your windlass? Soon as Frances has finished at the bottom, see if you can wind this paddle up.'

It reminded her of cranking the handle of the wind machine backstage – only fifty times harder. She could hardly move the wretched thing at all.

Luckily, some old man appeared from somewhere and took over with a lecherous wink and a grin.

Pip said drily, 'You won't be able to count on a lock-keeper every time. You'll have to be able to manage it yourself.'

The water rushed in to fill the lock and the boats rose up with it. Then the top gates had to be heaved open before they stepped back on board. More rope tricks from Pip as the motor overtook the front end of the butty, and they were off again with it trailing behind them. On a straight stretch, Pip handed over.

'Take a turn with the tiller – let's see how you do.'

Badly, as it turned out. At the first bend, she pushed the thing the wrong way and the boat headed straight for the bank. Pip grabbed hold of it and they veered away just in time. They went on veering this way and that. Shoving the tiller in one direction to make the boat's nose go the opposite way made no sense at all, and it was no help that the front end was miles away from her and that the boat was so slow to react. Still, after a while, with Pip constantly correcting her, she began to get the hang of it.

They were gradually leaving London behind, chugging north-west at a funeral pace along the canal – the cut, as she was supposed to call it. Another pair of boats came past them, from the other direction – not with trainees but with the gypsy-like people she had seen at the depot. Pip called out something and the man steering the motor jerked his head and muttered something back. Rosalind smiled and waved at him but he ignored her. So did the woman in the butty.

'Why are they so grumpy?'

'They're not grumpy. It's just their way, if they don't know you.'

They went through two more locks, and each time the gates were open for them.

'We're lucky today,' Pip said. 'We've got a good road. Sometimes they're all against you and it takes twice as long if you have to get the lock ready each time. Fill it, or empty it, as the case may be, before you can get in.'

Across the fields the sun was already setting, painting the sky with lovely crimson streaks. They did two more locks, both obligingly open and ready, before they stopped in a wooded spot above the second one, close to another pair of boats. She had to walk along the top planks to the front end to tie up, but it wasn't too difficult. Ballet lessons had taught her about footwork and balance. She'd been rather good at ballet and if she hadn't grown too tall, she might have become a dancer instead of an actress. The lock was called Black Jack. According to Pip, the boaters gave them all names – Black Jack, Copper Mill,

Springwell, Stockers, Batch, Rickey – one hundred and fifty-four of them all the way up to Tyseley, and the names had to be learned and remembered. There was no map to help, not in wartime. Maps, like signposts, could help the Germans if they invaded; they'd been burned, torn up, hidden away under lock and key. Pip had made her own notes of what she called Useful Information: names of locks and towns, pubs and good places to eat, shop, have baths, fill up with water, get repairs done. She'd written it all down in a book which she carried in the pocket of her jacket. By the time they'd got both boats tied up, one along-side the other – which took some doing with the three of them scrambling about and a lot of yelling from Pip – it was dark.

Pip said hopefully, 'I don't suppose any of you can cook?'

'I can.'

'Good. Then you can do supper tonight for us, Rosalind. We've got potatoes and a cabbage and a tin of mince. Think you can make something with that?'

'Any onions?'

'There might be. We'll have a hunt.'

She cooked on the little stove in the motor while the others kept out of the way in the butty cabin. Two onions had been discovered in the locker under the side bed – sprouting but still edible – so she fried those before she added the tinned mince. The potatoes went into the oven, in their skins, and the cabbage was cut up, ready to do last. She'd been cooking meals on all kinds of tricky stoves since she was about twelve, making up dishes out of any scraps she could find. Cooking bored her mother, but not her.

They sat down to eat in the butty cabin, next door, where there was a bit more room. Pip said, 'This is very good, Rosalind. Did you work as a cook?'

'No. I'm an actress.'

They all stopped eating, forks halfway to mouths.

Pip said, 'How *very* interesting. I don't think I've ever met an actress before. What sort of parts did you play?'

'Oh, lots of different ones. I've been acting since I was a child.'

'What did you do most recently?'

She told them about being with Sir Lionel's company, which impressed them no end.

Prudence said, 'Why ever did you leave?'

She embroidered that bit. 'Well, I thought if I didn't do my war bit soon, I'd get sent into a factory, or called up into the services. I thought this would be more fun.'

Pip frowned. 'I wouldn't exactly call it fun. It's very hard work on the boats and pretty uncomfortable, as you'll discover. And, speaking of hard work, we've got a long day ahead of us tomorrow, so we need to get off as early as we can in the morning – which means being up before dawn. We'll have to let the boaters go ahead first – they won't want us holding them up – and that also means that the locks are likely to be against us unless we're lucky with boats coming the other way. Rosalind, you can go on the butty with Prudence while Frances comes on the motor with me and does some lock-wheeling – that's taking the bike along the towpath to the next lock ahead and getting it ready for us, if necessary.'

They drank cocoa and smoked cigarettes – except for Prudence who didn't smoke – and they talked. Pip had once worked a narrowboat of her own on the Worcester Canal, so no wonder she knew so much about it. Frances said she came from Dorset and made her home sound like a ruin, though it was probably very grand. Poor Prudence had been working at a bank in Croydon, totting up figures all day long. They wanted to know more about the theatre, so Rosalind entertained them with stories of various disasters – forgotten lines, falling scenery, faulty props – some of them exaggerated, others made up, a lot of them perfectly true. And with tales about Sir Lionel – though not everything about him. There was no point in shocking them.

The stove in the motor cabin was still warm when she and Prudence went back there for the night. They let down the bed out of the cupboard, across the bulkhead, and she arranged her make-shift bedding. Prudence sat on the edge of the other bunk in her nightie and woollen dressing gown, winding her hair up in curlers to make the sausage curls. She kept scratching the bites on her face.

'Pip says they must be from bedbugs. She says they always get them on the boats. I haven't seen any, though.'

'You wouldn't, sweetie, they're too small. I've had bites like that before, as well.'

Many times, indeed, but she didn't say so. Prudence wouldn't have come across such things, any more than the bucket in the engine room. Her home in Croydon would be clean and neat and entirely bug-free.

Rosalind put on her flannel pyjamas – left behind by one of the travelling salesmen – un-clipped her silver earrings and curled up on the cross-bed. It was surprisingly comfortable and with plenty of room sideways, though she had to bend her legs to fit in lengthways. It must be the marital bed in the boat people's cabins, husband and wife cosily tucked up together. They'd have to like each other a lot, mind, and it wouldn't do to be tall – not that any of the boat people were, so far as she could see. Height seemed to have been bred out of them so they could live on the boats without bumping their heads. They were short, but they were very tough and they were very strong.

She did some more thinking. The evening performance would be ending at the theatre, with Felicia playing Portia, perhaps, though the role would be far beyond her range. Given the chance, she could have done it well. She recited the words in her head.

The quality of mercy is not strain'd,
It droppeth as the gentle rain from heaven
Upon the place beneath: it is twice bless'd;
It blesseth him that gives and him that
    takes . . .

Or maybe Kate – that was a meaty part that she'd always fancied. *If I be waspish, best beware my sting.* Or Ophelia, drifting around, out of her mind. *There's rosemary, that's for remembrance; pray, love, remember: and there is pansies, that's for thoughts.*

And the thought she was thinking right now was that maybe the narrowboats hadn't been such a good idea. From what she'd seen and heard so far, factory work would be a rest cure; so would the services.

She propped herself up on one elbow, watching

Prudence winding up the curlers. 'What happened to the girl I replaced?'

'She left.'

'Why?'

'She hated it. But then, she didn't really give it a fair try. And she never stopped complaining. We were rather glad when she went.' Prudence stopped winding and looked at her anxiously. 'Do you think *you'll* like it?'

'I don't know, to be honest.'

'But you'll give it a try?'

She flopped back onto the pillow. 'Yes, I'll give it a try.'

There was silence and she turned her head to see that Prudence was kneeling beside her bed. At first she thought she'd dropped something and then realized that she was saying her prayers. Just as well somebody was; they were going to need all the help they could get.

Seven

The boaters moored at Black Jack lock had already left before dawn. Pip swore that they could see in the dark, like cats, and they played all kinds of tricks to keep ahead. Time was money to them. The sooner they were off, the sooner they delivered their load, the sooner they got paid and the sooner they could start the next trip. They'd make sure of getting away first by quietly loosing off the mooring ropes and then bow-hauling or shafting the boats along the bank before they started up the engine. And if they had the luck to meet another pair coming the other way, they'd be getting a good road with the locks ready for them.

After a quick breakfast *Aquila* and *Cetus* set off just as the sun was coming up over the trees, making the overnight frost sparkle. Frances was on the motor with Pip, to lock-wheel for her.

'I'll put you and the bike off at the nearest bridge-hole. Your job is to see if the lock's ready for us. If it isn't, then make it ready so that by the time I arrive, I can go straight in. But if another pair's coming the other way and get there first, then you'll need to warn me so I can wait out of their way.'

Just hop off, Pip had said, with the bike under your arm. As they approached the bridge-hole where the canal narrowed and boat and land came close together, Frances misjudged the hop and fell in a painful heap on the bank. Pip shouted something which she couldn't hear and the butty went sailing by while she was picking herself up, with Prudence and Rosalind waving encouragement. Pip's bike was a rusty old wreck without working brakes and a saddle that kept slipping sideways. To make matters worse, the towpath was full of ruts and craters which made steering straight impossible. Several times she ended up in thorny bushes and, once, narrowly avoided plunging into the cut. Finally, she reached the lock, threw down the bike and ran up to the bottom gates.

All was silent. No lock-keeper. No angry boatman coming the other way to claim priority. Only the lock and the still water . . . waiting for her to do something and do it fast before Pip arrived. She stared at the lock. Was it ready, or wasn't it? Her mind went blank – refused to work. Come on, it was simple really. Pip had always said so.

Think of the steps of the staircase. Think of the levels. *Think, think, think.* No, the lock wasn't ready. Of course it wasn't. It was full, the top gates wide open, the paddles up. Pip would be coming along at the bottom of the step with the gates shut against her, so the water in the lock had to be let out and brought down to her level and the bottom gates opened so she could get in.

Frances wrenched the windlass out of her belt and ran to the bottom gates and then remembered just in time that, first, she had to shut the top gates and drop the paddles. If the paddles were left open at *both* ends of the lock, the water would simply go on rushing through and gallons and gallons would be wasted. An unforgivable sin on the cut, according to Pip, since all the water going through the locks had to be pumped back at night up to the summit level.

Fear of dismal failure and disgrace lent her strength. *Hurry, hurry!* She put her back against the balance beams, legs braced, heels dug in, summoning all her weight and strength. Down with the paddles as soon as both gates were shut – rattle, rattle, rattle – and then off to the bottom gates to crank the paddles open, feet slipping on the frosty walkway as she hurried across from one side of the lock to the other. She leaned over the lock-side panting and watched the calm surface of the water at the foot of the gates. *Oh*

God, nothing was happening. Nothing at all.
Then she saw a little tell-tale whirlpooling movement disturb the calm and grow into a churning
torrent as the water rushed out of the open sluices
into the cut below.

As soon as the lock had emptied and the lower
water levels were even, the gates could be opened
– but not until then. In the distance, she could
hear the steady pop-pop of *Cetus*'s engine. By the
time it came round the corner she'd got one gate
open and was battling with the other.

Pip brought the motor in and the butty
followed alongside with Rosalind more or less
steering. Pip ran up the steps.

'Jolly good, Frances. You can shut them now
and drop the paddles. I'll do the top ones.'

She leaned wearily against the beam, sucking at
a huge blister on her palm. A hundred and something locks ahead. And all the way back again.

Rosalind was rather proud of herself for steering
the butty into the lock, alongside the motor.
True, *Aquila* had banged its nose hard against the
sides once or twice, and for a moment she'd
thought they were going to keep on going and
crash into the gates at the other end, but Prudence
had already raced up the steps with a rope and
wrapped it around an iron post to hold the boat
steady. She lifted the butty tiller out to keep it

from getting bashed on the lock-side – another Pip lesson – and waved up to Frances, who was sagging against the balance beam as though the effort of getting the lock ready had nearly killed her. The boats were rising on their magic carpet, Pip was back on the motor, Frances opening the gates, the motor nosing its way out, Pip picking up the butty tow rope as she passed its fore-end, Prudence holding the butty back so it didn't try to barge out as well and get jammed up. Once the motor was clear, Prudence let go and hopped back on board. For once, it went like clockwork.

They had left London behind and it was very pleasant and peaceful with the butty trundling along quietly. The hatches were more sheltered than the flat steering counter on the motor and if Rosalind opened the cabin doors, the warmth from the stove below toasted her red boots. She could stoke up the fire, put on the kettle, reach for a quick snack, if need be. They passed under bridges, meandered through fields and woods, past houses and cottages and gardens and pubs, with ducks and moorhens quacking and scooting around the boats for any scraps of food they had left. Every so often, another lock had to be negotiated. They got easier, with practice, and after about the sixth one she could bring *Aquila* in without banging against the sides. No stopping for lunch allowed; they had it on the go. Prudence made tea and some corned-beef sandwiches and passed them up to her from the cabin. She ate and drank with one hand, steering with the other. After a while, she offered the tiller to Prudence.

'Want a turn?'

Prudence shook her head. 'No thanks. I don't want to get us stuck again.'

Life must have been pretty grim for her at the bank, Rosalind thought. No adventures. No excitement. No fun at all. Her own life had had its ups and downs but, on the whole, the ups had been more than the downs and there had been plenty of fun. She couldn't imagine how anybody could bear being shut up from nine to five, day after day, chained to a desk, doing some boring work. She'd done her share of ghastly jobs – waitressing, pulling pints, washing-up – but they'd only been temporary while she'd been resting. The same with this boating lark. It wasn't something she'd want to do for too long. How the real boat people stuck it all their lives was beyond understanding, but for the moment it was OK. As soon as the war was over, though, she'd go back to the stage. Everything would be starting up again. People coming home – directors, actors, writers. There'd be new ideas, new opportunities, new everything.

She was dreaming happily about this when they came to yet another lock and Pip had decided that she should swop over with Frances and do the lock-wheeling for a bit.

'Think you can manage it?'

Pip asked that all the time and it was never so much a question as an order to be obeyed, whether or not you felt you could do whatever it was. And she was far from sure that she could. Riding Pip's beastly bike would be bad enough but that was nothing to the prospect of dealing with a lock, alone and unaided.

She landed herself and the bike successfully and wobbled off along the towpath with the no brakes and the wonky saddle. The lock was about two miles ahead but it seemed like ten. She found the bottom gates firmly shut, the lock full and the top gates wide open. In other words, she was going to have to get it ready. On her own. There was no friendly old lock-keeper in attendance, not even a cottage where she could have knocked on the door and wheedled some help. Nothing to be done but get on with it. The first thing – *if* she'd remembered correctly – was to shut the top gates and drop those paddles. Easy to say; a different matter to do. She started with the gate on her side. Luck was with her, because it moved quite easily and when she wielded her windlass the paddle went down with a satisfying rattle. She went down to the bottom gates and crossed over to the other side. The second top gate wasn't quite so obliging and she was getting her back into the job when somebody started yelling furiously.

'What the bloody 'ell d'you think you're doin'?'

He was striding towards her – a boatman with a furious expression.

She said calmly, 'I'm shutting the gates. Getting the lock ready.'

'Not bleedin' likely, yer not.' He slapped a fist on the other side of the balance beam. 'We're comin' through. One of them bloody trainees, aren't yer? The ones they calls Idle bloody Women. No bleedin' use to nobody. Got no right ter be on the cut. You git out the fuckin' way.'

'Excuse me, but I was here first.'

'Where're yer bleedin' boats, then?'

'They'll be here soon – any minute.'

He leaned across the beam, thrusting his stubbled chin at her. 'And we're here right *now*. See?'

She did see and there was no denying it – the pair of narrowboats were waiting above the lock, all ready to come in. Not Grand Union ones, but with different markings belonging to some other company. The boatman was pushing the gate open again, and her backwards. There was no point in arguing, not unless she wanted to end up in the lock, so she retreated gracefully and watched him undo all her good work on the other gate in a matter of moments. He glared at her on his way back to his motor.

135

'Don't yer bloody touch a thing. We're comin' in.'

She watched the two boats sliding into the lock. There were several children of various ages on each one, the smallest chained by its ankle to the chimney on the butty cabin roof – all of them staring as though she was some kind of freak. The woman on the butty wore long black skirts but she stepped gracefully from boat to lock-side and did her part as though there was nothing to it. The top gates were shut, the paddles down, then the bottom paddles up all in the twinkling of an eye. When the lock had emptied they opened the gates and went out. The boatman delivered a parting shot over his shoulder.

'Bleedin' trainees! Yer oughta go back where yer come from.'

She watched them going off down the cut and saw Pip and *Cetus* already coming up, *Aquila* trundling along behind. It was only then that it occurred to her that, thanks to the angry boatman, the lock was now ready and waiting and she'd scarcely had to do a thing.

Frances lost count of the locks they worked through during the rest of the day – some of them so close together there was no time to breathe in between, and each one a struggle with unbudgeable balance beams and lethal winding gear.

Prudence – sent to lock-wheel after Rosalind – forgot the drill completely and they arrived to find her sitting on a bollard with her head in her hands and tears streaming down her face. They steered the boats into the mud so many times that Pip lost her saint-like patience and her temper and told them how hopeless and useless they all were. Then Rosalind fell into the cut, trying, yet again, to shove them off the bank with the long shaft, and had to be hauled out and sent to hang her wet clothes to dry in the engine room while Pip found her something else to wear. After that Prudence slipped and gashed her knee which poured blood everywhere until it could be staunched and bandaged and, finally, Frances, doing another stint of lock-wheeling, left her windlass behind. When they tied up for the night they had covered less than twenty miles, and supper was eaten in chastened silence.

At the end of the meal, Pip lit a cigarette and said brightly, 'I think it'd be a very good idea if we all go and have a drink at the pub. Forget about today. Tomorrow's bound to be better.'

They had tied up alongside other narrowboats, not all belonging to the Grand Union. Two pairs had the name Fellows, Morton and Clayton painted on the side. 'Known as Joshers on the cut,' Pip told them. 'They can be a bit rough. Best to stay well out of their way.' Another pair of boats at the end of the row carried no company name. 'Those belong to Number Ones – they own their own boats.'

The Feathers lay a short way along the towpath – an ancient tavern that had served generations of boaters and stabled their horses overnight. The boatmen were drinking, smoking, and playing darts and dominoes and a Mothers' Meeting of boatwomen occupied a corner, nursing their drinks on their aproned laps and gossiping. As they entered, faces turned towards them and there was a hush.

Frances had never drunk beer before and thought it tasted awful. So, by the look on her face, did Prudence, but Pip and Rosalind were downing theirs and lighting cigarettes. Pip offered her one too. Just as well that Vere couldn't see her now, she thought. Pubs and beer and fags. And boaters.

They were clearly unwelcome but Frances had the feeling that for all the turned backs, they were being closely observed – that every boatman and boatwoman in the pub had taken note of their presence and that they were watching. One of the boatmen sitting at the bar turned round and she caught her breath because he looked so like the gypsy she remembered in the woods at Averton: glossy black hair, red scarf knotted at his neck, gold hoop in one ear. But there was a difference:

he didn't smile. He stared at her without expression and went on staring until he turned away.

The beer was making Prudence feel sick but Pip had paid for it and she felt obliged to drink it all. The only alcohol she had ever drunk before had been the half-glass of Christmas medicine at the bank. Father would never have allowed it at home and she had certainly never been in a public house. He would be shocked to the core, and so would Mother, and they'd be even more shocked about other things like the bucket in the engine room and the bugs in the cabin and nobody bothering to wash much. It had been an awful day. She'd done everything wrong and then let them down completely at the lock. When she'd got there, she couldn't remember a thing that Pip had taught her. The lock had been empty, the dark water down at the bottom of its slimy walls. She had been terrified that she would slip and fall in and flounder around, unable to get out. She could swim, but not more than a few strokes and she always panicked if she couldn't put her foot on the bottom. The bottom, even if she could reach it, would be thick mud – the kind that sucked you down and swallowed you up. Her body had felt as paralysed as her mind and she had sat there crying. Pip had been very nice about it when the boats had arrived. It happened to lots of trainees, she'd said, putting an arm round her shoulder, and the main thing was not to worry about it or panic. She'd explained locks all over again to her, coaxed her across the gates from one side to the other, helped her raise and lower the paddles and push the balance beam to open and shut the gates.

Somebody had started to strum on the old piano in the corner of the bar – not very well and rather loudly. It was hard to hear, above the racket, what the others were talking about but she kept nodding as though she could, and taking tiny sips of the beer. After a bit, Rosalind said something and got up. She walked boldly over to a group of men playing darts – all boatmen, to judge by their clothes and their weather-beaten faces, and not at all pleased to be interrupted. But Rosalind didn't look afraid of them and she held out her hand for the darts. At first they shook their heads but she went on smiling sweetly, and, after a while, they allowed her a turn. Prudence knew nothing about the game, but she could tell that Rosalind did. The boatmen soon saw it too, and they didn't like it. Their faces grew more and more sullen as they watched her darts thud into the board. To finish, she scored a bullseye, smiled at them again and walked away. She sat down again at their corner table and picked up her beer.

140

Pip said grimly, 'You seem to know the game rather well.'

'I do,' Rosalind said. 'I've spent a lot of time in a lot of pubs.' She accepted another cigarette. 'I thought they needed teaching a lesson.'

'Well, I hope they won't decide to teach *you* one. Those are Joshers and they won't have taken kindly to it. You'd better keep well clear of them in future.'

On the way back to the boats Prudence tripped in the dark and banged her bad knee, which started it bleeding again. She sat on the side bed, mopping at the trickle of blood with a handkerchief and still feeling sick from the beer. After a while, she got out her curlers, started to wind one in and then gave up; she couldn't be bothered. It would mean straight hair in the morning but she didn't care. It didn't seem to matter much how they looked – not the way it had mattered at the bank. On the cut, they could wear what they liked, look as messy as they liked, and be as dirty as they liked and nobody noticed or minded. Except the boater people – they minded all right. Not how they looked, but about them being there at all. She'd seen the way the men and the women and the children stared at them – and it frightened her. After the light was turned out, she said, 'Do you think they'll come after us?'

Rosalind said sleepily, 'Who?'

'Those boatmen at the pub – the ones playing darts – the Joshers.'

A yawn. 'Oh, *them*.'

'They looked evil.'

'They're just pathetic.' Another yawn. 'God, I'm so tired . . .'

'Pip said we ought to be careful of them.'

'Mmmm.'

'Supposing they do?'

'Do what?'

'Come after us.'

'Don't worry, sweetie, they won't.'

'But if they do?'

'Just leave them to me.'

Eight

The next day they went by the Ovaltine factory at King's Langley where the company boats were unloading coal – beautiful, clean boats painted with roses and castles, and *Drink Delicious Ovaltine for Health* on the sides. The cut ran parallel to the railway on its right with a busy road on the left. *Cetus* pop-popped along between the two, hauling *Aquila* in its wake, overtaken by roaring trains and traffic. Five more locks followed, close together and called the New 'Uns though they were many years old. They took turns to steer butty and motor, with Pip bawling instructions, and when they weren't steering they were lock-wheeling. Thanks to the boaters just ahead, it was a bad road with every single lock against them. The frosty weather had turned to driving rain that soaked their clothes, made rat's tails of their hair, turned the towpath to mud and the ropes to slithery snakes in their hands. Pip kept up their spirits by promising fish and chips when they tied up for the night at Berkhamsted but by the time they got there, the shop had sold out of fish and they had to make do with soggy leftover chips.

It was still raining hard when they let go in the morning and their clothes were still wet. They had been climbing steadily since they had left the depot at Bulls Bridge and had worked through thirty-nine locks. There were six more locks before they reached Cowroast lock which marked the beginning of a three-mile flat stretch known as Tring Summit – a long stretch of water without a single lock, protected from wind and weather by high banks lined with trees and bushes. The butty, put on the sixty-foot snubber rope, trundled quietly along far behind the motor and they ate their dinner on the move – fresh bread bought from a lock-side shop, sliced thickly and spread with margarine and fish paste, and mugs of hot tea. But the peace and the rest lasted only an hour. Out of the shelter of the summit, they were back in the teeth of the wind and facing more locks – this time going downhill. Downhill locks, as they had already learned on the way to Limehouse, meant going into deeper water which required a different and slower technique. And there was a variation on the ever-present danger to the boats in locks. Going uphill, sterns could get wedged under the gate beam if allowed to drift too far back, so that the boat filled up with water as the nose rose. Going downhill, they could get caught up on the stone cill hidden under water, leaving a boat dangling helplessly as the bows sank. Almost as frightening, the motor steerer had to wait above while the boats were sinking, to open the gates, and then launch herself through space down onto a cabin roof far below. Not that an uphill lock was necessarily any safer when it involved standing on top of the cabin and springing onto the lock-side without falling between the lock wall and the boat to be crushed to strawberry jam.

Frances, steering the motor at the first lock, took the boat in much too fast, reversed the engine too late and crashed into the gates at the other end, sending waves of water slopping over the top and pots and pans and china flying round the cabin. And when Rosalind brought the unbrakeable butty in alongside, also too fast, Prudence, who had flung herself and her rope desperately onto the lock-side to check its head-long charge, dropped the rope so that *Aquila*, too, tore on and hit the far gates. When she had finally retrieved the rope she made the mistake of tying it to a bollard, as for an uphill lock, so that as the boat sank down, the rope snapped. They did little better at the next lock where the butty rudder came dangerously close to getting hooked up on the stone cill and was only saved by quick action from Pip, who rushed to drop and wind paddles and refill the lock.

That night they tied up at Leighton Buzzard and Pip took them to a pub where she said they might be able to get a hot bath. There *was* a bathroom with a bath, but the water was tepid, the room icy and the disappointment as bitter as over the fish and chips. They took turns, scrubbing the worst of the dirt off, and hurried back to the warmth of the cabins.

For the next part of the trip things went a bit better. It had stopped raining and they were gradually getting more used to handling the boats, their muscles hardening, their bodies growing stronger. Every day, they learned more things. How to recharge the dead battery which had to be dragged out from under the butty side bed and lugged to the engine room while the newly charged battery was heaved back in its place. How to clean out the bilge pumps and the well-named mud box which filtered water from the cut to cool the engine. The box filled up with a disgusting black slime that had to be scooped out by hand and flung over the edge. Couplings on the shaft had to be regularly checked for loose nuts and bolts and the rest of the shaft inspected. This lay, inconveniently, under the motor cabin floorboards which had to be taken up, a cap unscrewed and the inside rammed with thick yellow grease.

They'd also learned the trick of how to get from one boat to the other, without slowing down. Changing from the motor to the butty was quite easy. You hopped off at a bridge-hole where the cut narrowed and waited for the butty to come along; the reverse was more difficult. It meant getting off the butty at a bridge-hole and racing along the towpath to the next bridge before the motor reached it.

When they were not busy working the boats, they were kept busy with endless domestic tasks – refilling the coal boxes, making up the fires, swabbing away with the rag mop, scrubbing the hatches, polishing the brasses, black-leading the stoves, cleaning fenders and ropes, chopping firewood. And like foreigners in a strange land, they were learning the language. The boaters had their own words for things: the helm was the elum, the top of the butty rudder the ram's head, the sausage-shaped fenders on the motor's stern were tip-cats, and so on.

At Fenny Stratford lock they got their rations at the Red Lion shop – tinned milk, cocoa, sugar, tea. They bought some fresh vegetables as well and filled up the four-gallon water cans at the tap. From Fenny there was another long pound of four

147

hours before the next lock and then an iron aqueduct carrying the canal thirty feet in the air over the river Great Ouse which the boaters called the Pig Trough. The parapet on each side was no more than a foot or so high – not nearly enough to stop a heavy boat from going over – and the crossing easily the most frightening part of the journey.

A two-hour-long pound followed to the bottom of the seven locks rising to Stoke Bruerne, and they shortened the butty's snubber to work their way through them. There was little time to admire the canal-side village – the cottages, the church, the Boat Inn, the fine row of poplar trees along the towpath – before they plunged into the black mouth of the Blisworth tunnel, two miles long. In horse-drawn days, Pip told them, the narrowboats had been taken through the tunnels by leggers – men who lay on their backs and pushed the boats along by walking their feet against the tunnel walls.

They tied up that night at Heyford and were off early the next day working through the seven locks at Buckby. At Norton Junction the canal branched off in one direction towards Leicester, while they turned left towards Braunston, through another long tunnel and then six downhill locks. The canal split in two directions again – right for Coventry and the coalfields and to the left, which they took, for Oxford and Birmingham. There were no more locks until they reached Napton Junction where the canal divided yet again, and they turned onto the Warwick & Napton Canal towards Birmingham and thirty-two more locks spread out ahead.

They were beginning to get quite used to the whole procedure when Pip gave them the bad news that the next fifty-one locks were a different design from the ones before – wider, deeper, with paddles on the side of the lock instead of on the gates, and even heavier balance beams made of iron instead of wood. At Leamington they tied up outside the gasworks, but the smell was worth it for the fish and chip shop close by, which provided not only mountains of chips but big portions of crisp, golden fish, sprinkled with salt and vinegar and wrapped, mouth-burningly hot, in many sheets of newspaper.

At Warwick they filled up the water cans again before they came round the corner to the foot of the Hatton locks, rising before them up the hillside – a giant's staircase of twenty-one locks to be worked through and suffered through, one after the other, and every single one against them. *And* it was raining – a misty drizzle that would hamper their vision and make everything slippery.

Pip insisted on them eating before they began

the climb, and shared out the lock-wheeling and steering equally between them. It took them more than four hours to reach the top where Prudence crumpled to the ground like a wet paper bag and Frances and Rosalind collapsed like rowers after a race. Pip cooked supper for them that night – her speciality Boat Stew of tinned meat, potatoes, carrots and swedes, all in one big saucepan. But they were too tired to eat it.

An eight-mile-long pound the next day helped them recover from the Hatton locks. The five locks at Knowle seemed almost nothing by comparison, though the winding gear was stiff and the gates so heavy it took two to shift them. Joy of joys, there were no more locks between them and Tyseley where they were to unload. There was, however, Muck Bend which lived up to its name, as Frances learned when she took the corner too fine and sent *Cetus* straight into thick, slimy mud. *Aquila*, following dutifully behind, kept going, and her slackening snubber wrapped itself round the motor's propeller blades. It was just as well, Pip assured them calmly, that they learned to deal with the situation sooner rather than later, since it was bound to happen to them again. It was also just as well that, once they'd succeeded in unravelling the rope from the blades, a pair of boats came by with a steerer who not only gave them a snatch off the mud, but also gave them a smile and a wave as he went. They had learned another lesson: that boat people would help.

Tyseley Wharf, near Birmingham, was ugly and depressing. Trees and fields gave way to tin sheds, factories, warehouses, trams rattling and clanging and urchin faces appearing over bridge parapets to aim spit and stones. The towpath was an evil place, choked with soot and smoke, the roaring foundries beside it like gateways to hell. At the wharf where they tied up, the boatwomen were scrubbing away at their washing, their children playing in the dirt, their dogs nosing through rubbish for scraps of food. Unloading wasn't due until the next day so they went to the pictures in the evening and ate sausages and chips in a steamy dockside café. That night they listened to big rats scampering across the cabin roofs.

A heavy overnight frost froze the top cloths and the strings, and undoing them for unloading was a long and painful struggle. The boat people, who had somehow undone theirs with ease, watched in silence.

After the steel had been taken off, they spent the afternoon sweeping out the holds, and swabbing down the boats. When they'd finished, Pip broke the bad news that instead of going back the way they'd come and then branching off to Coventry to pick up the coal, they had been given orders to take the Bottom Road. The Bottom

Road, they soon discovered, meant three days of negotiating foul, undredged water and eleven locks oozing with black slime, so narrow they could only take one boat at a time. *Cetus* went ahead alone while *Aquila* had to be bow-hauled from lock to lock. They took it in turns – one to steer and one to drag the butty on the end of a long cotton line wound over the shoulder, stumbling along, harnessed like a beast of burden on a towpath black with soot, sharp with cinders and slippery with horse dung. A horse-drawn boat, loaded with coal, met them, and the boatman stopped his horse and let the line sink in the water so that the butty could cross over it.

At Hawkesbury Junction they tied up for the night and took the tram to the public baths in Coventry where they paid ninepence each for a towel, piece of soap and the use of a bath. They stripped off their filthy clothes and submerged themselves in steaming hot water. But the pleasure of being clean again was short-lived, and they might as well not have bothered. Pip had been given orders for them to be loaded the next day at Longford wharf, a few miles away. It was a dreadful place: black coal shovelled and carted and carried by an army of workmen, black dust hanging like a pall, and a traffic jam of motor boats and horse-drawn boats converging in chaos. For two hours, fifty tons of coal avalanched down chutes into the two holds, the boats sinking lower and lower under the weight. When the avalanche finally ceased, the coal had to be spread around until it was evenly distributed to Pip's satisfaction: an uneven boat was a nightmare to steer. Then they had to sheet up again. In dry weather the side sheets would have been enough to keep the water out of the hold, but this was winter and Pip decreed that top sheets had to go on too. And, before they left, the boats had to be washed clean, the cabins swept out. Washing themselves was the worst job of all. The gritty coal dust clung to their skin, coated their hair, irritated their eyes, tasted in their mouths.

The trip back to London, which would have taken a mere few hours by train, took a week. Seven more days of steering into banks and getting stemmed up on the mud, of snarled-up propellers and underwater snares, of battling with locks, of shredding fingers and gashing limbs and cracking heads, of dirt and mud and frost and wind and rain and such tiredness that they fell asleep the second their heads touched the pillow, and sometimes before.

The coal was unloaded at Croxley paper mills by Rickey and they brought the empty boats back to the lay-by at Bulls Bridge Junction early one evening. When they'd smartened the boats up yet again with more swabbing and scrubbing and polishing, they were free to go home for six days. Six days to sleep and rest and take baths before the second training trip. They packed their bags and took their bedding up to the store.

It was Frances who suggested that the three of them should celebrate their arrival and survival by having a slap-up dinner in London. The head waiter at the Ritz Hotel would remember her from visits with Aunt Gertrude which might be a good thing, considering the way they looked. They washed hands and faces in kettle-warmed water but nothing would remove the ingrained dirt and grease, and nothing could be done about the neglected hair, or the cuts and bruises, or the state of their clothes. Rosalind, alone, cut a certain dash in her breeches and boots, her swirling green cloak, her Robin Hood hat and her silver earrings.

They waltzed boldly through revolving doors into the swanky London hotel – or at least Frances and Rosalind did while Prudence, who had never set foot in such a place, lagged timidly behind. The kitbag, the carpet bag and the shabby suitcase were deposited with the porter and if the head waiter greeting them at the entrance to the restaurant was shocked by their appearance, he didn't show it. Certainly, he remembered Miss Carlyon . . . and how was her ladyship these days? Had they made a reservation? No? Unfortunately, as Miss Carlyon could see, the restaurant was very full this evening but, if they would wait a little moment, he would see what could be arranged. The arrangement turned out to be a table in a distant corner and to reach it they had to run the gauntlet of the other diners – the evening gowns, furs, jewels, black ties, gold-braided and be-medalled uniforms seated beneath softly shaded chandeliers linked by bronze garlands. An RAF wing commander glanced up as they passed.

'Good God, Frances! What on *earth* are you doing here?'

Nine

'We're here for dinner,' she said defiantly. 'The same as you, Vere. Any objections?'

He'd stood up, barring her path. 'Since you ask – yes. Have you any idea what you look like, Frances?'

'Well, we don't have smart uniforms like you, I'm afraid.'

'Frankly, I'm amazed they let you in.'

'They're not as stuffy as you.'

'Well, since you *are* in, you'd better introduce your friends.'

'When you've introduced yours. We don't know him.'

'This is Hugh Whitelaw. From my squadron.'

The fair-haired RAF officer, who had also risen, shook her hand. She said curtly, 'This is Rosalind Flynn, and this is Prudence Dobbs. We're trainees together.'

Her brother was issuing orders to the head

waiter, taking over in his usual bossy way. More chairs were being brought, more places set.

'Luckily, there's room for you to join us.'

'We're perfectly happy on our own, thank you, Vere.'

'I dare say, but it's never a good idea for young girls to dine out unescorted.' Her brother was still blocking her path to the corner table. 'People are staring, Frances. I suggest we all sit down as quickly as possible.'

Waiters were stationed behind chairs, her brother immovable, more and more heads turning towards them; she gave way, plonking herself down sulkily. Rosalind sat down, too, followed by Prudence who was pink with embarrassment. Rosalind's green velvet cloak, Prudence's matted tweed and her grimy gaberdine were whisked away to be hung up. Starched napkins were flourished and laid across their laps, menus brought, another waiter hovered.

Vere said, 'What would you all like to drink?'

'We'd like some champagne, please, Vere. We're celebrating.'

A pause. 'Very well. Hugh?'

'Champagne sounds a rather good idea.'

He looked so *clean,* she thought. Vere, too. Hair, hands, faces, clothes . . . all scrubbed and shining. Whereas the three of them looked a grubby mess. Greasy hair, crumpled clothes, grime . . . she wondered if they actually stank. Almost certainly, considering how little they'd washed in three weeks. She studied the menu and put it down; Prue, she noticed, was still clutching hers like a drowning man. Her brother leaned across.

'What would you like to eat, Miss Dobbs?'

Prudence said helplessly, 'I don't know. It's in French, you see.'

'How about some clear soup to start with? Then lamb cutlets afterwards, perhaps? They're usually very good here. Or would you prefer the Dover sole?'

Vere could be quite kind when he wanted to be.

'Have *you* decided, Miss Flynn?' Her brother had turned back to Rosalind.

Rosalind's lips were painted scarlet and her nose carefully powdered, but there was a neat little row of bedbug bites down one cheek and a big streak of oil down the front of her leather jerkin. She had removed the Robin Hood hat and her russet hair, released from its bit of string, looked like an abandoned stork's nest. The chapped and cracked hand that held up the Ritz menu had black-rimmed fingernails and knuckles skinned raw from wrestling with the stiff nuts on the mud box. She smiled brightly at Vere and said in a loud cockney voice, 'I'll 'ave the soup an' cutlets.'

He dragged his eyes away. 'Frances? What will you have, then?'

The food was ordered, the champagne opened and poured with a flourish. The RAF officer beside Frances said, 'What exactly are we celebrating?'

'Finishing our first training trip.'

'Training as what?'

She told him and he seemed surprised.

'I've never heard of women doing that. Almost everything else, but not working on the canals. Aren't the boats a bit of a handful for you?'

'We manage perfectly well, as a matter of fact.'

'So, when will you finish your training?'

'It takes two trips and we've just done one of them – steel from the docks up to Birmingham, then Coventry for coal and then back again – it takes us around three weeks because we have to learn as we go along. If we learn well enough, they let us take a pair of boats on our own – when we've finished the second trip.'

'The three of you together?'

'If we all stick it.'

There were two thick rings and one thin round his uniform sleeve which meant he was a squadron leader, and two medals sewn on his chest – the same as Vere's. Birds of a feather, flocking together. 'Have you known my brother long?'

'Sort of. We were at school together, but in

different houses and he's a couple of years older. I hadn't seen him for several years until we happened to be posted to the same squadron. I didn't know he had a sister.'

'He wouldn't mention it. We don't get on particularly well.'

'That's a pity.'

'He's always trying to run my life.'

'But I'm sure he means well.'

'No, he doesn't. He's just incredibly bossy. Do you have a younger sister to boss around?'

He smiled. 'I have a sister but she's older. She used to try to boss me until I grew taller than her.'

The hotel dining room seemed vast after the cabins. She had almost forgotten how to sit at a proper table and how to eat in a civilized fashion. They had become so used to grabbing and gobbling – one spoon, one knife, one fork making do for everything. It was an effort to remember how to use the right things and not to slurp the soup. Rosalind, she saw, had finished hers and was wiping a piece of bread round to clean the plate. Vere's face was a study. Serve him jolly well right.

She leaned across the table. 'By the way, Vere, what day is it today?'

He frowned. 'Thursday, of course. Surely you know that.'

'No, we don't. Do we, Ros?'

A chirpy smile and more cockney. 'No' a clue, darlin'.'

'Is this some sort of joke, Frances?'

'Not at all. We lose count of the days on the cut. It's either yesterday, today or tomorrow.'

'The cut?'

'The canal. It's called the cut. We don't know the date either. Or what's happened in the war, or anything else. No newspapers, you see. And no wireless. It's rather nice.'

The frown deepened. 'It sounds uncivilized.'

'Not at all. We're very civilized, aren't we Ros?'

A wide and innocent smile. 'Oh, yeah. Ever so.'

Her brother said slowly, 'Do you mind telling me what you're doing here in London, Frances?'

'I already did. We're celebrating.'

'I meant after dinner.'

'We go off on leave. We've got six lovely days before we do the next trip.'

'You're going home, I take it?'

'Tomorrow. I've invited Ros and Prue to spend tonight at Aunt Gertrude's flat – I knew she wouldn't mind.'

'I've got some leave as well, as it happens.'

'Oh? Are you staying the night there too, then? It'll be a bit of a crowd.'

'I'm staying at the RAF club and we can both go down by train tomorrow. I'll pick you up by taxi in the morning.'

'There's no need. I'm quite capable of travelling on my own.'

'I dare say you are, Frances. But we may as well go together.'

The soup was removed, the next course served. She crumbled her bread roll over the pristine tablecloth.

Hugh Whitelaw said, 'So, what were you all doing before you joined the boats?'

'I was doing nothing, Prue was working in a bank, and Ros . . .' she paused to make sure that Vere was paying close attention. 'Ros was an actress. Acting.'

Of course, the squadron leader then wanted to know what she had acted in and where, and Ros was more than happy to tell him about her theatrical life. There was a good deal of pleasure in watching Vere as he listened to the colourful recital with all the funny bits and the different accents – cockney, north country, Irish, Scots. Ros switched from one to another with ease and she tossed in some juicy scandals – illicit affairs, queer actors, lesbian actresses. It was a brilliantly shocking performance.

At the end of the dinner the waiters brought coffee – dainty little porcelain cups and a dish of lovely petits fours. Vere offered his cigarette case to the squadron leader.

She said, 'I'd like one, too, please. So would Ros.'

He lit Ros's cigarette and she blew a long plume of smoke up into the air as though she'd been doing it for years, which she probably had.

'Ta very much.'

Hugh Whitelaw lit hers. 'My parents' house is only a mile or two away from the Grand Union Canal – near Stoke Bruerne. If you ever need a bed for the night, I know they'd be glad to have you.'

'We always sleep on the boats.'

'Well, bear it in mind. Havlock Hall.'

'I will,' she said, instantly forgetting it.

In the taxi that Vere had insisted on ordering for them afterwards, Ros said in her normal voice, 'I don't think your brother approved of me very much, do you? Still, it was very nice of him and that other chap to pay for our dinner and for all the champagne. We might have had to wash up.'

Vere had paid for the taxi, too, but Frances was still cross at the way her brother had taken over their evening and spoiled it. And her leave would be spoiled by him being down at Averton.

She slept in Aunt Gertrude's room while the other two shared the spare room. After her side bunk on the *Aquila* the bed seemed too big, the mattress too soft, and she missed the warm glow of the stove and the gentle creaking of the boat.

*   *   *

Rosalind phoned her parents in the morning. Her mother sounded harassed.

'We weren't expecting you home for a while, darling. It's a bit of a problem at the moment.'

'You mean somebody's in my room?'

'I'm afraid so. He's playing at the Winter Gardens all this week – I can't really turf him out, you see.'

'Well, I'll just have to sleep on the sofa, I suppose.'

'Oh dear, that's occupied too. Only a walk-on, but she's very nice. We're terribly busy. I'm sorry, darling. If you can let me know well in advance next time, I'll make sure we keep your room free. Is there anybody you could stay with just this once? Otherwise, we'll manage something.'

'Don't worry, I'll find somewhere else.'

Frances said at once, 'Come and stay at Averton, if you can stand my brother being there too. It's not a bad place and you'll like my aunt.'

Prudence went off with her suitcase to catch buses to Croydon and Vere arrived in a taxi.

'Ros is coming as well,' Frances said without further explanation.

He took Rosalind's tatty old carpet bag and put it beside the driver. He didn't show it, but she knew he wasn't thrilled at the idea. Actresses were immoral and a bad influence, everybody knew that. You went to see them act on the stage, at a safe distance, but you didn't associate with them or invite them into your home – not if you were someone like him. She sat in the back of the taxi with Frances, and very comfortable it was too. The brother was sitting on one of the tip-up seats, staring out of the window, which gave her the chance to take a closer look at him. Nice eyes, nice hair, nice hands – men's hands counted a lot, so far as she was concerned. They had to be lean and strong, not plump or pasty. And the RAF uniform looked impressive. He didn't approve of her, or like her, but she didn't hold it against him. In fact, it was a relief. She'd had plenty of attention in her life, never a shortage of admirers of all shapes and sizes and ages and, more often than not, they were a nuisance. Sometimes a real pest. Right now she wanted nothing more than to do as little as possible and sleep as much as possible for six blissful days. She decided to abandon the cockney accent. She could have kept it up indefinitely, if necessary, but it really wasn't fair to go on teasing him.

At Waterloo station there was another argument. Officers of His Majesty's Forces were apparently expected to travel first class, not slum it.

'Ros and I can't afford that, can we, Ros? We're going third.'

'No you're not, Frances. I'm paying for both your tickets.'

'We don't want you to, do we, Ros?'

He won, of course, by simply going off and buying them. Not that she was going to protest. It was a treat to sit in style and comfort instead of squashed into a crowded compartment hopping with fleas.

When they arrived at the station, they took another taxi to the house which was much as Frances had described – sprawling, old, beautiful and run-down. Stone griffins guarded the entrance gates and inside it was stuffed with antique furniture and family portraits. It was also freezing cold. The aunt, Lady Somebody, was a nice old girl, straight out of the twenties. She chain-smoked and drank gin and since she loved going to the theatre they got on famously. What gossip Rosalind didn't already know about well-known actors and actresses she made up to amuse her. The father – another title there – was an old sweetie but rather weird and spent all his time in the orangery, growing orchids. Frances took her there on a visit and when she told him, quite truthfully, that she thought the blooms were lovely he cut one for her. It had no scent but its pure white frilled petals were perfection, and she wore it in her hair for dinner that evening. She slept until late every morning and bathed in a bath as big as a rowing boat. The water was never more than lukewarm, but she gradually scoured away the grime and grease from her skin and scrubbed her nails clean again. She washed her hair every day. The cuts and scratches started to heal, the bug bites and bruises to fade. Sometimes she practised speeches aloud to her reflection in the bedroom mirror – just to keep her hand in.

'Tis but thy name that is my enemy;
Thou art thyself though, not a Montague.
What's Montague? It is nor hand, nor foot,
Nor arm, nor face, nor any other part
Belonging to a man. O! be some other name;
What's in a name? That which we call a rose
By any other name would smell as sweet;
So Romeo would, were he not Romeo
  call'd . . .

She needed to remember it all. To keep rehearsing different parts. This was only an interval: the interval before the curtain swished up again, after the war.

'She's not the right sort of friend for you, Frances. You must know that.'

'I don't know anything of the kind, Vere. What exactly do you mean?'

'She's an actress. From quite a different background and with quite different standards. And since when did you start smoking and drinking champagne?'

'Actually, I usually drink beer.'

'*Beer?*'

'Yes, beer. In pubs. When we tie up for the night. There's nearly always a pub nearby.'

'You mean you three girls go to pubs alone?'

'Not exactly. Pip comes with us. The woman who's training us. She's very nice and very respectable indeed, if that's what you're worried about.'

'I dare say she is, but that's not the point.'

'What *is* the point, then?'

'The point is that I want you to give this whole thing up. Do as I suggested originally and find some other war work near here. Something much more suitable.'

They were walking across the fields with the dogs. Ros had stayed behind to play gin rummy with Aunt Gertrude beside the fire. She wished she'd stayed indoors too and avoided the inevitable lecture.

'I'm not going to give it up, Vere. Whatever you say. And I'm not giving up Ros as a friend, either. Or Prue. Or anyone else, just because you say so. I'll choose my own friends, if you don't mind.'

He was silent, striding along. She braced herself for what was coming next. At last he said, 'All right, Frances. If that's the way you want it, fair enough. I've said my say, and we'll leave it at that. I won't interfere.'

She wasn't deceived. 'You don't think I'll be able to stick it, do you, Vere? That's what you're hoping, isn't it?'

'Frankly I don't and, yes, I'm hoping you won't.'

They walked on up to the crest of the hill but it was too misty to see the sea.

She said, 'You're quite wrong about Ros, you know. She's a lovely person.'

'I'm sure she is.'

'So's Prue. We all get on awfully well.'

'You're going to need to, by the sound of things.'

She went up into the attics again, taking Ros with her on a hunt for sensible boat clothes. They foraged through more old trunks and tea chests and discovered a man's riding mac. It was a stiff and crackling affair with belt and straps and buckles – too big for Ros, but she could turn up the sleeves.

Frances wandered about the attic rooms – dusty repositories of the past. Boxes of letters and photographs, skittles, Vere's train set, her dolls' pram, an old steamer trunk covered with fading labels, a dressmaker's dummy. In one dark corner, she came across a crocodile suitcase stamped with her mother's initials. The knobbly skin was dull and cobwebbed but when she snapped open the clasps, the colours inside were as bright and fresh as when they had been worn. Evening gowns and day dresses, hats and shoes, long white kid gloves, silken wraps, a white fox fur . . . she fingered them.

Behind her, Ros said, 'Beautiful things. Whose were they?'

'My mother's. I'd no idea they were up here. I suppose Father kept them after she died.'

'What was she like?'

'Smiling. Lovely. Kind. My father worshipped her. He'd had a breakdown when he came back from the war and she helped him get over it. When she died he more or less gave up.'

'How sad.'

She replaced everything carefully in the suitcase and they went downstairs. In the hall she pointed out the portrait of the first John de Carlyon.

'He made his fortune looting galleons on the Spanish Main. I always think I'd like to have met him.'

'So would I.'

'Everybody thinks Vere looks a lot like him.'

'Hmmm.' Ros cocked her head to one side. 'I can see the resemblance. But your brother doesn't wear ringlets or an emerald earring. And somehow I don't think he'd ever have been a buccaneer. Do you?'

'Not likely. He'd never do anything like that.'

She turned to see that Vere had come into the hall.

'We've been up in the attics,' she said before he could cross-question them. 'Looking for things to wear on the boats.'

He was looking at Ros dressed in the riding mac. 'That's Father's, isn't it?'

'He wouldn't mind. He never goes riding now. Ros needs it for the boats.'

He was still staring at Ros. What on earth was the matter with him?

'It suits her. She's welcome to it.'

When Prudence arrived home her mother took one horrified look at her and sent her to the scullery, where her clothes were put straight into the wash. The bath was filled with hot water, Dettol poured in, carbolic soap and nail brush handed over. By the time her father came home from the bank she was wearing clean and neatly pressed clothes, hair curled with hot tongs, the bedbug bites camouflaged beneath dabs of pink calamine lotion.

'I ought to tell him the state you were in,' her mother had threatened. 'But it would only get him all upset and I don't want that this evening. I'll have to talk to him later, though.'

Her father didn't notice the bites or how her hands looked, and, naturally, she didn't say a word about the bugs or the bucket in the engine room, or anything else like that. She sat listening dutifully to him talking about the bank and the rumours that Mr Holland, whose health had seemed poor lately, might be retiring early. In which case, of course, her father would hope to be made manager.

'There'll be a position for you there after the war, Prudence. You don't need to worry.'

She did worry, but not in the way he imagined. The idea of going back to the bank made her feel sick.

She took her tweed overcoat to be cleaned and repaired and drew money out of her post office savings account to buy a pair of boy's lace-up boots and workmen's overalls which needed a lot of turning up and taking in. At a jumble sale she found some old woollen vests, thick socks and a cable-knit jersey.

There was nothing much to do at home except help her mother with the housework and the shopping and the cooking. They went to the pictures one afternoon to see Deanna Durbin. The Pathe News showed British soldiers fighting in Italy and American marines landing on an island far away in the Pacific Ocean, and the King and Queen shaking hands with American air crews. Afterwards, they had a pot of tea and toasted teacakes in the cinema café. Her mother kept on asking questions about the narrowboats but she only told her the good bits – like what an excellent teacher Miss Rowan was, and how nice the other two girls were. She mentioned that Frances lived in a big house in Dorset because she knew her mother would like to hear it, but not that Frances had said it was falling down. And she told her about them having dinner at the Ritz Hotel in London and meeting Frances's brother who was a wing commander in the RAF. She didn't mention the smoking and the drinking or the pubs, or that Ros was an actress. Her mother looked quite pleased about the good bits.

To please Father, she went to the bank one morning. Mr Holland happened to come out of his office when she was there, and actually stopped to speak to her. They would see what could be done about finding her a position after the war was over, he said. He couldn't promise anything, of course, but he would bear her in mind. Meanwhile, he hoped that she would never forget about the Psychology of Accuracy. It was very important. He looked perfectly well, and she thought that the rumours might have been wrong and Father's hopes falsely raised. To her relief, Mr Simpkins was away ill with influenza. She peeped through the door at her old desk below the frosted-glass window. The girl who had replaced her was sitting entering figures in the ledger, one after the other. Her head was bent so low that her nose nearly touched the paper.

The weather had been cold and dull, but the sun came out on their last day at Averton and Rosalind, wearing Sir John's riding mac and her red boots, took herself off alone for a walk – not the energetic hike up the windy hillside to admire the distant view of the sea, but a gentle amble along the valley. She crossed a stream by a little plank bridge, climbed over a stile and followed a pathway into the woods, wandering along until she came to a grassy clearing with a convenient fallen tree trunk. She sat down and discovered a brave little clump of violets growing in its lee.

I know a bank whereon the wild thyme blows,
Where oxlips and the nodding violet grows . . .

Oxlips were a kind of cowslip and it was still much too early for them or for any of the other things in Oberon's speech: woodbine, musk-roses and eglantine. Titania had been one of her best parts for Sir Lionel. No need for a wig, her own hair had been exactly right, so had her pale skin and green eyes. She'd worn a gauzy costume embroidered with silver thread and sequins, and a lot of glittery eye make-up. The scenes with Bottom had been fun.

174

*What angel wakes me from my flowery
bed? . . .
I pray thee, gentle mortal, sing again:
Mine ear is much enamour'd of thy note;
So is mine eye enthralled to thy shape . . .*

The two spaniels burst suddenly out of the trees
and bounded up to her, wagging their stumpy
tails. They were followed by Frances's brother not
looking quite so pleased.

'We were wondering where you'd got to,
Rosalind.'

'I went for a walk, that's all.'

'I was afraid you might get lost – it's an easy
thing to do in these woods if you don't know
them. They stretch for miles.'

'How did you find me?'

'I didn't, the dogs did. They picked up your
trail. Then we heard your voice.'

The spaniels had sat down beside her, tongues
lolling, and she patted their smooth heads.

'I was practising a speech from *A Midsummer
Night's Dream*.'

'Yes,' he said. 'I recognized it.'

She said, surprised, 'You know the play?'

'Doesn't everybody? I expect you've played
Titania.'

'Once, yes. And I was an extra fairy when I was
six years old.'

'You started very young.'

'It's in the blood. You rather disturbed me just now. I was rehearsing.'

'I'm sorry.'

'I like to keep in practice. For when the war's over.'

'You'll go back to the stage?'

'Of course. I'm an actress. It's what I do.'

'I'm sure you're very talented.'

'You've never seen me act, Vere, so you don't know. All you do know is that you'd much sooner your sister didn't have anything to do with me.'

He didn't trouble to deny it. 'She comes from a sheltered background; it's my job to protect her. Unfortunately, she takes considerable pleasure in doing stupid things just to annoy me.'

'And you think I'm a very bad influence.'

He didn't deny that either; instead he looked up at the sky, frowning. 'There are some rain clouds building up. We ought to get back before it starts.'

Presumably it came with the job. A wing commander commanded and everyone else obeyed. Snapped to attention and jumped to it. Except that she wasn't in the Royal Air Force.

'It's very nice here and I'm wearing your father's mac, so I won't get wet.'

'Nevertheless, I think you should come back with me. You could easily take a wrong turning.'

It was true about the black clouds and, anyway,

her peace had been disturbed. She sighed. 'All right. If you insist.'

The dogs ran ahead of them, snuffling through undergrowth, crashing about and scaring off Pease-blossom, Cobweb, Moth and Mustard-seed. The magic was gone, the wood just an ordinary wood.

They walked on in silence. When they reached the stile he tried to help her over, but she ignored his outstretched hand. To be fair, she had only herself to blame after her behaviour at the Ritz, but, even so, he had not only disturbed her peace, he had wounded her pride.

Cetus and *Aquila*, now fumigated and bug-free, were waiting for them at the Bulls Bridge lay-by and Pip had already been given their new orders: Limehouse docks again and a cargo of timber to be taken to the Midlands, another load of coal to be brought back. This time the trip was shorter, the weather better, the mistakes fewer, Pip more pleased. At the end of it, they were awarded their Inland Waterway badges, which they sewed on with pride, and were told that they would be assigned their own pair of boats. After six more days of leave they returned to the depot as fully fledged boatwomen.

Ten

The motor was called *Orpheus*, the butty *Eurydice*. They stood staring at them in awe, wondering how they were going to manage to manoeuvre the seventy-two feet of each of them out of the lay-by, let alone all the way down to the docks, all the way up to Birmingham and Coventry, and all the way back again.

'I've forgotten the story,' Frances said presently.

Ros sighed. 'It's very sad. When Eurydice died, Orpheus went to look for her in the underworld. Pluto liked his lute-playing so much that he agreed to let Eurydice follow him out of the underworld, so long as he didn't turn round to see if she was there.'

Prudence looked anxious. 'What happened?'

'Silly duffer. He couldn't resist a quick peek and she vanished for ever.'

The two narrowboats were newly painted and

varnished, but had, as yet, nothing inside them except rusty cooking stoves, empty coal boxes and empty cupboards. No brasses or curtains or decoration. All the essentials had to be bought from the depot stores with the five pounds provided: ropes and lines, batteries, windlasses, water cans, axes, tools, shovels, brooms, mops, kettles, dippers, pots and pans, china, cutlery, cleaning materials, engine grease, even handles and catches. One essential had been brought from home by Frances – a bicycle. It was a man's one, retrieved from a barn at Averton, as ancient as Pip's but in better condition. At least the saddle stayed in place and both the brakes worked. They cleaned and blacked the stoves, filled the cupboards with tins and packets of provisions, the coal boxes with company coal. A door at the back of the butty cabin opened onto a small storage place at the end of the hold which would take coats and coal, vegetables and all kinds of oddments. Prudence had found an empty Fry's Cocoa tin to use for a kitty and they each put ten shillings into it for food shopping.

At the lay-by, the boaters watched their to-ings and fro-ings impassively. Staggering back with a laden box, Frances passed by a young woman standing at the fore-end of a butty who smiled at her.

'Seen yer before, 'aven't I? Up at Croxley lock.

Yer the lady with the pretty scarf, if I'm not mistaken.'

'I've still got it, if you'd like it.'

'I would an' all – long as yer don' want it.'

When she returned, the young woman had disappeared down inside the butty and, remembering Pip's warnings about observing boat manners, she leaned over and knocked on the cabin, waiting for a formal invitation to step on board.

Her name was Molly Jessop. Her husband, who'd gone off to the depot, was called Saul. They'd been married eight months and she was to have a baby soon. She patted her rounded stomach under the pinafore she was wearing over her skirt. Any day now, she reckoned, by the way it kept jumping about. Like most boatwomen, she was short with strong arms – fit for cabin-living and working locks – and she wore gold rings in her ears.

The butty had been spotless outside – ropes scrubbed white, brasswork gleaming, roses painted over the big water can, the fairy-tale pictures of castles on the door panels, hearts and diamond shapes everywhere. Inside, the cabin was pin-neat and clean, with a stove that shone like black satin. When the kettle had boiled, tea was brewed in a pot decorated with roses and there were more roses painted over the dipper on its hook. Just inside the door by the stove, six shiny brass knobs were screwed to the wall and, opposite, a fretted china plate, slotted through with pink ribbon, hung on a nail. The cross-bed was down, framed by crochet lace curtains looped back with a red ribbon. Crochet runners edged the shelves and a pretty lace cloth covered the table.

'Brought it all with me, when we was wed,' Molly said. 'Me dowry, see. 'Cept Saul's mam give us the Banbury Cross plate up there. Sit yerself down.'

She sat on the side bed, Molly presiding on the cross-seat. The tea was dark and strong, the cups and saucers fine china. Frances took the silk scarf out of her pocket.

'This is for you. I'd like you to have it.'

Molly held it up, delighted.

'Prettiest one I ever seen. Look at all them flowers! Thanks ever so much.' She tied it round her head at once, knotting it under her chin. 'Saul won' know it's me.'

The scarf framed her smiling face. Frances wondered how long her nice looks would last – the bright eyes, the pink cheeks, the all-present white teeth. Most of the boatwomen she'd seen looked worn out, though they were probably not so very much older than Molly. After this baby was born, there'd be others – two, three, four, five, six, maybe more – and Molly would have to be boatwoman, wife, mother, cook, washer-woman, cleaner, mender, drudge for all the days of her life.

She looked round the cabin again. 'Do tell me, why do you always paint roses and castles and hearts over everything?'

'Dunno exactly. Allus been done like that on the narrowboats. Some say the roses are fer beauty, the 'earts fer love an' romance, an' the castles fer honour. Could be so.'

'Where did you find the brass knobs?'

'Off old bedsteads, an' such. See 'em dumped in the cut sometimes, or on rubbish tips, an' the Brum factories throw out the bad ones. They shine up nice.'

'What about that brass chain on the chimney?'

'Pinched those from Croxley mills when we was unloadin'. We all do that. There's sheds there full of army gas-mask cases they're goin' to make into paper an' they got these buckles an' clips on 'em. You cut them off, see, and put 'em together. Makes a pretty chain for keepin' yer chimney an' your water can safe.'

They chatted over the teacups. Molly had been born and brought up on the boats with five brothers and an older sister. Two of the brothers had died early of some kind of fever. The sister had married a boatman when she was sixteen and already had four children. Molly and Saul had been courting for three years before they'd got married in the church at Stoke Bruerne – Bruan, she called it, in boaters' talk. There'd been fifty guests, she said proudly – all boatmen and their families. They'd had the wedding feast round a long trestle table in the open air, with the boat tarpaulins at the ready, in case of rain. Luckily, it had stayed fine. The honeymoon had been a trip to Hawkesbury to load coal for London. She unhooked a framed wedding photograph from the wall and showed it to Frances – herself in a long white dress and veil, her bridegroom in a suit and stiff wing collar, the big family group dressed up in their Sunday best.

'We're cousins, see – but I never 'ardly knew Saul, cos we never spent much time together. Passed each other on the cut – him goin' one way, me t'other – and sometimes we met at a lock, or here at the lay-by, but that didn't 'appen often. Still, he's a good man and treats me right – not like some of 'em.' She poured more tea. 'What's a lady like yerself doin' on the boats? An' them others? It don' seem right. There's all sorts of accidents can 'appen if yer don' watch out – bones broke, fingers crushed in them ropes, drownin' in the locks.'

'The Government asked for women to train for the work – so we volunteered. We're not very popular, are we? Most real boat people seem to think we're just a nuisance, getting in their way.'

'Truth is they don' know what ter make of yer. There's some feared they'll lose the work or get called up cos of the trainees, an' others just don' understand what yer about or what yer sayin' cos yer talk different. Yer do everythin' different, an' yer dress different – in trousers an' such – an' yer don' really live on the cut, do yer? Just visitin', so ter speak. Yer a puzzle, see.'

'Well, they scare us sometimes – when they don't say a word and just stare.'

'It's just their way. Not showin' what they're thinkin'. Don' mean they won' do yer a good turn, if need be.'

'I hope so. We've finished training now and we've been given our own pair of boats.'

'We all knows that. News goes fast on the cut, see. Up and down in the wink of an eye. You'll allus be trainees, though, no matter how long yer stays. And they'll all be watchin' yer, waitin' to see how yer do when yer lets go, furst time. See if yer makes a fine mess of it.'

'I'm steerer, so I hope I get it right.' Being steerer was like being captain, but the responsibility was a worry.

'Yer wants to use yer shaft as yer turns so's yer don' get stemmed up.' Molly grinned. 'An' say yer prayers.'

184

*   *   *

In the depot canteen they were greeted with whistles and the usual ribbing.

''Ere they come, lads . . . the Idle Women . . . wish I had your job, love . . . nuffin' ter do all day . . . any room for me on board, sweetheart? I could do with a nice 'oliday . . .'

They checked through everything again to make sure nothing had been forgotten, then all they could do was sit around, waiting for the summons from the office. When nothing had happened by evening, they went to bed – Rosalind and Prudence sharing the slightly larger butty cabin, Frances alone on the motor. She had chosen to use the cross-bed rather than the side one since it was larger and more comfortable, but she couldn't sleep for worrying. Worrying about getting stemmed up on the turns, worrying about getting the snubber tangled up on the blades or getting the blades fouled with canal rubbish, worrying about the hundred and something locks that lay ahead, about something really terrible happening, like the butty getting caught up on the cill or one of them falling in to be crushed by the boat or chewed up by the propeller . . . about all the things that could so very easily go wrong. And there would be no Pip to put things right. No Pip to tell them what to do and what not to do, to shout encouragement or warning, to bear the brunt and take away the responsibility. Pip would be miles away with another set of trainees and she, as steerer, would be in sole charge. She'd refused the job at first but, as Pip had pointed out, she was the most competent at steering the motor and the most competent all round. A natural. She had copied Pip's little book of Useful Information into a notebook of her own – lock names, towns, pubs, water taps, shops, public baths . . . anything and everything that might come in handy.

There were the usual night noises on the wharf – footsteps passing, a dog barking, a baby crying, and then, just as she'd heard once before at the lay-by, the sound of a boatman playing the accordion and singing. Same voice, same song. She listened, comforted.

They were up early, bolting down breakfast and dressed for action with their windlasses tucked into the leather belts buckled low around their hips. The boaters all seemed to have been up long before. They hung about, fiddling nervously with things and waiting. Suddenly the loudspeaker came alive, blaring out names. A string of others first, and then, 'Steerer Carlyon, please report to the office. Steerer Carlyon, report to the office.'

'That's you, Frankie,' Rosalind said. 'You'd better get going.'

She got going, riding the bike down the tow-path at breakneck speed. There was a group of boatmen waiting in silence outside the office, shoulders hunched against the cold, stamping their heavy boots on the ground. Nobody said a word to her, or even looked her way. Every so often one of them went inside and came out again, carrying papers. Finally, it was her turn.

'Got your boats ready?' the stern-looking man at the desk asked.

'Yes.' Should she call him sir? 'We're ready.'

'Limehouse,' he said. 'Cement. You're to get down there quick as you can.'

She was given a trip card, loading orders and money. He stared at her as he handed them over.

'First one on your own, isn't it?'

'Yes.'

'Well, you be careful.'

Outside again, she threaded an apologetic path through the remaining boaters, who neither made way nor spoke. She heard a resentful mutter behind her: *Bloody women trainees . . . don' know what they're about. Oughtn't ter be allowed.*

Back at the boats, she waved the papers at the other two before she put them away in the cabin ticket drawer. 'We can go.'

The first hurdle was persuading the National engine to start. It refused, point-blank, no matter how many times or how hard they swung the starting handle.

Frances wiped her forehead. 'Let's try going a bit slower at first. And, Prue, you're doing it just a bit late. Be sure to pull the lever over *exactly* when I say THREE.'

It fired the next time and she pulled on the governor rod to give it an extra burst. They scrambled out of the engine room and Ros went to untie while Frances took up her steerer's position on the counter.

'They're all watching us,' Prue said unnecessarily.

The boaters were watching, sure enough, leaning in the hatches with their unreadable expressions. Waiting, as Molly had warned, to see if they made a fine mess of it. She took the motor gently out into the cut and, as she passed the fore-end of the butty, snatched up the short tow rope from Ros and shoved its hollow eye over the stud on the deck. She looked back over her shoulder to make sure that *Eurydice* was following and in those inattentive few seconds, *Orpheus* ploughed straight into the mud and weeds on the opposite bank.

'Prue . . . get the long shaft. *Quickly!*'

Prue, who could barely lift the twelve-foot shaft, wobbled along the planks and plunged it into the bank. It did no good. The motor sat there, fore-end firmly embedded, its engine ticking over merrily while Prue went on struggling.

The boy came from nowhere. He simply appeared beside Frances on the counter, edging her politely out of the way. The engine note changed, the motor moved backwards out of the mud and floated freely to one side. He grinned at her and wagged a grimy finger.

'Yer'd got 'er in ahead, miss. Should've put 'er in reverse, see.'

In her panic she hadn't noticed, but all the watchers would have done.

The boy said kindly, 'I'll take 'er up aways for yer. See yer safe round the bend.'

She perched on the gunwale, furious with herself, while he manoeuvred the motor and the butty effortlessly under the bridge and round the sharp right-hand bend. He was thin and scrawny, with bowed legs, like many of the boat children – the size of an eight-year-old, though from his speech and manner she judged him to be about twelve. His eyes were the colour of dark treacle, his face dirty, his hair wild black curls, his clothes a grown man's cut down or turned up to fit, or, in the case of the cap, simply twisted to one side. He wore his windlass stuck through a rope belt that held his trousers up, together with braces and hobnail boots. His name, he told her, was Freddy. Freddy Carter.

She thanked him. 'It was very kind of you to come to the rescue.'

'Me bruvver told me ter do it.'

'Your brother?'

He nodded. 'Me bruvver Jack. Back there at the wharf. Yer was oldin' us up, see. Get that bleedin' woman out me way, 'e says.' He grinned at her. ''E'll be by in a tick.'

With that, he slowed the motor so that the boats drifted to a stop. Round the corner, with the steady putt-putt of an engine, another pair approached and as the motor drew close alongside the boy leaped across the gap between them, and they were off and away down the cut. The motor's name was *Snipe* and a small black dog stood on the cabin roof. The steerer had ignored her wave of thanks, as had the woman sitting in the butty cockpit behind, her face hidden under a frilled black bonnet. But Frances had seen the man's face beneath his cap and recognized him. He was the one at the Feathers on their first training trip: the one sitting at the bar who had turned around to stare so hard; the one who looked so like her childhood gypsy.

Prue wobbled back from the fore-end. 'Who was that boy?'

'That was Freddy. I'd left the engine in ahead. All my fault. Sorry.'

'They weren't Grand Union boats, that pair, did

you notice? There was some other name on the side.'

She hadn't noticed, any more than she'd noticed her stupid mistake. All in all, it had been a very bad start to the day.

Prue joined Ros on the butty where they had nothing much to do since the empty *Eurydice*, towed close behind *Orpheus*, needed no steering. After a while, they disappeared down into the warmth of the cabin to make cocoa. Out on the motor counter, it was miserably cold under sullen skies. Frances dared not relax her concentration for a second for fear of making another mistake. There would be boats coming along behind them with boaters in them who would be very angry if they were held up. Delaying them, even for a moment, was a deadly sin and one which she had already committed in full view of them all.

They putt-putted on steadily, winding their way along the cut, through countryside at first before it gave way to London. Loaded boats came by, up from the docks, the butties trailing on the end of long snubbers, a steerer in the cockpit to guide the heavy weight. As Pip had taught her, Frances slowed down politely to let them pass and go through first under bridges. Sometimes they gave a curt nod, sometimes, slouched behind their chimneys, no acknowledgement at all.

Ros came up to the butty fore-end to pass over

a mug of cocoa. Half of it had got spilled on the journey, but it was warm and it cheered her. Things began to look rosier. She hadn't got them stemmed up again – so far – and nothing else terrible or drastic had happened. They came round a bend with another bridge ahead and she saw a pair of boats there, waiting by the bridge-hole for a horse-drawn barge to come through. She slowed the motor, preparing to wait too, but, as they drew nearer, she realized that the barge wasn't moving. Nor was the horse who was standing on the towpath, head hanging, looking bored, its rope slack. The bargee had got off and was peering into the bridge-hole, down the side of the barge. Presently he was joined by his mate and the two of them scratched their heads under their caps and then started shaking them. The steerer from the narrowboat ahead strode along the towpath towards them, his dog trotting at his heels. There were gestures and shrugs and more head-shaking.

She brought *Orpheus* to a gentle stop beside the bank, behind the other pair, and saw Freddy on the motor counter. He waved and came running along the towpath.

'Stuck fast, she is. Me bruvver's gone to see what's to be done. Reckon 'e'll try and pull 'er out.'

They waited and watched while the boatman

returned, the dog following, and took his motor down to the bridge-hole. A rope on the barge bows was fastened round a stud on the deck of the narrowboat, which reversed until it was taut. Gears shrieked, the rope broke and the barge stayed stuck. Freddy came running back.

'Me bruvver says she's overloaded, that's what's done it. Water's too shallow there an' she's grounded.'

Another pair of boats came round the corner behind them and joined the queue and passers-by were gathering on the bridge, leaning over for a better view. A new rope was fixed in place and the horse reattached to the barge to lend its power on the towpath, but all in vain. Both ropes broke, the horse went cantering off and the barge stayed stuck. Prue came over with a mug of tea.

'What do you think's going to happen next?'

'I don't know. I suppose I'd better go and see if we can help at all.'

Quite how they could, she'd no idea – unless maybe *Orpheus* could tug too – but it seemed the right thing to offer help wherever help was needed on the cut. That was what Pip would have done.

Freddy trotted along beside her on the towpath towards the bridge-hole. They came to the other butty, brightly painted, shining clean and crowned with a snow-white Turk's head. She saw that it was called *Godwit*, and the name *Alfred Carter* was painted in black on the side.

'What a beautiful boat.'

The boy looked proud. 'It were me grandad's afore 'e died, same as the motor.' He tapped his chest. 'Called arter 'im, only everyone calls me Freddy. Me gran's in there cookin'. Allus doin' somethin', 'cept at night an' then she drives 'er pigs to market.'

'Surely you don't keep pigs?' Chickens, rabbits, ferrets, canaries, cats and dogs, yes, but she'd never seen pigs on the narrowboats.

He grinned. 'Snorin'. We can 'ear it on the motor, Jack an' I. Keeps us awake sometimes, it's that bad.'

'Do the boats belong to her?'

'Naw. Grandad left them to Jack, 'im bein' the oldest. Our dad were already dead, see. Fell in the cut one winter when 'e were comin' back from the pub. Frozen stiff as a plank when they found 'im in the mornin'. Me mam died too, from the bronchitus.'

He pronounced the illness in a funny way, like boaters mispronounced words.

They had reached the butty's motor, *Snipe*, which was equally well kept. The bridge-hole where the three men were talking was a few yards further on. Freddy stopped.

'They'll try somethin' soon. Best to wait 'ere.'

'I thought I'd ask if I could help.'

He looked shocked and shook his head. 'Wouldn't do that, miss. Me bruvver wouldn't take no 'elp from a woman – even if yer could, which yer can't.'

'I'll ask, anyway.'

She approached the men. 'Excuse me.'

They turned round, fists on hips. The black dog sniffed at her shoes. She noticed that his master wore a fancily embroidered waistcoat under his jacket, and a broad leather belt with the windlass stuck through like a cowboy's gun.

'I was wondering if we could help in any way at all?'

The bargemen – beefy giants towering above her – started grinning all over their faces. Brother Jack didn't grin.

He said, 'Best help yer can give us, lady, is ter keep out of our way.'

He turned his back and they went on discussing the problem.

'Told yer so, miss,' Freddy said.

More boats arrived, forming a queue on both sides of the bridge, and more watchers gathered above and on the banks. A tractor was sent for from a nearby farm, but it was unsuccessful in dislodging the barge. Eventually it was decided to unload enough of the timber onto the towpath to lighten her. An hour or so later she was floating free, and the horse towed her out of the bridge-hole to the bank.

By the time they had managed to restart the engine on *Orpheus*, the boats were already proceeding under the bridge, one pair after another. Terrified of getting something wrong and of holding the boaters up, Frances let them all go in front. Nobody offered them their rightful place in the queue and they trailed along, last, and least, of all.

They tied up at Camden Lock for the night and discussed the day over the tinned sardine supper in the butty cabin.

'I ought to have pushed more,' Frances said. 'We were second in the queue. It was feeble to let them all go in front of us. They'll just think we're idiots.'

'Yes, they will,' Ros agreed. 'Even more so. But who cares? Let them think what they like.'

They made cocoa and Frances and Ros lit cigarettes. It had started to rain, pattering on the butty roof, making the cabin seem all the cosier. Prue was almost falling asleep over her mug. They turned in very early, planning to be up and ready to leave at first light.

In the morning it was still raining, but much harder. Frances rolled out of her cross-bed and when she slid back the cabin hatch the rain drenched her face. She pulled on her clothes without bothering to wash or even brush her hair. Ros and Prue had the kettle going on the butty stove and they swallowed mugs of hot tea and slices of bread and jam.

'We've got some leaks,' Ros said, pointing to trickles of water sliding down the walls, and to tins and pans strategically placed to catch drips. She looked at Frances more closely. 'And you've been bitten by a bedbug.'

They'd got leaks and bedbugs: *Orpheus* and *Eurydice* were not as romantic as their names. Once again, there was a titanic struggle starting the engine. The boaters, of course, had already gone and were well on their way down to the docks. They followed long after, negotiating the London locks with the empty boats breasted-up as Pip had taught them. The lock-keepers were kind and helped them in a fatherly way and they didn't do too badly, but they knew it wasn't a fair test. There would be many other locks that would have unhelpful keepers or none at all.

After the locks they singled out the boats and Frances carried on steering the motor, with Ros and Prue in the butty behind towed on its short strap. The rain carried on, too, all the way to Limehouse. It found its way down the back of her neck and into her shoes and, with the hatch open for steering, down into the cabin where it lay in cold puddles on the lino floor. The only respite was the tunnel at the Angel, Islington where they swopped the rain for unpleasant darkness and constant thumps and bumps as *Orpheus*, in spite of Frances's best steering efforts, ricocheted off the brick walls. She thanked God that they didn't meet a barge head-on – there was room for the narrowboats to pass each other, but not barges.

Loaded pairs were coming up from the docks. The boaters, she noticed, ignored the rain. They wore old overcoats, never any kind of water-proofs.

They reached the docks and tied up alongside the row of narrowboats, their ears assaulted by the noise from cranes and lorries and, every so often, by ships testing their guns. Molly Jessop appeared on the wharf above, wearing the silk scarf, and shouted down that they weren't loading yet, so would they like to come and have some tea?

In spite of the rain, Molly had somehow kept her butty cabin dry and the kettle was whistling a welcome on the stove. Saul, her husband, crossed over from the motor to join them, and they squeezed round the let-down table while Molly poured tea and handed out ginger biscuits. Frances asked Saul if he knew where she could buy oilskins. There was no reply, so she repeated the question.

He nodded. 'Heard yer first time, but I were

198

thinkin' what to tell yer. I don' 'old with oilskins, ter speak the truth. See, the wet runs off an' it soaks yer trousers and yer shoes, an' that makes a right mess in the cabin. An' they gets in the way, flappin' about. We wears our coats and then we 'ang them up in the engine room to get dry. Works better.'

He was a man of few words but they were always wise ones, and whenever he spoke they listened.

'Go stiddy, but keep a-goin' – that's the way. From when yer lets go in the mornin' till yer ties up at night. No need to rush it, but no call to stop – less somethin's amiss.'

Which, thought Frances, it assuredly would be many times. There was no hope that they would ever handle the narrowboats as well as the men and women who had spent their lives on them. She said as much to Saul, who chuckled.

'Us never stops learnin' neither – not till we dies. There's allus better 'n' quicker ways ter find. An', by the way, yer water can's in the wrong place – oughta be on t'other side of yer chimney – might's well get it lookin' right.'

They were loaded during the afternoon – bags of cement dumped by crane from the wharf into the holds, coating the boats and them in fine grey powder. If the rain hadn't stopped, they might have set like rocks. Then the sheeting-up – the battle with beams and stands and top planks, the struggle with heavy, unwieldy canvas and tarry strings, eyelets and knots. Their reward more cuts and blisters and bruises and sore knees.

They weren't to let go until the next morning, and Molly came round again and invited them to go with her and Saul to a pub. A nice glass of port and lemon did her and the babe the world of good, she said. Got them both to sleep sound at night.

The Volunteer lay outside the main gates to the docks. Inside, it was lit by gas lamps and there was sawdust on the floor, an atmosphere nearly as thick as a London fog and a hard-drinking clientele of seamen, dockers and boatmen. They sat decorously at a table and Molly sipped her port and lemon while the rest of them drank beer, except Prue who had her fizzy lemonade. With all the noise and chatter going on, it was hard to hear what anyone was saying. Frances was trying to listen to Molly when there was a shift in the crowd and she caught sight of Freddy's brother Jack. He was standing at the bar, pint mug in fist, talking to another boater. She gave Molly a nudge.

'That boatman over there – the one with the red scarf round his neck . . .'

Molly looked. 'Jack Carter? What about 'im?'

'He doesn't think much of us trainees. We held him up when we let go at the lay-by.'

'Well, 'e wouldn't, would 'e? 'E's a Number One. Owns 'is own boats. They don't stop for nobody an' nuthin'. Not if they can 'elp it.'

'His little brother, Freddy, he's nice. He helped us.'

'We saw 'im. Everyone likes Freddy. 'E's the youngest Carter. There's three more brothers an' a sister. The sister got married an' the other brothers work fer a company on the Oxford. When Jack got left the boats from 'is grandad, 'e took Freddy with 'im cos their mam and dad was dead. Ever seen the grandma?'

'Only once. Not properly.'

'She's like the boatwomen allus was. Bonnet, an' long black skirts an' lace-up boots, an' 'er cabin's got more brasses 'n anyone else on the cut. Ain't nuthin' she don't know about the boats an' the cut. Nor Jack neither. An' that's not all 'e knows. A proper lady-killer, is Jack Carter.' She giggled. 'If only 'e'd looked my way, I'd've gone wiv 'im, but 'e never did. Still, I reckon I'm better off with my Saul.'

Later, he came by their table and Molly stopped him. ''Ow's yer grandma, Jack?'

'Fine, Molly. An' yerself?'

'Not so bad, considerin'. These ladies are trainees.'

'I know that.'

'This is Rosalind and this is Prudence. And this one's Frances.'

Cement dust still caked their hair and their faces; they looked like old ladies. He nodded curtly.

'How d'y do.'

The fancy waistcoat, Frances now saw, was embroidered with a pattern of spiders' webs. She said, 'I'm sorry if we held you up.'

He stared at her with eyes that were the same colour as Freddy's, but a lot harder. 'Like I told yer, lady. Best thing is if yer keeps out o' the way.'

He moved on and Molly dug her in the ribs. 'See the way 'e looked at yer? 'E were watchin' yer close, all right. Did yer notice?'

Eleven

Tring Summit was one of Prudence's favourite parts of the trip. It wasn't as long as some other pounds, but the cut wound peacefully through quiet countryside and was well sheltered from wind and weather. For three miles there were no locks to worry about. There was time to drink and eat without gobbling and gulping on the go, as they usually did, and, if Ros was steering the butty, time to catch up on other things. Tidy the cabin, stoke up the fire, fill the coal box, even do some splicing which she found, surprisingly, that she enjoyed. In fact, she was rather good at it. There was something very satisfying about unlaying the strands of a broken rope, whipping them and then remeshing them neatly together. It was a fiddly job and Ros and Frances both found it boring, but she didn't and it was the one thing on the boats that she could do better than them. Frances could steer the best, Ros was the surest-footed, but she was the fastest at splicing.

She could manage steering either the butty or the motor, if she had to, and walking the top planks wasn't so frightening any more, but, given the choice – which she frequently was by Frances – she preferred lock-wheeling. So long as you kept calm and did everything in exactly the right order, it was really quite simple. Rather like Mr Holland's Psychology of Accuracy, which she still thought about sometimes. One, shut gates. Two, lower paddles. Three, raise paddles. Four, open gates and so on . . . The swirling lock water no longer held such terrible fears for her because, as she had discovered, it did exactly as it was bidden – came into the lock or went out of it, rose up or went down, controlled by paddles and gates and gravity. Unlike the sea, it had no mind or will of its own. And where there was a lock-keeper he was often helpful with heavy beams and stiff ratchets.

At one lock – to her horror – she had dropped her precious windlass into the water and the lock-keeper had gone into his cottage and returned with another for her. He had a box of them, so he told her. The trainees were always leaving them behind and even the boaters got careless sometimes, which had surprised her. The boat people carried their windlasses so easily and so nonchalantly – stuck through their belts or dangling from trouser pockets or hooked over their shoulders under their jackets, so that for a while she'd thought that a lot of the boatmen were humpbacked.

When she'd finished her splicing she went and stood with Ros in the hatches. If the butty was being towed on the snubber on a long pound like Tring Summit you couldn't hear the racket of the diesel engine, which was a relief. The thumping throb of it was with them all day, from the moment they got it going in the morning until the moment it was switched off at night, when a blessed silence fell and the boats were quiet and still. She slept well at night – they all did because they were always tired out, exhausted by labouring away non-stop for hours and by spending so much time out in the fresh air. For the same reason they were always ravenously hungry, wolfing down thick doorstep slices of bread and jam or bread and peanut butter, and scraping their plates clean of whatever Ros had concocted on the little stove. Ros would cook things as she steered the butty – reach into the cabin to stir the stewpot or test the vegetables. She could even peel potatoes with one arm hooked round the tiller, and chop and mix things going along, like the boatwomen did.

Out of the wind, the sun felt warm, which was

a change from all the cold and the wet. She lifted her face to it, shutting her eyes as they trundled along, thinking about the spring and the summer to come and how lovely it was going to be on the cut – much more like the recruiting picture of the happy, smiling girl. The alders and willows along the banks would be in leaf, there'd be flowers in the grass, lambs in the fields, crops growing, the woods and the countryside all turning green. Then Ros said something and she opened her eyes again.

'What did you say?'

'I said I hope that bloke isn't going to chuck things at us.'

'What bloke?'

'The one on the bridge ahead. Pass me a lump of coal.'

She fetched the coal and shielded her eyes. At that distance, all she could make out was a dark shape leaning over the parapet. 'I can't see him very clearly.'

'Nor can I. Let's hope he's friendly.'

People leaning over bridges were very often far from friendly – usually it was children throwing stones and clods of earth or spitting down on them, but sometimes it was older youths who threw harder and spat more and yelled abuse. *Dirty gippos!* It was a spectator sport and the narrowboats were considered fair game, never mind that they were helpless to defend themselves, except with lumps of coal. Ros was the best shot and had scored many direct hits. Prudence watched the figure apprehensively. The motor was getting close to the bridge and she could see the man leaning further over with his arm raised. She thought, at first, that he was going to throw things at Frances, and then she realized that he was waving and shouting. Frances was shouting back and pointing behind her in their direction. The man waved again and reappeared on the bank beside the bridge-hole.

Ros lowered the lump of coal. 'What's he on about?'

'I think he wants a lift.'

As the butty chuntered nearer, Prudence could see the man more clearly. He was wearing an RAF greatcoat and cap and he was waving.

'Do you think we should, Ros?'

'Don't see why not – if Frankie reckons he's OK. You'd better give him a hand as we go past so he doesn't fall in.'

As the butty drew closer to the bridge-hole, she leaned over and held out her hand towards him. He grasped it and she pulled him on board and down into the hatches – the three of them squashed up together.

'The name's Steve,' he said, grinning down at her. 'Steve McGhie.'

'I'm Prudence Dobbs. And this is Rosalind Flynn.'

'Hi there, both of you. Thanks for stopping.' He sounded American, though it made no sense if he was in the RAF.

'We didn't exactly stop,' she said. 'We couldn't, I'm afraid. Where are you going to?'

'Wherever's near a town. Somewhere where I can get on a train. I need to get back on duty.'

'There's Leighton Buzzard ahead, isn't there, Ros?'

'I can never remember, darling.'

'We don't have a map, you see,' she explained, in case he thought they were really stupid. 'And we've only just finished training.'

He whistled. 'You girls handling these big boats all on your own . . . that's incredible. What're you carrying?'

'I'm afraid we can't tell you that.' They'd been told never to talk to strangers about their cargo, or about where they'd been loaded or their destination. Careless talk cost lives. Anyone could be a spy. He didn't look like one but you could never be sure.

Ros was trying to manoeuvre the butty's heavy tiller. 'You'll have to put him in the cabin, Prue. I can't steer properly with the three of us here.'

She led the way down and, of course, he cracked his head.

208

'Sorry. I should have warned you.'

He took off his forage cap and stood, head bent, rubbing it and looking round. His hair, she saw, was almost exactly the colour of clean new straw.

'Say, this is real homey, but kinda small.'

He was much too tall to stand upright and what with the broad shoulders and the bulky greatcoat, he filled up most of the spare space.

'We're used to it,' she said. 'Would you like a cup of tea? Or there's cocoa, if you'd prefer.'

He gave her a close-up smile. White teeth, blue eyes, a snub nose. Everyone else looked so clean, while they always looked so dirty – always covered with grease or coal or oil or mud.

'That's real nice of you, Prudence. Cocoa'd be great, if you've got some.'

'Would you like to sit down?' She pointed to the side bunk. The bedbugs had hopped over from the motor but they only seemed to come out at night.

'Sure. Thanks.'

Once he'd sat down she could manage to edge past him to get to the stove and put the kettle on. He watched while she put the cocoa powder into mugs and opened a tin of milk.

'Do you take sugar?'

'Only if you've got enough.'

They were running low but he was a guest as

209

well as some kind of foreigner – she didn't like to ask exactly what kind – which meant he must be treated with special consideration. As soon as the kettle had boiled, she poured on the hot water and added evaporated milk and some sugar. She gave him one of the mugs and handed another out to Ros. It seemed rude to leave him alone in the cabin, so she perched on the edge of the coal box with hers.

'You're in the RAF?' Obviously he was, but she felt obliged to make polite conversation.

'Yeah. Stationed at a place called Cranborough. It's just a one-street village in the middle of nowhere with a great big airfield. I'm on Halifaxes.'

'Really?'

'Four-engined bombers,' he added. He took a swallow from the mug and she saw him flinch.

'Is it all right – the cocoa?'

'Oh, sure.' He lifted the mug to her. 'It's great. Thanks.'

'How far away is Cranborough?'

'To tell you the truth, I've no idea. I don't have a map either. They gave us a forty-eight so I took myself off to see a bit of England. I've only been over here a couple of months. Got on a train, then a bus, then I walked, and then I got lost. Couldn't figure out where I was at all. No signposts and no folks around to ask. Then your boats came along. First time I've seen any boats like that.'

'They're narrowboats,' she said. 'The real boat people paint them all over with pictures – the ones who live and work on them all the time. Would you like a biscuit?'

'Sure. If you can spare it.'

She reached for the biscuit tin and he took one of the rich teas. They were stale but maybe he wouldn't notice.

'Back home, we call these cookies.' He took a bite and chewed slowly. If he'd noticed the staleness, he didn't say anything.

'Really?'

'I'm from Canada,' he told her, tapping the side of his shoulder where there was a badge. 'Winnipeg, Manitoba. Know where Winnipeg is?'

'I'm afraid I don't – not exactly.' She'd heard of it, of course, and they'd learned about Canada at school. Lumberjacks and log jams. Fur trapping. The Hudson Bay Company. Mounties. Prairies. Rockies. 'Is it near the Great Lakes?'

'They're further east. Winnipeg's sort of in the middle of Canada, where two big rivers join together. One flows up from the Mississippi and when that floods we get them too. That's what the name means: muddy water.'

'Does it really?'

'Yeah. It's Indian. We get a lot of our names and words from those guys. They were there long before we were.'

'Yes, I suppose they were.'

'It's nothing like England,' he went on. 'Not round Winnipeg. It's prairie land and so flat you can see a dog coming thirty miles away. Then when he's gone past, you can see him going for another thirty miles after that.'

'Can you really?'

'Yeah, you *really* can.' He grinned. 'Pretty much, anyway.'

He was teasing her, of course, but in a nice way. He looked round the cabin. 'Where do you sleep in this place?'

'Where you're sitting,' she said.

'No kidding? How about the other girl? Where the heck does she fit in?'

'There's another bed that lets down out of a cupboard.'

'Well, it's real cosy. Not like our huts on the base. They sure aren't cosy. Those stoves they have don't heat a thing.'

'Is it very cold in Winnipeg in winter?'

'Boy, is it ever! Colder'n you'd ever get here. Twenty below at least. Frozen from November to March – lakes, rivers, every darned thing. Ice so thick you can drive a truck over it and snow six feet deep sometimes. But we're used to it. I tell you – I've felt a darned sight colder in England than I've ever felt back home.'

'Really?'

'Yeah, really. Our summers are a lot hotter than yours too – hot and humid with mosquitoes the size of your hand. We've got a cottage by a lake where we go to cool off then – not like your English cottages, though. What you'd call a log cabin. We go swimming and boating and fishing. And we cook the fish in the open over a fire. It's real nice there. Nice in winter, too, but then we have to cut holes in the ice to catch the fish.'

'Do you go skating?'

He grinned. 'Boy, do we go skating! I'll say we do. We learn to skate before we can walk. I tell you, we can get along better on ice than on the ground.'

Ros called down. 'Better get moving, Prue.'

'It's the Marsworth locks soon,' she told him. 'I have to go ahead and see if they're ready for us.'

'What if they're not?'

'I have to shut and open things to let the water in and out. There are six of them close together and then another one soon after. And there'll be some more after that before we get to Leighton Buzzard.'

He drained the mug and wiped the back of his hand across his mouth. 'Sounds like a lot. I'll come and give you a hand. Work my passage.'

The downhill locks were all against them, which meant twice the work. On her own she would have been rushing about, straining at beams and wrestling with paddles, but he made it easy. He moved the beams as though they weighed nothing, whipped the paddles up and down as though he understood all about locks.

'I'm an engineer,' he told her when she commented. 'I know how things work, specially engines.'

She was impressed. Engines were beyond them. They could start the National – eventually – and stop it, but they couldn't cope with anything in between.

At Leighton Buzzard they tied up for the night.

'How about we go to a movie?' he said. 'What you call the pictures.'

'I'll ask Frances and Ros if they'd like to.'

'I meant just you. We could find something to eat after, maybe.'

'But I thought you had to catch a train.'

'No rush. I'll get one later.'

She hesitated. 'I ought to ask the others what they're doing. See if they'd like to come too.'

'Sure. Go ahead.'

Frances and Ros smiled and said they didn't want to play gooseberry. They were going to find a bath and a decent meal, in that order. Ros offered the loan of her lipstick and powder, which was kind of her because there wasn't much left of either. Prudence washed her hands and face and combed her lank hair and wished she'd taken the trouble to do her curlers the night before. When she peered at her reflection in the powder-compact mirror, she wondered why on earth he had asked her. Why not Ros who was so glamorous? Or Frances who had such confidence? Why *her*?

He was waiting on the wharf, leaning against a wall and smoking a cigarette. He threw the butt away. 'All set?'

There was a long queue outside the cinema and when they finally got inside, the film wasn't very good but she scarcely noticed because of him sitting next to her, so close that his arm lay against hers. She wondered if he would put it round her, like most of the servicemen were doing with their girls, and what she would do, if he did. She'd never been out with a man to the pictures before, or anywhere else; nobody had ever asked her – except for Mr Simpkins and he didn't count. But the Canadian went on smoking a cigarette and watching the big screen where the Hollywood actors and actresses all looked so perfect that they hardly seemed like real people.

Afterwards, they found a café down a side street. It wasn't very good, either – a shabby place with smeary glass-topped tables, tarnished cutlery and a cracked linoleum floor. The menu was sausage and mash, or liver and mash, or bubble and squeak – she had to explain to him what *that* was. They both chose the sausage and mash, and the waitress who took the order was rude. She felt ashamed of England.

He looked at her. 'Have you got a handkerchief?'

'I think so . . .'

She fumbled in her trouser pocket and found one, grimy with engine oil. He leaned across the table and wiped the lipstick carefully off her mouth.

'Sorry, sweetheart, but it didn't suit you. Not that colour.'

'It was Ros's, actually.'

'Ros is Ros and you're you. And you're great just the way you are. How old are you, Prudence?'

'Eighteen.'

'That's about what I figured. I'm twenty-one.'

The waitress took a long time bringing the order and banged the plates down in front of them. When he asked for some mustard, she clicked her tongue and came back with a pot that had a dried-up scrape in the bottom. The sausages were full of gristle, the mash full of hard lumps. She thought of the lovely dinner at the Ritz in London and wished it could have been somewhere like that with him – but in different clothes. Her best frock and her high-heeled court shoes, the pearl necklace Granny had left her, her hair washed and curled.

He said, 'How come you got to work on those boats?'

She told him about the bank in Croydon and about the advertisement, and how it had been a chance to escape from entering figures in a ledger all day and every day.

He nodded. 'I guess a lot of people felt like that. I sure couldn't wait to get away from home and join in the Big Adventure. It's been a whole lot tougher than I'd reckoned, but I wouldn't have missed it. Something to tell the children one day. If I get to have any.'

He meant, of course, if he survived. But he was an engineer and surely that meant he was safe on the ground – not flying?

'*Flight* engineer,' he told her. 'I'm crew. I sit by the pilot and give him a hand when he needs it, and if anything goes wrong I put it right. Mr Fix-It – that's me.'

'You mean you go on bombing raids?'

'Sure.'

'Often?'

'We've only done three so far. Another twenty-seven to go.'

'And then you can stop?'

'Well, some of the guys do another tour – if they want to. I'm not too sure about that yet. I'm waiting to see if I get through the first one OK.'

He didn't seem in the least bit worried – but she was, for his sake.

'I do hope you do.'

'Yeah, so do I. I'm planning on going home one day and living to a ripe old age.'

'In Winnipeg?'

'Guess so . . . it's my home town and it's not a bad place. My folks've lived there ten years or more. Before that, we had a farm out on the prairies but there was a big drought in the thirties and the soil got blown away. Then the locusts came along and ate what crops were left. That's when we moved to Winnipeg and Dad got work in a store. After a year or two, he opened one of his own and it's doing just fine.'

'Is that what you'll do? Work in the store?'

'Not if I can help it. Engines are my line. And I've got these ideas . . . inventions. Could make my fortune.'

'What sort of inventions?'

He grinned. 'If I tell you, swear you won't breathe a word?'

'Of course I wouldn't. I swear.'

'Well, one's a gadget for unfreezing car locks that've gotten frozen up – size of a pen so it can go in a pocket or a purse so it's handy. See, I told you the winters're real cold in Canada.'

The rude waitress brought their puddings – tinned plums and lumpy custard – and cups of

218

what was meant to be coffee. He grimaced – more than over the cocoa.

She said, 'I'm sorry it's so awful – the food and everything.'

'Yeah, it is. But it's not your fault. You've been going through hell over here for more than four years and you've got a whole lot of other things to be proud of.' He lit a cigarette. Looked at her through the spiral of smoke with his blue eyes. 'How about you, Prudence? What're *you* going to do, when the war's over? Go back to that bank of yours?'

She shook her head. 'I don't want to do that ever. I don't know what I'll do. Some other job, I suppose.'

'Come and live in Winnipeg.'

She laughed politely at the joke. 'It sounds a bit too cold for me.'

'I'd keep you warm.'

She stopped laughing and blushed.

He paid the bill and they went into the side street and blackout darkness.

'I think the railway station's that way,' she said.

'I'm seeing you home first.'

'There's no need, honestly.'

'Yeah, *honestly*, there is.'

He had a torch that worked and he took hold of her arm so she didn't trip over things or bump into lamp-posts or fall into the cut. The narrow-boats lay along the wharf, *Eurydice* tied up at the end of the row.

He said, still holding her arm, 'You do these trips regularly on the canal – right? Back and forth, delivering stuff?'

'Yes.' They weren't supposed to talk about that either but she couldn't see the harm. Not with him.

'Here's the deal. Next time you're coming this way, go to a call box and call the Three Horse-shoes pub in Cranborough. I don't know the number.'

'I can find it out.'

'OK. Leave a message for me with Ron, the landlord there. We're down there most nights when we're not flying and he'll pass it on for sure. He's a real nice guy. Tell him where you'll be stopping next and when, and I'll try to get over. If I don't show up, it's because I couldn't make it. If that happens, next trip you do the same. Sooner or later we'll meet again.'

'I can't remember your last name.'

'McGhie. Sergeant Steve McGhie.'

He put his arms around her and started to kiss her, then stopped.

'Hey, something wrong, Prudence?'

'I've never done this before.'

'Where the heck've you been hiding?'

'In the bank in Croydon.'

That made him laugh. 'You'll soon get the hang of it.' Later, he said, 'See what I mean? Piece of cake.'

He shone the torch for her to step on board the butty and down into the hatches. He called after her, 'Steve McGhie. Don't forget.'

Ros was already in bed, reciting one of her speeches: something about Arabian perfumes and a little hand.

'Had a good evening, sweetie?'

'Yes, thanks.'

'He's nice, your Canadian. Very hunky. Are you going to see him again?'

'I'm not sure.'

'I would, if I were you.'

She washed her face and brushed her teeth, tipped the dirty water overboard, switched out the light and climbed into bed. No curlers or prayers any more. She always fell straight to sleep, exhausted, but this time she couldn't for thinking of him and the feel of his mouth on hers.

Twelve

As usual, they were the last to let go in the morning. And, as usual, the engine had been a pig to start. When, in desperation, Frances had tried giving it a good kick it had fired on the next attempt, so maybe that was the trick. They swopped round duties. Ros took over steering the motor while Frances did the lock-wheeling and Prue steered the butty. They were all doing jobs they didn't much like, but that way they kept in practice.

After Leighton Buzzard, four downhill locks came close together. There was one bad moment when Prue let the butty creep back over the cill as they were going down, but they saved the situation in time, and another when Ros took the motor out too fast, missed picking up the butty tow rope and had to reverse all the way back again. Luckily, there were no spectators to witness either piece of incompetence.

At Fenny Stratford lock Frances went off to the shop to stock up on rations, carrying the kitty cocoa tin, while Prue filled up with water, staggering from tap to boats with overflowing cans that she could barely lift off the ground. The four-hour pound that came afterwards gave them a breather before they had to cross the Pig Trough aqueduct with its low parapet and terrifying drop to the Great Ouse below. Frances, on *Orpheus* and with a good view of the butty bows behind her, yelled a stream of instructions back to a white-faced Ros steering *Eurydice*. 'Too far over to the left . . . no, that's too far to the right . . . watch out, still too far . . . you're OK now. Just keep going straight as you are.'

Towards the end of the next pound, two hours long, a pair of boats came past and Frances called out to the steerer.

'How many locks have you made ready for us?'

He shook his head. 'There's a pair of boats ahead of yer.'

Sure enough, when they came to the bottom of the seven locks climbing to Stoke Bruerne every one was against them. They worked their way up doggedly, from lock to lock. Shut top gates, lower top paddles, raise bottom paddles, wait for water level to drop, open bottom gates, take boats in, shut bottom gates and drop bottom paddles, open top paddles, wait for water to rise, open top gates, take boats out. Seven times over. It was still early and they could have continued through the Blisworth tunnel and on for several more miles before darkness fell, but they were very weary and decided to tie up. Two other pairs of boats were already moored along the towpath. One pair, Frances saw, belonged to Saul and Molly, the other to Jack Carter. Freddy stuck his head out of the engine room on *Snipe* and waved at her, looking downcast.

'Engine's conked out, miss. Me bruvver's mendin' it. We'd've been through Bugby by now, else.'

In boaters' speech, this translated as the Buckby locks by Norton Junction, much further ahead. They were learning the boaters' names for locks and used them too: Stockers, Rickey, Albert's Two, Fishery, Mathus, Finney . . . There was no point offering Jack Carter any help. They were neither capable of giving it, nor would it be accepted if they had been.

Saul came walking along the towpath towards her, looking anxious.

'The babby's comin',' he said. 'Sister Mary's seein' to things.'

Pip had told them about Sister Mary and pointed out her canal-side cottage. She was nurse to the boat people – dressed their wounds, doled out their medicines, treated their ailments, delivered their babies. 'She knows them all,' Pip had said. 'They trust her completely.'

While they ate their supper in the butty cabin they thought of poor Molly in labour, close by.

Frances said, 'Do you remember Melanie in *Gone With The Wind*? She had an awful time. She had to cling to the bedpost.'

Ros shuddered. 'Don't talk about it.'

There was a sudden loud, inhuman shriek, and then another, and then one louder still – like an animal in dreadful torment. They sat listening in horror. Another scream of agony and Ros put down her knife and fork.

'I can't stand this. Let's go to the pub.'

They slunk past Molly's boat with their fingers in their ears. As they passed Jack Carter's pair the clink and clang of tools sounded from the engine room. At the Boat Inn Prue had her lemonade but Ros and Frances treated themselves to a cherry brandy. It tasted sickly but it steadied their nerves.

'No babies for me,' Ros said, drawing deep on her cigarette. 'Not after hearing that. It sounded as though she was being tortured.'

The pub filled up with regulars – local men who stared plenty but left them alone in their corner. Three more men came in – boaters this time – bought their beers and began a game of darts.

Prue nudged Ros. 'It's the same ones you played that time when we were with Pip. The Joshers.'

'So it is . . . maybe they'd like me to join them again.'

Ros started to get up but Frances grabbed her arm and pulled her down firmly. 'Pip told us to be careful of them – remember?'

By the look of them, they were brothers. Swarthy, unshaven, mean-eyed – like the baddies in a Western film, the ones who ride into town and cause big trouble in the saloon. The ones who drink hard and cheat at cards and finger their guns.

Frances drained her drink. 'Anyway, I think we ought to go, if we want to get off to a good start in the morning.'

Ros refused to be rushed. She lit another cigarette, sipped at her cherry brandy. 'Speaking of good starts, I've just had an idea.'

'What idea?'

'Well, I bet those Joshers will have tied up ahead of everyone so they can be first off in the morning.'

'We can't very well stop them.'

'We can get up even earlier than them. Pull that old boaters' trick of bow-hauling or shafting the boats further along the cut before we start the engine.'

'They'll hear us.'

'Not if we're quiet as mice, they won't.'

'The engine wouldn't start first go. It never does.'

'Kick it like you did today. That worked.'

'They'll catch us up. Overtake us.'

'They can't very well do that in the tunnel. Then if we can get to the next lock before they do, they'll be stuck behind us, whether they like it or not.'

Frances frowned. 'There aren't any locks till Bugby – that's more than ten miles away. We'd never make it.'

She glanced over at the three brothers and one of them gave her a very nasty look. She thought, Ros's idea is mad; they'd sink us if we got in their way. Then she thought, but if we could reach Bugby first, it would teach them a real lesson. She said, 'All right, Ros. We'll give it a try.'

As they were leaving the pub, Saul came in, beaming all over his face.

'It's a boy. A fine boy babby. Yer can go an' see 'im, if yer likes.'

Ros and Prue thought they ought not to make a crowd, so Frances went alone. When she knocked on the cabin door Molly answered, sounding quite normal, and when she went inside she found her lying in the cross-bed with the baby asleep in her arms.

'We're callin' 'im Abel, after Saul's dad,' she said, and she turned the shawled bundle gently towards the lamplight. 'In't 'e lovely?'

227

The baby was a mottled red with a wizened face like a monkey's.

'He's beautiful, Molly. But are you all right?'

'Me? Course I am. Sister Mary said I were ever so good fer a first one. Next time it'll be easier, she says. Nothin' to it.'

But already some of the bloom had gone, gone with the birth of Abel. However easy the births, Molly's youth would fade away.

'Will you stay here long?'

'Oh, no. We'll let go in a day or two. Saul says we'll take it easy at furst, though.'

'But shouldn't you rest in bed for longer than that?'

'Gracious, no. Me mam never did. Nor Saul's mam, neither. No time fer that on the boats. Yer'll be off tomorrer, though.'

'We're going to let go as early as we can, before the others. Get a good road, if we can.'

'Jack Carter's 'ere, in't 'e? Jack'll beat yer to it, love. Allus does.'

'He's still trying to mend his engine.'

'It'll be done by morn. Knowin' 'im.'

'There's another pair of boats arrived, too. Some Joshers. They were in the Boat Inn just now. Three brothers, I think.'

'That'll be the Quills. Nasty bits of work, they are. Drink like fishes an' allus lookin' fer trouble. Saul 'ad a fight with 'em once when they took our lock. Give 'im a black eye, they did.'

'We're going to see if we can get ahead of them in the morning.'

'They'll never let yer.' Molly sank back, suddenly looking tired. 'No sense in tryin'.'

Just before dawn, with only the faintest glimmer of pearly light in the east, they were up and dressed. There was no sound or sign of life from the other boats, nobody about on the towpath. They untied the mooring ropes, shafted the boats away from the bank and poled them silently past the Quills' pair and a short way down the cut, beyond a row of willows. Frances gave the engine a sound kick before she and Prue swung the flywheel. One, two, THREE. Ros pushed over the compression lever at exactly the right moment, the engine fired and settled to its steady beat. They were off and away, Frances steering the motor with Prue in the cabin ready to lock-wheel later on, and Ros steering the butty behind. They chugged towards the opening of the Blisworth tunnel in the side of the hill. Frances shifted the water can to the middle of the cabin top and laid the chimney pot on its side so neither would get knocked off by the slope of the roof.

She had never cared for the tunnels: the scary feeling of being sealed off from life, as if in a tomb, the icy drips and drops, the eerie light from the ventilation shafts, the deafening beat of the engine. She switched on the headlight and *Orpheus* entered the underworld.

The cut continued straight at first, then there was a bend and the nerve-racking plunge into two miles of Stygian darkness. Forty minutes, or more, to reach the other end. The light at the motor's fore-end shone feebly on black water and on brickwork encrusted with a strange orange fungus. Without the chimney in place, the smoke and fumes from the engine blew in her face, making her eyes stream. Steering was always tricky and every so often the motor hit the wall with a mighty, echoing boom. And tunnels held special terrors. The engine could fail, boats could get stuck, people could fall off, roofs could fall in. And the mind started imagining all sorts of ridiculous things . . . phantom boats, underground caverns, rivers that lured the unwary deeper and deeper into the bowels of the earth. The boaters loved frightening tales, and the Blisworth tunnel was said to be haunted by the ghost of an old legger who had drowned walking a boat through.

The first of the five shafts appeared ahead – a narrow beam of pale and eerie light filtering down from above. *Orpheus* passed through it slowly, foot by foot, before returning to the dark. If Frances turned around she would be able to see *Eurydice* as she went through, but her mind was still playing silly tricks. Don't turn round. Don't look back or the butty and Ros might vanish for ever.

By now, the Quills must be catching up. They would move fast – much faster than she could go, bumping her way inexpertly along. They might catch them up in the tunnel, ram them into the wall and force a way past, and the noise of the engine would make it impossible to hear them coming. She took the motor a little faster – as fast as she dared – put the tiller over too far and scraped her knuckles painfully against rough brick.

And then the headlight failed. It went on and off several times and finally went out, leaving pitch blackness ahead. The motor, continuing regardless, crashed heavily into a wall, bounced away and headed for the other side, the stern hitting afterwards like the smack of a whale's tail. She slowed the engine to idle and Prue's anxious voice called up from the cabin.

'What's happened?'

'The light's conked out.' She tried to sound calm. 'Must be a loose connection.'

Whatever the trouble was, after a minute or two the headlamp suddenly went on again and she carried on. A flickering mote of light had appeared ahead and she heard the sepulchral echo of a horn. Not some underworld being, she told herself sternly, or a ghostly legger, but the head-light of another pair approaching. Passing in a tunnel left no room for mistakes. It was easy for the motors to collide or for the two buttys to get entangled. She slowed the engine, answered with her motor's horn and steered *Orpheus* as close to the right-hand wall as possible. Ros, she prayed, would be doing the same thing with *Eurydice* behind. The mote of light grew and grew until she could make out the fore-end of the approaching boat, hugging the opposite wall. They crawled past each other, separated only by inches. The steerer, a hunched shape, was so close that she could have stretched out and touched him. She saw his nod and nodded back; the usual polite exchange of words would be inaudible above the combined racket of the two engines. As the butty glided by, the boatwoman nodded too, and shouted out the kindly and useful bit of information that they'd made Bugby ready for them, which meant that there was no other pair ahead to stop them going straight in.

Had they mistaken her for a real boater in the darkness? Not likely. The boat people noticed everything on the cut, knew where all the boats were and who was on them. They would have known exactly who she was.

Further on, the darkness began to lighten at the tunnel's end and when they emerged into the world again, the sun was up and the day had begun. Six more bridges before the canal divided at Gayton Junction where they must take the left-hand arm. She consulted Pip's essential information in her notebook. Rothersthorpe, then Bugbrooke, then Hayford . . . the cut wound its way in a series of bends and wiggles towards the Buckby locks, still twelve miles away at least. At any moment she expected to hear the sound of the Quill brothers' motor boat and to see them come storming round the corner, but Ros kept putting her thumb up as though there was nothing whatever to worry about. Then, just past the Stowe Hill boatyards, just as she was beginning to believe that all was well, the engine began to cough and splutter and to pour out black smoke from the exhaust pipe. She drifted to a stop by a bridge-hole and a workman called from the bank.

'Yer blades is blocked up, luv. Got a bladeful of summat, you 'ave.'

He wore a cloth cap and blue overalls and looked like somebody who might be able to do something. Pip had warned that all kinds of things could get caught up besides the snubber – old bits of rope, wire, clothes, rags, tyres, branches, dead cats . . .

'Can you help us, do you think?'

'Dunno 'bout that.'

She gave him her best smile. 'Please . . . we'd be very grateful.'

'Give it a try.' He spat on the ground. 'Can't promise nowt, though.'

The stern of the motor was manoeuvred close to the bank. He poked about with the short shaft underneath. Nothing much seemed to be happening, and presently he was joined by another man, and then a third. It was barbed wire, they said at last, and it'd take time to cut it all loose. It were in a right mess.

After a while, as expected, the Quill brothers' boats came up and passed them by. One of them shouted something but Frances kept her back turned and pretended not to hear. It was another half-hour at least before the propeller blades were free and they could go on their way. The Quills would easily reach Buckby first and start their climb. And unless another pair came up from the opposite direction afterwards, all seven locks would now be against them – the very fate they'd planned for the brothers.

Two miles further on they rounded a sharp left-hand bend and there was the Quills' motor with its nose buried deep in the mud bank. The three brothers were very busy with long shafts and lines, but, by the look of it, they'd got themselves well and truly stemmed up. If it had been anyone else Frances would have offered to tow them off, but not the Quills. She steered *Orpheus* past at full speed.

But their triumph was short-lived. Before long they heard the clattering beat of an engine pushed deliberately to its limits, and saw that the brothers were behind them once again and catching up fast. The cut ran straight for the final mile to the first lock and Frances steered the motor down the middle, leaving no room on either side for the Joshers to pass unless they wanted to risk getting stuck in the mud again. They started blowing their horn and yelling at her to get over, but she took no notice.

The lock was ready for them, as the boatwoman in the tunnel had promised. The gates were wide open and all Frances needed to do was go straight in. They reached the concrete marker on the bank which officially gave them the right of way and Frances slowed, steering the motor to the right, ready to enter the lock. The Joshers were close behind, engine hammering, and, out of the corner of her eye, she saw the fore-end of their motor nosing close alongside, heard the steerer bellowing at her.

'Loose us by, else yer'll be sorry. Stupid bloody cow! Git out of our way.'

She shouted back. 'It's our lock. You get out of ours.'

He didn't and in another moment he'd be past

if she didn't stop him. She wrenched at the tiller and *Orpheus*'s fore-end lurched across his path. The Josher boat thudded into the motor's side and swung round close enough for one of the brothers to leap across onto *Orpheus*. He snatched at the tiller, shoving Frances aside so hard that she overbalanced and fell into the cut. When she surfaced, the Quill brother was reversing to clear the way to the lock. His head was turned away to look over his shoulder when Prue, brave Prue, emerged from the cabin, brandishing the poker, and set about him. Taken by surprise, he flung up his arms to defend himself, toppled over and joined Frances in the cut. They both swam for the bank and reached it at the same time. Somebody yanked her out onto the towpath and kicked the Quill brother back in. When she'd scrambled to her feet and wiped her wet hair out of her eyes, she saw that it was Jack Carter.

The other two brothers were coming along the towpath, one of them swinging a windlass menacingly, with the Carters' black dog snapping and barking at their heels and nimbly avoiding their kicks. The third was climbing out of the cut.

'Don' just stand there, woman! Git in an' git the bloody gates shut!'

Jack Carter yelled it over his shoulder as the three brothers fell on him and she ran for the lock.

Prue had brought the motor in exactly right and Ros the butty, in its turn. The gates were slammed shut, paddles dropped, paddles drawn, and water gushed into the deep lock. Back on the towpath a furious fight was taking place.

One Quill was thrown into the cut, another fell to his knees, but the third was still on his feet, windlass raised. And then the little old Carter grandmother came trotting along in her bonnet and long skirts and button boots. She carried a short shaft in her hand and she hurled it like a javelin. It hit the third Quill in the middle of the back, knocking him flat to the ground.

The lock was full. They opened the top gates and as Frances jumped back onto the motor, Freddy ran up, grinning.

'Jack's took care of 'em. Seen 'em off proper. 'E said to tell yer to git a bleedin' move on an' not 'old 'im up no more.'

She scrambled into dry clothes as they worked their way frantically up to the seventh lock with Jack Carter's pair following. After the way he'd saved them from the Quills, she ought to have waited at the top and let him go by, but, stubbornly, she didn't. It was too good a chance to prove themselves, to show him they weren't as hopeless as he thought. At the Norton toll office, after Buckby, their trip card was marked and the boats gauged, checking that their load was

237

all present and correct. They fled through the Braunston tunnel and on down the six Braunston locks. The Carter boats were only one behind them and Freddy kept biking up to lock-wheel for his brother. The bike was man-sized and he rode it very fast, standing on the pedals. He gave them a hand with gates and winding gear and the benefit of his wise advice.

'Let 'er swing, miss. Nice 'n' easy. No call ter shove so 'ard. Dig yer 'eels in, if she's a booger. That paddle's still oop, so yer won't be goin' nowhere. Forgot yer iron, miss. Left it on the beam. 'Ere it is.'

'We've got to manage on our own,' Frances told him. 'You mustn't help us.'

He nodded, understanding. 'Not doin' so bad, an' all. Considerin'.'

A long pound followed with more bends and treacherous mud. If they got stemmed up, Jack Carter might give them a snatch . . . or he might not. There was no way of knowing how a boater would behave – not if he was being held up, as he surely was. At Napton Junction they turned to the right. The Wigrams three came next and then the flight of ten downhill locks at Itchington, and then the Radford ten, followed by the Leamington pound, and all the time Jack Carter was chasing them, breathing hard down their necks. It was after seven by the time they tied up for the night above the Warwick locks and they were aching all over – backs, arms, legs begging for rest. With the engine stopped there was blissful silence. Peace after hours of racket, and in a pleasant mooring with tall trees and a nice old pub close at hand called the Cape of Good Hope. There were other boaters already there and presently Jack Carter arrived and tied up along the bank.

'We ought to go and thank him,' Frances said. 'Shall we draw lots for it?'

Ros shook her head. 'Your job, Frankie. You're the steerer. Off you go.'

'I'll do it later. He's bound to be at the pub.'

'You're not by any chance frightened of him, are you, sweetie?'

'Of course I'm not.'

But they'd held him up, blocked his way – committed the unforgivable sin in a boater's eyes. He was bound to be furious.

With the last of their strength, they refilled the water cans and changed over the batteries and chopped firewood for the morning. Ros heated up some stew and potatoes and when they'd eaten, they went over to the pub. The boaters were at their usual darts and dominoes and an old pianola machine was grinding out 'The Bluebells of Scotland'. But instead of blank looks and turned backs, there were some nods and smiles in their direction. They retired to a bench with their mugs, puzzled. There was no sign of Jack Carter but, at that moment, the Quills walked in.

Ros paused in the act of lighting her cigarette. 'Here comes trouble.'

The brothers, sporting a number of colourful bruises, passed by the bench on their way to the darts corner and, as they did so, they nodded. It was no more than the faintest jerk of the head, but an acknowledgement nevertheless.

We stood up to them, that's why, Frances thought, light dawning. Unpleasant though they are, they respect that. And the other boaters have heard about it.

They walked back to the boats under a starry sky, feeling well pleased with themselves.

'There's the Plough,' Frances said, stopping to gaze heavenwards. 'It's the only constellation I can recognize.'

Ros's earrings jingled as she craned her neck. 'Isn't that Orion, the Hunter?'

'How on earth do you know that?'

'I don't. I'm making it up.'

'Do you know any, Prue?'

'Only the Milky Way.'

'That's a galaxy – billions of stars and gas and dust held together, if I remember rightly.'

They walked on.

Ros yawned. 'I vote we don't get up so early

tomorrow. There's no point in exhausting ourselves like we did today.'

She and Prue disappeared down into the butty cabin; Frances stayed out on the counter, stargazing. She was very tired but the tiredness had a good side to it: the day's hard work had earned the night's healing rest. She would fall asleep the second her head touched the pillow, sleep soundly until the morning and awake refreshed. She had never felt fitter, or happier, or more satisfied in her whole life.

There was a patter of paws, the scrape of a boot and then the bright flare of a match. Jack Carter and his dog had come out of his cabin onto the counter, only a few yards away; the smoke from a roll-up cigarette drifted towards her. He didn't say anything, but she was ready with her little speech.

'Mr Carter, we want to thank you for coming to our rescue today.' It sounded horribly like Lady Muck being gracious, which she hadn't intended at all. She hurried on. 'It was awfully good of you. We're very grateful.'

'Are yer now?'

'Yes, we are.' It was too dark to see him properly – to know if he had any bruises like the Quills. 'I hope you weren't hurt – in the fight.'

'Nothin' to mention.'

'And we're very sorry if we held you up

afterwards.' It was the second time she'd had to apologize to him for doing that. 'We ought to have loosed you by at the top of Buckby.'

'So yer ought.'

'Next time we will.'

'Won't be no next time.' He sounded amused, not angry. 'I promise yer that.'

'No, I don't suppose there will. And, as I said, we're very sorry about it. We'll keep out of your way in future.' She fished for his approval. 'Did we do all right with the boats today?'

The cigarette glowed at its end and more smoke wafted her way. She waited for some small crumb of recognition, if not for actual praise. Finally, he answered.

'Considerin'.' Freddy's condescending word.

They'd nearly killed themselves in the attempt. Run themselves into the ground. Given their all.

'Considering?'

'Considerin' what yer are.'

Ladies playing at boats, was what he meant.

She said huffily, 'We do our best.'

'Didn't say yer didn't.'

'But you still think we're useless?'

'Didn't say that neither.'

There was another silence. She waited, still hopeful, but nothing more was forthcoming. 'I expect you'll be leaving very early in the morning.'

242

'Earlier 'n you.'

That would certainly be true – he'd make very sure of it. So would the Quills. She turned away.

'Well . . . goodnight, Mr Carter.'

'Jack's the name.'

She said, 'I'm Frances.'

'I know. Molly said.'

'What's your dog called?'

'Rickey. I got 'im thereabouts.'

'That's a good name.'

''E's a good dog.'

Something about his voice rang a bell with her; she realized suddenly what it was.

'Is it you I've heard singing sometimes?'

'Mebbe.'

'Playing an accordion?'

'Melodeon.'

The cigarette glowed again. A long silence. She knew he was watching her in the dark and, with his boater's eyes, he would be able to see her far better than she could see him. He had the advantage. Her heart was thudding . . . the nine-year-old child behind the tree, afraid, yet fascinated.

My mother said
I never should
Play with the gypsies in the wood . . .

It was a skipping rhyme from schooldays, repeated over and over again. Two girls each holding an end of the rope and swinging it round and round for the third to jump over. Jump, jump, jump. Jump, jump, jump. Until the rope caught them.

If I did
She would say
Naughty little girl to disobey.

Still he didn't speak. And still he watched her. She could feel his eyes fixed upon her; feel the gentle tug of invisible silken threads, pulling her towards him.

My mother said
I never should . . .

'Well, goodnight . . . Jack.'
'G'night, Frances.'
She lay in the cross-bed, wide awake. After a while, she heard the melodeon playing and him singing again. It was a different song, this time, and all about summer. About sunlight on the cut, and willows and wild flowers and good roads instead of bad ones, and about a fair-haired maid who'd stolen his heart. Foolishly and fancifully, she imagined that he was singing it to her. And, even more foolishly and fancifully, she imagined him lying in the cross-bed beside her.

When she woke in the morning he'd left. The way things went on the cut, it could be weeks before they saw him again.

They unloaded the cement at Tyseley and continued round the hateful Bottom Road to take on coal at Longford, which they brought down to the ABC bakery at Camden Town. The return leg was not without crises. An engine breakdown halted them for two days until a company fitter arrived. They were stemmed up at least a dozen times, the butty water can and chimney were swept off by an overhanging branch and had to be retrieved from the cut, and the bike slid from the cabin roof with the same result. Ros lost her windlass, the blades got fouled and the bilge pump failed. Back at the Bulls Bridge lay-by they cleaned, polished, mopped and scrubbed the boats. The cabins were stoved out with a formalin candle and the dead bedbugs swept up. Two more trips had to be made before another spell of leave. On the next, they carried a load of iron filings and on the one after that it was steel billets. Both times they brought back more coal. Winter had gone and it was spring.

Thirteen

It was depressing being back in the real world, Rosalind decided. On the boats, you were out of touch – no petty restrictions or boring regulations. You forgot about the news, the queues, the air raids . . . all the wartime miseries. But as soon as you went on leave, you realized that everything you'd left behind was just the same. The war had gone on without you and was still going on. In the train, she shared a third-class compartment with a group of soldiers who kept plying her with cigarettes. She smoked away and listened to them chewing over rumours that the Allies would invade France soon, and betting where they might land. Their money was on Normandy and, to hear them, you'd think that Winston Churchill himself had tipped them the wink. When she pointed out that she might well be Mata Hari, eavesdropping in her corner, they roared with laughter and said that spies never looked like her. Spies were people you didn't notice.

She walked from the station, carrying the carpet bag. A long convoy of lorries overtook her, with more soldiers hanging over the tailboards and wolf-whistling. They were heading west, which made her wonder about the rumours and whether the soldiers in the train had been right.

There was only one lodger at the house, so her bedroom was free. After three trips she was ready to drop. It was going to take several days to recover and several baths to get clean.

Her parents had no interest in the narrowboats, which was fine by her. The talk, as always, was entirely about the theatre. Who was acting in what, whether they were any good or whether they were terrible, who was sleeping with who, who was either on the bottle or on the wagon, who was up and coming and who was on the slippery slope down. The current play at the Winter Gardens was *Private Lives* and the leads, according to her mother, were going down: an ageing matinee idol with badly dyed hair and a well-past-it actress who would never see forty-five again. The second leads, apparently, were far better.

After three days, mainly spent asleep, she took a walk along the front and up to the chalk cliffs. Another convoy, this time of Royal Navy ships, was sailing westwards down the Channel and

RAF fighters screamed over her head. If it was true about the Allies landing soon in France, then the war wouldn't last much longer. Maybe only months. It might even be over by Christmas. Time to think about how she was going to get back into the theatre.

The Winter Gardens was on the seafront, not far from the pier – a dilapidated old place, long past its glory days. The stage door at the side was unlocked, nobody about. She wandered down a dingy passageway, past cubbyholes and storerooms. There was the familiar smell of Jeyes Fluid and then, as she opened a door at random, the heady scent of greasepaint. A dressing room! She switched on the mirror lights, picked up a stick of Leichner from the table and stroked some colour onto her cheeks. Another colour – strawberry red – went on her lips. She was just choosing one for her eyelids when somebody walked in.

'Who the fuck are you?'

She looked at his reflection: stockily built, shock-haired, wearing a grubby sweater and old grey flannels. A plumber perhaps, or somebody come to mend something?

'I'm Rosalind Flynn.'

'Well, I'm Ken Woods and this is my dressing room. So would you mind pissing off?'

The accent was north country, a far cry from

248

the way actors usually spoke. She put down the Leichner. 'Certainly. I only used a bit.'

He went on looking at her, fists on hips, like a brick wall between her and the door or she might have made a dash for it.

'You've got a bloody nerve, I must say. Barging in here. Tarting yourself up. You a loony, or something?'

'I'm an actress,' she said. 'As a matter of fact.'

'Oh, yeah? So what've you been in?'

She told him, starting with the extra fairy in *A Midsummer Night's Dream* and finishing with Sir Lionel, and adding a number of parts that she'd never actually played in between. Then, for good measure, she threw in the bit about going off nobly to do war work on the boats. 'As soon as it's over, I'm going back to the stage.'

He said, 'All right. I believe you. But you're still going to have to get out. There's a matinee. I need to get ready.'

He must be the plumber, after all. Having her on.

'It's *Private Lives* this week. You can't be in that.'

'It is. And I am. I'm the second husband that gets dumped for the first. I'll get you a complimentary seat, if you like. To show there's no ill feeling.'

She sat in the front row of the dress circle;

usually she was at the back of the gods. The tatty auditorium – all flaking gilt and bomb-damaged cherubs – was full of old ladies in moulting furs that reeked of mothballs. As she waited for the curtain to rise, her mouth was dry, her hands clenched, her heart racing – as though she were on the other side of it.

At first, she didn't recognize him. His hair was slicked down, the north country accent had vanished, the clipped speech, the mannerisms and movements were faultlessly upper class. He's good, she thought, and so is the girl playing the other bride. But her mother had been right about the leads. The matinee idol and the over-the-hill actress were painfully bad. Naturally this was lost on the mothballed audience, who had known them in their heyday. At the curtain call, the idol and his partner were loudly applauded, the other two rated a sprinkling of polite hand-claps.

She went round to the dressing room again. He was cleaning off the greasepaint and looked at her in the mirror.

'Rubbish, wasn't it? Should've warned you.'

'*You* were good,' she said. 'And that other girl. And the seat was very nice. Thanks.'

He wiped off the rest, roughed up the slicked-down hair with his fingers. 'I'm starving. Want to come and get some grub?'

There was a self-service café round the corner where everything was on toast – beans, pilchards, soft roes, dolloped out from hot serving dishes.

'I'll pay for mine,' she said.

'You'll have to, love. I'm skint.' When they sat down he fell on the pilchards as though he hadn't eaten for a week.

She said, 'I didn't recognize you on stage at first.'

'I'm a good actor, that's why.'

'Where did you learn to talk proper?'

'RADA. On a scholarship. They taught us how to speak with plums in our mouths. How now brown cow . . . the rain in Spain, and all the rest of it.' He waved his knife around. 'I'll let you into a little secret, though. I hate this bloody play. All those witty lines make me puke. Can't stand anything by Noel Coward. Or Rattigan. Or any of that lot. Matter of fact, I don't like acting that much. It's a nancy job.'

'Why do it, then?'

'I'm going to hop over the footlights one of these days. *Direct* plays. And they won't have balconies, or drawing rooms, or French windows, or any of that sort of stuff. They'll be plays about *real* people and *real* life.'

She could see he was serious, not just shooting a line. 'Anyway,' she said. 'Why haven't you been called up?'

'Asthma. They wouldn't take me. All that coal dust up north.'

'Don't tell me your father was a miner.'

'I *am* telling you. He was.'

'Back-to-backs, tin baths, clogs, jam butties, scrubbed doorsteps?'

'Not forgetting the pneumoconiosis. Dad died of that.'

He produced a crumpled packet of Woodbines and a matchbox. There were only two cigarettes left, but he gave her one and lit them with the last match. She wasn't sure about his hands. Too square, the fingers too blunt, nails too much like spatulas. Hands were important. They told you a lot about a man.

'What do you do next?'

'We move on tomorrow. Touring.'

'Then what?'

'Well, we won't make it to the West End – not with this lot. I'll see what I'm offered.' *The West End!* Three magic words. Even better, one: *Broadway!*

As they left the café, he said, 'Let me know when you're done with the boats and I'll see what I can do.'

'How am I supposed to find you?'

'You'll hear about me, don't worry.'

* * *

252

The KEEP OUT notice had been pinned to the orangery door, but, for once, Frances took no notice. The reason for it was a newcomer and her name was Clara Cooper. She had small ruby and white flowers growing on long stalks and was, apparently, extremely fussy about living conditions. Papa did the introduction while Frances stood several feet away, in case she contaminated her.

'Quite special, don't you think?'

'Yes, very beautiful.'

'Don't come any closer.'

'I won't.'

Other orchids had come into bloom and her father hovered from one to another like an attentive bee. He had been nonplussed to see her.

'I didn't know you were coming home, Frances.'

'I'm on leave.'

'Oh, I see. How are the Wrens?'

'I'm not in the Wrens, Papa.'

'But I thought you said something about boats.'

'Not those sort of boats. Narrowboats. A bit like barges. On the canals.'

'Yes, of course. I remember now. How interesting.'

He wasn't in the least interested, she knew. She followed him round the orangery for a bit, making admiring remarks about the orchids, and then gave up.

253

Aunt Gertrude was gardening. Frances found her wielding secateurs and uprooting weeds in a border of the Italian pool garden below the orangery. They sat on a stone seat beside the middle of the three stone pools. The water was stagnant, the lead fountains hadn't worked for years and the box topiary was quite beyond poor old Didcot and his lad.

'Vere's going to have to marry an heiress,' Aunt Gertrude said. 'Restore the family fortunes. Don't you know any?'

'Afraid not.'

'I thought he was rather taken with that beautiful red-haired girl you brought here last time – the actress. Pity she's not an heiress.'

'*Ros?* No, he wasn't. He disapproved of her like anything. He told me she wasn't the right sort of friend for me to have.'

'Just the same, I noticed the way he kept looking at her.'

'Finding fault, I bet. He wanted me to give up the boats, you know.'

'He feels responsible for you, darling.'

'Well, he's not. And I'm certainly not giving them up. Or any of my friends.'

'I think the war might be over soon, in any case. If the rumours are true.'

'What rumours?'

'About the Allies planning a landing in France.

Don't tell me you haven't heard?'

'We don't hear a thing on the cut.'

'Good heavens, everyone's been talking about it for weeks. There are army camps all along the south coast and thousands of American soldiers. They requisitioned a whole chunk of land – just turfed the villagers out – and their marines have been practising climbing the cliffs. Apparently every port's full of naval ships and landing craft. There's not much doubt about it – it's just a question of *when*, and I don't think it'll be very long now. I hate to think of all those young men who are going to die.'

Frances took the bus into Bridport to do some shopping and South Street was jammed with a long convoy of tanks rumbling through the town. People were running out of houses and shops with mugs of tea and buns and cigarettes, handing them up to the crews. She stood on the pavement, watching the unending procession. An American tank rolled past and the soldier in the turret smiled and winked at her. She lobbed the Crunchie bar she'd bought at the sweetshop in his direction. He caught it with one hand and, with the other, gave a thumbs-up.

'Hallo. Is that the Three Horseshoes pub? Could I please speak to the landlord?'

'He's not here.'

'Will he be back soon?'

'Couldn't say. Anyway, the pub's shut. We don't open till six.'

The woman who had answered slammed the receiver down. Prudence wasn't sure if she'd have the nerve to try yet again. When they'd stopped at Leighton Buzzard coming back on the trip with the iron filings, the telephone in the public kiosk had been out of order. On the next trip, taking the steel billets, there had been a long queue of American soldiers who'd kept bothering her and she'd had to leave. On the way back from Coventry she'd rung again, but nobody had answered.

Mother came out of the sitting room.

'Who were you telephoning, Prudence?'

'Just a friend from school. She was out.'

He would have given her up by now. And she didn't even know where Cranborough was, so she couldn't go and find him. The world atlas, kept behind the glass doors of the bookcase next to the set of encyclopedias, only showed cities and towns, not English villages in the middle of nowhere. Twenty-seven more bombing raids to go, he'd said. For all she knew, he might be dead.

The six days' leave had healed the cuts and bruises, rested the sore muscles and unstiffened the backs. *Orpheus* and *Eurydice*, lying picturesquely side by side at the lay-by, were greeted as old friends, their vices forgotten or forgiven. It was fun to be back on board, fun, even, to clean and scour and polish, fun to stock up with supplies, to arrange things in cupboards and along shelves, and fun to go to sleep, once again, in a narrow bunk on a narrowboat.

They left Bulls Bridge at seven o'clock on a May morning and wound their way along the cut to Brentford Dock. It was closer than Limehouse, but the slow-moving horse-drawn barges coming up delayed them. When they reached Brentford, *Orpheus* and *Eurydice* had to be winded before they tied up and many eyes were watching – bargemen, boaters and dockers alike. When their turn for loading finally came, the bundles of iron bars made the boats tip and rock as they were dropped from the crane into the holds.

'Watch out they don't shift,' one of the men told them helpfully. 'They're boogers for that.'

By the time they'd sheeted up, washed down the boats and got everything in order, it was too late to let go until morning and they went to the cinema. As they walked past the long row of boats, Molly called out to them from the butty hatches. She had the baby, Abel, in her arms, and she held him up for them to admire.

After the cinema, they called in at a pub before going back to the boats. One of the bargemen stood them drinks and told them they were bleedin' good, for a bunch o' wimmin. He wore a sack round his shoulders and a cigarette stuck to his lower lip, and when he laughed it was like bellows wheezing. Bargemen, they had already realized, were a very different breed from the boaters. There wasn't much love lost between the two. Bargemen lived on land, not on the cut, and went home to houses at the end of the day's work.

'Boaters, they're gypsies, ain't they?' the bargeman commented genially, quaffing his pint. 'Or near as makes no diff'rence.'

They let go early the next morning. By nightfall they were at Cowley lock, beyond Bulls Bridge, and Frances took the trip card into the office to have the date marked and the boats gauged while Rosalind and Prudence filled up the water cans. The next day began with a long pound before they started working their way through the forty-four locks that climbed gradually up to Tring Summit. The cut had changed with the season. Grass had grown up on the towpath, wild flowers were out, white hawthorn blossom laced the hedgerows like bridal veils, tall reeds edged the banks, willow trees trailed their fresh new leaves in the water. Moorhens and their chicks were scooting about, and ducks with ducklings, line astern, paddled after them in search of scraps; an iridescent blue kingfisher skimmed low across the water and a heron rose before them, wings flapping ponderously. A pair of boats went by, the steerer in rolled-up shirtsleeves, the wife in the butty hatches wearing a flowered frock, their baby sitting in the sun on the cabin roof, tied by its leg to the chimney and banging away happily with a wooden spoon.

Prudence lock-wheeled for the first stretch, biking along in the sunshine. A pair of boats ahead were giving them a bad road with every lock against them, but her muscles had hardened and the work wasn't so tiring. Gates swung more easily, winding gear turned more smoothly. A lock-keeper came out of his little house to chat and give her an expert and unhurried hand.

'Easy does it, little lady. Just give a quarter-turn at first. You don't want to swamp the boats.'

He cut a cabbage from his vegetable patch and a bunch of flowers from his garden for them, and they gave him a tin of sardines in return. Ros cooked the cabbage for supper that night with some sausages, while Prue arranged the flowers in an empty soup tin to decorate the table. They had tied up at the Fishery lock, beyond Hemel Hempstead, where the pub offered something even better than beer – a bath. Instead of the dipper of kettle water in the cabin, they could soak themselves clean. The black tidemark left round the bath took some scouring away with Vim, but it was worth it.

259

They crossed Tring Summit the next day and tied up for the night at Leighton Buzzard. Prudence summoned up the nerve to go to the public telephone box and try once more. This time there was no queue of Americans, only an old woman inside with rows of curlers under her scarf, her mouth working away soundlessly beyond the glass.

At last she came out and Prue went in with coins clutched at the ready. The operator answered in very refined tones and she pushed the coins into the slot, one after the other.

'The numbah is ringing for you, callah.'

She waited, heart racing. A man's voice answered and she pressed button A. The connection was made.

'Is that Ron?'

'Yep, it's me, all right. What can I do for you, miss?'

'Could you give a message to Sergeant McGhie? Next time you see him.'

'Steve? That's easy. He's here now. Want me to fetch him?'

'Yes, please.'

She waited, listening to the background noise – male voices, bursts of laughter, the clink-clink of glasses, a piano being played. Minutes went by and then more minutes, and then, at last, somebody picked up the receiver.

'Hallo. Steve McGhie here.'

He sounded as though he might be a bit drunk. Or more than a bit.

'It's Prudence Dobbs speaking. From the narrowboats. We gave you a lift, if you remember.'

'Sure, I remember. Been hoping you'd call . . . almost given up hope.'

'I'm sorry, I did try.'

'Great to hear from you, anyway. Where the hell are you?'

She was about to answer him when the operator interrupted.

'Another six pence, calla.'

She fumbled frantically in her pocket and dropped coins onto the floor.

'Ah'm afraid I shall have to disconnect you, callah.'

'Wait. Oh, please wait—'

The line went dead.

Frances had brought back a few home comforts – books, a brass candlestick and candle to go by her bed so she could read at night, some pretty china mugs that she'd found in Bridport, and a picture of Lulworth Cove to go on the wall. She had also brought a Primus – another relic of Vere's scouting days – for brewing up tea and cocoa without having to rely on the coal stove. Much as she liked Ros and Prue, she enjoyed having a cabin to

261

herself. She could arrange things as she liked, read as late as she liked, snuggled down in her cross-bed, the candlestick beside the pillow. And there was room to wash herself and her clothes and space to hang them on the brass rail above the range, where they usually dried before morning.

The trip wasn't going too badly – so far. There had only been one minor setback when Prue had misjudged a sharp bend and *Eurydice* had ended up with her nose in the bank. They had settled into a routine of two hours for each stint – steering the motor, steering the butty or lock-wheeling – before they changed around. And they ate on the hoof. Slices of bread and margarine for elevenses; something out of a tin for dinner and often eaten straight out of it; mugs of cocoa or tea. In the evenings, Ros performed miracles with whatever other food they had managed to scrounge along the way.

At Norton Junction, above Buckby locks, Frances biked down to the toll office to get their trip card marked. As she handed it over the counter the manager said, 'There's someone been waiting for you. An RAF officer. Your brother, he says he is. I told him you'd most likely be along soon.'

Vere was standing on the quayside, back turned, watching the boats and looking absurdly out of place in his gold-braided uniform. She thought, it's my turn to say what on *earth* are you doing here? He turned round when she called his name.

'Hallo, Frances.'

She said, 'How did you know we'd be here?'

'I rang the company office. Apparently they always know where their boats are. You all have numbers and they keep tabs on you. They told me you'd be coming through here, and more or less when. It wasn't very difficult.'

It wouldn't be – for him. Wing commanders got answers.

'What are you here for?'

'Not to make trouble – if that's what you're worried about. I simply wanted to see things for myself. I've got a couple of days' leave and I thought I might come along with you – if you've no objection.'

'There's not enough room. And nowhere for you to sleep.'

'You stop for the night, don't you? I'll find a room in a pub, or something.'

'We haven't got the food.'

'I'll buy my own.'

'Your uniform would get ruined.'

'I can get it cleaned. And I've brought some other clothes. I think that about covers the main objections, don't you? Why don't you show me the boats?'

Prue and Ros were waiting. Ros was sitting in the sun, smoking a cigarette, Prue industriously polishing the brass rings round the motor chimney. 'You remember my brother, Vere?' she said. 'He's come to spy on us.'

It was Rosalind's turn to steer the butty and Prue went on the motor with Frances to be ready to lock-wheel after the next pound, so the brother came on the butty and stood in the hatches beside her. He'd taken off his RAF jacket and was wearing a sort of seaman's white roll-neck sweater. The wind soon messed up his hair and made him look more human. He'd been taken aback by the tiny cabins and, naturally, he'd hit his head – twice, actually, and one of those quite hard. Nobody had yet dared tell him about the bucket in the engine room.

They were on the long snubber, trundling along far behind Frances and Prue on the motor. From time to time she reached into the cabin to stir the stew on the stove.

She said, 'Have you really come to spy on us?'

'Not at all. That's my sister's version.'

'Well, I fear you're going to find a lot of fault with us. We're going to horrify you.'

'Are you?'

'Oh, yes. We don't wash often – it's too much trouble. We're filthy and therefore we smell. Also, we eat like pigs and, as you can see, we dress like scarecrows. On the other hand, you could say we're doing quite a useful job.'

'I can see that you are.'

Another pair of boats was approaching and passed by. The steerer gave them a nod and a 'How d'you do?' Rosalind replied, inclining her head in return.

'I hope you realize that you're ruining our reputation on the cut. Every boater will hear that we've got a strange man travelling with us and they'll probably shun us completely. They're very moral. If they take a girl to the cinema, then they're courting. And once they're courting they won't look at another girl. They'll be shocked by you.'

'Well, I dare say they'll find out that I'm Frances's brother. That should make it all right.'

'I certainly hope so. We need their help when something goes wrong – which it often does.'

He said, 'But you seem to manage the steering very well.'

'You can take a turn, if you like. See how you do.'

'I'd like to.'

The butty was actually the harder boat to steer, having no engine to help. She'd been hoping very much that he'd get them stuck on a bend, but he didn't. He worked the tiller exactly right, pushing it out over the cut and back again, then out and back again, so that the butty flicked smoothly round the corners – something she'd never quite achieved. She noticed his nice hands again.

'You must have steered boats before.'

'We sailed a fair bit as children – though I must say this particular boat handles rather differently. It's quite tricky.'

'How about handling planes?'

'They're nothing like boats.'

'When I was home on leave last week there were lots of RAF fighters buzzing around the cliffs. Spitfires, I think. Or maybe Hurricanes. I'm never sure which is which.'

'Spitfires are quite easy to recognize. Just look for the shape of the wing.'

'What do you fly?'

'I used to fly Lancaster bombers. Now I fly Mosquitoes. Two-engined fighter bombers.'

'You mean they do both – fight and bomb?'

'Exactly. They fly very high and very low and very fast. Useful machines.'

'Do you have a crew?'

'Just one chap. He navigates, operates the radio, drops the bombs.'

'He sounds quite useful, too.'

'Couldn't do without him.'

He took them smoothly round another bend.

'I've never been in an aeroplane,' she said.

'Maybe one day. When the war's over. What's it like up there?'

'Rather difficult to describe.'

'Try.'

'Well, I suppose you could say that flying is like being set free. Tremendously exhilarating. The sky's a vast place . . . no frontiers, no boundaries, no shackles. You can soar through space, climb towards the sun. Reach for the stars.'

Fancy that . . . he was a human being, after all.

'There's a tunnel coming up soon,' she told him more graciously. 'You can carry on steering, if you like.'

'Fine by me.'

They passed from bright sunshine into the darkness of the Braunston tunnel and she switched on the cabin light and sat on the coal-box lid, out of his way and avoiding the icy drips. From there, she could observe him – or what she could see of him. The air vents spotlit him every so often – very upright, very noble, very English, very Henry V. The tunnels were wonderful places to belt out speeches because you could let rip at the top of your voice and nobody could hear you.

Once more unto the breach, dear friends,
  once more;
Or close the wall up with our English dead!

She'd enjoyed playing Princess Katharine, doing the fractured French. *Your majesty sall mock at me; I cannot speak your England . . . is it possible dat I sould love de enemy of France?* It was a pity that the flat-footed Paul hadn't looked more like Frankie's brother.

It took less than the usual forty minutes to get through the tunnel. Apart from one or two minor bumps, *Eurydice*, who was rather fond of crashing into tunnel walls, behaved as docilely as a spirited horse that has met its master.

Prudence lock-wheeled after the tunnel and, to her embarrassment, Frances's brother insisted on going with her to help.

'Just tell me what to do,' he said. 'And I'll do it.'

And so she found herself issuing orders to a wing commander – open that gate, draw that paddle, drop the other one. He did everything exactly as she told him, and when she'd taken the kitty cocoa tin to the shop at Braunston, he'd gone with her and bought a whole lot of extra things for them, out of his own pocket – biscuits and peanut butter and tins of useful supplies. She wanted to ask him if he knew where RAF Cranborough was, but in wartime people didn't ask, or answer, that sort of question.

They tied up at Warwick and ate Ros's one-pot

stew – one of her best ever. There wasn't much room for them all to sit in the cabin, so, later on, they went to the pub with Frances's brother. The boaters there cold-shouldered them at first, but then Molly's husband, Saul, came in for a pint and Frances explained to him in a voice loud enough for everyone to hear that her brother was on leave from the RAF and would be staying in the town.

Vere travelled with them until the middle of the following day, when they put him off at a bridge close to a railway station.

Ros said, 'Did we shock him, Frankie?'

'The bucket certainly did. And he still thinks the work's far too hard for women.'

'Well, we won't be doing it for much longer, if those landing rumours are true.'

'I asked him about that. But, of course, he wouldn't tell me anything, even if he knew.'

'I suppose he'll be mixed up in it?'

'Yes . . . I suppose he will.'

'I hope he's OK.'

'So do I, Ros. So do I.'

They delivered the iron rods at Tyseley but, to their relief, new company orders directed them to the Coventry coalfields via the Oxford canal, instead of by the dreaded and dreadful Bottom Road. Approaching the coalfields was just as depressing, though. Slag heaps, ponies dragging carts, huts and wash-houses, black-faced miners with lamps on their helmets, pit wheels turning, black coal dust thick on the ground.

They were loaded first thing the next morning and the coal roared down from trucks, filling the holds from sterns to fore-ends. Even with the doors tightly shut, the dust worked its way into the cabins and it got into their eyes and down their throats and up their noses. When the job was done, Prudence produced mugs of tea for the loaders, whose faces were as black as the miners. Frances noticed *Orpheus* was tilted to one side and pointed it out to one of the men.

He shook his head.

'Nothin' to worry about. She'll settle down when you gets goin'.'

'She might not. And it makes steering awfully hard if the load's not level.'

'We knows what we're doin', love. Bin doin' this for years. Done more boats than you'll ever 'ave 'ot dinners.'

She stuck to her guns. 'I'm sorry but we're not leaving till it's been levelled out.'

They grumbled and muttered, but they did it.

They carried the fifty tons of coal down to the Heinz factory near Greenford, where their hard labour was rewarded by a canteen dinner – a mouth-watering array of hot dishes and all for free. They stuffed themselves to the gills.

On the next trip they carried a consignment of American rubber and brought coal back to the Croxley paper mills, where Frances remembered Molly's tip. She found a shedful of canvas army gas-mask cases with brass clips attached, and put together two long chains for tying the chimneys and water cans to the cabin tops.

They were getting to know the boaters, passing them on the cut or meeting them at the tie-ups at night, or in the shops. The Granthams, the Skinners, the Suttons, the Taylors, the Gibsons who somehow found room for nine children, a dog, two cats, a ferret, four chickens and a canary in a cage. Nods and smiles were exchanged. Not much was said, but the words were friendly if sometimes hard to understand. Boaters' speech was like none other – a weird blend of Yorkshire and Midlands and cockney, rolled into one, and with odd bits of other dialects thrown in.

Sometimes they encountered the fly-boats – boats that carried barrels of Guinness from Park Royal to Birmingham and did the trip from London to Birmingham in two and a half days, non-stop, running all night through the blackout with masked headlights. They had right of way, and everyone let them by.

Jack Carter's boats passed them only once. He

gave them no more than a curt nod, but Freddy held up his fingers and shouted out, 'There's three locks ready fer yer, ladies.'

The following load was steel billets, and on the way back the kindly lock-keeper, who had kept on giving them things since the cabbage and the bunch of flowers, came out of his house.

'Heard the news, little lady?'

'What news, Mr Morton?'

'On the wireless. We've been an' gone an' done it.'

Prudence gave the winding gear another turn with her windlass. 'Done what?'

'Landed in France.' He handed her a freshly cut lettuce. 'Would you like some spinach?'

Fourteen

Prudence was home on leave in June when the first flying bombs landed on London. The siren started late one evening and the all-clear didn't sound until half past nine the next morning. After that, the buzz bombs kept on coming, by day and by night. Croydon was on their path to the City and on one afternoon, she counted five of them in the skies. They made a growling spluttering noise, like a motorbike with a faulty engine, and, at night, the tail flames looked like fireworks. Father said it showed what cowards the Germans were, sending planes without pilots. She didn't like to contradict him, but she thought it showed how clever they were to have invented such a thing.

Every so often one of the buzz bombs would come down on Croydon, and the most frightening thing about them was that nobody could tell when or where they were going to fall. The spluttering noise they made grew louder as they approached and everybody prayed it would go on, because if it stopped it meant the engine had cut out. She'd been shopping with Mother the first time that had happened. They'd been in the butcher's, queueing for the meat ration and chatting with the other women, when they'd all heard the sound. Everybody had fallen silent and stayed as still as stone statues – the women clutching baskets and string bags and ration books, the butcher in his straw hat and striped apron, cleaver aloft in his hand. The buzz bomb had come right towards the shop and then its engine had suddenly stopped. Everyone had flung themselves onto the sawdust floor and the bomb had come down two streets away and exploded with a mighty woomph and a blinding flash. After a moment, they'd all picked themselves up, straightening hats and brushing themselves down. The butcher had risen slowly from behind the counter, cleaver still in hand, his boater knocked over his nose. Mrs Pilkington who was at the front of the queue had said, just as though nothing whatever had happened, 'I'll have a nice piece of brisket today, if you please, Mr Ford.'

Father invited Mr Simpkins to Sunday lunch. 'An admirer of yours, Prudence, as I'm sure you're aware. And with a promising future.'

He sat opposite her at the table, looking at her in his creepy way. His hands were soft and white –

hands that never lifted anything heavier than a knife and fork, or pen and pencil. She wondered if he had noticed how rough hers were, and hoped he had. It might put him off. He leaned towards her.

'You'll be returning to the bank before long, Miss Dobbs, no doubt.'

Her father said, 'As soon as the war is over, isn't that right, Prudence? Not long now that we've got the Huns on the run.'

'Do you think we have, Father?'

'Of course. We've got the finest armed forces in the world. There's nothing to worry about now.'

It seemed to her that there was still quite a lot to worry about – not only the buzz bombs but what the newspapers had been saying about the trouble the Allies were having in Normandy. Far from being on the run, it sounded as though the Germans were fighting back hard, defending every town and hedge and orchard to the death.

After lunch they went out into the back garden, where Father had patriotically Dug for Victory and the lawn had been replaced by orderly rows of vegetables – potatoes, carrots, cabbages, broad beans, peas, spinach. Mr Simpkins, who lived in a flat, said all the right things and confided aside to Prudence that it might not be long before he, too, would be purchasing a property in Croydon. Was she acquainted with Princes Way, only three streets away from Mr Holland's Chestnut Drive?

That was the sort of select neighbourhood he had in mind. What did she think of the idea? All she could think was that she would sooner be dead than live anywhere with Mr Simpkins.

When he had gone and her father had sat down to read the Sunday newspaper, she crept into the hall and dialled the number of the Three Horseshoes pub. The same woman answered.

'May I speak to the landlord, please.'

'Can't hear you. You'll have to speak louder.'

'Could I speak to Ron?'

'He's busy.'

'It's rather urgent.'

'Huh.'

The receiver was banged down and then picked up after a moment.

'Yes? Who is it?' He sounded impatient too.

'This is Prudence Dobbs. I'm a friend of Sergeant McGhie and I just wondered if you had any news of him? Whether he's all right?'

'Haven't seen him lately. Not since the Landings.' The voice softened a bit. 'Do you want me to give him a message, if he comes in?'

'Could you just tell him I rang?'

'What did you say your name was?'

'Prudence Dobbs.'

'I'll do that. If he comes in.'

They paid a visit to Auntie Dot and Uncle Ted who lived in a house in Purley that was as big as

Mr Holland's. Uncle Ted had been very successful, buying and selling things. Father always said that that sort of thing wasn't like having a proper post in a bank, but Prudence thought he was secretly envious of the house. Her mother always went on about the parquet flooring, the convenient serving hatch to the dining room, the big Kelvinator refrigerator in the kitchen and the French windows from the lounge to the garden. Not that Father cared much about any of those; the thing he really envied was the car in the garage. The Sunbeam Talbot had been put away on blocks for the duration, but Uncle Ted liked to show it off. When they trooped into the garage after tea, Prudence was invited to sit in the passenger seat. It was upholstered in green leather and the dashboard was made of polished walnut, with a compartment at the side where Uncle Ted kept a road-map book of the British Isles. She took it out and ran her finger down the As and Bs in the index until she came to the Cs. Cramlington, Cramond, Cranage, Cranberry, *Cranborough*. Page 34. Mother started tapping impatiently on the window. The page, when she reached it, was a maze of roads, marked with towns . . . Luton, Hitchin, Toddington. The small black dots were the villages: Tebworth, Wellbury, Potsgrove . . . Tap, tap, tap on the window. Tap, tap, *tap*. Biddenham, Wootton, Millbrook.

She found it. South-west of Bedford and at least fifteen miles away from Leighton Buzzard. Mother opened the door and stuck her head inside.

'Whatever are you doing, Prudence? We're all waiting for you.'

On the next trip they transported scrap – shell casings from anti-aircraft guns. The flying bombs were coming over all the time and the boats got in and out of the docks as fast as they could. Doodle-boogers, the boat people called them. The weather was cold with heavy cloud and driving rain and nothing dried out properly. Bedding was sodden, clothes put on in the morning still wet. Deck surfaces were slippery as glass, locks even more so. Prudence lost her footing crossing a gate and toppled into the water just as *Orpheus* came charging in. The lock-keeper hauled her out just in time, choking and spluttering and badly shocked. Next day, the gears started to do strange things and they had to stop and phone for a fitter. It took hours before one turned up, and two days for a new gearbox to arrive. Then Frances caught her hand on a rusty nail. She bound it up with a handkerchief and it bled and throbbed and, finally, turned septic. Another hold-up while they went in search of a doctor. The only one to be found was off duty and drunk. He prodded about, poured something stinging from a bottle and managed a clumsy bandage. The bandage fell off the next day, but the gash felt better and began to heal.

They unloaded the scrap shells at Tyseley and, once again, were spared the Bottom Road. At Hawkesbury, three days later, they were given their orders from the Grand Union office. They were to load up with coal at Griff Colliery, six miles north of Coventry, and to unload at the ABC bakery again, almost as far down the cut as Limehouse. From there, they continued straight on to the docks to take on steel billets. After that it was more bags of cement. Then a few days' leave.

Instead of going home, Prudence took the train up to Bedford and, from there, a country bus out to Cranborough. It was a very small village with one street, just as Steve had described – a row of cottages, a church, a shop and the Three Horseshoes pub. Opening time was not for another hour, so she took a walk down a lane which led to the aerodrome a mile or so away. There was a barbed-wire fence all the way round the outside and an armed guard at the main gate. Inside, she could see Nissen huts and hangars and airmen going to and fro. She walked round the barbed-wire fence and saw the four-engined bombers standing out on the far side of the aerodrome. Halifaxes. One of them started up, engines roaring and fading several times. She watched it swing round and roll along the track to the start of the runway, turn and stop. The engines bellowed again, roaring and fading as before, and the bomber suddenly charged forward and lumbered down the runway until it left the ground and climbed slowly into the sky. It seemed a miracle to her that such a heavy thing could fly. She waited and, after a while, it returned and went back to its place. No other planes took off and there was no sign of preparations for a night raid.

In the early evening she went back to the village. The Three Horseshoes was open, bikes propped against the pub wall or thrown down on the ground. Inside, it was crowded with RAF.

'Hallo there, love.' An airman grinned at her. 'What's your name?'

'I'm meeting someone,' she said. 'Excuse me.'

She squeezed a way through, ducking under arms and around backs. And then she saw Steve. He was leaning against the bar, pint mug at his elbow, cigarette in hand, and he was talking to a WAAF. A very pretty WAAF in a smart blue uniform with shiningly clean, neatly curled hair. He was smiling down at her and she was laughing up at him.

'Not leaving already, are you?' the same airman said. 'What's all the rush, sweetheart?' He put a hand on her arm but she pulled herself free.

Fifteen

By August the weather had changed to blistering heat. Frances took to wearing her old school games shorts and aertex shirts, Prue a blue and white cotton frock she'd had for work at the bank, Ros a peasant skirt and blouse with a floppy straw hat tied with ribbons under her chin, appropriated from a stint as a simple country girl in *Babes in the Wood*.

The cabins were stifling by day – the butty cabin worse because the stove had to be kept going for cooking. At night they slid back the hatches, leaving them open to the stars, and lay coverless, sleepless, drenched in sweat. Fresh milk from friendly farms went sour in hours, margarine melted to a greasy pool, and any leftovers quickly turned bad. One good thing: they could hang their washing out to dry on a line across the decks, though they still dried their smalls in the engine room to avoid upsetting the boaters. In any case,

as most of their underclothes had somehow
turned a dingy grey, they were better out of sight.

Soon there was a water shortage on the cut.
Levels dropped and even the boaters were often
caught on the mud. Only sixteen pairs were
allowed to cross the Tring Summit each day, and
the lock gates after the Summit were chained and
padlocked sometimes from early afternoon. Those
that hadn't cleared them were left to wait until the
next morning. The first time that happened to
them, they tied up next to Molly and Saul's pair.

'Locked up fer the night with Jack Carter, lars'
trip, we was,' Molly told Frances with relish. 'Yer
seen him lately?'

She'd come over with Abel in her arms, and sat
on the motor-cabin coal box bouncing the baby
on her lap while Frances boiled the kettle on
the Primus. The baby had stopped looking like
a wizened monkey and had plump cheeks and a
thatch of dark hair.

'We towed him off the mud the other day.'

Molly's mouth fell open. 'Jack Carter stemmed
up! *Never!*'

'He was stuck fast on Muck Bend.'

'That's a bad one, an' all. Never known that
'appen to Jack, though. Fancy that!'

'We were rather amazed, too.'

She'd been steering *Orpheus* into the bend
when they'd come across *Snipe* marooned on the

opposite bank. At first she'd not known what to do. Being stemmed up dented a boater's pride. They might take help from another boater, but if offered it by an Idle Woman, they usually refused. Boaters would skulk in their cabin, or pretend there was something wrong with the engine, or that the load was too heavy. Anything to save face. And she was wary of Jack Carter. On the other hand, she owed him, didn't she? Ever since the Quills. She'd slowed down and shouted to Freddy who was on the counter while his brother was wielding the long shaft at the fore-end.

'Can we help?'

He'd looked doubtful. 'Dunno. I'll ask me bruvver.'

Surprisingly, the offer had been accepted, bows hitched to stern, but the manoeuvre was far trickier than she'd bargained for and she'd only succeeded in making matters worse. Without a word, Jack Carter had come back to the counter and sprung across to *Orpheus*. He'd taken over the tiller and towed *Snipe* clear. Her thanks had been a silent nod as he handed it back, a grinning wave from Freddy and the dipped brim of the old lady's black bonnet.

Molly drank her tea and bounced Abel some more. She looked round the cabin. 'Yer a scholar, then?'

'A scholar? Heavens no.'

'Must be with all them books.' Molly nodded at the shelf. 'Stands to reason, yer can read. An' write, too, I'll be bound.'

'Well, of course I can.'

'No o' course 'bout it. I can't read. Nor write neither. Nor Saul. Never 'ad the larnin'. Don't know a boater what can. Mebbe a word 'ere an' there, but that's all.'

She was stunned. 'But I thought everyone had to go to school, Molly. It's the law.'

'Can't make us, can they? Not when we're allus on the go, like. Got a schoolroom for the kids at the Bridge, but don't do much good cos they can't stay there fer long.'

'How on earth do you manage, if you can't read?'

'Easy. We notices things, an' we remembers 'em. An' we knows all 'bout money an' what things cost. We knows what we're owed, see.'

'Supposing you have to sign your name?'

'We puts our mark. Makes no difference.'

No wonder they mispronounced so many words. 'But wouldn't you like to be able to read? I could teach you, Molly.'

'Naw. Don't 'ave no time an' Saul wouldn't like it. Thanks all the same. I can look at pictures, if I wants. That don't need no readin'. An' there's plenty to look at all day, goin' along. No call for books an' such. Not on the cut.'

That was true enough. Even the ugly bits of the cut were interesting; the rest an ever-changing picture, different round each bend and with each season. Towns, villages, trees, fields, cottages, gardens, stately homes, ancient bridges, wild birds, the light on the water, sunrises, sunsets. And no two days were ever the same, so life could never be boring. The cut measured the boaters' existence. Their whole lives revolved around it: their work, their customs, their manners, their speech. Everything centred on the waterways they inhabited all their lives. They had little in common with the outside world and almost no interest in it. No interest in the war, or in politics, or in what other people did or how they lived. She'd never heard them talking about anything but their own world; never been asked questions about her own. So, if nobody else on the cut could read or write, what could it matter to them?

Abel spewed up some sick and Molly wiped it tenderly away with a rag.

'There's been talk on the cut that Jack Carter's sweet on yer. Ever since 'e done up the Quills fer yer.'

'Oh, but that's nonsense.'

'Wouldn't say that.'

'But he's never spoken more than a few words to me.'

'Don't need to, do 'e? 'E's got eyes in 'is 'ead.

285

An' I seen the way 'e looked at yer that time. Not frit of 'im, are yer?'

'No.'

'Cos 'e wouldn't lay a finger on yer. Not 'less you wanted it.'

In fact, he'd already laid several fingers on her – five of them, to be precise. When he'd jumped onto *Orpheus* and taken over the tiller from her, his right hand had covered hers for a moment. But that wasn't what Molly had meant.

Molly shifted Abel onto her shoulder and patted him on the back. 'Course there's lots o' girls on the cut as do want it, but I never 'eard of 'im goin' courtin' with none of 'em. Some say 'e only goes with girls off the cut, but I wouldn't know 'bout that.'

She could feel that her face had gone red. 'Anyway, we hardly ever see him.'

'Wait till you're locked up for the night with 'im.' Molly giggled. 'You'll see plenty of 'im then.'

It was harvest time. Tractors and reaping machines clattered across the fields beside the cut and binders followed to gather up the loose corn. Clouds of dust, the smell of hot oil and tractor fuel. Italian prisoners of war, stripped to the waist as they stooked the sheaves, stopped to wave and smile and sang out to them: *Bella, bella, bella!* The German POWs were different. They didn't smile or wave, but watched impassively. A group of them, crossing a bridge ahead on their way to work, stopped to lean over and stare and pass remarks to each other.

Ros said, 'At least they're not throwing rocks, but I'm rather glad we don't know what they're saying.' As the butty went under the bridge, she called up to them. *'Guten Morgen.'* And then, as *Eurydice* emerged the other side, she waved cheerily. *'Auf Wiedersehen.'*

Sometimes they came across local boys swimming in the cut, or using a full lock as a pool – diving and splashing and yelling. As the boats approached they would swim up to them and hang from the sides or attach themselves to the stern of the butty. The motor steerer had the unnerving job of keeping them away from the propeller blades, and they had to be fended off with shouts and threats and fierce brandishing of mops and shafts.

'They don't seem to mind that the water's absolutely filthy,' Frances said after a day spent repelling small boys.

'They probably don't know about the buckets,' Ros said. 'Either that, or they're immune, like the boaters. Look at the way they rinse their mugs in it and use it for making tea. Old Mrs Skinner told me that the water in Blisworth tunnel makes much the best cup. They always fill their water cans there and she recommended it highly.'

Prudence looked horrified. 'You're joking, Ros. It's not true.'

'For once it is, darling.'

They had tied up for the night and were sitting on the motor-cabin roof, eating fish and chips out of newspaper. Cod in lovely crisp batter and chips liberally sprinkled with salt and doused with vinegar.

Ros said suddenly, 'Well, fancy that . . .'

'Fancy what?'

'There's a picture of someone I know in this paper. An actor I met once. He's touring in a play . . . *Mr Kenneth Woods gives a most impressive performance in* Private Lives . . . *his deft touch and faultless timing set him above the rest of the cast . . . he is clearly a star in the making* . . . This is the local rag, so the company must have come here.'

Frances leaned over. 'He looks rather dishy. Maybe we could go into town and see the play this evening.'

''Fraid not. The paper's a month old. They'll have gone on somewhere else by now.'

'What a pity.'

'Yes . . . it is rather.'

*   *   *

In summer, the coal-loading was quicker and easier. There was no need to bother with the top sheets or the stands and they laid the planks on the coal itself and secured them with the side strings. On the way down to the Croxley paper mills, their tame lock-keeper gave them a freshly cut lettuce, some ripe tomatoes and the news that Paris had been liberated.

The hot weather went on for the rest of August and so did the water shortage. They crossed the Tring Summit early one afternoon and found the Marsworth locks already padlocked for the night. They tied up alongside other pairs and did some cleaning and polishing. Frances was swabbing down the motor-cabin roof with the mop when Freddy came biking fast along the towpath, standing on the pedals.

'Thought yer might be 'ere, miss. We 'eard yer was ahead of us.'

The cut telegraph had been at work in its mysterious way. She smiled at him. 'Looks like we're all stuck here till the morning. I don't suppose your brother's very pleased about that.'

''E says we'll soon make up the time. We allus do.' In spite of the heat he was wearing his coat and cap. He groped in a pocket. 'Got somefin' fer yer, miss.'

'For me?'

''Sright. It's a present.' He produced a brass bed knob and held it up; it gleamed in the sunlight. 'Got it off a dump, last trip. I give it a nice polish fer yer.'

She was very touched. 'Thank you, Freddy. It's beautiful.'

'Like me ter put it on the wall fer yer?'

'Could you do that?'

'Course I can. Easy. Got some screws an' a screwdriver?'

She found both and he soon had the bed knob fixed to the wall on the left of the doorway. They both admired it.

He looked round the cabin which, she realized, must seem very bare to him. 'If I sees 'nother, I'll git it fer yer. Yer could do wiv some more brass. An' some more pitchers, an' all. Look at all them books! What you want them lot fer, takin' up all that room?'

'I read them. At night before I go to sleep.'

He shrugged his thin shoulders. 'Can't read meself.'

'How about your grandmother and your brother?'

'They can't read neither. We don' 'ave to on the cut, see. No call fer it.'

She had scarcely believed Molly, but it was true.

'Would you like me to teach you some letters?'

'Larned some once in the school, but I've

forgot. Don't 'ave no fancy ter go agin. I keeps outta sight o' the kid-catchers.'

She coaxed him gently. 'I could write them out for you – with pictures of things to match. Things you see all the time on the boats and on the cut. You'd soon remember them again. And when you've learned all the letters you could start to read. And write, too.'

He rubbed his nose. 'I'd be a scholar, wouldn' I?'

'Yes, you would.'

'Don' know what Jack'd say.'

'We won't tell him. Or your grandmother. Let's keep it a secret between us.' She put a finger to her lips. 'Mum's the word.'

He grinned. 'Orlright, miss. Mum's the word.'

'We could start right now – with the letters.'

He shook his head. 'Got ter get back an' 'elp me bruvver clearin' out the mud box. Grandma said to tell yer to please come an' 'ave some tea wiv 'er on the butty.'

The invitation to tea, she realized, was something of an honour, and she washed her hands and brushed her hair for the occasion. She walked down the towpath while Freddy weaved his way back and forth on the bike in front of her, keeping to her slower pace. When they reached the Carter pair, tied up near the end of the line of boats, the black dog, Rickey, was sitting on the motor-cabin roof. Freddy disappeared into the engine room. The doors to the butty cabin, alongside, were both wide open but she knocked politely on the roof and waited to be asked to step on board. Everything was spotless and speckless: the coiled lines white as snow, the brass rings on the chimney shining, all surfaces swabbed clean. Molly had once told her that the old grandmother had more brasses than anyone else on the cut. Even so, when a voice answered her knock and she entered the cabin, the display made her blink.

There must have been almost twenty bed knobs and doorknobs and horse brasses screwed in the space by the doorway, all polished to a dazzling brightness. A waterfall of filigree china plates, gilt-edged and threaded on ribbons, cascaded down the opposite wall. A beautiful old brass oil lamp hung over the stove and the dipper on its hook was brass, too, with an ebony handle. Every inch of the cabin was adorned with something – framed photographs, crochet-work, a brass ladle, brass candlesticks, china ornaments, painted hearts and diamonds, roses and castles. But no books. Not one.

The old woman was sitting on the side bench, her hands folded in her lap. The frilled black bonnet partly concealed her face and her dark clothing was relieved only by a large gilt brooch pinned to the neck of her blouse. The invitation to sit was made with a slow, queen-like gesture of one knobbly hand. If Frances hadn't witnessed it herself, she would have found it impossible to believe that the same hand had hurled the short shaft and felled the Quill brother.

The flap table, like Molly's, had been covered with a lace cloth and set with cups and saucers. A kettle was simmering on the stove. Frances perched on the side bunk and wondered where the water in it had come from, and, as more moments passed in silence, whether Mrs Carter was ever going to utter a word. At last she spoke.

'Yer'll take a cup?'

'Thank you.'

The old woman rose to her feet, took a tea canister from a cupboard, spooned tea from it into the largest and most magnificent teapot that Frances had ever seen: brown glazed and decorated with bright flowers and the words *A Present From A Friend*. The lid was in the form of a miniature teapot and the old woman lifted it to pour in the kettle water and sat down again, refolding her hands. There was another silence. It was as unnerving as taking tea with Queen Mary.

Frances said, 'What a beautiful boat you have, Mrs Carter. With so many lovely ornaments.'

The bonnet dipped graciously.

'And what a lot of wonderful old photos. Who's that gentleman up there?'

'Moy Alfred. Jack's grandad. God rest 'is soul.'

'Well, he's very handsome.'

'Best-lookin' man on the cut. An' our Jack takes after 'im.'

She couldn't see any likeness. The man in the photo was all dressed up in a suit, collar and tie, not boater's clothes; he had a bushy moustache and his dark hair had been greased flat. 'And that lady in white?'

'Me sister, Peg. Took on 'er weddin' day.'

The old woman stood up again and poured the tea, handing her a cup. Blisworth tunnel water or not, the tea was very good – far better than anything they ever managed.

'Were you born on the cut, Mrs Carter?' She knew the answer before she asked the question but at least it kept the conversational ball rolling.

'Born on't an' lived on't all me life. I dare say I'll die on't, same as Alfred.'

'Where is he buried?'

'Stoke Bruan. All done proper. We knows how to do things right.'

'Yes, of course.'

Another silence. The stove was roasting her left leg and she could feel sweat breaking out on her forehead.

'You must be very proud of your grandson – Freddy.'

''E's a good lad, though 'e's a chatterchops.'

294

'And of your grandson Jack, too.'

'None better 'n Jack. 'E looks a'ter me.'

'That's nice.' Everything she was saying sounded false to her ears; Mrs Carter would surely think so too. Old she might be, but not stupid.

''E'll be gettin' wed one o' these days, will our Jack. There's plenty on the cut for 'im ter choose from.'

'Yes, I'm sure.'

'No sense lookin' elsewhere.'

'No.'

'Those that live off the cut don' understand our ways, see. That's why we keeps to our own. We bin on the boats 'undreds o' years. Don' do 'less a person's born to it.'

Mrs Carter lifted her head at that moment and, for the first time, Frances saw her face clearly.

It was a very old face – mottled, deeply lined, wrinkled, toothless and with grey hairs sprouting from the chin. But the rheumy eyes were knowing. If she'd heard the same cut gossip as Molly – which seemed likely – then she was probably warning her off her grandson. Perhaps that had been the whole reason for the invitation to tea.

She drained her cup, thanked her very politely and made her escape. Outside, arms plastered in muck to the elbow, Freddy was chucking stinking slime from the mud box into the cut. It was a chore that she loathed but he was grinning away. As his grandmother had pointed out, he'd been born to it.

A mouldy shop-bought pie had disagreed with Prue and she stayed behind when Rosalind and Frances walked along the towpath to the local pub in the evening. A group of American airmen in the bar immediately surrounded them. Ros had pinned her IW badge onto her peasant blouse and they were curious.

'What do you girls do? Some kinda special job?'

Ros smiled sweetly. 'I'll tell you if you give us some of your lovely American cigarettes.'

They were showered with packets of Camels and Lucky Strikes, and were bought drinks – proper gins, not the usual watery beer. In return they explained what IW stood for and what they did. The Yanks didn't believe them at first.

'You're kiddin' us. Beautiful girls like you doin' work like that.'

True, they looked cleaner than usual, having had time to wash their hair and themselves, but they displayed their ruined hands and the cuts and bruises as proof. Soon more drinks were bought, more cigarettes lit. The Americans were ground staff from a nearby bomber station – good company, with nice manners and bags of charm.

'I'm from Smithville in West Virginia,' one of

them told Frances in a drawling accent. 'Guess you don't know where that is.'

'Sorry, I don't.'

He proceeded to tell her all about his home town and his family and then got out several photographs. She dutifully admired the pretty wood-framed house, with the mother and father and the three small sisters standing on the porch. He was clearly very homesick and she didn't blame him. England in wartime was a horrible place to be and America, the land of plenty, thousands of miles away. As she listened to him talking at length about what a great country it was, she could see, over his shoulder, that Jack Carter had come in and was drinking at the bar.

'Ever seen a baseball game?' the American was asking.

'I'm afraid not.'

'Gee, you don't know what you've missed.'

After the next round of drinks, she began to feel decidedly tipsy and decided to go back to the boat. The American wanted to walk with her but she refused the offer. Ros, her pockets full of cigarettes, another gin in her hand, earrings jangling merrily, stayed.

It was almost dark, but not quite. Frances could still see the towpath and the cut beside it. Boaters returning from long evenings at pubs and many pints of beer had been known to fall in and drown. They had once passed a boatman crawling unsteadily on hands and knees along the wooden plank connecting his boat to the bank.

'Evenin', Frances.'

He'd come up behind her so quietly that she hadn't heard him. Her heart was thudding away.

'Hallo, Jack.'

Without his coat, the embroidered waistcoat was on full display. Boatmen wore loose white shirts and he'd rolled up the sleeves, showing his strong arms.

'Seen you with them Yanks.' His disapproval was obvious.

None of his business, she thought fuzzily. 'Yes, they were very nice. Real gentlemen.'

'Not from what I've 'eard. Yer needs ter watch out.'

'I can take care of myself, thanks.'

So saying, she tripped over something on the path and he grabbed hold of her to save her from falling flat on her face.

'Yer bin drinkin' too much gin, I reckon.'

'I most certainly have not.'

'Yes, yer 'ave. I bin watchin' yer at the pub.'

'Well, you'd no business to. Let go of me, please.'

He walked beside her, hands in his trouser pockets, whistling.

'Like ter go ter a fair?'

'A fair? You mean with merry-go-rounds?'

'With all kinds o' things. There'll be a big one by Leamington. An' it's a good tie-up for the night. I'll take yer if yer wants – that's if yer gets there soon enough. Can't be after dark with the blackout.'

She'd heard that boaters loved fairs. And so did she.

'But we won't be able to keep up with you, Jack. You'll be at Leamington hours ahead of us.'

'I'll wait.'

When they reached the boats, there was silence from *Eurydice* – Prue would be sound asleep. Nobody else was about.

'See yer at Leamington, then,' he said.

He was standing very close and she wondered whether Molly was right again. *'E wouldn't lay a finger on yer. Not 'less you wanted it.* Well, she did want it. She wanted him to lay his fingers on her – all ten of them this time. And if she took just a single step towards him, he'd know it. Instead, she took several cowardly steps backwards.

'You frit of me, Frances?'

'No.'

'Yes, yer are. Yer shakin' all over.'

'I'm cold, that's all.'

'Couldn't be. Not this weather. Yer frit. Frit I'm goin' to grab hold of yer. Could 'ave done

299

that back in the fields if I'd wanted to, and yer couldn't 'ave stopped me. But I didn't, did I?'

'No, you didn't.'

'Don't yer wish I 'ad?'

'Certainly not.'

He smiled slowly. 'Don't believe yer. Yer want me to, only yer frit. An' yer've drunk too much gin so yer'd best get to bed.' He held out his hand to help her onto *Orpheus*, steadying her when she staggered. 'G'night, Frances.'

As he walked away, she called after him. 'I'd love to go to the Leamington fair, Jack.'

'I'll wait fer yer,' he answered over his shoulder. 'Like I said.'

Prudence felt better the next morning and was up early, boiling the kettle on the Primus and cutting slices of bread. Ros made a groaning sound.

'Don't do any for me.'

'Did your pie make you ill too?'

'Not the pie, the gin. I drank too much at the pub. I feel ghastly.'

'Would you like a cup of tea?'

There was another groan. 'No, thanks. Not a thing.'

Frances came over from the motor and she had a headache, too.

'We'll have to untie and get on. Can you take

300

the motor, Prue? I'll lock-wheel and Ros ought to be able to manage the butty.'

Somehow they got down the Mathus seven. Ros was sick over the side and Frances forgot the safety catch when she was drawing a paddle and let go of the windlass by mistake. The handle whirled round, striking the back of her hand again and again before she snatched it away. Prudence made a hash of steering the motor, crashing wildly into gates and then dropping the butty strap on her way out. If the locks hadn't been ready for them, they would have taken all day to get through.

At Leighton Buzzard Prudence, still on the motor, looked out for Steve McGhie, although there was no hope that he'd be there. She searched fruitlessly among the faces peering over Leighton Bridge and among the people on the towpath. On they went through the Stoke Hammond three, Talbots, Finney and Cosgrove. Along the quiet, tree-lined stretches of the cut the anglers on the bank, their fish disturbed, scowled as they raised their rods in an archway to let them by. Prudence hid behind the chimney.

They came to the bottom of the Stoke Bruerne seven, confronting them like a Herculean trial of strength. At the top they tied up for the night. Ros had recovered her appetite and they had corned beef and mashed potatoes for supper with fresh carrots that she'd pinched from an allotment when she'd been lock-wheeling the day before, and some juicy apples that she'd scrumped from an orchard. Poor Frances could hardly use her hand.

After a good night's sleep they let go early the next morning and continued on their way through the Blisworth tunnel up to Gayton and on to the Bugby seven and Norton Junction, then through the Braunston tunnel and the Braunston six to the turn towards Napton and Leamington. Frances had taken over *Orpheus* while Ros had a turn at lock-wheeling and Prudence steered *Eurydice*. At Napton, Pip passed them with some trainees, going the other way, and shouted out something to Prudence that she couldn't hear. They worked on steadily down through the Wigrams three, the Itchington ten, the Radford ten and tied up at Leamington near the gasworks in the evening. She was giving the cabin roof a good swab-down when she heard someone call her name. She turned round and saw Steve there, standing on the bank.

'How did you know we'd be here?' she asked him later.

'I didn't. Figured there was a chance you'd be by, though, after I'd seen another boat with girls on it. There was an older woman in charge and she said she thought you'd be coming along soon.'

Pip, of course. And that was what she'd been shouting about.

He said, 'If you hadn't come along, I was going to go to Croydon – the place where you said you lived – and see if I could find you there.'

She thought of the pretty WAAF in the pub and the way he'd been smiling down at her, just like he was smiling down at her now. She ought not to believe him, or trust him.

'But you don't know my address.'

'I know your name: Prudence Dobbs. I'll bet there are not many Dobbses in Croydon and only one called Prudence. Wouldn't have taken me too long.'

'Anyway, I don't go home often. We spend most of our time on the boats.'

'That's why I came looking here first. I've got a coupla days' leave, so maybe I could come along with you. Like before.'

'We can't really take passengers.'

'I'm not a passenger. I'm crew.'

Frances's brother had been one thing – this was quite another. The boaters wouldn't approve at all.

'You couldn't stay on the boats at night. The people on the cut would talk.'

He pretended to look shocked. 'Can't have that. Hey, I can kip down anywhere . . . haystack, hedge, wherever . . . I'm used to living rough. Do it all the time back home when we go hunting.'

'Hunting?' She couldn't imagine him doing that, wearing a smart red coat and following the hounds. 'You mean for foxes?'

'Heck no. Big animals. Moose, elk, white-tailed deer . . . Some guys go for bears. Not me, though.'

'You have *bears* in Canada?'

'Sure we do. Big ones. More'n five foot tall when they stand up, with great long claws like this.' He held up crooked fingers to show her. 'They can be mighty mean. We go hunting in fall right through winter – my brothers an' me. Mostly I use my grandpa's Winchester – same as he used years back, when he was alive – other times we shoot with longbows.'

'Bows? Like Robin Hood?'

'Yeah . . . I guess like your Robin Hood. Only it's not like Sherwood Forest, that's for sure. Canada's a real big place, an' real wild out of the cities.' He grinned at her. 'So you see, it won't bother me sleeping rough – if I come along.'

She hesitated. 'I'll have to ask the others.'

'Sure. And while you're asking, tell 'em I'm an engineer. It might come in handy.'

It did. He started the engine first go in the morning – one easy swing on the handle and off it went – and when it broke down later he mended it straight away. And that wasn't all. He cleaned out the mud box, checked the bilge pump, tightened up the bolts on the shaft couplings, hauled up the cabin floor to grease and check the rest of the shaft and the stern gland – all horrible difficult dirty jobs that they hated.

When they'd tied up that evening, she went for a stroll with him along the towpath beside the fields. It was still daylight, still very warm and very peaceful, the sun just beginning to go down. The corn had been cut, the sheaves stooked in neat rows. They climbed over a stile into one of the fields so that she could pick the scarlet poppies growing along the edge, then sat down by the hedge. Except for some rooks cawing away over a wood on the far side, there was scarcely a sound.

He stretched out, propping himself up on one elbow and chewing on a piece of stubble, while she sat at a little distance from him, hands clasped round her knees, the bunch of poppies laid beside her.

'Right now,' he said, 'you'd never know there was a war on, would you? It's kinda strange.'

'We hardly see anything of it on the boats. Only when we're going through London or when the cut runs past an aerodrome and the planes fly over us.'

'Too bad you don't come by Cranborough.'

'I did once.'

He stopped chewing and stared at her. 'You came by and you didn't let me know? Why the heck not?'

She told him about seeing him in the Three Horseshoes with the girl.

He shook his head. 'You got it all wrong. I talk to different WAAFs all the time. I don't even remember which one that was. It's *you* I'm crazy about, Prudence. I thought you'd have cottoned on by now. You're my kind of girl. I knew that when I saw you coming along in the boat, wearing those overalls, with dirt all over your face – remember? You held out your hand to me and that was real dirty too. I thought you were the cutest thing I'd ever seen.'

She said stiffly, 'I don't usually look like that. At home, I look quite different.'

'Sure. And I bet that's cute too. But I'll always remember the way you were the first time I saw you. I want us to get married, Prudence, just as soon as this goddam war's over. I guess we could do that in England or we could wait and get married back home in Winnipeg. Whichever you like.' He chewed some more on the straw, watching her. 'But maybe you hate the whole idea. Maybe you'd never want to leave England. Maybe you'd hate to live in Canada.'

She turned away from him, gazing across the cornfield, trying to imagine what it would be like to live in a place thousands of miles away – a place where it snowed and froze from November to March, where they had log cabins and fished through holes in ice so thick you could drive a truck across it; a place so wild they went hunting for bears; a place where, when the snows had melted at long last, it got swelteringly hot instead, with mosquitoes the size of your hand. To leave dear beautiful old England and go and live in such a place among total strangers.

'I'd look after you,' he said, as though he knew exactly what she was thinking. 'Take real good care of you. If you'd take the chance.'

The rooks were circling lower and lower over the treetops, like planes coming into land. She could hear a church clock striking somewhere in the distance. One, two, three, four, five, six . . . a gentle English sound.

'Prudence? Do you reckon you could take a chance on me?'

She turned her head towards him. 'Yes, I do.'

'Kept my promise,' he said. 'Waited fer yer.'

'Sorry we took so long.'

'Didn't do so bad, considerin'. What's 'appened ter yer 'and?'

'Forgot the safety catch and let go of the wind-lass by mistake.'

'Yer want ter take more care. Could've broke yer bones.' He stared at her with his dark eyes. 'Yer look beautiful in them clothes.'

She'd put on a cotton blouse and skirt instead

307

of the old games shorts and shirt. Washed her hair, too, and brushed it properly, for once. Taken trouble. Playing with fire, Ros had warned her. With a man like that.

'Where's Rickey?'

'Left 'im behind, guardin' the boats.'

They heard the sound of the fair from some distance away – organ music blaring, machinery roaring and rattling, shrieks of delight from the crowd.

'What d'yer want to do?' he asked when they arrived at the glittering lights, the stalls, the rides.

'Everything.'

They queued to see the Fat Lady and the Tattooed Lady and the Siamese Twins. They rolled pennies, threw quoits, shied for coconuts, went on the Big Lizzie and the Big Dipper and the Helter Skelter. When he hit the Test Your Strength machine with the sledgehammer, the bell at the top rang loudly, first try, and he knocked down all the targets at the shooting gallery. The prize was a gold-rimmed china plate decorated with roses and slotted with a blue satin ribbon, which he presented to her with a flourish.

'Wouldn't your grandmother like to have it?'

'I dare say, but 'tis not fer her I won it.'

'How did you get to be such a good shot?'

'Rabbits an' hares,' he said. 'Pheasants an'

pigeons. Anythin' for the pot. I shoots 'em an' Rickey fetches 'em back fer me. Sometimes 'e brings back ducks' eggs. Jumps off at a bridge-'ole and jumps back on at the next with one in 'is mouth.'

'What a clever dog!'

'Yer won't find better.'

He wanted to go in for the boxing contest. 'I could beat 'em all easy.'

'I know. I've seen you in action. But can we go on the merry-go-round now?'

'Anythin' yer likes.'

They'd passed by it several times but it had always been on the move. Now the painted horses had come to a stop. They paid their sixpences and she chose a dappled grey on the outside – a prancing steed with a flowing mane and tail and flaring nostrils. Jack put his hands on her waist, lifted her sidesaddle on to its back and swung himself up behind her. As they started to move he kept one hand on her waist, the other on the barley-sugar pole, steadying her in the crook of his arm. They went slowly at first, the dappled grey rising and falling gracefully beneath them; then faster, and faster still until they were at a full gallop. The steam organ in the middle was belting out 'Roses of Picardy', the people watching had dissolved into a dizzy blur. Her hair blew about her face, her skirt ballooned above her knees; she turned to him, laughing, and he bent his head and kissed her. He went on kissing her as they whirled round and round and round.

It was still light when they left the fair and walked back towards the cut – the last hour of the late summer day, with the August sun turning everything golden. They stopped by an orchard gate and she rested her arms on the top bar; crooked old apple trees, laden with fruit, cast long purple shadows on the grass. He stood beside her, one foot propped on the lowest rung.

'I don't want to go back yet, Jack.'

'No need ter.'

He rolled a cigarette and lit it with a match, blowing smoke into the air.

'Can I try one of those?'

'They ain't fit fer a lady.'

'I wish you wouldn't call me that. I'm not a lady. I'm just an ordinary girl.'

'Ain't nothin' ord'nary 'bout yer, Frances.'

'There's nothing ordinary about you either, Jack. And it was kind of you to take me to the fair.'

'Weren't kind,' he said. 'I wanted ter.'

'Well, I had a wonderful time. Thanks.' She held up the china plate. 'And for this. I'll hang it on the cabin wall. Are you sure your grandmother wouldn't like it?'

'Like I said, it's fer you. Ter keep.'

She was silent for a moment.

'Those Siamese Twins weren't real, were they? It was all faked.'

'Reckon so. The Fat Lady were real, though. Fattest I ever saw.'

'How about the Tattooed Lady?'

'She were real, too. Tattooed all over, far as I could see.'

She stole a sideways glance at him – the handsome profile, the glossy black hair curling on the nape of his neck, the gold earring, the red knotted scarf, the embroidered waistcoat. And she looked at his mouth and remembered how it had felt when he'd kissed her, and thought how much she wanted him to kiss her again.

'How old are you, Jack?'

'Twenty.'

Younger than she'd guessed, but then most boat people looked much older than their years.

'Will you stay on the cut for ever?'

'Thought o' leavin' once. Me Uncle Bill went off ter be a sailor in the war – workin' the barges for the navy. Might've done the same meself, but I can't leave the boats – not with Grandma an' Freddy.'

'I suppose not.'

'It's a hard life,' he went on. 'But it's a good one. We're free, see. Nobody's servants. Nobody bosses us.'

She understood. Boat people weren't trapped in

311

factories and offices or ordered about. They were free spirits. But it *was* a hard life on the cut. Work, work, work, and almost no play.

The shadows were getting longer, the golden light fading. She said, 'Do you think they'd notice if I took some of those lovely apples?'

He grinned. 'Fancy a lady thinkin' o' such a thing.'

'I told you, I'm no lady. I could take just a few.'

'I'll get yer some.'

He squashed his cigarette under his boot and was over the gate in a flash. She followed more slowly, being careful with the fairground plate, and he came to her with his arms full of fruit. She made a pocket with the hem of her skirt and he tipped the apples in.

'We'd better go, Jack. Before someone catches us.'

'Still frit o' me?'

'I'm frit of whoever owns this orchard.'

'Nobody'll come. An' it's a nice place, this. We could stay awhile.'

He set his hands on her shoulders and she could feel their strength.

'Mind the plate, Jack.'

'I'll win yer another if it gets broke. Do yer like me, Frances?'

'Very much.' Her voice sounded croaky.

'Thought yer did. I could tell from the start. An' I've allus liked you, since I first saw yer.'

'You've had a funny way of showing it.'

'We don' show our feelin's, see. Only some-times.'

When he kissed her again it wasn't in fun, like it had been on the roundabout in front of the crowds. It wasn't in fun at all. With her skirtful of apples bunched up in one hand and the fair-ground plate clutched in the other, she couldn't have stopped him – even if she'd wanted to.

After a bit, the apples started rolling to the ground, one by one.

He said, his cheek rough against hers, 'Not frit no more, are yer?'

'No . . .'

The rest of the apples tumbled out of her skirt and down into the long grass.

He pulled her down beside them.

Sixteen

The last of the summer faded away. Autumn came in like a lion with fierce winds that tore down the dying leaves, with heavy rainstorms and sharp morning frosts. They took *Orpheus* and *Eurydice* up and down the cut, delivering the loads of steel, iron, cement, timber and rubber and returning with coal for paper mills, bakeries, factories. The landmarks along the way were now familiar to them. They had learned more of the boaters' names for the locks, all along the cut – Salters, Sewerage, Sweeps, Casey, Berker, Stoke, Wigrams, Catty Barnes . . . the names of bends and bridges, and of every bridge-hole with a nearby village store so that the lock-wheeler could step off with the bike under her arm and go shopping. They had learned every good tie-up where they could get fish and chips, a decent café meal, or a hot bath, and which were the best pubs to frequent. They had learned every twist and turn of the cut, and where the deepest channel ran, and where the hidden obstacles lay in wait. They knew where the mud was always thickest – at the sides or on the inside of a bend – and the peculiarities and perils of all the locks from London to Birmingham to Coventry and all the way back again. With the darker, colder evenings, the cabins went back to being cosy retreats instead of stifling ovens.

Molly came over to see Frances at one of the tie-ups, carrying Abel.

''E's took sick an' I'm fair worrit.'

She sat on the coal box with the baby's head lolling against her shoulder. Abel had his eyes closed and his skin was frighteningly pale. He seemed to be struggling for breath.

'Have you taken him to see a doctor?'

'Seen one a day or two back an' 'e give 'im some medsun but it done no good. Dunno what ter do now. Saul don' know neither.'

'We must find another doctor this evening. I'll come with you, Molly.'

'Would yer? That's ever so good of yer. Saul'll mind the boats.'

They walked into the town and up and down streets until they came across a doctor's brass plate outside a door. The surgery had closed and the doctor's wife who answered the door was unhelpful.

'He's having his supper.'

She began to shut the door again but Frances put her boot in the way.

'This child is very ill and needs urgent attention. Please ask the doctor to come.'

'He's in the middle of his supper, I told you.'

'Then we'll wait until he's finished.'

They sat in the waiting room – a cold and comfortless place – and eventually the doctor appeared, grumpy at being bothered. He examined Abel.

'You'd better get him to hospital. The child's got a severe bronchial infection.'

''*ospital!*' Molly started weeping. 'I'm not takin' me babby to no 'ospital.'

'Do you want him to die?'

Frances said angrily, 'Of course she doesn't.'

'Then I suggest you talk some sense into the woman. I'll give you a note.'

At the hospital they waited again until a nurse came to take Molly and Abel away.

Later, the nurse returned to tell Frances that they were keeping both of them for the night. She went back to the boats to tell Saul who looked worn out with worry. He was wringing his hands.

'I seen the mark o' death on 'im – like I seen it on others. Yer can allus tell.'

316

She tried to cheer him up. 'He's in good hands, Saul. They'll make him better.'

'Is't the bronchitus?'

'I don't know. They didn't say.'

He stood shaking his head in distress, not knowing what to do next. She made him sit down and boiled the kettle on Molly's shining stove for a strong cup of tea. Boat people might know all there was to know about the cut, but they were ignorant about the ways of the land and how to help themselves. Whatever Molly had said, not being able to read or write was a big disadvantage.

Abel didn't die. He recovered, and after a few days Molly brought him back to the boats.

'Saved 'is life, yer did,' she told Frances when they next met up on the cut.

'No, I didn't. The hospital did that.'

'Wouldn't never 'ave got there, but fer yer.'

Since the fair, Frances had seen Jack Carter only twice – passing on the cut, with no more than the chance to wave and shout. Then one evening they happened to stop at the same tie-up. It was already dark when Freddy turned up and banged on the motor-cabin door with another brass bed knob he'd found – or stolen – for her.

He spotted the fairground plate that she'd hung on the opposite wall.

'Where'd'yer get that?'

'Your brother gave it to me. He won it shooting at the fair.'

Freddy grinned proudly. 'He allus wins things. 'E's clever, Jack.'

She gave him a thick slice of bread and treacle, and the home-made alphabet book that she'd done for him on leave. She'd drawn pictures to go with the letters – all things he'd know and recognize on the boats: A for apple, B for butty, C for chimney, D for dipper, E for elum, F for fender, G for gunwale . . . They went through them together, the boy repeating each one after her.

'That's very good, Freddy.'

He beamed. 'I ain't forgot, see. Can yer larn me to write me name?'

She wrote it out in capitals and he stared at it for a moment.

'That's me?'

'It certainly is. Freddy Carter. Of course, your full name is Alfred, isn't it? Like your grand-father.' She wrote Alfred Carter.

'I seen that on our boats. Looks just the same.'

'That's what reading's about. Recognizing a word from its letters. If you learn your letters, then you'll soon be able to tell the names of all the boats on the cut.'

'I knows them already. We all does.'

'Ah, but you'll be able to *read* their names properly. And other things, too. Names of places.'

'I knows all the places, too.'

'Well, you'll be able to read notices and sign-posts . . . useful things like that. Let's go through the alphabet again.'

He was no fool, she could tell. Sharp-witted and eager to learn. A good schoolteacher could have had him reading in no time – if only there was the chance. She gave him the book to take away.

'Don't say nuffink to me bruvver nor me gran.'

'I promise I won't.'

Jack came over later – not down into the cabin because that wouldn't have been proper by boaters' standards, but staying on the counter outside.

'Like to go to the pictures?'

They went to see a Hollywood Technicolor film with Esther Williams swimming around in clear blue very un-cut-like water, and diving from a great height to surface with a smile, perfect make-up and not a hair out of place. She wondered what on earth Jack made of it all. The odd thing was that boaters loved going to the cinema, even though the films were so far removed from their own world. They couldn't read the title or the names of the film stars, but she'd seen them examining the stills outside to see if they liked the look of the film or whether it was one they'd watched before.

When they came out, it was raining hard. He knew of a fish and chip shop nearby, and then a pub afterwards where they washed down the greasy food with beer. He rolled up one of his cigarettes, licking the paper and pressing the edges neatly together.

'Yer done a good turn fer Molly an' Saul Jessop, so I 'ears.'

'It was nothing.'

He stroked the cigarette-paper edges from end to end. 'Not as I bin told. Can't do nothin' on the cut without everyone knows 'bout it. An' we knows everythin' 'bout you trainees.' He stuck the cigarette in his mouth, struck a match. 'Yer'll be leavin' afore long, I dare say. Goin' back to yer 'omes.'

'Not till the war's over.'

He blew the match flame out slowly, making it flicker and dance before it finally died. 'If I asked yer, would yer stay? Come an' live with me on the boats?'

She'd dreamed about it many times.

'Do you mean . . . marry you?'

'Didn't mean nuthin' else.' He put the matchbox away in his pocket. 'Wouldn't do, though, would it?'

'Why ever not?'

'Yer bein' a lady an' not born to the cut.'

'Not that nonsense again.' She put her hand on

his arm. The sleeve of his old jacket was damp from the rain and badly frayed around the cuff. She would have liked so much to buy him a new one, but he'd never accept it. 'I'd go anywhere with you, Jack. If you asked me.'

'Would yer now?' He looked at her for a moment, in his steady way. 'Would yer really?' Then he smiled suddenly. 'But I ain't arsked yer yet.'

They got soaked walking back to the tie-up and when he kissed her goodnight by the boats his mouth was cold and wet against hers.

She said, 'It'd be drier in the cabin. And warmer, too.'

'People see me go in there, they'll know what to think.'

'It's dark and they won't see. And, anyway, I don't care if they do.'

She sat on the edge of the cross-bed and watched as he crouched by the stove with kindling and coal, and got it going faster and better than she'd ever managed. In a trice, the fire was blazing, the cabin warming up.

'Will you teach me to do that, Jack?'

'Nothin' to it.'

'I want you to teach me everything about the boats.'

'Mebbe,' he said. 'One day.'

She had dreamed about it – how it would be,

living on a narrowboat with him. Sleeping with him, eating with him, working with him. Loving him.

She said, 'I meant what I said . . . about going anywhere with you, Jack.'

He turned his head towards her, still crouched by the stove. 'Yer don't know what yer sayin'.'

'Yes I *do*. And I really mean it. I'd go to the ends of the earth. Don't you believe me?'

He got up and took off his wet jacket. Looked down at her with his dark gypsy eyes. Touched her mouth. 'Best ter say nothin' more, just now.'

'*Two* brass bed knobs,' Ros said, admiring them on the cabin wall. 'And the fairground plate. It's beginning to look like the real thing in here, Frankie.' She perched on the edge of the coal box, puffing at a cigarette. 'How's it going with Jack, then?'

'He wanted to know what I'd say if he asked me to marry him and live with him on the boats.'

'And what did you say that you'd say?'

'That I'd go anywhere with him. And I would – like a shot. Only he hasn't actually asked me yet. He says it wouldn't do. I'm a lady and not born to the cut. All that sort of thing.'

'But he's got a point, hasn't he? I know you're loopy about him, sweetie, but you wouldn't last long as a boater's wife.'

322

'I don't see why not.'

'Simple. You have to be born to it, like he told you. The way things are now, you can go home any time you like, back to civilization. Hot baths, soft beds, good food, nice clean clothes. But if you married him and tried to be one of them, you couldn't do that and I bet you'd get fed up with the life in no time. Do you want to end up like poor Molly and the rest of them – endless kids, non-stop grind, worn out by the time you're thirty? And I doubt the boaters would ever really accept you, which would be a bit grim. You know what they can be like. It's just a dream of yours, darling. A romantic dream. You're going to have to wake up one day.'

'Jack could always leave the cut.'

'He wouldn't transplant to shore very well, would he? And it wouldn't be fair to ask it of him. It's the only life he knows. And I dare say he likes it. They all seem to, God knows why.'

'I thought you'd understand, Ros. You, of all people.'

Ros scratched her head. 'It's just that I've been around a lot more than you. And I've never been madly in love with a man, like you are with Jack. It must be rather like when people go and commit suicide – the balance of the mind is disturbed.'

'What about Prue and Steve? He wants her to

go and live in Canada after the war. Somewhere ghastly, by the sound of it. Much worse than the canals.'

'Winnipeg. It may be a bit chilly there in the winter, but it'll be a lot more comfortable. And miles better than going back to work in that bank of hers. I just hope Steve survives the war. She's started saying her prayers again at night and I can tell she's worried sick about him going on those bombing raids.'

'Poor Prue . . . I know what that's like. Vere and I always seem to quarrel whenever we meet, but I dread anything happening to him.'

'He'll be all right, Frankie. He knows his job.'

'That's what I keep telling myself. You keep doing that, Ros.'

'Doing what?'

'Scratching your head.'

'So do you. So does Prue. Do you think we've all got nits?'

Dear Prudence,

I'm sending this to the Grand Union Canal Company, like you said to do, so I hope you get it OK. I had a great time on the boats with you – only wish I could have stayed longer. Maybe there'll be another chance.

They're keeping us real busy here, so I guess I won't be able to get away for a while.

Don't forget about Canada. You'll like it there. Love, Steve.

Dear Steve,

Thank you for your letter. It was waiting for me here at Braunston in the Grand Union office today. We've tied up for the night and so I thought I'd write you a letter back at once so that I can try to post it before we leave tomorrow.

It's been a horrible trip so far. The rain hasn't stopped since we left London. We can't get anything dry and all sorts of things have gone wrong. Something went wrong with the engine again and we had to wait for a fitter to come and mend it. If you'd been there, I expect you would have got it going at once – like you did that time when you were with us. Then the butty elum got knocked off in one of the locks – Ros had forgotten to take it out. The pin got bent and we had to crawl all the way to Norton to get it repaired. Then the bilge pump blocked up. The engine room flooded and the fly-wheel sprayed everything with black oil. Frances had to unscrew the pump and poke around with a piece of wire to unblock it. It was a bit of grit, or something. It took us ages to clean up the mess. And after we unloaded at Tyseley, *the wind was so bad it kept blowing the empty boats onto the mud. We had an awful job getting them off. Of course, the engine never starts first go in the mornings, like it did with you.*

Anyway, we're on our way back to London at last. We don't like going there much because of the V2 rockets. One of them hit a factory near the docks when we were down there last time and the blast damaged our boats and smashed things up in the cabins. They're much more frightening than the buzz bombs. You can't hear them coming and they blow everything to bits. This is our third trip on the go, so we'll have six days' leave when it's finished.

A Halifax bomber, like yours, went very low over us when we were going along the cut near Leighton. We all waved, just in case you were in it and could see us.

Please write again, when you have time. I won't forget about Canada.

With love from Prudence.

In November the fogs began – not the skeiny mists of October but clammy clouds shrouding the cut and, in London, pea-soupers. Coming back from leave, lugging her carpet bag, Rosalind groped her way to a theatre in Shaftesbury

Avenue. She bought a ticket for the gods – the very back row because all the other seats were taken. When the curtain went up it was like looking at the stage through the wrong end of opera glasses.

Ken was even better than in the Coward play. It was Rattigan this time – another of his despised la-di-da playwrights – and he had the lead part. He played it to perfection. Just the right touch and timing, no trace of the Yorkshire accent, oodles of charm and a presence that kept all eyes riveted on him at every appearance on stage. Star quality that was God-given and could never be taught. At the end the audience gave him the loudest and longest applause.

She went round to the stage door where a little group of torch-carrying fans had gathered in the fog. As he came out – coat collar turned up, tousled hair, cigarette in the corner of his mouth – autograph books were thrust towards him, the torches held for him to sign his name. *Kenneth Woods*. She waited until he'd done the last one and then stepped forward with a scrap of paper and a stub of pencil. Her torch battery was almost flat and he had to find his. He scrawled his name with a flourish.

'You were plain Ken when we last met,' she said.

'Last met? Have we?'

'At the Winter Gardens. You were playing *Private Lives*.'

He traversed the torch to her face. 'I remember you. You're the girl I found in my dressing room, making herself up. The redhead.'

'That's me. Rosalind Flynn.'

'Worked on the barges, or something, didn't you?'

'Narrowboats. War work. But I'm an actress. Always have been.'

'Yeah, I remember that too.'

'I thought you didn't like Rattigan. French windows and things.'

'I don't. But it's the West End. And the lead. Couldn't say no, could I?' He lowered the torch. 'Want to come and have a bite round the corner? I'm bloody hungry.'

'So am I.'

Last time it had been a self-service caff; this time it was a full-blown restaurant – a theatrical watering-hole with signed photographs of actors and actresses hung all over the walls. She dumped her carpet bag with the coats and the head waiter came forward.

'Your usual table, sir?'

She recognized some famous faces at the tables and there were smiles and nods and waves, airily acknowledged by Ken as they were conducted to a corner.

'You've gone up in the world a bit,' she said, pulling off her woollen hat. 'We had pilchards on toast last time.'

'They do things like that here, if you want. Good plain grub. They stay open late and nobody bothers you, that's why I come here. What in Christ's name have you done to your hair?'

'Cut it.' She'd hacked it off with blunt scissors. 'We caught head lice – from a fair, or the flicks, or somewhere like that. So I cut mine short and washed it in paraffin. It seems to have done the trick.'

'I've had those. Used to get them at school. Mam'd fetch out the carbolic and a fine-tooth comb. They were always coming back, though. What're you eating, love?'

She wolfed down kidneys in a delectable wine sauce, creamy mashed potatoes and buttery cabbage.

He said, 'You haven't got worms, as well, by any chance?'

'Not that I know of. We're always starving because we work so hard.'

'Don't they feed you?'

'We feed ourselves – on whatever we can get. By fair means or foul.'

'You mean you nick stuff?'

'*I* do. We're always passing allotments and fields full of cabbages and sprouts and carrots

329

and things. Sometimes kind farmers take pity and give us free eggs and milk. One of them gave us a chicken once.'

'Alive or dead?'

'Dead. But with the feathers on. I used them to stuff a pillow. Nothing's ever wasted. Have you got a cigarette?'

Offstage, in the flesh, he wasn't much to look at – nothing like onstage when he was made up and lit up, and wearing nice clothes. But he had loads of sex appeal. That was the secret weapon.

'So, you're planning on coming back to the theatre – soon as you're done with the barges?'

'Narrowboats.'

'Whatever the hell they are. Got an agent?'

'Not yet.'

'You want to get yourself a good one, when the time comes. There'll be lots of others like you looking for work.'

'I was hoping you'd help. When you start directing.'

'Told you about that, did I? Yeah, a couple more years or so of this acting lark and I'm changing horses.' He grinned. 'I'll bear you in mind, love. If you're any good.'

The bread-and-butter pudding was the best she'd ever eaten and after it there was real coffee and another cigarette.

'Where're you staying tonight, then?'

'I was going to phone Frankie. Her aunt's got a flat in Knightsbridge and she'll be staying there. We have to be at the depot early in the morning.'

'You don't want to go wandering about in this fog. Never know who you'll bump into. Why not come back to my place instead? It's not far. We could talk some more.'

She'd be a fool not to go with him. Hitch her wagon to his star.

The flat was on the top floor of an old building with a rickety lift. Attic rooms without much furniture but, he assured her, wonderful views on a good day. He did the blackout, lit a gas fire and fetched a bottle of brandy. Poured it into glasses.

'OK. Pretend this is an audition. What do you know by heart?'

'What do you want to hear?'

'How about your namesake in *As You Like It*?'

Funny he should pick that. And lucky, because she knew the play so well. He lounged on the sofa, fag stuck in a corner of his mouth, head on one side, watching her and listening.

I will weary you then no longer with idle talking. Know of me then, – for now I speak to some purpose, – that I know you are a gentleman of good conceit . . .

When she'd finished the speech, he nodded

slowly. 'Not bad. Not bad at all. And you've got the looks all right.'

'Do you want to hear something else?'

He stubbed out the cigarette. 'Not now, love. Come over here. I've got another idea.'

'Jack Carter's courtin' yer, then?' Molly said. 'So I hears.'

'Actually, I hardly ever see him.'

'Were just the same with me an' Saul. Passed each other on the cut – a word an' a wave an' 'e was gone. If we was lucky, we 'ad the same tie-up an' then we could go fer a walk, or ter the pictures.' Molly hitched Abel higher on her hip; her stomach was already swelling with another baby, due in the spring. 'Yer bin with 'im?'

She understood the meaning very well. Like all boatwomen, Molly loved a gossip. 'Of course not.'

'Wouldn't blame yer if yer 'ad. But courtin's different. Gettin' wed. Yer don' know what it's like, livin' on the boats.'

'We've been working on them for almost a year.'

'That's not *livin'* on them, like we does. Wouldn't be right fer yer, an' that's a fact.'

'But I love the boats, Molly. And I love Jack.'

'I dare say.'

*   *   *

The manager in the company office at Coventry handed Frances a telegram and she tore it open.

Vere wounded on ops and taken to hospital at Northampton. Can you go soonest to see him. Aunt Gertrude.

Ros said, 'Off you go. Prue and I can manage.'

'Two-handed? We've never done that before?'

'We'll potter along slowly. You can catch us up somewhere later on. You ought to go, Frankie. It says "soonest". That means right now.'

The cross-country train journey took hours. During it, her imagination painted all sorts of horror pictures: Vere hideously burned, horribly mutilated, lying unconscious at death's door – perhaps already dead. At the hospital, she followed a nurse down a long linoleum corridor. Swing doors led off into gloomy wards with rows of beds filled with sad-looking patients. They'd put Vere in a small room on his own at the far end of a corridor. He was lying with his eyes closed, so still and so white that at first she thought he must, indeed, be dead. There was heavy bandaging across his chest and over his right shoulder.

'He's been sleeping a lot,' the nurse whispered. 'But I expect he'll wake up now you're here. You won't be able to stay long, though. He's not up to it.'

She sank down on the chair near the bed, numb

with fear. Vere wasn't dead but he was obviously very badly hurt. A chest wound was never a good thing – not from all she'd ever heard or read. In films, if people got shot in the chest, it was almost always the end. She spoke his name and he opened his eyes slowly.

'Frances? What on earth are you doing here?'

She pulled the chair closer. 'Aunt Gertrude sent me a telegram. She said you'd been hurt.'

'Damned nuisance . . .'

She wasn't sure if he was referring to her being there or to being hurt. 'How are you feeling?' What a *stupid* question.

'I don't feel anything much. They keep giving me stuff. Where am I, by the way?'

'Northampton Hospital.'

'You shouldn't have come. What about those boats of yours?'

'Ros and Prue are looking after them.'

'Can they cope?'

'I should think so. We're quite good at it now.'

'You're doing a very good job. I'm sorry I tried to stop you.' There was a pause. 'But I still think you shouldn't be doing it.'

He closed his eyes. She waited but he seemed to have drifted off again, and presently the nurse came back and said that her time was up. Out in the corridor she bumped into an RAF squadron leader whose face seemed familiar.

'Hugh Whitelaw,' he said. 'We met at the Ritz, remember? I've come to see how your brother's getting on.'

'He doesn't look very good. In fact, he looks dreadful. What happened?'

'His Mosquito was hit by flak, that's all I know. And he managed to fly it back. God knows how.' He took her arm. 'You don't look so good yourself. There's a canteen here, if you'd like a cup of tea, or something. It might make you feel better.'

He sat her down at a table and fetched her a cup of tea – the stewed kind that she used to dispense from the urn in the Bridport canteen.

'Cigarette?'

'Thanks.'

Her hand was shaking as he lit it for her.

He said, 'Try not to worry too much. Vere's incredibly tough, you know. He'll pull through all right.'

'We've never got on very well . . .'

He smiled. 'Yes, you told me when we first met. Big brothers can be a drag – from the best of intentions. He told me once that he's worried about you since your mother died, and that your father isn't up to things. He feels you're his responsibility. Responsibility is a big thing with him, you see. Looking after people he's in charge of. He's a hero to his men; they worship him in the squadron.'

Tears were trickling down her cheeks. 'I've been pretty foul to him, one way and another. Now he's going to die and I won't get the chance to be nicer.'

He handed her a very clean handkerchief. 'He's not going to die, Frances. He'll go on bossing you about and you'll go on being foul to him – until you get married and he can hand over the responsibility to somebody else.'

'He won't approve of my husband at all.' She mopped at her cheeks.

'You've someone in mind?'

'Yes. And he'll disapprove like anything.'

He found her a room in a hotel for the night – a depressing place with elderly residents dozing in wing chairs and run by staff almost as decrepit – and then took her off to dinner in a nearby pub. After a large gin and tonic she began to perk up.

'Do you mind telling me the latest war news, Hugh? We don't hear much on the cut.'

'I assume you know that President Roosevelt has been re-elected?'

'No. I'm afraid not. What else?'

'Let's see . . . RAF bombers sank the German battleship *Tirpitz*.'

'We haven't heard that either.'

'Our army has been doing amazingly well in Burma.'

'That's wonderful.'

'And the Yanks have been steamrollering across Europe.'

'So the war'll be over soon, won't it?'

'Don't count on it. We've still got a good way to go, I'm afraid. In Europe and the Far East.'

'How much more?'

'Impossible to say. Will you stay on your narrowboats until the bitter end?'

'Yes, of course.' She twiddled her glass. 'Actually, I might stay even longer. Perhaps for ever.'

He didn't ask why, which saved her having to lie about it in case he spilled the beans; he wasn't the sort of person it would be easy to lie to. Over dinner, she took a closer peek at his face. Grey eyes, firm mouth, strong chin, but marked with the same lines and shadows as Vere.

She said, 'Do you fly Mosquitoes too?'

'I do, indeed. Fantastic planes. Mostly made of wood, you know.'

'*Wood!* Isn't that a bit dangerous?'

He smiled. 'War *is* dangerous.'

'Vere will never tell me exactly what he does.'

'I can't tell you either, I'm afraid. But it's all pretty routine and boring.'

She didn't believe him for a moment. It was hideously dangerous – whatever they did – and he could easily be killed doing it.

'Don't forget about my parents' house at Stoke

Bruerne,' he said when he dropped her back at the depressing hotel. 'If you're ever in need of some decent food and a bed. Havlock Hall. It's easy to find.'

She stayed in Northampton for two days, spending most of the time at Vere's bedside. It would be a long haul, the hospital doctor told her. A large piece of flak had entered his chest and done a lot of damage. But there was every chance that he would make a full recovery – eventually. Predictably, Vere, whenever he woke up, still tried to give her orders.

'Time you went back, Frances. There's no point in hanging about here.'

'I'm not hanging about. I'm making sure you're all right.'

'Well, I am – as you can see. I'm in perfectly good hands, and you're needed on your boats. You're the captain, or whatever it's called. It's your responsibility.' He shut his eyes again.

She caught the boats up at Berkhamsted, where the railway passed close to the cut and the station was only a stone's throw away. She wriggled through the fence onto the towpath and presently *Orpheus* and *Eurydice* came trundling along in smooth and stately fashion towards her – Ros steering the motor, Prue the butty. She wasn't quite sure why but the familiar and beautiful sight made her start crying, and when they saw her face

338

they thought, at first, that it was bad news until she tried to explain.

They'd been quite OK, they assured her, except for getting stemmed up once, but the Quill brothers had come along and given them a snatch.

'The *Quills*?'

'They were charming about it – for them,' Ros said. 'And we gave them mugs of tea as a thank-you. We're all friends now.' She put an arm round her shoulders. 'I'm so glad Vere's going to be all right.'

Seventeen

The boy had been standing on the towpath by the top lock when they came in – not a boat child but one from some nearby slum. He was about the same age as Freddy, but without Freddy's lively spirit. His hair was dull and matted, his face and hands filthy, his eyes wary, his clothes like rags. He followed Prudence around as she drew the paddles.

'Give yer an 'and, miss.'

Children could be an awful nuisance and it was dangerous to let them get too near. 'I can manage, thank you.'

''Elp yer wiv the gate.' He set his hands on the beam and leaned his skinny frame against it. His boots were split open and tied on with string.

She hadn't the heart to chase him away and he stuck to her like a burr, all the way down the flight of locks. At the bottom she gave him a biscuit from her coat pocket. He crammed it in his mouth, swallowed it almost whole.

'Can I come wiv yer, far as Shrewley. I won' be no trouble.' His eyes pleaded.

'What do you want to go there for?'

'Me gran lives there.'

'Don't you have a home here?'

He shook his head. 'I run away. Me dad thrashes me.'

'Didn't your mother stop him?'

'She's dead.'

She looked at him unhappily. 'We can't take you. I'm so sorry.'

'Please, miss . . . I got nowhere else ter go.'

He followed her down the towpath. Every time she turned round he was still there.

Frances said, 'I suppose we *could* take him . . . it seems awful to leave him here.'

They stared at the child with his sad eyes and in his pitiful state; he was shivering with cold.

Ros smiled at him kindly. 'What's your name?'

'Billy, miss.'

'Billy what?'

'I forgot the rest.'

He was probably terrified that they'd give him away to some authority.

'Do you know where your grandmother lives at Shrewley?'

'Yes, miss. I bin there once when me mam took me. I can find it.'

In the end, they gave way and Billy scrambled

eagerly onto the butty. Cleaning him up was a hopeless job, but they fed him thick slices of bread and peanut butter and gave him hot cocoa. By the time they reached Shrewley it was getting too dark to go in search of the grandmother so they tied up before the tunnel and shared their supper with him. It was like feeding a starving animal.

Frances tried some more questions. 'What's your grandmother's name, Billy? Mrs what?'

'Dunno. I calls 'er Gran.'

'Does she live in a house?'

'A little 'un. Right by the water.'

'Does it have a number? Or a name?'

'Dunno. But I knows what it looks like.'

They opened a tin of rice pudding for him and he scoffed the lot, then half a packet of biscuits.

'He can sleep in the side bed on the motor,' Frances said. 'We'll go looking for the grandmother first thing in the morning.'

She dragged out blankets and a spare pillow. He crawled into them, like a creature bolting into a safe burrow. She drew the blanket up over his shoulders and tucked it gently round him.

'Sleep well, Billy. We'll find her for you.'

But he was already asleep.

In the morning they washed his hands and face in warm water and gave him breakfast – porridge with treacle and evaporated milk and a precious boiled egg with more slices of bread. Ros stayed to look after the boats while Frances and Prue set off with Billy. They walked along the towpath, past a long row of cottages, stopping at each one. The boy kept shaking his head until, finally, they came to one on its own with a front door of faded blue.

'This is Gran's.'

'You're sure, Billy?'

'Yes, miss. I remembers the door.'

Frances knocked, waited and then knocked again. The door was opened by an old woman – a sour-faced creature in hairnet and curlers, indignant at being disturbed.

Billy gave a loud wail of disappointment. 'She ain't me gran.'

Prudence took his hand in hers. 'This little boy's looking for his grandmother. He thought she lived here.'

'Must've been Mrs Smith. She died last summer. I live 'ere now.'

They walked back to the boats, Billy between them, and Ros took him down into the butty cabin and gave him some more biscuits.

'We can't possibly keep him, Prue,' Frances whispered. 'It's not like a stray dog, or something. We're going to have to call the police.'

'But they might send him back to his father.'

'I know. But we still can't keep him.'

'Couldn't we look after him, between us? He

could live on the boats and we could take turns to have him home for leaves.'

'It would be kidnapping – against the law.'

'Not if he wanted to stay with us.'

'It doesn't make any difference. He's under age. He doesn't belong to us.'

'Oh, Frankie . . . it's so sad. Do we have to tell the police?' Tears were running down Prudence's face. 'He trusted us. He came to us for help and we're betraying him.'

She said heavily, 'I'm afraid we do. I'll go and phone them now.'

They came in a car and took him away. He was crying bitterly as he went – despairing sobs that broke their hearts.

By mid-December the weather was very cold – colder than they had ever known it on the cut. At night they hung a hurricane lantern in the engine room to give some warmth for starting it in the morning, and they went to bed with jerseys over their pyjamas, coats piled on their bunks, socks on their feet.

In the morning they opened the cabin doors onto the glitter of thick frost and shut them hurriedly to stoke up the fire and put on the kettle. Dressing took two minutes – wriggling back into the triple layer of jerseys that had been shed like a cocoon the night before, pulling on trousers, more socks, coats, scarves, hats, boots. Frances had acquired a heavy leather jerkin from an RAF mechanic whom she had met in a pub. It had a warm lining and no sleeves, which left her arms wonderfully free, and it came down well past her thighs. The mechanic had been rash enough to let her try it on and drunk enough later to part with it. Outside, the decks were a skating rink. Frozen knots had to be prised open or thawed with hot kettle water, the engine coaxed into life. They clasped hands round hot mugs and round chimneys, stamped feet, swung arms. The lock-wheeler, racing ahead on the bike to wrestle with paddles and gates, was the only one to feel warm.

The boy, Billy, haunted Prudence for days. As she went about her work, she kept seeing his sad face and his pleading eyes, and hearing his sobs. Whenever they passed children by the locks or on the towpath, she looked out for Billy. Sometimes she imagined him living happily with them on the boats, growing fit and strong. They could have taken him to the public baths for a good scrub, found him other clothes, taught him some table manners. She saw herself – though rather less easily – taking him home to Croydon, where he might not have been quite so welcome. At other times, she even pictured taking him across the sea to a new life in Canada. When she wrote to Steve, she told him all about Billy.

Poor kid! He had written back. *But you've got to put him out of your mind. He'll be OK. They'll find a good home for him.* I could have given him one, she thought sadly. I know I could.

Christmas found them halfway through a trip. They had carried fifty tons of steel to Tyseley wharf and taken the empty boats on through rain and sleet to a colliery near Nuneaton. When they tied up on Christmas Eve, the place was deserted – no workmen waiting to load them, no other boats, nobody about: nothing but slag heaps, black dirt, empty trucks and the all-pervading smell of coal. In the morning they boiled kettles, washed themselves, put on the cleanest trousers and jumpers they could find, raided the cocoa tin and walked into the town in search of a meal. The streets were as quiet as the colliery, with every café closed, and the only option a grim Victorian hotel where they were banished to a table in the furthest recess of the dining room, well away from respectable diners.

The food was awful: tough chicken, sulphurous Brussels sprouts, cardboard potatoes and congealed gravy, and the Christmas pudding contained far more breadcrumbs than any dried fruit. Ros had ordered a bottle of red wine which

346

they polished off between them. It tasted sour, like vinegar, but made them feel better. They behaved rather badly in their lepers' corner, talking much too loudly, giggling like schoolgirls, and ignoring all the disapproving looks. On the way back to the boats, arms linked and singing carols, they stopped at a pub and bought a bottle of rum to take with them. They drank most of that, too, battened down cosily in the butty cabin with the stove well stoked. Luckily, the colliery was closed on Boxing Day while they nursed their hangovers, and by the following morning, when the men appeared and started wheeling their laden barrows up planks to tip coal into the holds, they had recovered.

The Christmas orchid with pretty sprays of small white flowers was in full bloom when Frances returned, on leave, to Averton.

'*Calanthe Harrisii*,' her father replied, when she asked the name. 'It goes on flowering for another month. I take it out of the pot in February and separate the new bulbs from the old. As soon as the new roots appear, they're planted back into five-inch pots.'

He went on talking about loam and sand and leaf mould, all mixed up with dried cow manure and one-year-old sheep droppings.

She interrupted him. 'Isn't it wonderful news

about Vere? About him coming out of hospital soon.'

'Yes, indeed.'

'Aunt Gertrude says the doctors think he'll be able to come home to convalesce for a while, when he's fit enough.'

'Excellent.'

Another bloom had claimed his attention. He had no idea how badly Vere had been wounded because Aunt Gertrude had kept it from him. In any case, the orchids were all that mattered to him. He would probably have borne Vere's death quite calmly, so long as his precious plants survived. No wonder she hated them all – even the Christmas one.

Rosalind had to sleep on the sofa. Her bedroom was occupied again, this time by an obnoxious and tenth-rate actor appearing in a third-rate revival. Like most mediocrities, he was jealous of success.

'Personally, I think Kenny Woods is overrated, don't you? I mean, what's all the fuss about?'

She said, 'The fuss is because he's very good.'

'Well, you're entitled to your opinion, darling, of course. Most of the rest of us wouldn't agree. I mean, he can't even speak the King's English properly.'

'Have you ever seen him on stage?'

He hadn't, of course – not that it would have made any difference. And Ken, she knew, wouldn't have given a jot for his opinion. Or for most other people's, either. Ken was going places that this little twerp would never go. With any luck, she'd go with him.

'There's someone on the telephone for you, Prudence. It sounds like an *American*.'

Mother followed her into the hall and hovered pointedly while she picked up the receiver.

'Hallo.'

'Prudence? It's Steve. I figured you might be home on leave.'

'How are you?'

'Just fine. Got your letters. It's sure good to hear from you. You get mine?'

'Yes. Thank you.'

'How are you doing?'

'Very well, thank you.'

'How long leave did they give you?'

'Six days. I've got three left. Then we do another trip.'

'Looks like I won't be able to get away for a while . . . too much happening here. Maybe next time we can meet up.'

Mother was still hovering, listening to every single word. She couldn't speak freely – say all the things that she wanted so much to say to him.

'That would be very nice.'

'Hang on a second . . . I gotta put more coins in. Darn it . . . I've only got a couple of pennies left. You still there, sweetheart?'

'Yes.'

'You sound kinda funny. Haven't forgotten about Canada, have you? Changed your mind?'

Before she could answer the line went dead.

Mother said, 'Who was that man, Prudence?'

'Oh, just someone I met. He's in the RAF.'

'But he sounded American.'

'He's Canadian.'

'Well, you'd better not tell your father. He always says Canadians are even worse-behaved than the Americans. Is he an officer?'

'He's a sergeant. In a bomber crew.'

'You said your friend's brother was a wing commander.'

'Yes, he is.'

'Then I don't understand how you could have met this sergeant. And how did he know your telephone number?'

'I gave it to him.'

'You should never do that, Prudence. It's very unwise. You don't know what sort of person he is.'

'Yes, I do, Mother. He's wonderful.'

Her mother stared at her. 'We should never have let you go on those boats.'

The boatwomen were busy with their washing at the Bulls Bridge lay-by, scrubbing away and gossiping as Frances passed on her way to *Orpheus* and *Eurydice*. It was miserably cold and the boats were damp and cheerless, brass tarnished, decks dirty, stoves rusty. She made a half-hearted start on the clean-up and was scouring the stove on the motor when Freddy knocked and stuck his head round the cabin door.

'Saw you goin' by, miss. Got another brass fer yer.'

'Oh, Freddy, that is nice of you. It's a lovely one. You didn't pinch it, did you?'

He looked aggrieved. 'Course not. There was two of 'em on an old bedstead fell in the cut. Gave one to me gran an' kept this one fer yer.'

'How have you been getting on with your letters? Have you learned them yet?'

'Naw. Got no time fer it.'

'That's a pity. Maybe I could help you.'

'Me brother don' want that.'

'Is he here?'

'He's gone ter see them as works in the office. To tell 'em we're leavin' tomorrer.'

'Leaving? You mean on a trip?'

'Not fer the Gran' Union. We're goin' back to the Oxford. Number Ones can work anywheres, see. An' me other brothers've got boats on the

Oxford. Jack says it's fer the best an' it'll make me gran 'appy. Reckon yer won't be seein' us much no more. Still, yer'll be all right.' He grinned at her. 'Yer not so bad on the boats now. Considerin'.'

She waited outside the company office until Jack came out. It had started to snow – white flurries drifting and settling along the wharf. His coat collar was turned up, his cap pulled down; she couldn't see his face clearly.

'Freddy told me that you're going to work on the Oxford canal, Jack.'

'That's right.' He was smoking one of his roll-ups: blew smoke up into the air and looked at her. 'I found that picture book you did fer 'im, Frances. You bin larnin' 'im letters. Givin' 'im ideas o' bein' a scholar.'

'He wants to learn to read. Surely there's nothing wrong with that?'

'Freddy belongs to the cut. We none of us reads. Yer knows that. We got no need ter.'

'What did you do with the book?'

'Threw it away. Weren't no good to 'im.' He stared at her. 'Yer want to change Freddy an' next thing yer'd want to change me. Want me ter read and write an' speak an' act different. Make me like a gentleman.'

'No, I wouldn't.'

'Yes yer would. Yer couldn't stop yerself. Yer'd

352

try ter larn me, an' I'd never do it. Wouldn't want ter.' He drew again on the roll-up, blew more smoke, looked at her. 'I fancied it might do, at first – us two wed an' workin' the boats together, livin' on the cut fer allus – but 'twere a dream, that's all. A dream fer both of us. An' I woke up.'

'You're angry because I taught Freddy a few letters. That's silly.'

''Tis more than that. An' I ain't angry. Ain't yer fault. Yer just don' understand. No reason why yer should.'

'What don't I understand?'

'Us on the cut. We're different, see. Yer not like us. Couldn't never be. Yer've got ter be born ter the boats, like I told yer. Else it don' work.'

'But I love the boats. And I love life on the cut.'

'I dare say – fer the moment. Fer a bit more, mebbe. But not fer ever. Yer've just bin playin' at it, not livin' it. Pretendin', like it were a game. Same with all you lady trainees.'

'That's not true!'

''Tis too. I'm not a scholar, like yer, Frances, but I got a lot more sense. An' that's why I'm goin'.'

She started crying. 'If you loved me, you wouldn't go.'

'Yes, I would. I'm leavin' so's yer'll go back to yer own world, where yer belong. I'm doin' what's right. Savin' yer from makin' a mistake.'

353

She caught hold of his coat sleeve. 'Please, don't go, Jack. I love you so much.'

'I got to.' He jerked his arm free. 'G'bye, Frances.'

'Wait, Jack. Please wait. Jack! *Jack!*'

She ran after him but he shook her off roughly. The snow flurries had become a swirling blizzard of thick white flakes that swallowed him up as he strode away.

Eighteen

The ice made a peculiar sound – groaning and creaking in protest before the motor's bulldozing advance, and breaking into lumps that skittered across the frozen surface.

They climbed slowly up through the forty-five locks from Cowley to Cowroast. A tyre puncture meant the lock-wheeler had to go on foot – trudging from one lock to the next through several inches of snow to wrestle with frozen gates. At Cowroast lock, slabs of ice the size of table tops had to be poked and prodded and pushed out into the cut with shafts and brooms before the gates could open wide enough to let the boats in. It was exhausting, back-breaking, arm-wrenching work. They tied up beyond the lock, stoked the stoves into blazing furnaces, piled yet more coverings on their beds and slept for twelve hours. It snowed again during the night and froze hard by dawn. Before they let go, they spread cold ashes from the stove onto the treacherously slippery gunwales and round the butty-hatch edges and along the top planks. The wind sliced at their faces like a sharp knife, reddening their eyes, chapping their lips, making their ears ache, freezing their fingers. Gloves were useless: they got in the way of anything fiddly.

Crossing Tring Summit, they were sheltered for three miles. The trees and bushes lining the banks were prettily laced with thick hoar frost and the snowy ice on the cut sparkled like powdered glass. At the end of the Summit, they were back in the teeth of the wind and the ice was worse, creaking and cracking louder than ever and thickening up along the banks. There were no boats behind them and none coming from the other way. They stopped to have dinner in the butty cabin and thaw out their faces and hands and ears.

Ros ladled out hot soup which she'd spiked with the last of the Christmas rum. 'So, what do we do next, Frankie?'

'Go on, I suppose. The cut is probably completely frozen up ahead but we may as well get as far as we can. We don't want the boaters thinking we're feeble.'

'You're the boss. I ought to mention, though, that we're running out of coal. Enough for one more day, that's all.'

They battled on alone down the seven Mathus

locks. It had started to snow again and was almost dark when they reached Finney lock. They stopped the boats by the bridge without bothering to tie up, heated up tinned stew and rice pudding. Both stoves were out by morning, both coal boxes empty. The cut-side water tap had frozen, so they filled the cans at the Red Lion and stocked up on rations from the shop. They wouldn't die of thirst or starvation, but, very likely, from cold.

After Finney there was the long, wiggling pound which took them six hours instead of the usual four, and then the terrors of crossing the Pig Trough high over the Ouse. It was Ros who spotted the snow-covered pile of coal hidden in some bushes below Cosgrove lock.

'But it must belong to someone, Ros. We can't just take it.'

'This is a question of survival, Frankie. Ours. Fetch the buckets.'

They had filled both coal boxes to the brim and started up the engine when a man appeared on the towpath, shaking his fist and yelling.

'Time to leave,' Ros said, waving back at him from the butty hatches.

After climbing the Stoke seven, they tied up and spent the evening in the Boat Inn in company with other boaters and a group of soldiers from a nearby camp. One of them sat down to play the piano and they all roared out the old songs.

Pack up your troubles in your old kitbag . . .

and

If you were the only girl in the world . . .

and

It's a long way to Tipperary . . .

When they woke up in the morning, the boats were frozen in; the cut completely covered with ice inches thick, the broken-off lumps piled up like boulders.

'What now, skipper?'

'You heard what the boaters were saying in the pub last night, Ros. We're stuck here till the ice-breaker comes, or till it thaws. Personally, I don't mind – as long as the coal lasts, and the food.'

'We'll need more cocoa soon,' Prudence said. 'We forgot to get some at Finney.'

They spent the morning sweeping the loose snow off the boats, chipping away at ice and cleaning up the cabins. After dinner they walked to the village shop and found it had run out of cocoa: a disaster. Cocoa fuelled them as much as diesel oil fuelled the engine.

'There's a shop at the next village,' the woman told them. 'About two miles from here. They might have some. The shortest way's across the fields.'

They padlocked the boats and took the route that she had pointed out to them, floundering through deep drifts of snow, clambering over gates and stiles. When they reached the village, the shop had a sign tacked to the door. *Regular customers only.* And another below it. *No bargees served here.*

There was a man standing behind the counter in a very clean white overall and with a very dour expression.

'Didn't you see the notice? Or can't you read? No bargees served.'

Frances drew herself up. 'We're not bargees.'

'From the boats, aren't you? I can tell by the look of you. Same as gippos, you are.'

She advanced to the counter and glared at him. 'We work for the Inland Waterways on the narrowboats. Doing very important war work, as it happens. And we'd like some cocoa, please.'

'We haven't got any.'

'Yes, you have. You've got a stack of Rowntrees on the shelf there, behind you. We'd like two of them.'

'They're reserved for regular customers.'

'I don't believe you.'

'Are you calling me a liar?'

'Yes. I am.'

A dumpy woman in a flowered apron had

359

emerged from the back of the shop. 'What's going on, Len?'

'These women are from the barges. I'm not serving them. Just look at them.'

She turned to do so – to stare at their swaddled layers of clothing with the rents and the grease stains, at their dirty hands and faces, at the snow melting into muddy puddles round their boots. They stared back in silence.

'Why not, Len?'

'I'm not having people like them in here.'

'What do they want?'

'Cocoa.'

'Give it to them, Len. These aren't real bargees, you fool. Can't you tell?'

They left in triumph with the cocoa and set off back to Stoke, taking the longer route by road rather than face the trek across fields again. It was bitterly cold, the arctic wind making their eyes water. After about a mile they passed a large gateway with stone lions pawing the tops of the pillars.

Ros stopped. 'That must lead somewhere very grand. Do you think they'd give us a cup of tea?'

Frances said, 'As a matter of fact, they probably would. It's where Hugh Whitelaw's parents live.'

'Who's he?'

'We met him at the Ritz when we went there to

dinner – don't you remember? He was the other RAF bloke with Vere.'

'Oh, yes. He was nice. He took quite a shine to you, but you were in such a bait with your brother, you didn't even notice. So how do you know the parents live here?'

'Because he said so. He told me that his parents lived at Havlock Hall, near Stoke Bruerne, and that's the name that's carved on the pillar over there. We were to go and see them if we were passing and needed dinner and a bed for the night.'

'Why on *earth* didn't you tell us before, Frankie? Here we are, marooned in the ice, probably for days and days, and through that gateway lies warmth, food, hot baths, bug-free beds . . .'

'We can't go barging in there, Ros. We've never even met his parents.'

'Well, we're going to meet them now. We have an open invitation.'

'People say those sort of things, but they don't really mean them.'

'Of course he meant it. I told you, he fancies you. Come on.'

Ros marched off with Prue following more slowly, Frances hanging back crossly. The driveway was bordered by large trees, and snow-covered parkland rolled away into the far distance. There were acres of woods and a frozen lake with a mock-Grecian temple beside it. The house itself was hidden from them by banks of rhododendrons until they reached a bend.

'Blimey!' Ros stopped and put her hand to her mouth.

Havlock Hall was massive. Rows of mullioned windows, crenellated walls, twisted chimneys, turreted towers, pinnacled roofs – every feature and embellishment known to and beloved by the Victorians.

Frances said, 'We can't do this, Ros. It's an awful cheek.'

'We're very cold and we're very hungry – aren't we, Prue? So we're doing it.'

The front door, studded with iron nails, looked rather like the entrance to a prison. Undaunted, Ros tugged firmly at the bell pull.

'You do the talking, Frankie.'

'*Me?* Why should I? It was all *your* idea.'

'But you're the one he gave the invitation to.'

'I'd no intention of taking it up.'

'Too late now.'

One half of the prison door had opened and an old man stood there, dressed in butler's black with a starched wing collar. He looked at them without speaking. They must, Frances thought, be a horrible sight. If the man in the village shop hadn't wanted to serve them, then this aged and dignified retainer wouldn't even allow them over the threshold.

Ros gave her a shove. 'Go on.'

'Squadron Leader Whitelaw invited us to call,' she said. 'He's a friend of my brother's, Wing Commander Carlyon.' She could see the butler assessing and reassessing the situation rapidly. 'We wondered if his parents were at home?'

There was a pause while he reached his decision: 'Perhaps you would care to step inside, madam.'

They stepped into a vast hall with a tiled floor, stained-glass windows, stags' heads, a minstrels' gallery and a majestic staircase of elaborately carved oak. An enormous, full-length portrait of a bewhiskered Victorian gentleman dominated the far wall.

'Who is it, Mathews?'

The woman coming down the staircase was dressed, not as some frightening grande dame, but in slacks and a jumper with her wavy hair cut short. Frances repeated her piece and she smiled.

'I'm Hugh's mother and I know all about you. Your Aunt Gertrude is an old pal of mine and your brother has been to visit us. How is Vere?'

'Much better, thank you. He's out of hospital. They've moved him to a nursing home.'

'That's good news. Do introduce me to your friends.'

363

She made the introductions apologetically. Ros, with her hacked-off locks and ragged scarves, looked like a wild Irish peasant; Prue resembled a penniless refugee from some poor and remote corner of the Balkans. They were shedding lumps of ice and snow over the tiled floor.

'It's an awful intrusion, I'm afraid, and we're very dirty.'

'Well, you work on the narrowboats, don't you? You're bound to be. Are you tied up at Stoke?'

'Actually, we're frozen in there.'

'Good heavens! I didn't realize it was that bad. You poor things . . . you'll be wanting a hot bath and food, and you must certainly stay the night.'

The bath was a claw-footed roll-top with big brass taps and the water was steaming hot. Frances, who had won the toss to go first, ignored the five inches economy rule, added rose-scented salts and wallowed blissfully. She dried herself with a fleecy towel, dressed in the most presentable of her layers and combed her hair with the help of a proper looking glass. Downstairs, the butler showed her into a sitting room where there was yet more bliss – a roaring log fire and a crystal glass full of sherry.

Mrs Whitelaw said, 'My husband's away in London at the moment but Hugh will be arriving this evening – in time for dinner, I hope. He's got leave – a whole week. Isn't it marvellous?'

It wasn't marvellous at all, Frances thought. They'd imposed disgracefully and the situation was already embarrassing enough.

'We really ought to go back to the boats tonight.'

Ros had appeared from her bath, magically transformed from wild Irish peasant to beautiful actress. 'No we oughtn't, Frankie. It's already pitch dark and it's snowing again.'

'We're not supposed to leave them unattended.'

'The cabins are padlocked and nobody's going to make off with fifty tons of steel, are they, sweetie?'

Hugh's mother intervened. 'But of course you must stay the night, Frances. You can't possibly go out again in this weather. And dinner is arranged. I hope you all like pheasant?'

The dining room was oak-panelled, the table twelve feet long and there was another log fire burning in a fireplace big enough to roast an ox. They sat up one end of the table and the old butler bore in a tureen of soup. They'd just started on it when Hugh arrived. If he was taken aback to see the three of them sitting there, guzzling away, he was too polite to show it.

As soon as he'd sat down opposite her and next to Prue, Frances said, 'I'm afraid we had the most tremendous nerve, turning up on the doorstep. Your mother has been very kind. She insisted on us staying the night.'

He smiled at her. 'Of course she did. It's terrible out. It took me hours to get home and it's getting worse. Apparently the freeze-up could last at least a week.'

'Could it? Oh dear.'

'Don't worry, you'll be more than welcome here.'

'We'd never have dreamed of coming here, if it hadn't been for the weather.'

'But I'm very glad that you did.'

'Ros was determined.'

'Very sensible of her.'

'We can't stay, of course. We have to look after the boats.'

'By all means. You can walk over in the day and make sure they're all right. It's not far. Come and go, just as you please. By the way, I went to see Vere at the nursing home a couple of days ago. He's making good progress but I think it's going to be quite a while before he's back with the squadron again.'

'He'll hate that.'

'Yes . . . he's a bit like a caged tiger at the moment.'

For once, the soup wasn't out of a tin and the pheasant from the estate had been roasted to perfection, with lovely trimmings. Somewhere, beyond the green baize door, there was a treasure working miracles with the rations. The butler poured smooth red wine into polished glasses. Ros hissed in her ear.

'You go back to the boats, if you want, Frankie. Prue and I are staying put.'

After breakfast – porridge and real eggs – they walked to the village, crunching through the fresh layer of snow. *Orpheus* and *Eurydice* lay shrouded in lace-edged white, still gripped fast in the ice. They shovelled snow off the surfaces and swept away with brooms. Then they cleaned the stoves, polished the brass and wiped over the engine with diesel oil on rags. When they'd finished, there was another argument between Frances and Rosalind over what should happen next.

'I think we should stay here, Ros. We've got enough coal to keep us warm for the next few days, and plenty of food. I'm the steerer, so it's my decision.'

'I just don't see the point of us being martyrs when we've got such a lovely alternative.'

'We can't go on accepting the Whitelaws' hospitality.'

'Well, I don't have your finer feelings, I'm afraid. What's the matter with you, Frankie? Is it because Hugh obviously likes you and you don't want him getting any wrong ideas? If you had any sense, you'd let him get them. The family must be loaded and he's a wonderful catch, as well as being extremely nice.'

She said furiously, 'I don't give a damn.'

'Don't tell me you're still moping after Jack Carter?'

'He's got nothing to do with it.'

'Hasn't he? I bet you're still dreaming those dreams about him and picturing yourself living on the cut with him for ever and ever amen. How gloriously happy you'd be, spending the rest of your days cooped up in a rabbit hutch with a man who can't read or write—'

'Shut up, Ros!'

Prue looked upset. 'Please, don't let's quarrel.'

'We're not quarrelling, Prue. I'm just pointing out to Frankie how silly and selfish she's being. Wouldn't *you* sooner stay in comfort with the Whitelaws than be here?'

'Well, yes, I suppose so.'

'There you are, skipper. You've got a mutiny on your hands.'

In the end she gave way, and they collected their sponge bags and the most respectable clothing they could find and trudged back to the Hall.

In the afternoon they built a giant snowman on the lawns, played ping-pong in the games room and Monopoly in the sitting room beside the fire. Hugh had spent the day out rough shooting and didn't reappear until dinner time – venison pie, apple turnover, wine flowing. What with the food and the wine and the warmth, Frances began to feel quite at ease until, after dinner, Hugh came to sit beside her. He offered her a cigarette and lit it for her.

'Tell me honestly, Frances, what do you think of this house?'

'It's very . . . impressive.'

He smiled. 'You don't have to be so polite. It's actually quite hideous. My grandfather made a fortune from coal and cotton and decided he wanted to live somewhere pleasant, away from the mines and the mills, so he built this enormous white elephant.'

'Is that his portrait in the hall?'

'He never did things by halves. I'm very fond of the place, actually. It grows on you.'

She said, 'We're not used to space. We don't have any on the boats.'

'I know. I've seen inside them when I used to hang about the Stoke Bruerne locks as a child. I was fascinated by the narrowboats and the boat people. I remember wanting to run away with them – like children dream of running away with a circus, or going off with the gypsies, or sailing away on a pirate ship.'

'I have an ancestor who was a pirate. He built our house in Dorset with his booty.'

'Did you ever dream of running off with pirates?'

'Not pirates,' she said slowly. 'With gypsies.'

'The boat people are very similar.'

'They'd hate to hear you say that. It's a big insult to them.'

'It wasn't meant as one. Far from it. They're both nomadic people – very proud and with an enormous amount of dignity. And they both lead very tough lives. When I grew up I realized that and stopped wanting to run away with them.' He smiled at her again. 'Are you still thinking of staying on the narrowboats after the war?'

'I don't know,' she said. 'I don't know what I'll do.'

They went skating on the lake and tobogganing down the hills and walking through the woods, collecting bundles of sticks for the cabin stoves. Sometimes Hugh came with them, other times not. Three days later, they heard that the ice-breaker had got through as far as Stoke.

When she said goodbye, he kissed her cheek briefly. 'After the war's over, Frances, I hope we meet again.'

Then he kissed Ros's cheek, and Prue's too, and said exactly the same thing to them. As she pointed out triumphantly to Ros, she'd got it all wrong about Hugh liking her.

370

Ros looked at her. 'No, I hadn't, darling. He's just waiting for you to wake up, that's all.'

The ice-breaker had cut a pathway of open water down the centre of the cut and they followed in its wake. Blisworth tunnel was clear, the air inside almost warm, but further on they faced the Bugby seven all alone. The boats nosed great lumps of loose ice into the entrance to each lock, which then had to be propelled out before there was enough room for them to go all the way in. It was a long battle and they took it in turns to be up on the wall, wielding the long shaft from a height, or staying down in the butty hatches which meant using the short shaft and working on their knees for fear of overbalancing into the water. The blocks of ice kept slipping and sliding away from them and floating off in the wrong direction. The trick, as they discovered, was to harpoon them firmly in the centre and pass them on until they could be pushed firmly out into the cut. Struggling through the first lock took more than three hours and they had to stop and rest. After sitting down to a proper dinner they had recovered, and went on to the next where the lock-keeper appeared, shaking his head.

'You'll not get far today, ladies. There's more trouble ahead.'

With his help, they manoeuvred the boats into

the lock and got the bottom gates shut. The lock filled, the top gates opened and they went very slowly on their way. The open channel was already freezing over and, once again, *Orpheus* had to act as ice-breaker as well as pulling the loaded butty. If the engine breaks down now, Frances thought grimly, we've had our chips. But, by a miracle, it didn't, and they climbed laboriously through the third lock before tying up for the night. They had been on the go for more than nine hours and slept like the dead for twelve more.

It was another two days before the ice melted enough for them to continue and deliver their cargo of steel to Birmingham, where the snow had beautified the normally ugly scene. When they loaded up with coal at Longford wharf it had been churned to a dirty grey. There was snow all the way down to the Glaxo factory where they unloaded. Back at the Bulls Bridge lay-by with the empty boats, Frances reported to the company office and collected their mail. Ros's family rarely bothered to write, but there was a letter from Vere and another from Aunt Gertrude and a small package for Prue. She took them all back to the boats and started to read the one from Vere.

I seem to be making progress, at last, though they're keeping me in prison for a while

372

*longer, though I'm determined to return to
the squadron as soon as possible. For once, I
have to take orders, not the other way round.
I expect that will amuse you.*

Prue gave a choked sob; she was staring at the
piece of paper in her hand.

'What is it, Prue?'

She didn't answer and Frances took it from her.
It was a brief letter and rather badly typed.

*We regret to inform you that Sergeant
Stephen McGhie is listed as missing on active
service, believed killed. We are therefore returning your letters to him herewith.*

'Oh, Prue . . . I'm so sorry. So *very* sorry.'

Nineteen

She remembered where his flat was and went up in the rickety lift to the top floor. He opened the door, yawning and scratching.

'Remember me, Ken?'

'Of course I do, love. Once seen, never forgotten. Come on in.'

She picked up her carpet bag and went inside.

'I've been having a kip. Generally do that, if it's not a matinee. How've you been, Rosalind? Still sailing those boats?'

'You can't sail them. No sails. One has an engine and pulls the other.'

'Yeah . . . Like some tea? I've got some somewhere . . . make us both a mug, would you?'

She found the packet of Lyons Green Label and a teapot in the cubbyhole that passed for a kitchen, and put the kettle to boil on the gas ring. When she carried the mugs into the other room he was lying on the sofa, smoking. He heaved himself up and made room for her at one end.

'Thanks, love. Have a fag.'

He was still doing the Rattigan, he told her, and had reached the stage where he went through every performance like an automaton, speaking the lines but thinking of something else entirely – like what he'd have for supper afterwards – the steak and kidney or the bangers and mash, or maybe the liver and onions.

'I come to when the audience starts clapping at the end and I can't remember a bloody thing about the bit in between.'

She laughed. 'I don't believe you.'

'It's true, love. And it looks like we're going to run for another three months at least.'

'Lucky you.'

'Yeah, but I'm getting sick of it. I'm ready for something else.'

'Such as?'

'Well, a bloke from Stratford came backstage the other evening . . . wanted to know if I'd be interested in auditioning for them.'

'What did you say?'

'I said I'd think about it – which I'm doing.'

She would have given her right arm for the chance. 'Sounds exciting. But I thought you wanted to direct.'

'Yeah, I do. I don't want to get bogged down in

Shakespeare. Prancing about in doublet and hose, doing what some airy-fairy git tells me.' He waved his arms around and launched into an excruciating parody.

To be or not to be, that is the question . . .

'I'm thinking of starting up my own company – putting on brand new plays, not ones written three hundred years ago. Trying out new things, new ways, new ideas. What do you say to that?'

'I say, don't forget me when you do.'

'Not likely. Not with your looks. Are you staying here again tonight?'

'I have to be back at the boats first thing in the morning.'

'Up to you, love. I can get you a ticket for the play this evening. And we'll go and grab some nosh after. We can have another chat then.'

She sat in the front row of the stalls and he was just as good, close up, as from the back row of the gods. If he was thinking about something else entirely, nobody in the audience would ever have known.

It was bitterly cold again when they let go from Bulls Bridge and took the empty boats down to Limehouse. They were all afraid of the docks. At first it had been because of the German bombers, then the doodlebugs and now the V2s. The boats were sitting ducks trapped in a landlocked basin, and they'd seen what blast could do, let alone a direct hit. Rather than sit there waiting for a rocket to arrive, they clambered up the vertical iron ladder and went off to the Prospect of Whitby pub to spend the evening in the rowdy company of merchant seamen, who bought them drinks and treated them with perfect courtesy.

The foreign sailor who had stared so hard at Prudence in the Chinese restaurant that Pip had taken them to, came in and stared at her again. She tried to ignore him but, after a while, he came over. His name was Aleksei, he told her, and he was Russian. He had seen her once before and had hoped very much to see her again. He would like to know her name. Also, where she lived. Everything about her. His English was hard to understand, but his pale eyes weren't. She had a fiancé, she said quickly, looking away and going red. A Canadian airman. They were going to be married after the war.

'But you have no ring.'

'We haven't bought it yet.'

'Where is he, this airman?'

'I don't know at the moment.'

'You do not know?'

'Not exactly.'

He moved closer and she retreated until her back was up against the wall.

'But I am here. And he is not. So we can talk together. Please to tell me your name.'

In the end, Frances and Ros rescued her and they went back to the boats. She wept silently into her pillow. *But I am here. And he is not.*

In the morning, they were loaded with bundles of rusty iron bars which thudded and clanged into the holds, making poor *Orpheus* and *Eurydice* shudder as they sank lower and lower and lower. The holding chains slithered away like snakes and the job of sheeting-up was painfully done with frozen fumbling fingers. When they finally let go and moved away from the wharf, the loaders, already busy on another pair, stopped work to whistle and wave.

With Ros steering the motor and Frances the butty, Prudence occupied herself making a new fender for the motor's stern. The old man in the sailmaker's shop at Braunston had shown her how to work the cotton line into a beautiful round shape, like a great fat ball of woven string. When it was done, she was going to start on a pair of hemp tip-cats to hang each side of the fender, so that the blades and the elum were protected. Keeping busy helped her not to think so much about Steve. He'd talked a whole lot more about Canada and how much she'd like living there. About his family – mother, father, two sisters and two brothers, aunts and uncles and cousins. And he'd talked about where they might live and how in summer he'd take her to the cottage on the lake and they'd catch fish and cook them over a fire. Even how many children they'd have. Four, at least, he'd said – if she didn't mind. He liked big families. And he'd told her about his other ideas for inventions: a machine that cleared away snow from pathways, a heated steering wheel, heated driving gloves. They'd talked and they'd talked and she could remember every single thing he'd said. She'd never give up hope. *Missing, believed killed* wasn't at all the same thing as *killed in action*. It meant that there was a chance. Nobody had actually found Steve dead, or knew what had happened to him. But missing where? Over the sea – in which case there was really no hope at all. Or over land – over France or Germany – which meant that there was some, but that it would be a long while until anything was officially reported. One of the cashiers at the bank had waited nearly six months for news of her son who'd been missing after Dunkirk. The Red Cross had eventually sent word that he was a prisoner of war in a camp in Poland. Only, since Prudence wasn't officially next of kin, nobody would notify her. Only Steve himself would do that. All she could do was wait and pray and never give up hope. Every night she prayed, not kneeling like she used to but in bed, in the dark, before she went to sleep. *Please God, let*

Steve be alive. Let him come back safely. She said it under her breath, over and over again.

At Cowley it was her turn to lock-wheel. She stepped off at the bridge-hole, bike under her arm, and cycled along the towpath to the next lock. The chain kept coming off and she had to keep stopping to put it back on, so it was a rush to get the lock ready in time for the boats. At Black Jack the old lock-keeper came out to help her shut the top gates and draw the bottom paddles as *Orpheus* and *Eurydice* approached.

'Half a paddle first, missy. We don't want to swamp the boats. More haste, less speed, that's the trick. An' make sure that safety catch is on.'

Like most lock-keepers, he moved slowly and steadily, never seeming to hurry but getting it all done with time to spare while Prudence scurried hither and thither.

'Good news, isn't it?' he said as they were standing waiting for the lock to empty.

'What news?' For all they knew, Hitler was dead, which would certainly be good.

'Thought you would've heard by now. They're over.'

'Over what? Who?'

He clicked his tongue at her ignorance. 'The Yanks. Over the Rhine. And they've took Cologne. Nothing to stop them now. The war'll soon be finished.'

That evening, after they'd tied up at Rickey, they toasted the Americans at the pub.

'God bless America,' Ros said, lifting her beer mug high.

'And Canada,' Prue added.

'And Canada, sweetie. God bless them too.'

Next day they crossed Tring Summit. Frances took a turn at lock-wheeling and went off on the bike for the Mathus seven. Ros steered the motor, Prudence the butty. There was another pair of boats not very far ahead and so the downhill locks were all against them, and what with the hard frost the night before everything took longer. Prudence could see Frances sliding all over the place. They reached the last lock and the boats sank down side by side as it emptied. Ros, who had opened the bottom gates, launched herself onto the motor-cabin top below and slipped and fell heavily as she landed.

She lay there, not moving, and, to begin with, they thought she'd broken at least one leg, if not two. She waved them away.

'It's my ankle, that's all. No need to fuss. I'll be OK in a minute.'

But she wasn't OK. When they helped her up she could hardly walk and her right ankle was swelling fast. Between them they got her into the cabin where she collapsed onto the side bed.

'We'll go on to Leighton,' Frances said. 'We can get a doctor to look at you there.'

'I hate doctors.'

'Well, you're going to have to see one, Ros. It might be broken for all we know.'

'I can still steer.'

'Don't be an idiot. You can't even stand properly. Prue and I will manage the boats perfectly well between us. It worked OK with you two when I had to go off.'

At Leighton Buzzard Frances went in search of a doctor, who agreed to come to the boats. They waited outside the cabin anxiously until he emerged, cracking his head. The ankle wasn't broken, he told them tersely, but it should be X-rayed and treated. The probability was that the ligaments were badly torn and he'd left some painkillers. Ros, apparently, had refused point-blank to go to hospital.

He very plainly disapproved of the whole situation. 'You young girls shouldn't be doing this job. It's much too dangerous. She'll have to go home anyway.'

'Silly old goat,' Ros said when he'd gone. 'It'll be fine in a few days.' But her face was sheet-white and she was biting her lip with pain.

Frances shook her head. 'I don't think so, Ros. You must go home – he said so. We can get a taxi

382

to take you to the station and ask the driver to see you onto the train.'

'I *told* you, Frankie, it'll be all right soon. Probably fine by tomorrow.'

'It won't. You're supposed to get it X-rayed and treated. And how are you going to manage on the boats if you can't walk properly? You'll just get in the way and be a nuisance.'

'Well, there's not much point going home.'

'Why not? They can look after you properly.'

Ros laughed ironically. 'I'll be sleeping on the sofa. They usually let my room.'

'Not if you need it, surely?'

'I wouldn't count on that. I think I'll just stay here.'

'You can't do that, Ros. You can't be a passenger – the company won't allow it. And we're going to have to get someone else to help us till your ankle's better. Actually, I've just had a brilliant idea. You can go down to Averton and stay there. Aunt Gertrude would love to have you – remember how well you both got on? I'll send her a telegram to say you're on the way. You can leave tomorrow.'

There was another argument, of course, just like there'd been over Havlock Hall but the other way round, with Ros saying it wouldn't be right to impose and Frances asking why on earth not, and that she hadn't minded at all about doing that before. Prudence listened to them going on at each

383

other. This time it was Ros who gave in, but Prudence saw the tears shining in her eyes before she wiped them away.

The ankle was worse by the morning and the doctor's bandage looked rather like a fat cushion on the end of her leg. She could only hobble slowly and the journey ahead would probably be a nightmare. News of her accident had spread up and down the cut, and one of the old boatmen appeared to present her with a walking stick. He made them as a hobby, cut from the hedgerows, and he'd carved the top of this one into a beautiful duck's head which fitted neatly and smoothly into the palm of her hand. As well as the walking stick, he gave her a toothless smile and called her 'little lady', though she towered over him. If it hadn't been for the strict code of the cut she would have given him a big kiss on his leathery cheek.

The taxi driver who took her to the station handed her carpet bag to a porter, who carried it to the train compartment where an RAF sergeant slung it up on the rack. When they reached Euston the sergeant saw her into a taxi across to Waterloo, where a very charming army major took over and insisted on escorting her to the right platform and finding her an empty seat. Three hours later the train steamed into Bridport station, and the naval rating who had been entertaining her all the way with salty stories jumped up to convey her and the carpet bag gallantly onto the platform.

At first she thought the platform was empty, but then a figure detached itself from the shadows and came towards her. She saw, with surprise and rather a shock, that it was Vere.

He'd come to collect her in a van – one they used on the home farm, he told her, which qualified for extra petrol coupons. 'You're lucky I didn't come with the horse and cart.'

'I wouldn't have minded.'

'I'm sure you wouldn't. You've cut your hair. That's a pity.'

'I had lice. We all did. We were lousy. I'm growing it again.'

'Good.'

'About the lice?'

'No, about growing your hair again. I see you're still wearing Father's riding mac.'

'It's been very useful.'

'That's good, too.'

There were two strong-smelling dustbins sitting behind her seat in the back of the van.

'Pigs' swill,' he said. 'Sorry about that. I've been collecting it from one of the hotels. They save us all their peelings and scraps.'

'It's better than having the pigs in here. I'd no idea you were home, Vere. Aren't you supposed to

be convalescing, not driving about the countryside?'

'I got fed up with that. It's your turn now.'

'But are you really better?'

'Much. I'll be back with the squadron very
soon.'

'Flying on operations?'

'That's the general idea.' He looked very un-
wing-commander-like in an old tweed jacket with
leather patches on the sleeves and the sort of
well-worn country clothes that his kind always
looked so good in.

'How did it happen – your ankle?'

She told him. 'We've jumped down hundreds of
times. This time, I slipped on the ice. Very careless
of me.'

'None of you girls should be doing that job . . .
it's far too risky.'

'That's what the doctor said. But we don't
happen to agree. And what about *your* job? I bet
that's risky.'

'With respect, Rosalind, it's not quite the same
thing.'

'You mean it's all right for you to take risks
because you're a man?'

'Yes, that's exactly what I mean. Men have
to take physical risks in wartime; it's expected
of them. Women shouldn't have to, unless it's
absolutely necessary.'

'You really are an old-fashioned stick-in-the-mud, Vere.'

He gave her a brief smile. 'Yes, I know. Frances has told me so many times.'

'Anyway,' she said. 'The war's going to end soon, isn't it? So none of us will be taking risks any more.'

'It's not over yet. Not by a long chalk. We've still got to defeat the Germans in Europe and then there's the Far East and Japan to deal with.'

'That's depressing. It'll go on for ever.'

'Not for ever,' he said. 'It'll end one day. Then what are you going to do?'

'Go back to the stage.'

'Yes, of course, I remember you saying.'

'What about you?'

'I'll probably have to leave the RAF and come home and do something about Averton. Try to get the place back on its feet again. It's been neglected for years and there's a hell of a lot to be done.'

'Wouldn't you miss the RAF?'

'Very much. But I miss Averton too, when I'm away. And it's my responsibility.'

It was getting too dark to see the house properly – only the pitch of its ancient roofs against the western sky, the solid mass of its stone walls. The aunt greeted her like a long-lost friend, pressing her uncomfortably to a necklace of lumpy amber. With the aid of the duck's-head walking stick – much admired by all on her long journey – she reached the sofa in front of a blazing log fire and Vere brought on the gins. It was rather like coming home, she thought wryly; in actual fact, a great deal better.

The local doctor called the next day and man-handled the ankle. He didn't think it was broken, either, but wanted her to have an X-ray. Vere drove her to the hospital in the van, and they sat around waiting for hours. If he hadn't confiscated her walking stick, she would have made a bolt for it. After the X-ray, another doctor held up a large negative of some bones which, apparently, belonged to her, and announced, tracing bits of them with a pencil, that there was no break. No break but damaged collateral ligaments, whatever they were. Heat treatment was prescribed, massage and exercises.

'I'm not going back there,' she said as Vere drove her away. 'It'll get better on its own.'

'Don't be ridiculous, Rosalind. Of course you must. I don't like hospitals any more than you, but you've just got to put up with it.'

She hobbled down to the orangery and paid a visit to Sir John, who gave her a tour of the orchids and cut off a lovely mauve flower for her. She would have worn it in her hair like she'd done with the one he'd given her before, but unfortunately it clashed, so she pinned it on her blouse instead. Vere drove her to the hospital for the heat treatment and the massage, collecting the pigs' swill from the hotel afterwards. Otherwise she spent a great deal of time with her foot up on the sofa in front of the fire, playing card games with Aunt Gertrude – poker, pontoon, gin rummy – and a funny old-fashioned game with bits of bamboo and ivory called mah-jong. The aunt usually won, but not always. In between games they chatted and Rosalind thought up more theatre gossip. Once they talked about Vere. Gertrude was worried.

'I simply hate the thought of him going back to fight in this wretched war.'

'He's not flying Lancaster bombers on raids any more, is he? It must be safer.'

'Far from it. An old RAF friend of mine told me about this Mosquito squadron. Apparently, they're given all the really tricky targets. He said it's hideously dangerous.'

She went on to talk about what a kind little boy Vere had been, and what a good older brother to Frankie.

'He was always taking care of her – making sure she was all right and not doing anything stupid. He still does, of course, and Frances hates that, especially when she *is* doing something stupid.'

'Perhaps he'll stop soon.'

'Not until she gets married. Has she met anyone yet, do you know?'

Ros hesitated. 'Well . . . she fell desperately in love with someone, only it didn't work out.'

'Oh? *Do* tell me. Who was he?'

'A boatman – working on the canals.'

'Oh dear . . . that's rather typical of Frances. What was he like?'

'Very dark and very handsome. Like a gorgeous gypsy.'

'No wonder she fell for him. I'd probably have done so myself, at her age. Awfully romantic. Lucky she came to her senses.'

'She didn't. *He* did. He told her it would never work and went off to another canal.'

'That was decent of him. And jolly sensible.'

'I thought so, too. Frances was very cut up about it, though – still is. I wouldn't mention it to her – or to Vere.'

'Not a word, I promise.'

'There's another man who's rather smitten. Someone called Hugh Whitelaw. He's in Vere's squadron. He told us that his mother's an old friend of yours.'

'She is indeed. Joan and I were at school together. And I've known Hugh for years. How did you come across him?'

'We met him at the Ritz. We went to have dinner at the hotel and Vere happened to be there with him, so we all sat at the same table. Then we stayed at his parents' house when the boats were frozen up a few weeks ago. Hugh was home on leave at the same time.'

'Really? What a piece of luck! He's a charming young man. And he'll inherit Havlock Hall and the estate, of course, as well as a *great* deal of money. Not to be sneezed at in these uncertain times. How smitten is he?'

'Very, I'd say. But Frances isn't interested. She's still pining for her boatman.'

'That's a shame. She'll get over it, though, in the end.' Aunt Gertrude screwed another cigarette into the ivory holder and lit it. 'As a matter of fact, I'm more concerned about Vere in that respect. It's high time he found a nice girl.'

'You needn't be. He must have umpteen WAAFs falling at his feet.'

'I dare say, but he doesn't seem interested either – like his sister. On the other hand, he's very interested in *you*.'

'Me?' Ros laughed. 'Somehow I don't think I'm quite his type. And I'm not a nice girl.'

'I don't agree on either count. To be perfectly frank, my dear, I'd always hoped it would be some rich heiress who'd snaffle Vere and bring her money to Averton, but since I've come to know you better, I've rather changed my mind about that. I'm not a bad judge of people and I think

you'd be the *very* thing for him. Make him extremely happy. Do him the world of good. Didn't
you realize how much he likes you?'

She frowned. 'No, I didn't.'

'Oh, yes. Enormously. And you bring such a
wonderful blast of fresh air to Averton.'

The clock on the mantelpiece made pre-chiming
noises. Cigarette holder clamped at an acute
angle, like President Roosevelt's, Aunt Gertrude
scooped up the cards with the dexterity of a
Mississippi riverboat gambler.

'Jolly good! Time for our gin.'

Every night they listened to the nine o'clock
news. The V2 rockets were still raining down on
London, but the RAF was busy bombing German
cities by night while the American Air Force did it
by day, as well as dropping incendiary bombs on
the Japanese. Meanwhile, the Allies were forging
their way across Europe. The end of the war was
nigh and that meant the end of being on the boats.
She wasn't all that sorry. She'd miss Frankie and
Prue a lot, but she didn't think she'd miss the
boats quite so much. How could you miss being
cold, wet, uncomfortable, filthy, tired, bruised
and aching? On the other hand, though, there had
been the good bits . . . the sun on your face and
the wind in your hair, gliding through miles and
miles of the most beautiful and peaceful countryside in the world, meeting the most extraordinary

people and – perhaps most of all – feeling free in a way that wasn't possible on dry land. Vere had once said much the same thing, she remembered – only he'd been talking about flying. She watched him covertly when they were listening to the news, and she could tell by his face that he was desperate to get back into action. Hideously dangerous, Aunt Gertrude had called it, which sounded frightening.

The ankle was improving fast, the swelling almost down and she could walk without the duck's-head stick. The next time that Vere drove her to the hospital for treatment, the doctor told her that there was no need for any more.

'I'm as good as new,' she said to Vere. 'You won't have to take me there again.'

'Back to the boats?'

'The sooner the better. Frances wrote that my replacement is hopeless. I ought to leave tomorrow.'

'I'm leaving too,' he said. 'We could travel to London together.'

They called at the hotel to collect two more bins of pigs' swill. He said, 'I'll take you the scenic route home. There are some rather amazing views.'

They followed a bumpy one-track lane, climbing and twisting and turning, the pig bins going clatter-clatter in the back. There were early primroses under the hedgerows and buds on the trees. It would soon be looking lovely along the cut, she thought – the willows trailing their long thin leaves, wild flowers dotting the bank, ducks and moorhens nesting, herons flapping around. At the top of a steep hill Vere stopped the van. The land dropped to the south in front of them, sweeping down in soft green folds until it reached the sea, twinkling away in the far distance.

'Averton's behind us,' he said. 'But you'll have to get out to see it.'

They walked along the ridge, the wind blowing her hair into a wild tangle. He pointed out the chimneys and rooftops of the house, just visible beyond the woods, with the square tower of the little church beside it.

He said, 'All the land in this direction belongs to Averton – as far as you can see.'

'*All* of it? My God!'

'Beautiful, isn't it?'

'Very.' She thought: how extraordinary it must feel to own so much of England, and so much beauty. 'You're incredibly lucky, Vere.'

He turned to her. 'I want you to share it with me, Rosalind. I love you very much and I'm asking you to be my wife. To marry me in that church down there, as soon as the war's over, and come and live at Averton.'

For a moment she didn't speak, because she

couldn't think of a blessed thing to say. Liking her was one thing, fancying her, even, but *loving* her and wanting to *marry* her was something else entirely.

'You can't mean it, Vere. You're not serious.'

'I do mean it. And I'm deadly serious. I adore you.'

'Since when?'

'Since you first came to Averton – after we'd met at the Ritz. I fell in love with you then. Probably before that. Probably when I first saw you.'

'But you couldn't have done. You disapproved of me like anything. You thought I'd be a bad influence on Frances.'

'I did – at first.'

'You hurt my feelings.'

'It was unforgivable of me. And I was wrong. You must hate me for it.'

'I don't hate you, Vere. I've never done that.'

He smiled. 'I'm very thankful to hear it.'

'And, anyway, it was my fault for behaving so badly at the Ritz. I did that on purpose, you know.'

'I realized that. Later.'

She was silent again. He'd paid her a huge compliment. Made her an offer that, as dear old Aunt Gertrude would have put it, wasn't to be sneezed at. All those acres, as far as the eye could see, the lovely old house – even though it was falling down – the hundreds of years of family and tradition, going back to that rather gorgeous buccaneer with the emerald earring. To be a part of all that and have a title too, one day: Lady Carlyon. For a moment, she saw herself swanning around, playing the part – charming the villagers, being gracious to forelock-tugging tenants, opening the summer fete, sitting in the front pew. Then she saw the turned-up noses, the snide asides, the sniffy looks.

'Only you were quite right in the first place, Vere. I'm not at all the sort of wife you should have. You'd be shocked if you knew everything about me.'

'I very much doubt it.'

'Yes, you would. For a start, I tell lies.'

'So do most people.'

'And I make up stories.'

'They're extremely entertaining.'

'And I steal things.'

'Such as?'

'Clothes, food, coal – anything I need. I do it quite often.'

'You wouldn't be in need of them if you married me. What else would shock me?'

'I've been sleeping with men since I was sixteen – just to get parts in plays.'

'Isn't that what actresses do?'

'And I want to go on acting. I'd hate to give that up.'

'You wouldn't have to give it up. Actresses get married, like anybody else.'

'You'd want me to have children to carry on the family name and I'm terrified of childbirth.'

'Only one's necessary – a boy called John.'

'He'd probably have my colour hair, you realize that?'

'I hope he would.'

'So might any others.'

'I hope they would, too. What else?'

'My parents run a boarding house.'

'I know they do.'

'And I've got an uncle who's a bookie.'

'He could give us some good racing tips. And Aunt Gertrude would be especially delighted. Well, is that all?'

'For the moment.'

'So, what's your answer?'

She pressed her hands to her cheeks; shook her head fiercely. 'I don't know, Vere. I'm not sure how I feel. About you. About anything. I'm not sure I could ever belong here. You must give me time.'

'You can have as much of it as you need.'

They walked back to the van. She was silent as they bumped down the hill to another clattering chorus from the pig bins.

'Penny for your thoughts, Rosalind.'

'They're worth much more than that.'

'A shilling, then.'

'Still not enough.'

'Five shillings.'

'Done.'

She held out her hand, palm up, and he dug out two half-crowns from his pocket.

'But no fibs.'

'No fibs,' she agreed.

'So, what were these expensive thoughts?'

'Well . . .'

'A deal's a deal.'

'Actually, I was just thinking to myself that I've never gone to bed with anyone who was in love with me. And I was wondering if it's any different. If you see what I mean.'

He kept his eyes fixed on the road ahead. 'You could easily find out, you know. If you wanted to.'

Twenty

They hugged Ros when she came back to meet
them at Bulls Bridge. They carried her carpet bag,
offered tea and her favourite ginger biscuits. Prue
had cleaned the butty stove, polished everything
and swept out the cabin, and Frances had bought
her a brass vase to put wild flowers in.

'You've no idea how much we missed you, Ros.
The other girl was useless, wasn't she, Prue?
Never did a thing right, and bone idle with it. All
she did was sit around and eat all our food. She
got off at Rickey, thank heavens. If we had a flag
we'd have run it up.'

Ros looked more beautiful than ever: she
seemed to glow. Her hair was growing long again,
all the usual cuts and bruises had healed, as well
as the ankle, and she looked wonderfully clean –
skin, hair, clothes. A normal human being from
another land – except perhaps for the clothes. She
was wearing a strange assortment of garments.

Aunt Gertrude had given her one of her jumpers and unearthed some plus-twos in the Averton attics, as well as a pair of long green shooting socks. With her leather jerkin and the belt round her waist, the overall effect was pretty striking.

Vere had apparently donated his old RAF battle jacket and Ros wore it slung jauntily across her shoulders.

'How was he?' Frances asked.

'Fine. He's gone back, you know.'

'Not on ops, I hope.'

'I'm not sure. He wants to, as soon as they'll let him.'

'He would. I hope they don't. And I hope he was nice to you, Ros.'

'*Very* nice.'

'He must be improving.'

'Yes, I know him much better now.' Out of Prue's hearing, Ros asked, 'Any news of Steve?'

'None, unfortunately. Prue keeps ringing that pub to see if they've heard anything, but they haven't. She hasn't given up hope, though. She's still convinced that he's alive.'

'Well, he could be.'

'It doesn't seem very likely though, does it? One piece of good news, though: Molly's had her baby – a girl.'

'Is she all right?'

'Seems to be fine. They're back working on the cut. She said the second one's easy. Like popping peas in a pod.'

'I don't believe it.'

'They've named it after me.'

'That's quite a compliment.'

On the last trip, when they'd stopped at the Hawkesbury office to get the coal loading orders, Frances had met Saul who'd told her that the baby had been born the day before. They were tied up round the back of the sheds on a quiet stretch of the cut which acted as a sort of boaters' maternity ward, with a midwife and local doctor in attendance. Molly had been sitting up in bed with the baby tucked beside her and Abel bouncing around at the foot.

'We're givin' 'er yer name as well as me mam's – that's if yer don't mind. Frances Sara. She'll be christened 'fore we move off. Yer'll come to the church, won't yer?'

It was a great honour, she knew, and she'd been very touched. The baby had worn a beautiful gown of old lace and the church had been full of Jessops gathered to make sure that everything was done properly. Afterwards they'd celebrated at the pub and it had been quite a party.

'I 'ear Jack Carter's courtin',' Molly had said to her at one point. 'A girl on the Oxford. One o' the Stokes.'

'From the boats?' She tried to look as though she didn't care – but she did. And it hurt.

'Course. You still thinkin' 'bout 'im? Wouldn't never 'ave done, see. Jack knew that. Best to fergit 'im.'

They let go early the following day with orders to take the empty boats to pick up a consignment of tinned food at Brentford. Brentford was much closer to the lay-by than Limehouse and they went breasted-up since the locks on that arm of the cut were broad enough to take both boats side by side. Frances steered, while Ros and Prue lock-wheeled for the eleven locks. The big horse-drawn barges coming up, loaded with coal or timber, made progress very slow. At Brentford Frances had to wind the boats before they could tie up – the tricky turning manoeuvre that was closely observed, as usual, by the boaters. No matter how long they spent on the cut, to the true boaters they would always be *them trainees* and sometimes, still, *them bleedin' trainees*.

The consignment of tinned foods included several crates of oranges. One of the loaders let a crate crash heavily onto the wharf side. It burst open and oranges rolled merrily in all directions.

'Whoopsa-daisy,' he grinned at them. ''Elp yerselves, girls.'

None of them could remember how an orange tasted. They unpeeled them, prised away the segments and ate them with the juice dribbling down their chins.

'We ought to make marmalade,' Prue said.

'No sugar,' Ros pointed out. 'Anyway, they're better like this.'

By the time they'd sheeted up it was too late to let go that night, so after cleaning the boats and themselves they went off to the cinema and then, afterwards, to the pub, where Frances saw Jack. He was standing at the bar, back turned, like he'd been the first time she'd ever set eyes on him – dark clothes, red scarf, thick black hair curling on his neck. Ros had seen him too.

'I'd leave it, sweetie. No point stirring things up again.'

Frances stood up and walked over to him.

'Hallo, Jack.'

He turned round. 'How d'yer do?'

'Fine, thanks. How are you?'

'Not so bad.'

'It's a bit of a shock to see you here.'

'I goes where the work is.'

'How's Freddy?'

'Same as ever.'

She said, 'I heard you were courting. A girl on the Oxford.'

'That's right. Rosie Stokes.'

'You'll be getting married, then?'

'Reckon so.'

'Soon?'

'Reckon so.'

''Scuse me, love.' A bargee shouldered his way to the bar.

There was a sing-song going on round the piano. The usual din. The usual songs. They'd started another one.

We'll meet again . . .

She probably never would meet Jack again and it broke her heart.

'Well, goodbye, Jack. Good luck.' She tried to smile at him.

He nodded. 'Goodbye, Frances.'

'I'll never forget you.' She couldn't help saying it.

He stared at her for a moment in his boater's way. 'I'll tell yer somethin', Frances.'

'What?'

'I'll never forgit yer, neither.'

It was raining again, pattering lightly like fairy fingers on the cabin roof instead of the usual heavy-footed rats. Prue was lying quietly but Ros knew that she was saying her prayers into her pillow and knew exactly what she was praying for. She hardly ever spoke of her Canadian now, but it was obvious that she hadn't given up hope of him being alive.

While Prue was doing her praying, Ros lay thinking about Vere and wondering what to do. The doubts niggled away. How long would it last once he'd taken off the rose-tinted specs and seen, like everyone else would have seen straight away, that she was never going to measure up? That she'd never be able to live up to those portraits of Carlyon wives at Averton. She didn't behave like a Lady, or dress like a Lady, or speak like a Lady or do anything like a Lady. And would he really let her go on acting, as he'd promised? Would he stand by without kicking up a fuss, while she skipped off for weeks or months on end? Would he *really* do that? And what about the little matter of the necessary son called John? All very well for Molly to talk happily about popping peas in a pod, but it hadn't sounded as though childbirth was anything like as easy as that: more like being stretched on the rack.

And then there was Ken. He didn't love her, of course, but he was going to be a big success and he was going to help her to be a big success too. Her parents' hopes and dreams, ever since she'd played the extra fairy, could all come true one of these fine days, if she had the sense to stick to him.

Last, but far from least, there was Vere himself. Old-fashioned, stick-in-the-mud Vere who was, as she'd been intrigued to discover, neither of those things – far from it – and who deserved a much better wife than she could ever be to him. It would be so easy to say 'yes, please, Vere'; and so easy to love him. All so, so easy . . . if only the rest of it were right.

Prue must have finished her prayers because all was silent. For her sake, and for nice Steve's sake, Ros hoped they'd be answered.

After a bit, it started to rain harder, drumming loudly on the cabin roof, finding ways through. She listened to the water dripping into the pots and pans carefully positioned to catch it. *Ping, ping, ping.* Her face started to itch – more bloody bedbugs on the rampage. They could never get rid of them. *Ping, ping, ping.*

They took the crates of oranges and the tinned food to Birmingham and brought coal back from Coventry to the ABC bakeries. On the next trip the load was aluminium bars and coal for the Heinz factory, but when they got back to Bulls Bridge and tied up at the lay-by there were no new orders. Frances hung about outside the offices until, finally, she was told to take the boats empty to Hawkesbury for coal.

'*Empty?*'

The man tapped the papers. 'That's what it says.'

'But we've never done that before.'

'There's always a first time for everything.'

The war was coming to an end – that much was clear from the news and rumours. V2s had stopped falling on London, the Russians were surrounding Berlin, Hitler was holed up in an underground bunker, the Allies were unstoppable, the Germans ready to surrender. She biked back to the boats.

'I suppose they're not going to need us so much now.'

Ros said, 'We've almost done our bit, Frankie, don't you think? We were only filling a gap.'

'We can still be useful, surely.'

'For a while. But we'll end up taking work away from the boat people, if we're not careful. They'll want us to go sooner rather than later.'

Go! Leave the cut for ever! Say goodbye to a way of life which suited her so perfectly. Goodbye to freedom, to never-ending variety, to a wonderful, colourful people and wonderful, colourful boats. All very well for Ros who was longing to get back to the theatre, and for Prue who was still clinging stubbornly to the belief that Steve had somehow survived, but she had nothing like that. It would be back to some depressing job, incarcerated from nine to five and bored to tears.

She said heavily, 'We'll let go first thing in the morning. May as well get on with it.'

They did the empty-boat run in record time and

then had to wait around at Hawkesbury for several days before they were given loading orders. To pass the time, they took the bus into Coventry where they went to the public baths, wandered round the shops in the rain, ate nasty food in cheap cafés and sat in the cinema where it was dry and warm, watching newsreels about the war coming to an end.

They unloaded the coal at Croxley mills and worked their way steadily down through Walkers, Rickey, Stockers, Springwell and Copper Mill. At Black Jack the keeper was grinning all over his face.

'War's over,' he shouted at them from the lock-side. 'They've said on the wireless. We've beaten the buggers at last!'

In Trafalgar Square bells were pealing, bands playing, fireworks exploding, people singing at the tops of their voices. They were laughing, hugging and kissing, dancing, waving flags, climbing up lamp-posts, hanging out of windows, splashing around in the fountains.

The middle-aged woman next to Prudence was crying, not laughing. The tears were streaming down her face and she kept wiping them away with the back of her hand.

'My son Joe's in the Far East, still fighting,' she said. 'I don't know when he'll come home – or if he ever will. I can't join in all this – not yet. Not till he's safe home.'

She said, 'My fiancé's not back either.'

'Far East too, is he?'

'No, he was shot down over Europe.'

'POW?'

'I'm not sure. But I know he's still alive. I'm sure of it.'

The woman nodded. 'You have to keep hoping – that's the only thing to do. I'm sorry for the ones that can't – the ones with sons and husbands and brothers they know they'll never see again. It's very hard for them today.'

Frances was jitterbugging with a GI and Ros had climbed up onto one of the lions with some drunken naval ratings and was wearing a sailor's cap on her head. She waved and Prudence waved back.

They did several more trips, mostly taking empty boats to bring back coal. Other Idle Women were starting to leave the cut and return to life on the land.

When they met Pip at the lay-by even she was talking of going.

'Time to hand the cut back to the boat people,' she said. 'It belongs to them and we're not needed any more.'

She'd spoken briskly but she looked sad.

Frances realized that there was no point in them hanging on for much longer. Ros was more than ready to go back to the theatre where her actor friend was going to help her. And poor Prue seemed to be losing heart as the papers printed more and more pictures of prisoners arriving home and there was still no news of Steve.

They packed up all their belongings and cleaned out *Orpheus* and *Eurydice* for the last time, sweeping and scrubbing and polishing to leave them looking their very best.

She stood alone in the empty cabin. The brass knobs would stay with *Orpheus* because the boat people would appreciate them, but the fairground plate would go with her. She lifted it off its hook, last thing of all, and traced its golden rim with her finger, remembering the summer's day at the fair, and the merry-go-round, and the apple orchard, and Jack.

Twenty-one

Prudence left the house in Lime Avenue with her father at eight fifteen precisely, walked down the front path and out of the sun-ray gate to go to the bank. As they approached the building, she hung back a little to allow him to go in first – just as she had always done.

Everything inside was exactly as it had always been: same staff, same customers, and Mr Holland still hurried out of his sanctuary to pacify old Mrs Harper. Miss Tripp still didn't smile and Mr Simpkins was still a creepy-crawly nuisance. On her first day back he had kept coming to her desk on any excuse, leaning over to pretend to check something in the ledger, touching her arm with his pudgy white hand, breathing in her ear.

She had tried to find work somewhere else – anywhere else – but there were hundreds of other people back from the war, all looking for jobs too, and Father had been shocked and hurt by the idea of her not wanting to return to the bank. Mr Holland, he had pointed out, had been very generous in offering to take her back at her original salary. She was a very fortunate young lady. She had even been given the same desk and the same ledger with the same customer accounts. The only difference was that the blackout blinds had been taken down, the brown paper strips unpeeled from the frosted-glass windows and the sand buckets and stirrup pump removed.

There were still photographs in the newspapers of homecoming troops and of prisoners of war arriving back from camps all over Europe, but there was no news of Steve. She had not quite given up hope – not yet – but there wasn't much of it left.

Sometimes, posting the figures in the ledger, her mind wandered back to the cut. She saw the open skies, felt the warmth of the sun, the wind blowing her hair. She heard the putt-puttering of the motor's engine, the clang and thud of lock gates, the rattle and crank of paddles, the water rushing through, and, at the end of the day, the stillness of the night.

She started to make mistakes in the ledger and crossings-out to correct them, and ink blots on the pristine pages. Mr Holland summoned her into his office and delivered a stern lecture on the Psychology of Accuracy. Her father delivered another one on the way home. There was no room for careless work at the bank, he told her, rapping the steel point of his umbrella against the pavement as they walked along. She would have to pull her socks up. In his view, she had learned very bad habits on the canals. It had been a grave mistake to let her work there. She should have stayed at the bank, just as he'd always preferred.

One day they were home a few minutes later than usual, and her mother came into the hall from the kitchen. She looked quite put out.

'There's someone to see you, Prudence. Some man.'

Her heart gave a wild leap. 'Did he give his name?'

'He may have done, I don't remember. I couldn't make him out at all. He's wearing a Royal Air Force uniform, but he speaks just like an American. I told him you were at work but he insisted on waiting. I've put him in the dining room. You'd better go and see what he wants.'

She walked towards the closed door, praying hard. *Please God, let it be him.* She turned the handle and pushed the door open inch by inch by inch. *Please, please God . . .* She peered slowly round the edge.

*   *   *

413

'I simply can't decide which one to have. What do *you* think?'

Frances didn't care which handbag the customer chose, so long as she got on with it. It was amazing how long it took some people to make up their minds; they dithered for hours, opening and shutting the bags, looking inside, picking them up and putting them down, carrying them over to the long mirror and then coming back and starting opening and shutting them all over again. Sometimes they asked for her opinion but she'd learned never to give it because it invariably prolonged the agony of decision.

'I think they're *both* lovely, madam. I'm sure you'd be happy with either one.'

'Do you? Of course black is always so useful. And it has a little more room inside and an extra pocket.'

'Yes, indeed.'

'But the navy blue has such a nice coloured lining.'

'Yes, it's very nice.'

'And it would match my shoes perfectly.'

The opening and shutting had started again, the clasps snapping away like crocodiles, then the woman was off to the mirror again with a handbag hooked over each arm.

Her high heels were killing her; she stepped out of them and wiggled her toes around. It was a ghastly job, standing behind a shop counter all day and being polite to customers, but at least the handbag department was by one of the main doors to Knightsbridge so she could see people coming and going. And sometimes a friend would turn up and stop by for a chat.

The woman was coming back with the handbags.

'Oh dear, I just can't decide . . .'

The war in Europe had finished in May, the one with Japan in August. Millions and millions of people had died. There had been the most sickening photos of death camps in Europe and of the prisoners of war liberated in the Far East. Suffering and misery of an unbelievable kind. But this silly woman in her silly hat couldn't make up her mind which silly handbag to buy.

She said, 'I don't think it actually matters a row of beans which one you have, madam.'

The woman stared at her through the hat veil. 'Oh, but I wouldn't want to make a mistake.'

'In that case, I'd definitely choose the black. It's more useful.'

In the end she chose the navy which, of course, was the one she'd looked at in the first place.

Soon after that, Hugh Whitelaw came in through the swing doors. She was dealing with another customer who couldn't make up her mind either, and spotted the blue RAF uniform out of the corner of her eye before she saw that it was him. If Hugh was back from the Far East, then Vere could be.

He waited until the customer had left before he came up to the counter.

She said, 'Have you come to buy a handbag, sir?'

'No, I've come to see you.'

'Is Vere back too?'

'The whole squadron is. They posted us home.'

'Wonderful! How is he?'

'He's absolutely fine.'

'Is he in London?'

'No. He went off on some mysterious errand.'

She straightened some bags to look busy.

'How did you know I was working here?'

'Your aunt mentioned it to my mother. It doesn't seem the sort of job you'd enjoy.'

'I don't. But the alternative was a secretarial course and I thought I'd enjoy that even less.'

'Are you missing your narrowboats?'

'Yes, I am rather, as a matter of fact.'

'I thought you might be. What are Ros and Prue up to?'

'Ros has joined a repertory company in the Midlands and Prue's just got married to her Canadian boyfriend. He came back from the dead.'

'Good for him. How did he manage that?'

'Apparently he'd been on the run in Germany

for weeks after he was shot down. When he got caught, the Germans sent him to some camp miles away in Poland. Then the Russians turned up and kept him for quite a while before they let him go.'

'He was lucky. They might not have done.'

'That's what he said. Are you sure you don't want to buy a handbag? Don't you have a girl-friend who'd like one?'

'Not at the moment.'

'I get commission.'

He smiled. 'Will you have dinner with me this evening instead?'

'Thanks, but I'm usually pretty tired by the time I get out of here.'

'How about at the weekend?'

Another customer was approaching – a battle-axe of a woman decked out in heirloom jewellery. Probably a dowager duchess. She braced herself for trouble.

'Frances?'

She shrugged. 'Saturday's OK. I only work half a day then.'

'Saturday it is. Where are you living?'

'My aunt's flat. For the moment.'

She gave him the address. She watched as he stopped to talk to a debby-looking girl on his way out. The girl was all over him, putting a hand on his arm, throwing back her head and laughing like a hyena. Well, he was a wonderful catch, as well as very nice. Ros had pointed that out, quite unnecessarily. She went on watching him holding the swing door open for an elderly woman before he went out into the street. He'd be bound to choose somewhere good for dinner. The Ritz perhaps? That would be ironical. This time she'd wear something a bit more respectable.

The battleaxe was rapping on the counter, glaring at her.

'I'd like some service, young lady. If you don't mind.'

It wasn't the Ritz. Instead, he took her to a rather smart French restaurant in Mayfair; luckily, she'd taken the trouble to dress up. The head waiter bowed and scraped and they were ushered to a corner table.

'Very nice,' she said, looking round. 'Do you come here often?'

'Whenever I can.'

'To impress the girls?'

He smiled. 'I didn't bring you here to impress you, Frances. I know you better than that. I brought you here for the food.'

The war was over but the rationing wasn't. Not at all. From the look of the menu, though, the French restaurant seemed to have got round it somehow.

'*Real* steak?'

'Real steak.'

'Not whale?'

'Definitely not whale.'

'And real chicken, not rabbit?'

'Real chicken.'

'I *am* impressed.'

But she thought nostalgically of Ros's boat stew, of the doorsteps of bread and marg and treacle, of porridge covered with evaporated milk, of oily sardines eaten straight out of the tin, sizzling fish and chips wolfed down straight from the newspaper, of spam fry-ups and Heinz baked beans, and of endless mugs of hot cocoa, sweetened with Nestlé's condensed milk . . . Nothing would ever taste quite as good again.

He said, 'You asked for champagne at the Ritz. Would you like some now?'

'I only did that to annoy Vere. I'd never drunk it before, or since.'

'Well, we could celebrate the end of the war, don't you think?'

He beckoned to a waiter and when the champagne had been popped and poured, he raised his glass to her. 'To the future – whatever it may hold.'

She drank and wondered what the future *did* hold. Unthinkable to stay for ever at the handbag counter – in any case, she'd probably be sacked soon for being rude to a customer. Unthinkable, too, to do one of those dreadful secretarial courses, bashing away at a typewriter and learning to make shorthand squiggles in a notebook so that she could end up as an office slave. What else? Work in an art gallery? Or a flower shop? Or a dress shop? Be a waitress? None of those were much better than the handbags. The fact was that she couldn't settle down to anything – not after the canals. *We're free, see. Nobody's servants.* Jack's words, and he'd known what he was talking about.

She said, 'Are you going to stay in the RAF, Hugh?'

'For the time being. I rather enjoy it.'

'I expect Vere will have to go home to Averton and save it from falling down.'

'Yes, he told me. I gather he has some other plans, too.'

'Plans? What plans?'

'For getting married.'

'Getting *married*? *Vere*? Who on earth to?'

'He hasn't said. I thought you might know.'

'Well, I don't. I'd probably be the last person he'd tell. It's one of the WAAFs, most likely.'

'No, it's not a WAAF.'

'Well, I hope she's nice, whoever she is.'

'I'm sure she will be.'

'And she'd better like Averton. Has he taken her there, do you know? It's not everyone's cup of tea.'

'She's been there, apparently. So he said.'

She frowned. 'I can't think who it could be.'

'I expect you'll know soon enough. How about you, Frances?'

'What about me?'

'Have you any plans for the future?'

'Oh, nothing special.'

'No ideas of going back to work on the canals?'

'We're not wanted there any more. They don't need us.'

'Life has a habit of moving on, whether we like it or not. The trick is to accept the fact. To look forward, not back.'

'I'm still looking back.'

'Not for ever, I hope.'

'I'll never forget the boats . . . or the people.'

'I don't expect you will. But there's a lot to look forward to – the rest of your life, in fact.'

'I don't much care about that – just at the moment.'

He looked at her steadily. 'You will. I promise.'

She remembered Ros's remarks about him. All complete rubbish. He'd have plenty of other girls – girls like the laughing hyena in the store. Girls falling over themselves to nab him. No need to wait around for anyone or anything.

As he drove her back to Aunt Gertrude's flat, he said, 'By the way, my mother would very much like you to come and stay next weekend.

Do you think you could manage that?'

'I have to work on Saturdays.'

'Only for the morning, though. I could collect you as soon as you've finished and we'll stop for lunch on the way.'

He reminded her of Vere – taking charge – though he did it very nicely. And she'd liked his mother. And Havlock Hall was very near the cut.

'Well, if you're sure she really means it.'

'Quite sure. My father will be there, too, and I know he'll enjoy meeting you. He'll want to hear all about living and working on the boats. And so will I. That's settled, then.'

'Is it?'

'Definitely. I'll pick you up outside the store.'

The Saturday morning was spent standing on one aching foot, then the other, while customers tried to make up their minds.

'Which one do you think looks best?'

'They both look very nice, madam.' Her stock answer.

'Yes, but which would *you* choose?'

'I think I'd have the brown.' In fact, she thought they were both ghastly.

'But it wouldn't go with black, would it?'

'Then I'd take the other. Maroon will go with anything.'

'I'm not sure I like the colour, though. And it's a bit small.'

422

She gritted her teeth. 'In that case, I'd choose the brown.'

'Actually, I don't think I like either of them quite enough. Could you show me that black lizard one over there?'

Hugh was waiting in his smart and shiny car outside the staff entrance and they drove out of London, stopping to eat at a pub before heading on north-west towards Northamptonshire. She realized that they were following much the same route as the Grand Union Canal, but travelling at more than ten times a narrowboat's speed. Once or twice she caught a tantalizing glimpse of it in the distance and, nearing Stoke Bruerne, they crossed over one of the old bridges.

'Would you stop for a moment, please, Hugh. I'd like to look at the cut. On my own, if you don't mind.'

He pulled in at once and opened the car door for her. 'I'll wait for you here.'

'Thanks.'

She walked back onto the bridge and gazed at the quiet stretch of water meandering peacefully along in the sunlight. She knew that particular bit of the cut rather well – the low-lying meadows on each side, the gamekeeper's cottage by the woods with the orderly vegetable patch and the Buff Orpington hens scratching away in their run. The keeper's wife had given them cabbages and carrots and warm new-laid eggs and Prue, lock-wheeling, had picked bluebells from the woods. Round the next bend lay the Stoke Bruerne locks – seven of them climbing up to the village – and after that came the Blisworth tunnel, then Gayton Junction, then Heyford and the Bugby seven where they'd beaten the Quill brothers – thanks to Jack.

After a while, she heard the putt-putter of a National diesel engine and, presently, a pair of narrowboats came chuntering round the bend. She watched them approach, smoke puffing merrily from the chimney, bright paint gleaming, brass shining. The motor and its boatman passed under the bridge, followed by the butty towed on its long snubber and steered with ease by an old boatwoman. She knew they would both have seen her because boat people noticed everything, but neither of them gave any sign. To them, she was an outsider, from another world. One of the gongoozlers, as they called them, who gawped at them from banks and chucked things at them from bridges and got in their way at locks. *Yer not like us. Couldn't never be.* She waited, watching until they had gone out of sight.

Hugh was standing by the car. He ground out his cigarette. Smiled at her.

'Ready to go on now?'

She nodded.

The audience had been better than usual. An almost full house and laughs in all the right places. People loved anything by Noel Coward, specially the fun plays like *Blithe Spirit*, and Elvira was a part which suited her. The local rag had given her a glowing write-up, but it was hardly *The Times*. Nor was provincial rep exactly the West End.

She started to take off her stage make-up and then stopped, still looking into the mirror but no longer seeing her reflection. Instead, she was seeing herself knocking at the door to Ken's flat and Nadine, her old enemy from Sir Lionel days, answering it. She'd looked surprisingly good for her age, but then she hadn't spent eighteen months working on narrowboats.

'What the hell do *you* want?'

'To see Ken. Is he in?'

'He's busy.'

Luckily, Ken had come to the door just then – or not so luckily, as it had turned out. She heard all about the company he was going to set up and the old bomb-damaged theatre he'd found for lease in south London. He was raising money and reading brand new plays by brand new authors, searching for the right one. Meanwhile, he was stuck in a corny old chestnut at the Globe and Nadine was playing opposite him. Would she like a ticket to see it? What she'd really like, she'd told him, would be a part in the brand new play. He'd call her, he promised, as soon as he'd got something worked out.

He wouldn't call her, of course – not if Nadine had anything to do with it. There were clear signs that she'd moved in to stay as long as possible. She was cradle-snatching but she'd probably be quite useful to him for a while. Contacts, names, old lovers, angels to back the new play. So, that was the acting profession, and if you didn't like it, too bad. There were the lucky breaks and the unlucky ones, the ups and the downs, the hits and the flops. But you had to keep going, whatever happened.

Somebody knocked at the dressing-room door and opened it. She saw Vere in the mirror. Spun round.

'I thought you were thousands of miles away.'

'I was. I just got back.'

'On leave?'

'For good. Didn't you get my last letter?'

'I haven't been home for ages. How did you get in here?'

'I bribed someone.'

'Were you out front?'

'I was. And you made a wonderful Elvira. It's the first time I've ever seen you act and I'm extremely impressed.'

She turned back to the mirror and the make-up removal. 'I act all the time, Vere. You know that.'

'Not all the time.'

'Most of it. Anyway, why have you come all this way out to the sticks?'

'I've come for my answer.'

'What answer?'

'I asked you to marry me. Remember?'

She peeled off her false eyelashes. 'I'm still thinking about it.'

'No, Rosalind – you said that before. I want a straight answer, right now. Yes or no. If it's yes, we'll get married as soon as possible, before you can change your mind. If it's no, I'll walk out of here and never bother you again.'

'That's not fair, Vere. I need more time.'

'Time's up. Yes, or no?'

'I don't know. I'm not sure.'

'You said you loved me.'

'I tell lies.'

'It didn't seem much like one at the time, as I recall.'

'Well, I'm very good at pretending.'

'You didn't need to with me. Did you? Not like with the others. You found that out.'

She looked at him in the mirror, her face serious. 'The truth is, Vere, I'm scared.'

'Of what exactly?'

'I'm scared you'd regret marrying me. End up realizing what a horrible mistake you'd made.'

'I'd never regret it – not for a single moment – and nor would you. Don't you trust me?'

'Yes. Of course I do. You're a very trustworthy sort of person.'

'Then there's nothing whatever to stop you marrying me. No more feeble excuses left. What's the answer?' He put his hand on the doorknob. Turned it. 'Yes? Or no?'

'I suppose,' she said slowly, 'I may as well.'

'May as well what?'

'Marry you. If that's what you really want.'

'You know perfectly well it is.'

'Are you quite sure, Vere?'

'*Quite* sure.'

She turned round, fluttered her fingertips coquettishly and put on her Princess Katharine fake French accent. '*Den it shall also content me, your majesty.*'

'I take it,' he said drily, moving away from the door, 'that means yes.'

Epilogue

She'd noticed the signpost bearing a name very familiar from the past and, on impulse, had turned the car down the country lane leading across fields to the village. She parked by the pub and walked through a narrow passageway to the canal. Not surprisingly, after more than half a century, there had been a lot of changes. The pub had sprouted a modern extension, cottages had been gentrified and the boats were now all pleasure craft, hired out to holidaymakers. Tourists were drinking at tables outside the pub, licking ice creams on the towpath, gathered in a gaggle by the lock to stare at boats passing through. It was a hot day in midsummer; blue skies, sun shining, water sparkling, trees in full green leaf. She could remember it, very differently, in midwinter with grey skies, bare branches, driving rain, icy wind, sleet, snow, mud, and not a soul about.

The top gates of the lock were closed and she used them to cross over to the other side of the canal, negotiating the narrow ledge with ease and barely touching the handrail. A boat was coming in through the open bottom gates, heading uphill – a hired boat converted from an old narrow one and painted in the same bright colours, though without all the boaters' beautiful castles and roses and lozenge shapes.

In place of the cargo hold there were cabins. She could see jazzy curtains at the windows and bunk beds, a kitchen fitted with cooker, sink and fridge, a dining table with padded vinyl seating, and, if she interpreted the two frosted-glass windows correctly, a shower and lavatory. She thought, smiling to herself, of the bucket in the engine room and the dipper on its hook.

The steerer was bare-chested and dressed in baggy shorts, an open can of beer set before him on the cabin roof where a blonde girl sunbathed at full stretch, wearing two minuscule strips of Day-Glo pink. The old boaters would have been deeply shocked at such nudity. Another young man, also in shorts and bare-chested, mounted the steps to the lock-side. He had curly hair, a deep tan, and a look of confidence. Cockiness, in fact. Showing off to all the gawping gongoozlers. She saw the way he applied his weight nonchalantly to the beam to close one bottom gate while an eager helper on the opposite bank closed the other. Then he pushed past her, windlass at the ready.

'Keep out of my way, please.'

She watched him draw a top gate paddle with a flourish, cross over the gates to reach the winding gear on the far bank – just as she had done, though not quite so adeptly – and then come back again to stand close to her, hands on hips, windlass slotted into the leather belt of his shorts.

The water in the lock below began to swirl and bubble and to rise steadily, and the young man waited expectantly for it to reach the required level. And went on waiting. And waiting. With the lock about three-quarters full, the narrowboat remained obstinately stuck, going neither up, nor down. The blonde lifted her head and looked about her, sensing something amiss. Another girl poked her head out of the cabin door.

'What the bloody hell's going on, Mark?'

She stepped forward. 'Excuse me.'

He turned his head. 'Yes?'

'That bottom paddle's been left open. Water's running out as fast as it's coming in.' She could tell he'd taken her for some batty, interfering old biddy, and his sunburned good looks were marred by his irritated frown. She pointed. 'You can see the ratchet sticking up several notches – if you look.'

He obeyed, reluctantly.

She went on mildly, 'Your boat could be sitting

431

there in the lock for ever if you don't go and drop it.'

He moved then and did as she'd told him. The water level immediately began to rise, the lock to fill up. He swaggered about again, confidence restored, shouting to the beer-swilling youth at the tiller. The blonde had lain down and the other girl's head had disappeared back into the cabin. Presently he passed by her again and paused.

'How come *you* knew about that?'

'I worked on the old narrowboats during the Second World War.'

'Oh, yeah?'

'Women were recruited to help out, carrying essential supplies on the canals – coal, steel, cement, timber – all that sort of thing. Three of us to a pair of boats.' She smiled at him, though he didn't deserve it. 'They called us Idle Women because of our badges. IW standing for Inland Waterways, you see. Actually, we were anything but idle; it was really very hard work.'

He stared at her, and she could see that he didn't believe a word of it. Well, she couldn't really blame him.

'Never heard of them,' he said.

THE END